Grisham's Juror

TIMOTHY BRAATZ

The Disproportionate Press

ISBN-13: 978-0615526041
ISBN-10: 0615526047

The Disproportionate Press

GrishamsJuror@lunycrab.com • www.lunycrab.com

GRISHAM'S JUROR

ALSO BY TIMOTHY BRAATZ

NONFICTION

From Ghetto to Death Camp: A Memoir of Privilege and Luck
(published as *Undermensch* by Deutscher Taschenbuch Verlag in
Germany, 2010)

Surviving Conquest: A History of the Yavapai People (University of
Nebraska Press, 2003)

PLAYS

Cossacks Under Water (2009)
When Saints Go Marching In (2007)
Paper Dolls (2005)
The Commistar (2004)
Paper Cuts (2003)
Gun, Lies, & Lullabies (2002)
One Was Assaulted (2001)
New and Nobler Life (2000)
Helena Handbasket (1999)
Gabriella's Garden (1996)
The Devil & the Wedding Dress (1994)

www.lunycrab.com

GRISHAM'S JUROR

1

How does one avoid jury duty? I thought I had it figured out. You 1) write a letter explaining that while you'd love to fulfill your civic duty, one hundred fifty algebra students would lose their hard-won appreciation for least common denominators and seize the opportunity to terrorize some bewildered substitute instructor provided, at no small expense, by the school district taxpayers. If the jury assignment happens to hit during summer vacation, you 2) request a change of date due to serious, lingering, infectious illness and, when a new date is approved, refer back to 1. If 1 somehow fails to secure your release, you can always 3) simply ignore the summons—what are they going to do, send out the highway patrol?

Actually, what they're going to do is send out a nasty letter refusing further medical postponement without extensive documentation and threatening contempt of court and several hundred dollars in fines. Now what? Marissa suggested I consult her John Grisham novels.

-If you want to outsmart the judicial system, you should find out how it works.

Open a Grisham? Desperate times, desperate measures. The first book I looked at was about jury members being assassinated one by one. If that's how it works, just kill me now and spare me the time in court. The second suggested ways to get yourself on a jury and see justice served, not sidestep it altogether. Not real helpful, Marissa.

-I guess you're just going to have to go.

-A courtroom in July? I'll die.

-It's just one day.

-Unless I get selected.

-The odds are against it.

-With my luck—

-Be obnoxious. You're good at that.

My friend Pete seconded the motion.

-Dude, just ask the bailiff where you can score some weed.

In the third Grisham I attempted, this hotshot young attorney takes a position with a major partnership, works his butt off, gets lots of perks, then discovers the entire operation is corrupt, basically organized crime, only he can't quit, he's compromised, so he ends up taking it down single-handedly. The way he does it is pretty ingenious. Okay, I confess, I caught myself enjoying Grisham. Go ahead and laugh—I know I did, whenever Marissa brought home his latest bestseller. If the masses are buying it, how good can it be, right? Which is why I hadn't told her that I'd read number three cover to cover and then picked up a fourth, being the story of a tax lawyer who loses his job, apartment, girlfriend, and goes to work defending the poor and homeless. The pleasure, I discovered, comes in Grisham's everyman prevailing over corporate villains. Human decency triumphing over the power of money. The underdog on top at last.

I was over halfway through number four, the fired lawyer now sticking it to his evil ex-employer, when the bailiff called all rise and the judge came in. I had planned not to stand—surely that would get me home by lunch—but I popped up with the rest of them. A woman judge—short black hair going gray, half-moon reading glasses on a beaded chain, a friendly librarian smile, like a younger, taller version of that Supreme Court justice. She apologized for the long wait this morning, reminded us no cell phones in her courtroom, and went to work. A murder trial, she explained, and it might last a week or more. This is Mr. Sloan, the prosecutor. Meet the defense attorney, Mr. Lawson.

-They're going to ask you some questions, some of you will be excused, don't take it personally.

Not to worry, Your Honor, no hard feelings, I promise.

-Any reason why any of you can't serve?

She surveyed her kingdom—a few assorted court personnel and sixty attentive citizens in a dingy room, twelve of them seated in the jury box, the lucky winners of the court clerk's initial lottery.

-Any reason why you can't be fair and impartial?

That was my cue. Your Honor, I read about this case in the paper, I don't recall all the details, but I know he's guilty of something. Your Honor, the prosecutor and I once had a heated argument over a parking spot, he may not remember it, but I'll never forget his weasely face, that haughty smirk, the dismissive tone: Tough luck, buddy. Your Honor, my best friend in high school was murdered, and I just…I just can't…I'm sorry, Your Honor.

A quiver full of arrows, and I couldn't let one fly. Some old guy got excused for a bad back, no doctor's note requested. A single mother of three couldn't afford childcare. Someone actually did know the prosecutor. Her Honor, Judge Silverson, was a soft touch. She released eight prospective jurors without arching an eyebrow, even the woman who claimed her mail-order business would suffer. Yet I remained silent. My palms were sweating, my throat was dry, I knew she would see right through me. Lying was never my strong suit. So much for Plan A.

Probably it didn't matter. I'd read on the internet that attorneys want jurors they can persuade—not too stubborn, not too sharp. Lowest common denominators. That was Plan B, I'd play it smart, if it went that far. Most likely, though, they'd have a jury chosen before my number was called. Marissa was right, the odds were in my favor.

My cell phone vibrated in my pants pocket. From the bench, Judge Silverson was explaining peremptory challenges. Attorneys can excuse prospective jurors without cause, although according to my internet source, the Supreme Court has ruled they can't reject candidates solely on race, gender, or ethnicity. Of course, if anyone pressed the issue, a clever attorney could always find other, more acceptable explanations for having removed an unwanted demographic. Interesting, but Her Honor was holding forth on basic procedures, not case law, so I slid the phone out of my pocket and onto my lap and read the new text message: How is it going? Ignoring a scolding glance from the prospective juror to my right, I texted back: Murder. Guy named Jack. Home by 2.

-Have you ever made a big mistake, a serious mistake, that you immediately regretted?

Mr. Lawson, the defense attorney, was approaching the jury box. He was a large man with thick hands that he held open, palms up, a gesture of congeniality. Practiced, I'm sure. And that hitch in his step—wouldn't a slight limp make a big guy less intimidating, more human? It was all calculated, all theater, I knew that from the Grishams, and I was on to him. But what was he going for with his opening question? A big mistake, immediately regretted—wouldn't that include everyone, if they were honest? Of course it would. He wasn't looking for mistake makers, he was trying to identify sympathetic jurors who might understand that we're all just a bad decision or two away from a felony, jurors who might be inclined toward leniency. Except doesn't someone who readily admits to a mistake believe in owning up and taking responsibility, and wouldn't a defense attorney want to keep Mr. Stand-Up-And-Be-Counted off the jury? Quick, if I were in the box, would I raise my hand? No. Attorneys don't like stubborn jurors.

Juror Number Four, a heavy-set white woman, once agreed to a puppy, knowing full well she was allergic. Juror Seven, it turned out, told his wife don't be silly, went up on the roof to clear gutters during a rainstorm, and snapped his ankle in two places when he hit the ground. And Juror Two, with her straight brown hair and awkward slouch, what was her big mistake?

-I got married.

She said it quietly, and Mr. Lawson softened his voice to match hers.

-You regretted that?

-I was only eighteen. I wasn't ready.

-That must have been difficult.

-We got divorced. But I'm remarried. It's better now.

-Good. That's good. Now tell me, is there any reason why you can't give my client a fair hearing?

-No.

-Do you think it could be possible the police have arrested the wrong person? Is that possible?

-I guess so.

-Do you have any relatives who are policemen? Any friends?

-No.

-Do you believe that police can make mistakes, big mistakes, even when they're doing their best?

-Anyone can make mistakes.

Indeed. My mistake is I didn't get Sharon to marry me. I was probably too uptight, too critical of her dramatic personality. She had a great sense of humor, she was hysterical, she could be a bit much. If we had gotten married, life would certainly be more interesting. I should have found a way. Or maybe not. Pete says marriage is like cheese, it makes everything taste better, until it goes bad. Then it can kill you.

Somebody near me chuckled. Juror Five, the only African American in the box, was entertaining the court with his big mistake.

-I bought a hundred shares of my brother-in-law's company, and it tanked.

I was reminded of those education seminars where everyone states their name and tells us a little about themselves. Hi, I'm Joe, I teach chemistry, that's about it, oh and I enjoy sudoku. I'm Jane, A.P. English, two cats. And then there's always some oddball who enjoys sharing his foibles with strangers over bad coffee at eight in the morning.

-About a year later the stock came back up, way up, there was a buyout, and I'll be honest with you, I had to tell my wife that I'd sold it six months earlier. At a loss. A big loss.

The laughter was surprisingly loud—a roomful of strangers releasing tension. But Juror Five was no oddball. His beard was perfectly trimmed, his tie was powder blue and expensive—more expensive maybe than defense attorney Lawson's entire suit—his voice a rich baritone, a serious man by all appearances, yet still able to laugh about a failed investment. If we were making a movie here, he'd be the defense attorney, unfazed by some redneck prosecutor's insinuations. No, if we were making a movie, he'd be the judge. Mr. Lawson asked him about his business: home entertainment systems. Mr. Lawson asked him about his MBA: USC.

-No way they'll keep him.

Was the man to my left whispering to me or talking to himself? I turned to look. So far as I could tell, he was the only other African American in our jury pool. Two out of sixty. He noticed me looking and shook his head.

-Gonna make it all white if they can.

For a county population that's only two percent black, two out of sixty is significant overrepresentation, but I chose to point out a more obvious calculation.

-There's gonna have to be some Latinos.

The southern end of Orange County is rich and white, Reagan land. The rest of the county, once middle class and white, becomes browner and poorer by the day, and the jury pool appeared to reflect that. Lots of Latinos or Hispanics or whatever the proper term is, and also a number of Asians. An all-white jury was highly improbable. My new friend didn't agree.

-Wait and see, I'm telling you.

Mr. Lawson had finished getting acquainted with the twelve in the box, thanked them twice, a little too heartily if you ask me, and sat down, making way for Mr. Sloan, the prosecuting attorney, a much shorter and quicker man. No limp, no open palms, just a brief greeting and thank you for your attendance let me remind you, ladies and gentlemen, of a juror's obligation to the truth. Where's the charm, Mr. Sloan, the play for our sympathy?

-I have just one question for the twelve of you.

Oh, I get it, the efficient public servant, no unnecessary flourishes, no wasted tax dollars, a man with no pretense, a man you can trust.

-Do any of you believe it's okay to take the law into your own hands?

Come on, Mr. Sloan. What juror, sitting twenty feet from a black-robed judge, is saying yes to that? No one, see, no hands. Mr. Sloan didn't hesitate.

-What if you felt like you'd been cheated?

Juror One came to life. Dark hair slicked back, effortless mustache— Hispanic down to his *dedos*.

-Yeah, I would.

-You would what?

-If I'd been cheated I'd do something about it.

-So you would take the law into your own hands?

-Man, if the cops ain't doing it.

So I'm not the only one here with an exit strategy, only this poor guy can't sit back and play the odds, not in chair one.

-Would you say it's acceptable to kill someone who cheated on you?

-I'm not saying it's acceptable...

Don't back down, amigo. ¡*Ándele, ándele!*

…but if you let a dude walk over you, he won't be the last one.

That's what I'm talking about!

-I just want to be clear on this, Juror One. If you shoot someone who cheated you, should you be charged with a crime?

-No, he should.

Adiós, muchacho. Mr. Sloan consulted his papers.

-Juror Number Six, do you agree with Juror Number One?

-No.

Pale skin, long black curls, dark eyes. I wouldn't mind being sequestered with her.

-No?

-Not really. The police should handle it.

Mr. Sloan seemed surprised. What did he expect—all Hispanics would think alike?

-What if the police are too busy?

-I don't know.

-Shouldn't you do something about it yourself?

-Not if it means breaking the law.

I leaned to my left and whispered.

-He's gonna keep her.

My neighbor shrugged

-Maybe.

-She's not white.

-White enough.

-She's…she looks Mexican.

-If he keeps her, she's white.

I once had a sociology professor like that. You couldn't argue against her sophistry. Any outcome proved her proposition, it just required the proper analysis, which she generously supplied. We called her The Spinster. But if the guy on my left was a sophist, the woman on my right was a hypocrite. That disapproving glance when I pulled out my phone, reminding me the judge had insisted we give the proceedings our full attention, even us back-benchers, and now here she is with a paperback open on her knees. And she was smooth. She looked up, eyes on the jury box while turning a page, then dropped her head and returned to reading. Head lifting and dropping, like a swimmer coming up for air between strokes. Is it possible to read that fast? Oh, I know. It had to be. I caught a glimpse of the book's spine. Yep. Grisham.

According to the original twelve, at 10-1 with one abstaining, taking the law into your own hands is not acceptable. The abstainer was Juror Seven, who couldn't give a confident answer, he said, because he'd never been faced with such a decision. Is that honesty or stubbornness? He's the guy on the roof in the hurricane, so I'm going with stubbornness. Mr. Sloan will dismiss him—that was my prediction—and El Numero Uno of course, and I bet Number Four goes too, the allergic woman with the dog, for being dangerously stupid. That will be three of the prosecution's six allotted peremptory challenges. The defense I was less sure about. Mr. Lawson might toss Number Twelve, an elderly man thrice divorced who admitted to no regrets, and Number Nine, a mother of three including a military policeman. That would leave seven jurors in, five sent packing, and the court clerk calling five replacements into the box. Five out of the forty of us still sitting behind the bar, with only seven peremptory challenges remaining. I liked my chances.

-Juror Number One may be excused.

Judge Silverson had asked if there were any challenges for cause, both attorneys had declined, and now Mr. Sloan was jumping right in with the peremptory challenges. El Numero Uno picked up his jacket—a jacket in July? crazy *vato*!—and exited the box. You did it, bro. *Vaya con Díos.*

Mr. Lawson spoke next.

-Juror Number Two may be excused.

Huh? That's the woman who regrets her first marriage. She thinks cops are fallible—why would the defense toss her?

-Juror Number Eight may be excused.

Sloan dismissed an Asian woman who barely spoke English. I should have known.

-Juror Number Nine may be excused.

That's more like it—Lawson ousted the MP's mom.

-Juror Number Seven may be excused.

And next time listen to your wife and stay off the wet roof.

-Juror Number Twelve may be excused.

That seemed to be the end of it. Sloan and Lawson were at the bench, whispering with Judge Silverson. Three used challenges apiece, and I had picked four out of six. Not bad for an amateur. The remaining six included a black man and the lovely light-skinned Latina. No all-white jury today. I gave The Sophist on my left a smug grin. This ain't Alabama, brother, this ain't 1960.

-Juror Number Five may be excused.

The black MBA stood up. Mr. Sloan thanked him. The Sophist tilted his head toward me and raised an eyebrow.

-What'd I tell you.

It was like the NBA draft, only in reverse. You identify the most talented individual, the guy with the leadership skills and the presence, and if the opposition doesn't beat you to it, you use one of your picks to have him removed from the league. Ladies and gentlemen, with their first pick, the Chicago Bulls cut Michael Jordan. A reverse draft and then a reverse lottery. No number 51, please, anything but 51. The clerk called out seven numbers, none of them 51. Yes! Seven new candidates heading for the jury box, thirty-three prospective jurors still safe behind the bar, five total peremptory challenges remaining.

When we broke for lunch, I wandered the courthouse hallways, eating a sandwich and doing the math. At worst, if I was figuring this right, a fifteen percent chance of spending the week with Sloan and Lawson, attorneys at law, an eighty-five percent chance I'm eyeing bikinis while finishing my Grisham on the beach tomorrow, with my jury obligation satisfied.

After lunch, Mr. Lawson started again with the same question about a big mistake. One guy said he'd purchased a used car and the transmission blew. The next guy had even less imagination.

-Yeah, same thing, bought me an old Isuzu, never shoulda did that.

The website said trial lawyers try to identify leaders and followers in the jury pool. What they want is a jury filled with followers and a leader or two sympathetic to their side. Mostly I was seeing followers. A short Hispanic woman who regretted dropping out of high school with her friends. Follower. But now she was working on her GED to set a better example for her two kids. Leader? Maybe at home, not on a jury, no way. A young white woman who teaches yoga. Leader? Says she makes mistakes all the time, doesn't believe in regret, tries to live in the moment. Not real inspiring, lady. So who was going to lead this bunch? Anyone with even a hint of initiative—roof man, black MBA—was already on the freeway going home.

Mr Sloan wanted to know more about the yoga instructor, who sat in chair ten.

-Do you have an open mind about this case?

-I believe so.

Duh.

-Would you be able to find someone guilty, even if it meant sending him to prison for the rest of his life?

-I think so. I mean, if he's guilty and everything.

-Did you grow up in Orange County?

-No, I'm from back east. Baltimore.

-Oh. What brought you to California?

-I needed, you know, a change. The yoga scene is better here.

-Have you ever been the victim of a crime?

-No, not that I...yeah, our house got robbed once, when I was little, but it was just some kids, nothing serious.

-Do you believe a person has the right to take the law into her own hands?

-You know, I was thinking about that when you asked it before, and I think maybe there are things we could solve ourselves. I don't mean like hurting someone, but you know maybe talking to them, telling them what they...what you think they did wrong.

-Okay. But what if they won't listen to you?

-I still think you should try.

Mr. Sloan smiled and thanked her. Would he want her on his jury? The Sophist to my left didn't think so.

-She's outta here.

-A white woman?

-A crazy white woman.

-He needs to save his challenges.

-He gets ten.

-Isn't it six?

-Criminal trials it's ten.

-You sure?

He was sure. And if he's right, I'm up to—I did the math: oh, shit—a forty percent of getting picked. Calm down. Even if I get called into the box, there's still Plan B, there's still stubbornness, there's still man, if the cops ain't doing it. That's it: I'm not staying without a fight.

-It's twenty.

What? The Hypocrite on my right had joined the conversation, but kept her eyes on her book, even when I whispered in reply.

-Ten each, right?

-No, twenty.

-Each?

-If it's for a life sentence.

She still hadn't looked up. Her nonchalance was troubling.

-Is there a problem, sir?

Judge Silverson! Her welcome-to-my office voice had become something sterner. Her stare honed in on me. The Sophist was suddenly busy checking his watch. The Hypocrite stayed deep in her paperback, not even a ripple on the pond. The Sophist and The Hypocrite—I was surrounded by Greeks, but I was in this alone, just me and the judge. Our eyes met, and she asked again.

-Sir, is there a problem?

I shook my head no. She held my glance a beat longer, a schoolmarm's reprimand, then instructed Mr. Sloan to resume his examinations. The bailiff, though, a rather extreme looking man—very serious, very short, very bald—continued sizing me up.

Is there a problem, sir? How many times have I used that tired line? What it means is I'm pretending to give you the benefit of the doubt, pretending that there might actually be a legitimate reason for you to be talking when you should be factoring equations or filling in bubbles on a standardized test, when we both know that if there was a legitimate reason for your conversation then you wouldn't be whispering while pretending not to be, only this way you can save face, and I can appear respectful, and we can both avoid escalation. What it means is shut up.

Actually, Your Honor, there is a problem. If The Hypocrite is correct, if each side gets to disqualify twenty, then I'm still in play, we all are. It's no longer about simple odds. If the attorneys don't like what they see, together they have enough challenges to march each one of us prospective jurors into the box and pop the question. A big mistake, immediately regretted? Actually, I'm regretting that I just missed my second escape opportunity of the morning, so please, Your Honor, could we try it again? Is there a problem, sir? Yes, Your Honor, I've developed such a crush on Juror Number Four that I can hardly think straight, I need to be dismissed. Is there a problem, sir? Yes, Your Honor, I neglected to tell you that I'm army reserve and I've just been called up, a text message from Uncle Sam, they've located bin Laden and need all boots on the ground, boo-yah! Is there a problem, sir? Yes, Your Honor, I'm having a stroke.

My pocket vibrated again: another text message. Wouldn't it be weird if it really was from the government, like the Pentagon is wiretapping brains now? You have a random thought—joining the army might be cool—and two minutes later a text message says Be all u can be and a recruiter is knocking on your door. That would make a great Grisham: a small town lawyer takes on the government, only the government can read his mind, so he has to think fake thoughts to misdirect them, then he sneaks out of town and plots his strategy in a cave in the mountains where the brain-tappers can't reach him. Can a person think fake thoughts? Could the small town lawyer drive down main street thinking he was going to his old aunt's house for Sunday afternoon pie when really he was heading for the cave? Wouldn't the brain-tappers know he was thinking about thinking fake thoughts? Probably too science fictiony for a Grisham.

The bailiff seemed to have lost interest in me, so I risked a quick peek at my cell phone: Get on the jury!

Huh?

Marissa works as a masseuse—forgive me, massage therapist—at a fancy hotel in Laguna, and when she has a time slot with no customers—sorry, guests—there isn't much to do except refold towels and send text messages to her few friends and her boyfriend—oops, guy she is seeing—so maybe she is just goofing around, but I don't get the joke. Or is the exclamation point supposed to be a question mark? I doubt it. But why would she want me on a jury? Maybe because when she has an afternoon off, she'd rather hang out with that artist guy, not the math teacher. Artist might be too generous a term. She says he paints landscapes, and in Laguna that usually means sun-drenched cliffs dappled with flowers overlooking a stretch of sand and a pale blue sea, sold to tourists wanting a splash of ocean in their suburban living rooms. Interior decorator is more like it. I'm sure he has a beard.

I typed Huh?, hit SEND, and waited for Marissa to reply.

Meanwhile, on the other side of the bar, Mr. Sloan was still working his way through the new talent. The guy with the bad transmission was the second Juror Number Five, having moved into the dismissed MBA's seat, and the difference was, well, night and day. Mr. Amiable replaced by Mr. Terse.

-Juror Number Five, have you ever met the defendant?

-No, sir.

-Do you have any independent knowledge of this case?

-No, sir.

-Any opinion on his guilt or innocence?

-No, sir.

His no-sir's had that aggressive matter-of-factness you hear from ex-military who, faced with the chaos of civilian life, take refuge in their certitude, their lack of ambiguity. The other guy with a bad car tried the same pose, but couldn't pull it off.

-Juror Number One, have you ever met the defendant?

-No, sir.

-Any independent knowledge of this case?

-No, sir. Uh, what do you mean by independent knowledge?

-Had you heard anything about this case before you came into the courtroom this morning?

-Oh. No.

-Maybe you read about it in the newspaper?

-Not really.

-So you don't have any opinion on his guilt or innocence?

-I don't know what he did, if that's what you mean.

In high profile cases, they sometimes have trouble filling a jury because most prospective jurors have already formed opinions about the accused, but that wasn't our situation. I read the newspaper, and I'm pretty sure this case went unreported. A drug deal goes bad in a rough neighborhood, some poor fool gets shot in the head—that doesn't even make the tv news any more, never mind the front page or even the local section. Rough neighborhoods don't matter. A guy named Jack is arrested, accused of first degree murder—murder!—and, yawn, nobody cares, nobody even knows.

I was beginning to think even the defense attorney didn't care. In comparison to Mr. Sloan's hurried efficiency, Mr. Lawson's friendly questioning now seemed lackadaisical. When it came time for challenges, he didn't even stand. He looked tired. Maybe the limp was real after all. Mr. Sloan employed four more peremptories, including one to dismiss the Hispanic GED mother. He was shaping a jury, he knew what he was looking for. Mr. Lawson disqualified only the bad car guy in chair one, an obvious move, and without much enthusiasm. Is Lawson bored? Ambivalent? Maybe he's sure his adversary will knock out anyone unpredictable, so he lets him do it, lets Sloan use up challenges, saves his own for when he needs them most. Like rope-a-dope. The slow guy with the bad hip wins in the end. That would be brilliant. Or maybe Lawson knows he's drawn the short straw, the losing card, knows once the damning evidence is presented the jury composition won't matter much at all. That's probably it. He's thinking let's just get this finished and go home. Or was it the other way around? A defense attorney excusing jurors left and right would appear desperate, and Lawson was sitting pretty with an ace up his sleeve. Hell, Sloan, you pick 'em this time, my witnesses are unimpeachable, my defense is jury-proof. Or maybe Lawson was just the typical public defender you read about—overworked, underpaid, uninspired, incompetent. Brilliant or incompetent, it's a fine line, right? If he was brilliant, he would have graduated top in his class and taken a big money job with a big money firm, like that character in my third Grisham. So, incompetent then. Maybe incompetently brilliant, like that genius mathematician who quit MIT and sought political asylum in France because he thought men in red ties were stalking him. Maybe crazy old Lawson has the perfect defense sketched out on his legal pads but won't reveal it, not even to the jury, fearing assassination if his legal genius becomes known? Or maybe his legal pads are completely blank, he's brilliantly incompetent, like Inspector Clouseau. Like he's actually the courthouse janitor pressed into service when he discovered the real public defender passed out in the bathroom. Don't worry, Jack, he'll bumble his way to an acquittal.

Or maybe I think too much. Marissa says so. Maybe that's why she likes the plein air artiste, whatever his name is, sitting dumbly at his easel, daubing distant seagulls onto his tedious seascapes.

Sloan and Lawson accepted Lady Yoga and Sir No-Sir, giving them seven total jurors. Judge Silverson asked the clerk to call five more numbers. Please, not 51. The clerk called 52. Whew, close call. The Sophist stood up. I hope they retain him—keep the black guy who predicted an all-white jury—how would he spin that? The clerk called 26, 18, 22. Sounded like a locker combination.

Suddenly, I could feel it. It's hard to describe, and I'm not psychic or anything, but sometimes when I'm concentrating intently, my mind will open up, my thinking will kind of relax, almost cease, and a physical sensation will emerge, at first just a hint, then growing stronger to where my thoughts and feelings reach perfect alignment, a unity, and then I just know. Only it's stronger than knowing. It's an awareness. Physiological certainty. I was now aware of what was happening, what was about to unfold. My number would be drawn.

And...bingo! When the clerk called 51, I was already standing. Five minutes earlier I had been dreading this moment. Now it was here, and I felt relief—the battle finally joined, nothing left to do but fight. And I was ready,

I had my strategy: the stubborn, biased, obnoxious jury candidate was on his feet and heading for chair number one. Ready or not, Loan and Slawson, bumblers at law, here I come.

When Mr. Lawson, the brilliant or incompetent attorney or janitor limped or faux-limped toward me and repeated his perfunctory or crafty question, I finally got it. It wasn't a question at all, it was a mantra. Each time he said mistake immediately regretted, he was telling us that his man hadn't intended to kill, the gun just went off, an accident, regrettable, but not murder. It was a subliminal message aimed for a juror's unsuspecting subconscious, planting seeds of doubt in fertile ground. I should have been a lawyer. I mean, was anyone else catching all this? Does Juror Number Eleven, for example, a gray-haired woman with bifocals, realize she's being carefully cultivated? I doubt it, otherwise she would knock off the incessant smiling. She smiled at the attorneys when they questioned her, and positively beamed at me when I entered the jury box. What did the old bumper sticker say?—if you're not worried, you don't understand the situation. Something like that.

-What about you, Juror One, ever make a big mistake?

Mr. Lawson's face wasn't quite fat, more like round and fleshy, and, like most white people stuck indoors all day, his skin was closest to pink. He, too, was smiling—real or fake? or delusional?—as he waited for my big confession. But I wasn't ceding a thing.

-Sure, I suppose.

-Can you give us an example—a big mistake you made?

-I don't know. I try to forget them.

-I see. You're a teacher, right?

That was from the juror questionnaire: single, thirty-five, Dana Hills High School, no criminal record.

-That's right.

He paused, encouraging me to provide details. Not a chance, Mr. Public Defender, you're on your own.

-What do you teach?

-Math.

-Oh, math. How are the students these days?

-Fine. On vacation mostly.

-Right, yes, summertime. Do your students have trouble with drug use?

-No. They're experts at it.

Down in chair twelve, The Sophist laughed. Thank you, brother, I got a million of them. Judge Silverson wasn't amused. I could feel her eyes on me, waiting for me to go too far. Mr. Lawson managed a patient smile, but didn't relent.

-Ever make mistakes with students? I don't know, maybe yell at a kid and then wish'd you hadn't?

-Yeah, sure. It happens.

-Ever yell at the wrong kid? Like you thought he cheated and turns out he didn't.

-Actually, I try not to yell.

-Ever accuse the wrong kid of cheating?

-Probably.

-You don't remember?

Am I the one on trial here? Shouldn't we be asking Jack over there about his big mistake? Lawson hadn't shown this much interest in the other jurors. It was like my resistance had inspired him, and he was determined to break me. I didn't give an inch.

-Like I said, I try to forget.

-Right. Now tell me, can you look at my client seated at that table and say right now that you think he's innocent?

-Yes. No. I mean, I don't know.

-You don't know?

Don't blow it. Here's your chance. *Ándele.*

-I mean, when I see him sitting over there, I....

My phone vibrated in my pocket.

-Yes?

Mr. Lawson hovered over me, suddenly enthusiastic about his job. Blood rushed to my face. Focus, focus.

-It's like on tv, him sitting there, like the bad guy, and so I think something in my head assumes he's guilty. I can't help it.

Attaboy! That ought to do the trick.

-Thank you for your honesty. That's actually a pretty normal thought. Do you think you could set that thought aside and carefully, objectively, weigh the evidence?

-I'm not sure. I've never done this before.

Mission accomplished. Enough reticence to suggest stubbornness. Hints of sarcasm without bringing down a scolding from the bench. Clear admission of bias. And Mr. Lawson moving on to Juror Number Two.

Marissa's new message was burning a hole in my pocket, but it was too risky to check my phone while Lawson was talking to my immediate neighbor, while the spotlight was still so close. I waited until Lawson made it down to The Sophist.

-Juror Number Twelve, ever make a big mistake?

-I went up the Eiffel Tower, I thought I had enough time, but I ended up missing my flight back to the States.

-What were you doing in Paris?

-I had a layover, flying back from Morocco.

I leaned forward as if trying to get a better look at the globetrotting African American, propped my elbows on my knees, and read the new text message: Dude Angels game my place beers. That was Pete, not Marissa. If that was Marissa, I'd get down on my knees and beg her to marry me. I'd teach summer school for extra income. I'd give her the latest Grisham for Christmas. Her mother could move in with us. And bring her cats. But Marissa doesn't like beer. She doesn't even like sports. Sometimes I'm not sure she likes me.

From the box, I could now see the defendant's face. Jack looked to be in his thirties, six feet tall, lean—not all that different from me, actually, if I were wearing a coat and tie, not jeans and a polo shirt, and if I were a black man accused of shooting someone, not a white guy being accused of indifference. He was sitting at Lawson's table and staring, I swear, right at me. Stone cold. Like my future is in your hands, asshole, and you're playing with your cell phone? I'm usually suspicious of cops, but the two burly uniforms by the door were suddenly a comfort. I could easily imagine Jack with a handgun, no, a shotgun, and the same cold eyes watching his victim fly backward across the hood of a car. I looked away. I'd love to stick around and hear your side of the story, Jack, hear all the lurid details, hear your big regret, but it's seventy-five and sunny at the beach and summer vacation goes by in a flash.

Mr. Sloan wanted to hear more lurid details from my illustrious career.

-How long have you been teaching?

-Ten years.

-Would you agree that student behavior has gotten worse over time?

-I don't know. People say that.

-Do you consider yourself a disciplinarian?

-What do you mean?

-Well, do you tolerate student tardiness?

Okay, Sloan liked my bias against the defendant, thought I was a keeper, he just wanted to make sure I wasn't too forgiving. Time to shift gears.

-Students are going to be late. There's no point making a big deal out of it.

-Do you assign detentions?

-Rarely.

-What if a student is disrupting class?

The truth is, students don't disrupt my class because they know I'll send them out, call their parents, have them suspended, see them kicked off sports teams. And for tardies, same thing, zero tolerance. It's the only way to survive. But never mind.

-I usually ask a disruptive student to solve a few equations on the board. That calms them down.

If only.

-So let me ask you this. Would you be able to find someone guilty, even if it meant sending him to prison for life?

Competing mantras. Lawson says his client made a mistake he regrets. Sloan tells us to send the accused to prison for life. Judge Silverson must have understood what they were doing, trying the case in advance, yet she didn't halt their foreplay, their premature enunciations.

-I guess if I were truly honest, I'd say that life imprisonment is a waste of taxpayer money. Why keep a senior citizen locked up?

Sloan frowned and gave up. Fish Number One isn't a keeper after all. The only question that remained was who would excuse me first, Sloan or Lawson?

Well, there was one other question: had I committed a crime? Before jury selection began, we had all sworn to answer accurately and truthfully, failure may subject you to criminal prosecution. My responses to the attorneys now were definitely not in the spirit of the whole truth and nothing but. But did I actually lie? It would be tough to prove. They had mostly asked about my opinion, and opinions change. Did I really assume the defendant was guilty? Probably. Probably I probably did, I can't be sure. Was I really skeptical about life imprisonment? In the context of public expense, probably. With regard to justice and deterrence, probably not, but again, I'm not certain. If they had framed more succinct questions they could have pinned me down. Sloan hadn't asked for my opinion on the value of life sentences. He had asked if I could find someone guilty, my answer was a non sequitur actually, and he let it slide. It's not my fault, Your Honor, if these bumbling lawyers didn't help me clarify my thoughts on issues I don't normally contemplate. That's it: I wasn't being dishonest, I was confused.

As it turned out, no one was concerned about my possible perjury. As it turned out, my ambiguousness wasn't interpreted as evasive or hostile. At least so far as I could tell. At the other end of the box, my friend The Sophist was far better behaved. He was cooperative and forthcoming, kept his cynicism under wraps. He presumed innocence but was willing to convict. He rejected vigilantism. He didn't know any policemen, agreed they could make mistakes, but had called them when his car was stolen and sure was grateful when they recovered it without a scratch two hours later. He managed a family restaurant and coached Little League baseball. Mr. Sloan sent him home.

-Juror Twelve may be excused.

Judge Silverson nodded. The Sophist shrugged and departed.

But neither the particular Mr. Sloan nor the brilliant or incompetent Mr. Lawson saw fit to dismiss the math teacher with the attitude. They were both sitting down, Sloan shuffling papers, Lawson whispering to Jack. It took a moment to sink in. I gave up on Lawson, but kept expecting Sloan to rise up and end my misery. Come on, buddy, you don't want a wild card like me, I'll hang your jury, I swear I will. Nothing. The clerk called two new numbers to replace The Sophist and one other lucky escapee. I stopped paying attention.

It was over. I wouldn't be at the beach tomorrow, or the next day, or the day after that. I would be sitting in a stale courtroom, bored to tears, while Sloan, Lawson, and Silverson debated some arcane point of order.

My phone vibrated. A text from Marissa: Bud Jack? Get on the jury!

Well, there's a murder mystery for you, sports fans. Marissa rarely leaves bucolic Laguna Beach, avoids newspapers because they're too depressing, works in the hushed spa of a resort hotel tending to the aches of the rich, tan, and pampered, and somehow knows the name of a black man accused of murder sitting in the bustling county courthouse in Santa Ana, twenty freeway miles and a world away.

-Juror Number One, is that a cell phone? Sir?

Busted!

-I'm sorry, Your Honor. I—

-Perhaps you'd like to spend a night in lockup?

Busted, like my students say, big-time!

-No, I—

-I won't tolerate this.

-My dog is sick.

Where did that come from?

-I don't care. Is that clear to everyone? No cell phones in my courtroom. How sick? Mr. Fletcher?

-What?

How did she know my name?

-How sick is your dog?

-I took her to the vet last night. She was vomiting. And bleeding from the other end. It was pretty bad.

If you're going to lie, lie big, right? My heart was going a mile a minute. My face was on fire.

-Why didn't you say something earlier?

-I don't know. I thought it would be okay. But I just got a message from the vet. They needed my permission to run more tests. They said it was urgent, so I....

Judge Silverson looked out at the remaining jurors beyond the bar, then back at me. Her frown was gone. Maybe she's a dog person and knows what it's like when your little darling is hanging by a hair. Maybe I'm a better liar than I thought.

-Would you like to be dismissed?

That, then, is how you avoid sitting on a jury: lie through your teeth, perjure like a politician. Plan A was right from the get-go. Not that I'm proud of it. Not that I knew what I was doing. The dog story wasn't premeditated. I've never even owned a dog. Inspector Clouseau flashed to mind: Eet's naht mah dahg. The irony, too, was unintended. After all the calculating, all that agonizing, I'd finally found the way out, only there was one problem.

-No, Your Honor, I wish to serve.

2

After the jury selection, after they had sworn us in again and dismissed us for the day, I drove back to Laguna, taking the canyon road as it cuts narrowly through the hills then opens up to downtown and the beach. The canyon is beautiful, especially in spring when the hillsides are green and yellow with wild mustard, but the canyon road has become an industrial strip. Downtown Laguna is reserved for luxury—art galleries, hair salons, fashion shops, and quiet restaurants beyond the reach of a high school teacher. The lower canyon is home to the Pageant of the Masters, an enterprise I don't understand. Why would someone volunteer to get dressed up and stand motionless, night after night, in living, breathing, life-size re-creations of classic paintings, and why would someone pay to look at them? But they do, and they come by the busload. The few practical shops in town—auto repair, surfboard shaping, hardware store, lumber yard—crowd against the steep slopes farther up the canyon road. Behind the businesses, where the canyon widens, there is a small residential area. Driving toward the beach after, say, a long day in court, turn left at the used car lot, follow the road as it winds into a side canyon, and park in front of the first yellow house on the right. There's an old wood-frame guesthouse around back, hidden from the street by a beat-up fence and a stand of bamboo wrapped with morning glory vines.

Marissa opened the door with a frown. She didn't like me coming by without warning.

-I'm sorry. I tried calling. Your phone—

-I was taking a nap.

Does the beach painter get the same cold greeting, or is he allowed to show up unannounced?

-I'm in.

-What?

-I'm on the jury.

She hugged me tightly. That's more like it.

-Thank you. I'm so happy.

-I'm happy you're happy.

Inviting myself in, I stepped past her into the living room. Futon couch, Mexican blanket, throw pillows with third world designs—she knew how to dress up a dumpy place. On one wall, a framed Van Gogh print announcing the dates of a museum show. On another wall, shelves with music CDs, a few ceramic pieces, one for burning incense, and books—new age self-help, Neruda poetry, Grishams.

-He needs your help.

-Who does?

-Bud Jack. It's a case of mistaken identity. He's not a violent person.

-Says who? How do you—?

-Sigrid. My client.

That would be Sigrid who had her breasts enlarged and quit her job as a community college art instructor when she remarried, Sigrid who knows all the local gallery owners and organizes an annual fundraiser for the sea mammal rescue foundation. And her new husband is in television. And they have a house in Laguna. Just a small house, Sigrid says, we live modestly and I don't understand these people with their mcmansions ruining the village atmosphere, it's not right. Her husband spends three nights a week at his apartment in LA near his work, but no way he's cheating on her, he calls every night from the apartment to say he loves her, and anyhow there was no prenuptial, if he ever tries anything Sigrid will dump him in a heartbeat and leave him with nothing. And the maid lives in Santa Ana, so when her bus to Laguna gets stuck in morning traffic, Sigrid ends up late for pilates class. She can't just leave a list of chores because the maid, bless her heart, has trouble reading English, you just have to give specific instructions if you want things done properly. And the gardeners are supposed to come and go in the late afternoon when Sigrid is off playing tennis, but they often arrive unfashionably early with their screaming leaf blowers and desecrate the sacred quiet of Sigrid's meditation hour.

I knew all this—late maid, early gardeners, small house, big breasts— because one morning a week, once the maid understood her marching orders, Sigrid had her middle-aged skin scrubbed, peeled, oiled, and kneaded while she poured out her troubles and explicated her life. A massage therapist—the licensed professional, not the forty-dollar-an-hour Prettiest Asian Girls! advertised in the back of the sports pages—must be confidante and confessor. It's part of the process, Marissa insisted. The body work opens up emotional blocks, and her clients—sometimes they laugh, sometimes they cry—you have to let them flow.

I knew all this because a week earlier, the last time I'd seen Marissa, it was all she talked about—Sigrid and her stress.

-I'm like, Sigrid, just relax, that's why you come here. And she's all, I know, I know, but I've got to vent. She says this time her neighbors submitted an architectural design that doesn't totally block the ocean, they would still see Catalina Island but they lose their whitewater view, the beach and everything. She went on for like twenty minutes about view equity. I wanted to strangle her.

-Why didn't you?

-That's one of the rules. Don't kill the clients. Ever since the new management.

Marissa can be funny—if she's had a little wine.

-What's view equity?

-I don't know. It's like your neighbors have as much right to see the ocean as you do, so you can't stop them from putting on a second story. She's like I don't understand it, we welcomed them to the neighborhood, had them over for dinner, they even admired our picture window and they never said a word about planning to remodel. That is pretty cold, you have to admit. And then her husband got into an argument with them and kept shouting, I'm a very serious man, I'm a very serious man.

How much of human communication is complaining? Sigrid complained to Marissa about the help, Marissa complained to me about Sigrid, and then I complained to Pete about Marissa.

-I mean, she says she can only stay a few minutes or she'll be late to yoga, and then I swear she spends the whole time talking about her clients' problems. I guess they're more interesting than a math teacher.

-Sigrid's the one, you said, with the big—?

-Yeah. Would you say we're serious men? I mean, more serious than some guy who paints beach balls, right? We're teaching the youth of America.

-We're very serious.

-So why doesn't Marissa take me seriously? She takes Sigrid seriously.

-How big are we talking?

-Honkers.

I'd never met her, never seen the woman, but according to Marissa, when Sigrid was face down on the massage table, she was propped up. Which apparently was the scenario—Sigrid propped up and flowing, Marissa working her lower back—when the topic of my jury duty came up.

-Yeah, because I just got your text message before her session started, and she asked what the case was about, and I said what you said, some guy named Jack or whatever, no big deal, and then like fifteen minutes later her head pops up and she goes, is it Bud Jack? I've never seen her like that, like agitated or, I mean, even when she's complaining about the neighbors, she's usually laughing, but now she was like, Marissa, the trial, the jury, is it for Bud Jack? I said maybe, because your text just said Jack.

I sat down on the couch, hoping she would join me. No such luck.

-And then she has to call her husband. She knows we don't allow phones in the spa, but this was like a big emergency all of a sudden, and she leaves and comes back and goes, Marissa, listen to me, this guy Bud Jack, his trial is starting today, he's accused of murder, but it's not true. Turns out her husband knows someone who insists there's no way the guy would shoot anyone or even own a gun. He lives with his grandmother in Long Beach. He supports her. He has his own business, the kind that washes your car in your own driveway.

-You shouldn't be telling me this.

I could still hear Judge Silverson ordering us not to discuss the trial. I could still see her chastising glare.

-I know, but if he goes to prison, his grandmother will lose the house. He's a normal guy, not like some gang-banger.

-A normal guy?

-That's what Sigrid said. Why?

-Let's just say if he knocked on my door and offered to detail my car, I think I'd keep the door closed.

-Because he's black?

-No, because he's scary looking. His eyes.

She gave me an irritated look. Whenever she and I talked about race, I always ended up sounding racist, at least according to her, so I quickly changed my answer.

-Okay, he's not scary. He's…he looks like a point guard.

-What's that?

-A basketball player.

Another irritated look. Here it comes.

-Of course. How could a black man be anything else?

She went into the bathroom and shut the door.

To be honest, she might have had a point, only it's not my fault. I happen to live in a white community. I just happen to have been hired at Dana Hills High, with almost no black students—under one percent, I think. There was one black woman I used to encounter regularly in Laguna. She was frail and weather-beaten, skin like leather, she panhandled in front of a downtown grocery store, my guess was she slept on the beach. The only other black women I ever see in town are gorgeous, usually in the passenger seat of a large SUV, usually with a white man driving. The only black men I see regularly are athletes on television, basketball players especially, you see them up close and personal—muscles, tattoos, facial expressions. So they're a point of reference for me. But that doesn't make me racist. Point guard isn't a value judgment.

-Who else is on the jury?

-Marissa, please.

She was still in the bathroom. Should I sneak another Grisham off the shelf?

-It's not like it's a secret. Are there any blacks?

I wanted to talk about the case, just to spite Judge Silverson. It didn't feel right though. In the courthouse parking lot, I had run into The Sophist, and he was still going on about the race issue.

-You see how it works, man? They should've cut you loose after that song and dance you gave them. Any trouble with drugs?—no, they're experts. That busted me up. But they should've cut you loose.

-Yeah, I was kinda—

-You're the only one who said you thought my man was guilty. The only one. And they keep you on the jury. Presumption of innocence, my ass. I could've been justice herself, blindfold, scales, and they still excuse me.

That's when we shook hands. The normal handshake at first, then you rotate the heel of your hand down and your fingers up into more of a clasp. This requires a deeper elbow bend, bringing the two people closer together, tighter. I doubt he was expecting it from a white math teacher in a polo shirt, but he went with it.

-Alright now.

And the way he said it was cool: Alright now. I felt a connection, even if we never exchanged names. So I know I'm not racist.

Marissa came back into the room.

-So it's all whites?

-There's a Hispanic woman.

-This is what Sigrid said would happen. It's totally unfair. She said you had to get on the jury.

-Does she think I'm black?

-No, but I told her you would do the right thing.

The Sophist had one last comment for me before he got into his car.

-It's up to you now, brother.

-What is?

-Justice, baby. I'm counting on you.

And now Marissa.

-Fletcher, he needs your help.

-What if he's guilty?

-Sigrid said—

-Sigrid said her husband said somebody said. This is crazy. I should tell the judge I've been compromised.

I was serious. First thing in the morning. Your Honor, my sort of girlfriend—I mean, our relationship is she doesn't want commitment right now, she needs to explore her freedom, that's just the place she's at, and under these circumstances, my status being already precarious, if we find him guilty it's going to be ex-sort of girlfriend, so I don't think I can be impartial. But I could already hear Judge Silverson's scold: this is the last straw, Mr. Fletcher, your cell phone, the sick dog story, now this. You are going to sit on that jury like a model citizen and you are going to listen to the arguments and weigh the evidence and make the right decision, do you understand? Not that there was any chance of this conversation taking place.

-Promise me you won't. Promise me you'll stay on the jury.

Marissa was hugging me again. She knew how to get what she wanted, Pete was right about that. I could hear his voice: Dude, she's got you pinched, she hangs out with that painter guy, and you can't even *look* at another woman. Well, he was half right. I looked at other women all the time. I even smiled. Rarely, this being Laguna and me driving an old Honda, did they smile back. Marissa had said go ahead, see whoever you want. But if I did, if I had a dinner date with the nice Spanish teacher for example, Marissa would be hurt. That much I knew. She'd feel betrayed, get angry, and that would be the end of us.

-Okay.

-That's a promise? You'll stay on the jury?

I really didn't have a choice.

-Yes. But listen, if the evidence says guilty—

-Of course. Thank you.

Another hug, then she went for her cell phone.

-I need to text Sigrid. I told her I'd let her know. Do you want to go to First Thursday?

She can type a text message and carry on a conversation at the same time.

-I told Pete I'd come over. How about dinner tomorrow night?

-Okay, dinner tomorrow. I can't wait to hear about your day in court.

She closed her phone. Message sent.

-Marissa, I'm serious, I can't talk about the trial. I don't want you to—

-To what?

Hug number four. And this time a kiss. I didn't know a juror was such a turn-on.

-You know. Sway my opinion.

-Sway your opinion? I can't even get you to go to First Thursdays. Sigrid says there's great new stuff.

On the first Thursday of the month, the numerous art galleries in downtown Laguna stay open late and entice locals with free hors d'oeuvres and the promise of a cultural outing, only the paintings on display always seem so self-conscious, like they're trying hard to be something, whimsical or cubist or I guess mostly they're trying to be sold. Also, I'm not big on cheap white wine served warm in plastic cups. I'd rather drink beer.

-I promised Pete I'd watch the Angels game. I'm sorry.

-It's okay, I'll find someone else.

Great. Someone, for example, who appreciates bright sunny oil paintings, someone who doesn't talk sports. What *do* they talk about? Sigrid, I hope. I hope Mr. Seascape has to listen to all the updates on Sigrid's heroic struggle against injustice.

-I'll go next month.

-Right. Is Bud Jack's lawyer good?

-Hard to say.

-Sigrid says he couldn't afford a decent one.

I knew it. Lawson is incompetent. I knew it all along.

-You know what she told me? Public defenders almost always go for a plea bargain. They know they're probably going to lose, it's their word against the police, so they tell the defendant to take the smaller sentence, guilty or not. What do they care? They get paid the same and it's less work. A poor black guy doesn't stand a chance in that system. That's what she kept saying—Marissa, he doesn't stand a chance. She can be dramatic sometimes, but you have to admire her passion.

-Why doesn't she hire him a lawyer? I mean, if she's so concerned and everything.

Sigrid went on and on to Marissa about her causes—the malnourished sea lion pups that wash ashore, the scandalous lack of art in public spaces around town—and then Marissa went on and on about Sigrid, such a generous woman, such great energy, you know she won an award from the city council, she's amazing. But a few hours of charity work squeezed in between the spa and the gym and a salad at the natural food café downtown doesn't impress me. Try being in a high school classroom for thirty hours a week, grading papers all weekend, taking phone calls from parents who are absolutely shocked by the D on our daughter's progress report, she's never had any trouble in math before, we're very concerned, maybe you're using the wrong approach. Try having nightmares about students who refuse to take their seats and keep flipping the lights on and off, on and off. If Bud Jack is innocent and the jury is racist and grandma's losing her house and the system is a fraud, why doesn't the amazing and passionate Sigrid skip the eco-vacation—they'll be on a sailboat for two full weeks, she told Marissa, one island to the next, no carbon footprint except the plane ride but how else can you get there?—and hire a defense attorney clever enough to excuse the one juror who said the defendant looks guilty?

-She is. I mean her husband. I wasn't supposed to say anything. She wasn't even supposed to tell me. She said her husband doesn't want anyone to know because they don't like to wear their generosity on their sleeve.

-They're paying Bud Jack's legal expenses?

-That's what she said. Because even if he did it or not, everyone deserves competent representation.

Oh.

For the record, I'm no math whiz. Yes, I teach algebra and geometry and enjoy solving logic puzzles. And I'd done a little research. I knew a "small" house in Laguna started at a million bucks. I knew Sigrid was spending over $200 a week on spa treatments. I knew the two-week all-inclusive Galapagos excursion cost seven grand, I had looked it up online. Don't ask me why, but for some reason I was curious how much money Super Sigrid threw around. But I wouldn't know where to begin to figure the odds of a jury member dating the masseuse of the wife of the man secretly funding the defense counsel. In a mega-sprawling population center. And finding out about it. I mean, that's one hell of a coincidence.

On the drive over to Pete's, I stopped at a burrito shop on Pacific Coast Highway. Pete lives in a condo too close to school and refuses to shop within a five-mile radius because he will run into students or former students or, worst of all, other teachers.

-They're going to want to chat.

-So?

-So I don't want to chat.

So it goes without saying that when we watch a game at his place, I pick up dinner. Inside the restaurant, next to the front window, a small woman was sitting by herself reading a paperback, a half-eaten meal in front of her. I couldn't help myself.

-Excuse me. Sorry to interrupt. How are you enjoying that book?

-I can't put it down. Have you read it?

-No, I…is it about a jury?

-No, this billionaire rewrites his will right before he jumps out a window. He's got it all planned out, he leaves the entire fortune to a missionary in Brazil because his heirs are…well, you'd have to read it.

I usually feel bad for someone eating alone. I wonder if they're lonely, if they wished they had someone to talk to. For me, eating alone is like filling your gas tank, something you do quickly, when you have to, something to keep you moving, not a time to savor and enjoy. This woman, though, seemed quite content. When I left the restaurant with a warm bag of takeout, she was back in her novel and didn't look up.

-So she was reading a Grisham. So what?

Pete was sitting on his couch, watching the baseball game, eating his burrito straight from the wrapper, dripping hot sauce onto his lap.

-It wasn't just her. The woman next to me in the courtroom had one. And so did I. We're both reading Grisham while waiting for a murder trial. Kinda weird, huh?

He wasn't impressed.

-Yeah, spooky. What does the guy look like, anyway?

-Grisham? The picture on the back of the book—

-No, the defendant.

-He looks like a point guard.

-Small and quick, or big like Magic Johnson?

Pete knew exactly what I meant—a physical description, nothing more.

-Small and quick, like John Stockton.

Stockton who, for the record, happens to be white, very white, as white as the walls in Pete's condo.

-Well, we know the guy can shoot.

White walls, brown carpet, a couch-and-tv living room, common walls with neighbors on two sides—it's not a charming home. Pete pretends to love it, says it's cool, he can plug the cord in behind the couch and the vacuum reaches every room. I call the place The Cave. There's almost no natural light, just a sliding glass door that leads to a tiny, walled patio facing north. I guess you can't be picky if you want to live walking distance from the beach on a science teacher's salary—walking distance, but the roar you hear when the television is off is not crashing waves, it's traffic on the nearby highway.

-You think he did it?

-I don't know. The trial hasn't really started yet. And anyhow, I'm not supposed to discuss it.

I turned my attention to the ball game.

-Or what?

-Or I'll get kicked off the jury.

I took a big bite of food.

-I thought that's what you wanted.

Pete wasn't getting the hint.

-Yeah, well….

I had planned on telling him, man, they stuck me on a jury, there was nothing I could do. I didn't want him to know how the judge gave me a chance to escape and how, after weeks of anguishing over jury duty, I had declined the judge's offer simply because Marissa's text message insisted I stay. I knew what he would say. But when I stopped chewing and opened my mouth, the same mouth that lied under oath in a court of law, the truth came out, the whole truth. Go figure.

Pete, for one, couldn't believe it.

-You're kidding. You told the judge you wanted to serve?

-Crazy, huh?

-I don't know.

That surprised me. I had expected to hear dude, she's got you pinched. I wasn't expecting him to be understanding. I mean, Pete had never really warmed up to Marissa. I think partly he wanted me to be in his situation, without a date on Friday night and no prospects for Saturday. Misery loves company. Mostly, though, he was concerned that Marissa was stringing his friend along. He understood the physical attraction—she was tall and thin, with green eyes and long straight hair dyed some shade of reddish-brown depending on her mood, and every once in a while, not often enough, she invited me to spend the night. But he wondered if she and I were otherwise compatible. I guess I did too. We liked watching movies together. We made each other laugh with horror stories from work—the drunk student throwing up under his desk, the obese client with old toilet paper caught in the thick folds of skin below her hips. We enjoyed walks on the beach. If sometimes our conversations got stilted, it was because she was afraid of being too vulnerable. She had suffered through an unfriendly divorce and she was wary. Pete should have understood that, that's what I told him, he'd been through the same thing. Marissa said it was like starting over, figuring out who you are and what you want, trying to get past the anger and the blaming. No, she should stick with the blaming, Pete said, it comes in handy. Marissa was thinking about going back to college, studying sociology, or maybe just starting a private massage therapy practice. Pete said I was the guy between her ex and her next. I disagreed. I thought that once she decided to trust me, once she was ready, she would be able to open up.

-Pete, I'm grabbing another beer. You want one?

Feeling relieved at not being criticized, I headed for the kitchen, a room so narrow you can't have the refrigerator and oven doors open at the same time, not that Pete ever opens the oven door.

-You sure Marissa won't mind? Maybe you should text her.

-Funny.

I was opening the refrigerator when it hit me—not the refrigerator, though it should have been that obvious all along: the whole thing is like a Grisham. Sigrid's husband hires Lawson who knows he can't win the case on its merits, so with money to burn, what does he do? He hires professional jury consultants to analyze all the potential jurors, everything about them—education, political affiliation, automobile type, racial attitudes. Only I hadn't seen anyone in the courtroom who could be a jury consultant. No one was scrutinizing body language, taking notes, whispering knowingly to Lawson. Just anxious prospective jurors, bored court personnel, and two mismatched attorneys. And I hadn't seen Lawson putting much effort into building a sympathetic jury. Maybe he figured a hung jury was the best he could do, so he only needed one juror who would decide not guilty and refuse to be swayed. That's it—he only needs one. So Sigrid's husband arranged my jury summons. I don't know how he did it, but he did. Maybe he bribed someone in the courthouse or hacked into the computer system. With enough money, you can do anything. Then he used Marissa—Bud Jack? Get on the jury!—to persuade me to serve. The whole thing was set up to make sure the math teacher who drives an old Honda and knows how to shake hands with a black man will get on the jury and...The Sophist! Why was he still outside the courthouse when we were dismissed for the day? He had been excused much earlier, but there he was, waiting to say that justice was up to me. Obviously, someone put him up to it.

But when I presented my hypothesis to Pete....

-Dude, that's the most stupid-ass thing I ever heard.

-Have you ever read a Grisham?

He deftly ignored the question.

-Okay, suppose you're right, suppose the woman's husband wants you on the jury to make sure the guy isn't convicted. I mean, there's no way, but for the sake of argument, a rich white guy in Laguna, what does he care?

-Good question.

-What's the guy's name—the husband? I'll look him up.

He had his laptop computer open.

-All I know is he's Sigrid's husband.

-Oh, that's helpful. Sigrid's husband. Let's see. Two thousand hits. Sigrid and her husband Otto own a German bakery in Cincinnati. Is that them?

-Search for Sigrid and Laguna Beach marine mammal rescue. Something like that. She arranges their annual dinner.

Pete frowned as he typed, deepening the furrows on his expansive forehead. Marissa complained to me about Sigrid, I complained to Pete about Marissa, and Pete complains about his hairline, which is receding faster, he gripes, than the goddamn glaciers. Just looking at him he is hard to place, a grocery store manager or maybe he sells insurance, just your average guy, unremarkable to be sure. But usually he wears a baseball cap, and with the baldness concealed, you can see the lanky first baseman he used to be, the energetic teacher-of-the-year and weekend warrior he still is. Funny what a bare scalp suggests. Thank God for my thick, unruly mop. You swing like my sister, Pete razzes me when we golf, but I'd kill for your hair, so would she.

-Here it is. Benefit dinner. Sigrid Wilhite?

-That's it. That sounds right.

-Richard and Sigrid Wilhite.

-Really?

-There's even a picture. Richard and Sigrid. You weren't kidding. Holy shit.

-What?

-The woman has disproportionates.

Fake breasts come in two categories. Proportionates seem genetically plausible, at least size wise, though their defiance of gravity gives them away. Disproportionates are just absurd. You can see them from behind, reaching out wider than the ribcage. From the front, they look like separate entities unrelated to the torso, two cantaloupes on a cello, they simply don't fit. But they do get your attention. When they're bearing down on you in the canned goods aisle or making a mockery of a bikini top on the boardwalk, you can't not look. Pete thinks they're fantastic, says they're the reason he loves south county: Dude, there's a disproportionate number of disproportionates here. Actually, some scientists believe the breasts of American women are, on the whole, larger than in previous generations. The causes are not clear— hormones in meat, microwave radiation, pesticides? I argue for natural selection, Pete's in the high fructose corn syrup camp, but we agree that further observation and analysis are in order. We're academics, it's what we do.

Reluctantly, Pete left the photo behind and resumed sleuthing. A search for Richard Wilhite was too broad to be helpful. A search for Richard Wilhite in television led us to a salesman in Indiana. A search for Richard Wilhite in television in Los Angeles gave us two stories about a high school football player. A search for the point guard who washes your car in your driveway turned up one useful news sentence: Bud Jack, 28, of Long Beach was charged in the death of Juan Castro, 22, of Huntington Beach. A search for Juan Castro could go on for days. Something wasn't adding up. I had thought Bud Jack and I were about the same age. Turns out he was younger than he looked. That's an honest mistake. But how can a philanthropist in the entertainment business who smiles happily to the photographer at the marine mammal benefit dinner be otherwise completely off the internet radar?

-Dude, I got it. Where does he live?

-Laguna somewhere. Marissa might know. Why?

-Call her. We'll stake out his house.

One problem with being around high school students all day is you end up thinking like one. Pete teaches biology mostly to sophomores, and it shows. One time he stood up at an emergency faculty meeting, with the principal and two vice principals seated nearby, also the campus safety officer, and suggested we encourage the students to smoke more, especially the angry, alienated ones.

-Not cigarettes. I mean pot.

-Thank you, Mr. Repetti.

-Some of them, we could probably get medical approval.

We were gathered in the wake of the latest school shooting—three dead including the shooter at a junior high in Nebraska. Captain Safety had come up with a remarkably long list of recommendations, most of them (hallway cameras, panic buttons) intended to get him (sniper rifle, body armor) on the scene as quickly as possible, some of them (classroom telephones, remote-locking doors) with great potential for student pranks, and none of them preventive. Which is where Pete came in.

-I'm telling you, no way a stoner shoots up the cafeteria.

-Mr. Repetti, thank you.

He thinks like a sophomore, but he's always thinking—and now, in hot pursuit of the Wilhites, he was inspired.

-Dude, you said her husband was arguing with the neighbor over their ocean view, right?

-So?

-Design review board. You can't remodel your house without approval from the city. It's all public.

Through the magic of internet, within seconds Pete was able to find the city website, pull up the minutes from board meetings, scroll through the addresses of designs under dispute, and there it was, a complaint against 327 Hummingbird Lane by Richard Wilhite, immediate neighbor to the north.

-Let's go. We'll take my car. It's a stake-out vehicle.

He was up off the couch, searching for his keys.

-A minivan?

-They always sit in a van when they're tapping your phone. The guy in the back has those big headphones on his ears. Come on. I've got binoculars. We'll park across the street and watch.

-No.

-We'll bring beer.

-You're crazy.

-On your feet, soldier. We've got a mission.

When Pete Repetti gets the impulse for an adventure, there's no stopping him, and when he designates you as an accomplice, it's harder to dodge than jury duty.

-Someone will see us and call the cops.

-Okay, then we'll just go knock on the front door.

-And say what?

-Dude, oh, dude, this is brilliant. We'll buy a pizza and pretend we're pizza delivery with the wrong address. Grab the beer, will you.

Keys and wallet, cap and flip-flops, he was ready to roll.

-I don't see how this is going to tell us why her husband wants me on the jury.

-No, I just want to get a glimpse of those disproportionates.

3

If you are going to lie, don't hesitate—that's what I learned from the Holocaust. Every year, the students in Mrs. Dietz's English class read the memoir of a Jewish concentration camp survivor, or at least they carry the book around school, and I've thumbed through it once or twice. When the guy is caught stealing potatoes, he has his lie ready. He smoothly gives the German guard his old phone number instead of his prisoner number, and later the guard can't pick him out of the work crew. That's why he was a survivor. Some prisoners, he wrote, didn't know how to lie, didn't know when to steal, no street smarts, and they didn't last long. That would be me.

-How's your dog doing?

-My dog?

-Didn't you say your dog was sick?

It was Juror Number Four, the heavy-set woman.

-Oh. Yeah. He's better. Thanks.

-Good. I'm glad. Dogs are wonderful. I wish I could have one. I thought you said it was a she.

-Really?

-Because that's what reminded me of Sugar. She was such a sweetheart. I had to give her up because I'm allergic. You didn't say she?

We were in the hallway outside the courtroom on a recess from the morning proceedings, twelve perfect strangers forbidden to discuss the one thing we had in common.

-My name is Cheryl, by the way. What kind is he?

-What?

-What kind of dog?

-A mutt, I guess.

Heavy-set is a euphemism and, in this instance, an understatement. There was no way around it, Cheryl-by-the-way was obese. No way around her, either. My back was to the wall, she had planted herself in front of me, and she wanted to talk.

-Mutts make great pets. Very loyal.

A pudgy smile. Layers of chin.

-Sugar was a cockapoo. Such a little sweetheart.

Arms the size of my legs.

-I thought a cockapoo would be okay for me. They don't shed.

Memory like an elephant's.

-I'd swear you said she.

The arrival of the yoga instructor saved me.

-Hi, I'm Cheryl. Didn't you say you were from Baltimore?

I fled down the hall to where three other jurors, three paunchy men, were testing the limits of free speech. I casually listened in.

-So whata you think?

-Kinda slow so far.

-That guy sure can talk.

They looked to be in their fifties, graying hair half-heartedly combed, probably veteran fathers and husbands, guys who come home from work and flip on the tv.

-How long you think this'll last?

-Judge said a week, right? And the deliberations of course.

-That probably won't take too long.

A pause. Was that too far? Judge Silverson had started the day with a pleasant welcome back, then sharply reminded us we weren't to discuss the case—Are we all clear on this?—not even with other jurors. Well, a little vague patter about courtroom conduct can't hurt, Your Honor, not among responsible adults.

-Ever been on a jury before?

-No, first time. You?

-Once, ten years ago. Just a civil case.

-Seems like this might get interesting.

-I don't know. After hearing that attorney—

-The first guy?

They noticed me eavesdropping and checked themselves, as if I might object to a few harmless words about a lawyer's demeanor. I wanted to say something to put them at ease, let them know I wasn't the obnoxious jerk with the cell phone from the day before.

-The first guy reminds me of that sports announcer, the one who does college football.

They turned toward me and nodded. They weren't Laguna types, and definitely not Newport Beach, no dismissive airs, not enough energy invested in appearances, maybe north county, like from Brea or Fullerton. One of them grinned.

-Sure, I know who you mean. Guy they caught with the hooker.

The others chuckled. It seldom fails—you mention football or baseball, and everything's cool. The male sports bond, Marissa called it. They resumed the color commentary.

-Reminds me more of a salesman. Ladies and gentlemen this, ladies and gentlemen that.

-I guess they gotta be a salesman.

-The second guy—I liked him better. His way of talking, I mean.

First guy meant Sloan, whose opening statement had kicked off the morning show.

-Ladies and gentlemen, the defendant Mr. Jack killed Juan Castro, shot him in the head in cold blood, and I'm going to prove it to you. Some cases are complicated, in some cases the evidence is confusing and it's hard for a jury to decide, but in this case, ladies and gentlemen, you will see the case against Mr. Jack is simple and straightforward. You will hear from eyewitnesses who saw Mr. Jack fleeing the crime scene. You will hear an expert on street gangs explain Mr. Jack's motive for killing Juan Castro in cold blood. You will hear a confession. That's right, ladies and gentlemen, Mr. Jack confessed to the crime. So it's going to be a straightforward case. The defense attorney, Mr. Lawson, is going to try to confuse you. That's his job.

Sitting in the jury box, struggling to stay awake, I was already confused. How is this going to take a week? If the defendant confessed, let's just hear what he said and call it a wrap. I could still get back to Laguna and be napping on the beach before the morning fog burned off. Maybe a certain dark-haired juror would go with me.

My alarm had bleated at six a.m., plenty of time to eat breakfast with the sports section and pick up a latte on the way to the freeway, except I slipped right back into unconsciousness. A late night stake-out will do that to you. I woke up in panic at seven, out the door by seven-fifteen, and, mother of all miracles, Friday morning traffic on the 5 Freeway was moving. Inside the courthouse, the wait at the security checkpoint was short, no metal detectors going off. When I reached the elevator, the door was opening. The stars were aligned. I entered the fifth-floor courtroom two minutes before eight, sleep still in my eyes as I looked around for a cup of coffee. Surely Judge Silverson would want her jurors alert and perky on day two, surely the county taxpayers will provide for our waking needs, surely I jest. The only refreshment the county provided was the drinking fountain outside the restrooms, and I can't manage plain water on a morning stomach. I could, however, manage a morning smile for a lovely Latina. I'm not sure what the stuff is properly called—shadow? pencil?—but her eyes were sharply drawn and her long eyelashes seemed to wave hello when she smiled back. Better than caffeine, almost. Her dark curls fell softly on a crisp white blouse. Obviously, she hadn't overslept. Did she notice my same green polo shirt, two days running? I hoped not. I should have introduced myself, said good morning, something. I wasn't at my best, I wasn't sharp. I hesitated, and The Elephant moved in.

-Hi, I'm Cheryl, by the way.

-I'm Roya.

-You're the dental hygienist, right?

I already knew what I would say to Pete: I could use a good flossing.

After Mr. Sloan had finished laying out his case—Motive, opportunity, confession, ladies and gentlemen, all crystal clear—Mr. Lawson stood up to muddy the waters. Once again, the slight limp, the open palms.

-I ask you to keep an open mind. Eyewitnesses can be unreliable, so-called experts can be wrong. I will show you—no, you will see for yourselves—that there was no confession. My client, Bud Jack, is a decent man. He didn't shoot anybody. No one saw him shoot anybody. No one saw him with a gun. In fact, there is zero material evidence tying my client to this unfortunate event.

Bud Jack caught me looking at him. He betrayed nothing, just the same cold stare.

-My friend, Mr. Sloan, told you that the case is clear. What is clear is that the case against my client is entirely circumstantial. Bud Jack was walking down the wrong street at the wrong time and the police picked him up. He didn't confess to anything because he had nothing to confess to. Just because he was walking down the wrong street does not make him guilty. Just because he was arrested does not make him guilty. Just because he is sitting over there, worried and scared, does not make him guilty. Remember, unless the prosecutor can convince you otherwise, convince you beyond a shadow of a doubt—and I don't think he will—you must find Bud Jack not guilty.

Mr. Lawson kept looking my way and frowning. He had to convince at least one juror that the surly black man at the defense table, the only black man in the entire courtroom, had been wrongly arrested, and his most likely candidate, his great white hope, could barely keep his eyes open. Sorry, Lawson, I had a rough night, but whose fault was that?

Pete had been in rare form. A warm summer evening, a couple of beers, nothing but midseason baseball on the television—a recipe for pointless recklessness, the one dish Pete can cook. Pete and his wife once had a patio table until she went to visit her mother and Pete decided we needed to remove the legs and use the round tabletop as a raft. The Voyage of *The Bagel*, he kept calling it. We made it halfway across Dana Point harbor. The marriage sunk three months later. The following July, after Pete had resurfaced from his depression and ensconced himself in The Cave, we filled his minivan with every box of rock salt available from every nearby grocery store in an inspired attempt to corner the market during homemade ice cream season. Pete kept the car running—Just in case, dude—while I filled the grocery carts. A speculative failure, perhaps, but a certain PE teacher who had called Pete an asshole at graduation in June soon learned how difficult it is to remove two hundred pounds of sodium chloride from a dying front lawn. The dumbest ideas, we agree, have the greatest potential for mischief, which was why Mission Disproportionates worried me. It was also why, at nine on a Thursday night, I was riding shotgun rather than heading home for a decent night's rest. If things got crazy, I wanted to be there.

-One more thing. When you listen to the prosecution's witnesses, you may find yourself believing them. These witnesses are going to tell you what they presume to be true about my client, Bud Jack. But listen closely and you will realize that they don't know him. They know nothing about him. This is not one of those crime-and-punishment television shows where the prosecutors are the good guys and the defense attorney, who you never really meet, is simply an obstacle to justice. Jurors sometimes mistake those shows for reality, and they mistake true life trials for one of those shows. Bud Jack is not just the expendable bad guy on the latest episode. He is not a television actor. Bud is a human being, just like you, just like me, with friends and family, a job, hopes for the future. And he's relying on you to give him a fair hearing.

Lawson's eyes came to rest on me. If I hadn't been so tired, I might have stared back and defiantly folded my arms, let him know I'm no pushover: you want me to hang this jury, Mr. Defense Attorney, you're going to have to earn your paycheck. If I had been more disciplined, I would have held back, played it tight, close to the vest. Instead, I grinned. I couldn't help it. I like it when I know something about someone, something they would prefer kept secret, and they don't know I know. Marissa said it comes from a need for control. Whatever, it's still fun. Lawson asked that we afford his client a fair hearing, and I grinned. His eyes narrowed, like some grave thought was crossing his mind, and I smiled, I almost laughed. That's right, big guy, I might look half awake, one more ill-informed citizen-juror for you to patronize and persuade, but I know who has retained your services, I know who's funding Bud Jack's defense, and that's not the half of it.

Finding Hummingbird Lane had been easy. We parked around a corner and walked back up the street. I thought we should stay in the van, but Pete insisted there was no reason to be sneaky.

-Relax. We're just two guys taking a nighttime stroll in Laguna.

-You don't think we look suspicious?

-No, we look gay.

-Oh, that's a comfort.

The property of interest, like the entire neighborhood, like every neighborhood in Laguna—people hunkered down in front of the tv or computer, no porch-sitters shooting the breeze, no children playing tag in the street—was quiet, almost sterile, like those comfort-food paintings they sell downtown with everything perfect—the glowing cottage, the pastel sunrise reflected in the placid creek, the gentle footpath, no people. Just north of 327, a hand-painted mailbox indicated 331. Rose bushes surrounded a neat patch of lawn. A tastefully placed bench, flanked by flower pots, invited you to sit and ponder the patch of lawn next door. Garage door closed, no car in the driveway, no sign of life in the front rooms of the house, yet light blazed from every window. Not exactly eco-friendly, Sigrid. We circled the block— no alley, no way to peer into the backyard. Now what?

-Dude, let's hop the fence.

-And get arrested? No, thanks.

-Then I'm ringing the doorbell.

-No, keep walking. There's a car coming.

Four houses down, we stopped and looked back. The car had pulled into Sigrid's driveway. A car door slammed.

-Come on. Hurry.

-Don't run.

We should have run. When we got close, a large man was disappearing through the front doorway. I recognized him immediately.

-I know that guy. You know who that was?

-Her husband. The smug guy in the photo. But that's not who we came to see.

-No, that was the guy's lawyer. The defense attorney.

-Is this more of your Grisham stuff?

-No, I swear.

Would I? Would I swear in court it was Mr. Lawson entering 331 Hummingbird Lane? Would my testimony hold up on cross-examination?

-Tell us, Mr. Fletcher, could you see his face?

-Not really.

-Not really? Was he facing you?

-No.

-Did he turn and look your way?

-No.

-How far were you from the house that night?

-Maybe one hundred feet. Maybe a little less.

-How long was he in your view?

-Not very long.

-Would you say one second—one-thousand-one?

-Maybe.

-Maybe half a second? A split second?

-It's hard to say.

-So you really can't be sure it was him, can you, Mr. Fletcher?

-It was him. When he stepped into the house, I knew. I could feel it.

-Mr. Fletcher, had you been drinking?

It didn't matter. After Lawson had finished his opening statement, taken in my sleepy grin, and limped back to his chair, I was more convinced than ever—like when I knew my juror number would be called, that same sense of calm, the same physiological certainty. That was his Lexus parked in Sigrid's driveway last night, that was definitely his big frame filling the doorway.

After the recess, after I had escaped The Elephant and talked sports with the guys, we solemnly filed back into the jury box, and Mr. Sloan called as his first witness the police detective who had surveyed and documented the crime scene. On television, this goes quickly—signs of struggle, scattered wallet contents, pool of blood. In our true life trial, as Lawson had put it, this took several hours. Sloan apparently thought it critical that we learn the precise dimensions of the fateful parking lot, the location of the street lamps, the amount of graffiti decorating the dumpsters, and the detective was happy to comply. All those hours pounding the pavement, and he finally had an audience. And a diagram.

-The corpse was located here, behind what I've designated Refuse Receptacle A, face down, head due north, feet to the south. Underneath the corpse we found a plastic bag containing desiccated orange peels, also various glass shards and three pennies. Incidentals, most likely. Refuse Receptacles A and B were empty, all doors open, refuse collection was the day before.

When it was his turn, Lawson had only one question.

-Did you find anything—fingerprints, shoe prints, blood drops, hair samples, food crumbs, clothing fibers, personal items, a gun—anything at all tying Bud Jack to the crime scene?

-No, we didn't.

The killer, it occurred to me, must have been a professional, leaving no trace like that. My stomach clenched. My scalp released a chill. Why this unsettled feeling? It wasn't the horror of a cold-blooded assassination. You hear about this stuff so often, it almost doesn't register. It wasn't hunger, a long morning without a bite to eat. I was used to that too, having started enough school days on an empty stomach. No, it was Pete and I, being amateurs, had left behind more crumbs than Hansel and Gretel.

We'd found a side gate unlocked, the side walkway into the backyard was dark, Pete's adventure gauge was on full—no one's going home till we have a story worth telling. Once our eyes adjusted, we could see a swimming pool, deck chairs, a wet bar. Beyond the pool, a forest of trees and ferns rimmed the yard. I'd never actually been in a layout like this. You see them all the time in glossy real estate ads and the local fashion magazines. From the front, another nondescript upscale home. In the back, a secluded little paradise.

-Let's sit in the hot tub.

-That would be gay *and* suspicious.

-Dude, seriously, I'm getting naked.

-Don't.

-Hold my beer.

-No. I'm leaving.

Pete's momentum builds upon itself, an autocatalytic reaction—something he acknowledges, at least later, after the battle, in moments of subdued reflection: It's my prefrontal cortex, Fletch, it never fully developed, I get these impulses, probably too many Twinkies as a kid. When *The Bagel* went down, leaving us treading water in the dark harbor, he had wanted to crawl aboard one of the yachts anchored nearby.

-Dude, they gotta take us in, it's maritime law.

We swam past *Retirement Package* and *All Aboard*. Is there a law mandating yacht owners congratulate themselves with a smug christening? The good ship *Our Happy Hour* caught Pete's fancy.

-Arr, we'll show them a happy hour. Come on, me hearty, let's hoist the jolly roger.

He started climbing. The lights of a harbor patrol boat were bearing our way. I had to pull him back into the drink. He's the id. I'm the superego. I protect him from himself.

-Pete, I'm not kidding. No hot-tubbing.

-Okay, okay, you're right. Stick to the mission.

Mission creep averted, we stood in the dark backyard. An electric motor hummed. A waterfall gurgled over large rocks and streamed into the pool. What had Marissa said Sigrid had said?—We put the cascade opposite the barbecue, you know like hot and cold for balance, and three boulders, the landscaper wanted two but we had it feng shui-ed, the splashing water focuses your chi. It sounded to me like a running toilet.

The only light in the rear of the house came from upstairs. At one point, we could see a woman near a window, too briefly though to declare success. We backed away from the house hoping for a better angle. When a dog barked next door, we took refuge beneath some trees, in case someone poked their head outside. Another dog barked in reply. What were they saying to each other? Woof, woof, everybody, there's two guys sneaking around next door, I can smell them! Woof, woof, I smell them too, they had burritos for dinner! According to Pete, dogs have a sense of smell so acute they can detect hormonal levels in humans. Woof, woof, one of them suffers from jealousy! Woof, woof, yeah, the other one's prematurely bald! Pete nudged my chest with his beer bottle. I took it, took a swallow, had to laugh. Seven hours earlier, I had been in a courtroom, my first time ever in the halls of jurisprudence, and now I was trespassing in someone's backyard, spying on the defense attorney. So it's true what they say: the criminal justice system creates criminals.

When quiet returned, the dogs having lost interest in our glandular secretions, my accomplice had disappeared.

-Pete?

No response. This could be bad.

-Pete?

-Dude, I can see them.

He was up a tree, his binoculars trained on the window.

-What are they doing?

-He's just standing there. She's gone now. Into the bathroom, I think.

-What does he look like?

-Hard to say. Now he's gone too.

A deep growl from the dog next door: Grrr, don't you assholes even think about traipsing through my yard!

I was getting anxious. If that was my dog making that guttural sound, I'd be going for the flashlight. And the baseball bat. Suppose we get caught—the neighbor calls, the police arrive—what would we say? We needed a lie ready. Officer, we were tracking a coyote a bobcat a baby bobcat my friend is a biologist the bobcat got separated from its mother we followed it this far the gate was open we think it's still up in these trees.

-Dude, you're not going to believe this.

-What?

-I think it's John. In the window. Yeah, it's definitely John.

-John who?

-Grisham.

-Very funny.

-Wait, he's back in the room. So is she. He just—I think he just kissed her.

-You're kidding. Is it the husband?

-I can't tell for sure. Whoever it is, he's kissing her. Oh, yeah.

-What?

-Oh, yeah. They are getting it on.

-Seriously?

-Oh, baby.

-What are they—?

-He's all over her.

-Yeah, right.

-Come see for yourself.

-I will.

-Wait. Now they're gone.

-Yeah, exactly.

-They might be on the bed. I need to climb higher.

I know when Pete is putting me on, but it was a funny thought, pie-faced Lawson and Super Sigrid having an affair. Officer, we're private detectives dicks for hire that's our summer job missing persons marital infidelities and, officer, I think you'll find no one here wishes to press charges we don't want anyone embarrassed this can all be handled discreetly.

A branch cracked. Pete hit the ground with a thud. A loud groan followed.

-Are you okay? Pete?

-I think I busted a rib.

The canine chorus started up again. The lights went off upstairs.

-Try not to move.

-I'm okay. Just help me up.

We were standing behind the tree when the outdoor lights came on— Chinese red lanterns on the patio, swimming pool glowing blue, the waterfall backlit. Pete groaned again.

-Looks like my damn honeymoon. The hotel.

A second set of lights flickered on, illuminating the ferns around our feet. This wasn't good.

-Let's get out of here. Can you walk?

We moved from tree to tree along the perimeter of the yard, crushing plants underfoot, then paused in some shadows, checking the house. Still no one on the patio. Had a motion detector triggered the outdoor lights? Had the people inside heard Pete's crash landing, and were they now standing by a dark window, peering nervously into the luminous garden? Ahead of us, ten feet of exposed fence stretched to the side walkway. No trees, no cover. Maybe they'll see us, maybe they won't, but if we wait and someone comes outside, we're sitting ducks.

-You ready?

-Yeah, go.

A few quick strides, and we were safely in the dark walkway between the garage and the fence. Pete was still making pained sounds.

-You okay? Pete?

-I never should have listened to you.

-To me? This was your idea.

-No, the hot tub. I wouldn't have fallen out of that.

We stood listening. No voices, no doors, no sirens. The dogs were calming down. So far, so good. I carefully pulled the gate open and snuck a quick peek around the corner. No one in the driveway.

-You go first, I'll close the gate. Go ahead.

With his right hand cradling his left arm like it was broken, Pete hobbled out past the Lexus and was gone. After a couple of tries, I latched the gate, turned, and walked smack into Sigrid.

-Oops. Sorry.

I assume it was Sigrid. She definitely fit the description.

-What are you doing?

She was tough, she held her ground, unfazed by a strange man emerging from her backyard late at night.

-Looking for—

I kept moving.

-For what? Excuse me.

The *excuse me* was an accusation, not an apology.

-Wrong address. Sorry.

I was almost off her driveway.

-I'm calling the police.

I ran down the street and found Pete leaning against the van.

-I saw her. I saw her rack. Mission accomplished.

-You gotta drive.

If Pete's juvenile humor is gone, adventure gauge on empty, he must be in serious pain.

-Okay. We're going to the hospital.

-Have you got my beer?

-No.

I started the engine. Pete eased himself into the passenger seat.

-I need a beer. Don't tell me you left it.

I turned onto Pacific Coast Highway, still busy after ten p.m., and drove cautiously. Still no sirens, a clean getaway, but they would find it—one glass beer bottle, two sets of prints, saliva samples for DNA testing. I must have set it down when I helped Pete to his feet under the tree. But I didn't notice it when the lights came on, so maybe it had rolled underneath a fern, out of sight, and two weeks from now the gardeners will stumble upon it and throw it in the trash. Okay, no reason to panic, just get Pete to the emergency room. He was hunched over, looking suddenly old.

-Pete, where's your hat?

-Probably with my binoculars.

Sorry, officer, we were just looking for a dark place where we could watch the meteor shower there's too many lights where we live we didn't mean any trouble the tree branch uh what tree branch? Even with time to prepare, my lies aren't very good.

Fortunately, the painstaking detective on the witness stand worked Huntington Beach, not Laguna, and wouldn't be called in to audit the odd refuse and incidentals left behind in Sigrid's backyard. Fortunately, he was done testifying, excused, and it was time for lunch. There's no such thing as fresh air in Santa Ana in July, no point in leaving the courthouse, so I sat on a bench in the hallway, hoping the dental hygienist with dark curls might sit down next to me and notice the apple and celery sticks I had grabbed from the refrigerator in my morning rush.

-Hi, I'm Roya. That's a fine lunch. Good for healthy teeth and gums.

-The apple's organic.

No such luck. Instead, it was the smiling gray-haired woman, a retired church secretary, it turned out, with three grandchildren.

-Here's a picture. Aren't they adorable? Five, eight, and the oldest is nine. They keep me on my toes.

She thought it was nice having a teacher on the jury.

-You'll explain everything for us, won't you? All this information is hard to follow. I would hate to have to decide all by myself.

She thought it was nice they sell water in the cafeteria.

-Usually I bring my own, but I'm glad they have it in case I forget.

Right. A wealthy county in the wealthiest state in the wealthiest country in the history of the world, and we have to pay for a bottle of water? I bet jurors in Canada get a decent sandwich. I bet jurors in Denmark get the whole damn smorgasbord. In my next life, I once told Marissa, I'm living in a social democracy, a real one. You won't like the winters, she replied. I could hear Pete's voice in my head.

-It takes more water than they hold to manufacture those stupid little bottles, never mind the BPA.

-BPA?

-Yeah, dude, chemical shit, leaching from the plastic. Makes you impotent.

The smiling woman reminded me of my mother, and I'd hate for someone to be rude to my mother, so I nodded and smiled back. Life must be easier for people like her, people content with what they're given. I should work on that. Accept what is. Marissa's better with acceptance. Everything is okay right now at this exact moment. That's how she got through the divorce. I gave it a try: right now I'm sitting here in an air-conditioned courthouse, I'm breathing, I'm alive, my throat isn't sore. But doesn't acceptance breed complacency? If no one speaks up and complains, will anything ever change? Was Marissa seeing her painter pal today? Should I complain about that or just accept it?

-That's not enough lunch for you, dear, would you like a peanut butter and jelly? I packed an extra one just in case. It's strawberry jam.

-No, I—

-Here, it's okay, I won't eat it.

Another warm, gray-haired smile. I wanted to hug her, I don't know why. If Lawson could get Bud Jack to smile like that instead of staring us down, he'd be home free. Of course, it's probably not so easy to accept what is when what is is indictment for first-degree murder.

The first witness after lunch was a Huntington Beach fireman, and he looked the part—broad-shouldered, dark mustache, a respectful nod to Judge Silverson, like a cop without the attitude, a little self-conscious in jacket and tie. On the night Juan Castro was killed, the fireman had gone out late to buy cold medicine for his ailing wife, and driving home he saw this guy running down the street. Sloan led him through his account.

-By running, do you mean like jogging, for exercise?

-No, he was kind of half walking, half running, and he would kind of stop and look behind him and start running again. It looked suspicious.

-What did he look like? A physical description.

-A physical description? Black guy, kind of average build, wearing a hooded sweatshirt.

-Running shorts?

-No, definitely not. Long pants. He wasn't out jogging.

-So you thought it looked suspicious. What did you do?

-Yeah, I drove past him and something didn't seem right, so I turned right at the next street and circled back through a residential street, and then came back up behind him.

-What was he doing?

-Same thing. Kind of running, kind of walking. He wasn't jogging. But then he kind of looked over at me. I'm pretty sure he could tell I was watching him.

-What did he do?

-He stopped walking and just looked at me.

-What did you do?

-I kept on driving. That was it. I figured it was probably nothing, or maybe he was on drugs, just acting weird.

-When did you call the police?

-Next day. I had kind of forgotten all about it, but the next day it started bothering me again, and I know some of the guys on the force, so I called over there and told them what I saw. You know, it's probably nothing, I just saw this guy acting weird, that kind of thing. But then a couple days later they called me back and asked me to come down to the station and see if I could identify the guy.

-Identify him how?

The fireman turned toward the jury box, as if to say this is for your benefit.

-In a lineup. They had six or seven guys. Maybe more. It was like you see on television. I picked him out right away.

-The defendant sitting over there—is that the man you saw running down the street?

-Yes.

-Are you sure?

-That's him. Absolutely.

Taking a step backwards, Sloan looked over at the defense table. So did I. I'm sure the whole jury did. Bud Jack was staring at the fireman and shaking his head slightly. Lawson placed his hand on his client's shoulder and leaned in to whisper something, shielding him from our collective gaze. An effective turn, I thought, meant to remind us that Bud Jack was a real person, someone with whom you could quietly confer. Effective and rehearsed. Everything seemed rehearsed. The dialogue between Sloan and the fireman—not jogging, suspicious—the fireman turning to address the jury, Bud Jack's glower, Lawson's protective, almost intimate motion. Lawson was right, this really did feel like television. Then, abruptly, he stood, his chair banging against the wooden barrier behind him. Another neat move, breaking the tension of the fireman's accusation. No open palms this time, almost no limp. Sloan was finished, and Lawson was on the attack.

-Do you know where the victim's body was found?

-I think so. Parking lot off Palm and Seventeenth.

-That's correct. Firemen know their streets. Did you see the suspicious walker-runner in that parking lot?

-No.

-Did you see him come out of that parking lot?

-No.

-How far was he from that parking lot when you saw him?

-Half mile.

-You wear glasses?

-Only for reading, not for driving.

-Were you wearing your glasses that night?

-I don't need them when I drive.

-So you weren't wearing them.

-That's correct.

-The suspicious walker-runner was on the sidewalk, yes?

-Yes.

-On the same side of the street as you?

-No.

-Across the street?

-Yes.

-Were there cars passing between you and him?

-A few, but I could see him clearly the whole time.

-Did you stop your car?

-No.

-You were driving the whole time you saw him?

-I slowed down.

This was getting interesting. Under Sloan's encouraging direction, the fireman was just trying to be helpful, fellow citizens, probably it was nothing, just kind of telling you my experience. Lawson's rapid grilling was evoking something else.

-Just so we're clear so far, you were driving, but looking over your shoulder, across the street, through traffic, without your glasses—

-I don't need—

-At night, and you saw him clearly the whole time.

-There were street lamps. The sidewalk there is well lit.

There it was again, defensiveness, a hint of I know what I saw.

-From above?

-What?

-These street lights shine light from above.

-Yes.

-You said the suspicious walker-runner was wearing a hooded sweatshirt. A hoodie.

-That's correct.

-Was the hood up, on his head?

-Yes.

-Are you sure?

-Yes.

-How much of his face did it shade?

-What?

-If he had his hood up, and the light was coming from the street lamp up above, his face would be shaded, like a shadow across his forehead and eyes. Do you recall what was shaded?

-No.

-Where was the suspicious hooded walker-runner standing when you last saw him that night?

-Corner of Palm and Twelfth.

-The northwest corner?

-Uh, yeah.

-I have here a photograph of that corner. Does this look like the same corner?

-Yes.

-What does that street sign indicate? The blue one.

-That's for a bus stop.

-Do you know what time it was when you last saw the suspicious hooded walker-runner at that corner?

-10:28.

The pedestrian's behavior was so suspicious, the fireman explained, that he had checked his watch and jotted the time on the cold medicine receipt. Lawson next produced a bus schedule and had the fireman confirm that a bus was due to arrive at the corner in question at 10:29 on the night in question.

-You told Mr. Sloan that you thought the man looked suspicious, but that it was probably nothing, correct?

-Yes.

-What did you mean by probably nothing?

Mr. Sloan must not have seen that one coming because the fireman wasn't prepped for it. He searched for an answer.

-That it was that nothing was…I guess there was probably nothing to be suspicious about.

-Would someone hurrying to catch the last bus of the evening fall into the category of probably nothing to be suspicious about?

Score one for the defense. Sigrid's husband was getting value for his dollar—a humanizing touch with the defendant and a clever rattling of the prosecution's sturdy eyewitness, not to mention the after-hours house call. I was still puzzled about that. Lawson arrives to confer with Sigrid's husband. Sigrid is alone upstairs where we saw her in the window. Lawson and the husband must have been in some inner room, a study, conferring in private. After his passive performance during jury selection, I would have said Lawson could use help from anybody, even a guy in television. Now I'd say he knew what he was doing. So it had to be the in-television guy who requested the late night summit meeting. But what was so urgent? In the Grishams I'd opened so far, there was always a secret plan, carefully plotted down to the smallest detail. Everything happens for a reason, nothing left to chance. What's the plan, Lawson, what's the big secret? I know where you were last night, I just don't know why.

On the way to the emergency room, Pete and I had carefully plotted our own conspiracy. If the police find our crumbs—beer bottle, hat, binoculars, broken branch—they might go checking hospitals for someone who fell out of a tree.

-Tell the doctor you tripped down some stairs.

-No.

-Why not? You were drinking, you fell down the stairs.

-It'll get out. Mr. Repetti was so drunk.

-It won't get out.

-Some nurse will tell her kid, and then the whole school will know. I'll just tell them you backed into me with your car.

-Mr. Fletcher was so drunk he ran over Mr. Repetti. I don't think so. How about you fell off your couch?

-No.

-You slipped in the shower.

-I'm not telling them I'm a total klutz.

-How about you were being an idiot and I kicked your ass?

-Who would believe that?

-Okay, here's an idea. Tell them you broke into a woman's backyard and climbed a tree so you could peep into her window and see her fake tits.

-I should have sat in the hot tub.

While Lawson interrogated the fireman, the unsettled feeling in my stomach gradually dissipated. Perhaps it had been hunger after all. Or I was finally calming down. I mean, so what if the police found our crumbs?—I understand, ma'am, a man in your backyard trespassing, not exactly breaking and entering, maybe put a lock on that gate and keep the shades pulled, anything turns up missing call us. I mean, police in coastal communities have better things to do, like track down shadowy black men suspiciously late for the bus.

-So you went home, gave the cold medicine to your wife, went to bed, and forgot all about it, correct?

-I didn't really forget.

-Isn't that what you just told Mr. Sloan? We could check the transcript.

-I mean, yes, I forgot about it, because I was sleeping, but the next day I remembered and it started bothering me again.

-According to the police report, you were shown the lineup and picked out Mr. Jack on the fourteenth, three days after you first called them. Do you accept that?

-Yes.

-So you forgot all about it, then you remembered it, then three days later, not a couple, but three days later you identified Bud Jack. Tell us about the lineup. What was the lighting like?

-The lighting?

-Yes, was there a street lamp in the lineup room?

-No. I don't know.

-Was Bud Jack wearing a hoodie?

Lawson got the fireman to admit that conditions in the lineup were nothing like the street that night, then he sat down. Sloan came forward and asked the fireman if the suspicious man looked like someone racing to catch a bus. Over Lawson's objection, Judge Silverson instructed the fireman to answer, and with Sloan's friendly guidance he was able to conclude that a man hurrying for the bus probably wouldn't keep stopping and looking back over his shoulder in the opposite direction from which the bus would be approaching. When the fireman caught Sloan's drift, a smile softened his face, his confidence returned, he was going out a winner.

-One last question. Are you still convinced that the defendant sitting over there was the person you observed acting suspiciously that night?

-It was him.

And then we were done for the day. Her Honor wanted to meet with the lawyers.

-Jurors, thank you. Remember, you are not to discuss the case with anyone, not even spouses. Have a nice weekend. Court recessed until Monday morning.

I stepped outside, into the afternoon heat, heading for the parking lot. In thirty minutes, I'll be home. Thirty-five, I'll be asleep on my bed.

-Long day, huh?

Long day, long eyelashes, long black curls. Roya! Say something, you fool.

-Yeah, long day.

No, say something clever, something witty. She smiled. Perfect teeth. I couldn't think.

-How's your dog doing?

-She died.

At least I didn't hesitate.

4

At first I didn't realize how little I liked south Orange County. I thought I was living the sun and sand California dream. Eighty degrees on Christmas Day, a bike ride along the beach with our shirts off, and Pete says, can you believe we get to live here, they pay us to live here. Then I met Sharon, and she set me straight.

-This place has all the misery of a city and none of the advantages, too many people, infuriating traffic, nothing to do, don't even pretend you're happy here, darling, I'm not buying it.

Always it was darling. I don't like my given name, and she refused to call me Fletcher.

-Too chummy, darling, I'm not your chum.

Not the drawn-out, aspirated *daahling* of an overwrought matron, it was primarily businesslike—she had to call me something—but it could stray anywhere from condescending to almost affectionate, depending on her mood.

-Darling, darling, please. No need to overanalyze.

We dated for a year, then she moved to northern California, the Bay Area.

-Can't take it anymore, darling, sorry, it's oppressive, uninterrupted sprawl filled with anxious people, a cultural wasteland.

I begged her to stay. She didn't ask me to go. I suggested she had a case of the grass is greener. She suggested I had a case of get a fucking clue.

-The only reason to stay here, the only possible reason, darling, is to avoid being challenged, no surprises, no scary strangers on the street, no trash cans out the night before. People just sit here, warmed over and rotting, thinking they've got it good. Look around you sometime, really look.

She jabbed a finger against the passenger window as we sped down the 5.

-You're a prisoner in a cushy gated community, it's an honor farm.

A stupid thing to say, I told her, seeing how at the time I lived in a decidedly ungated apartment complex on a busy street across from a noisy gas station in a small bedroom community called Lake Forest.

-Ha! Lake Forest, Aliso Viejo, Laguna Niguel.

She flailed her arms above her head as if fending off a swarm of gnats, a frequent gesture I never understood. One of many. Teaching high school drama was her vocation, dramatics were her life's work.

-Mission Viejo. Rancho Santa Margarita.

She rolled the r's with contempt.

-One big gated community, south county, guarded by the high cost of living and a tragic lack of history, don't let the quaint names fool you.

She looked at me sadly, shook her head and sighed, then chuckled to herself, signaling satisfaction with her performance. I pondered ramming the car into a center divider.

Pete and his wife lived in a gated community. No guard, just a gate that swung open in slow motion after you punched in the passcode, and even that was usually unnecessary as you could just slip through with the car ahead of you. One time I parked in Pete's driveway, walked in the front door without knocking, and found myself in an unfamiliar living room. A woman screamed, ran upstairs, slammed a door. I was still driving in circles, trying to pick out Pete's house, when the police car, full lights and sirens, arrived at the gate and couldn't get in. After five minutes, someone else drove up and opened the gate, the cops roared through, I drove out. It was an honest mistake—the same white stucco house and red tile roof, wrong damn gated community. Acapulco III not Acapulco II.

-Maybe put your name on your mailbox, Pete.

His wife vetoed that.

-We'd rather not draw attention to ourself, people will steal your identity, you know, or worse.

-Then how about a lawn ornament or planting a tree?

She smiled and shook her head at my foolishness.

-That's not allowed. Only an American flag. We all want to keep the neighborhood neat.

I could hear Sharon's *ha!* I had a sudden urge to flail my arms.

So I moved to Laguna Beach, to a smaller apartment at double the rent, and gave up any hope of ever owning my own home. At least the town had an identity, a sense of place, protected from the sprawl by the last few unravaged hills and the canyon. At least the town was a town, I could be sure where I was living. Sharon scoffed when I called her with the good news.

-I don't see the difference, darling.

-Well, for one thing, Laguna has character.

-Ha! You mean *had* character, it's fading fast, the hippies are long gone, you're thirty years too late, Lake Forest by the sea.

-That's not true, Sharon. For one thing, the houses in Laguna don't all look alike.

-Proud of you, darling, really pushing the diversity envelope, and good luck dining out, all that pretentious inelegance, you'll need a bank loan.

She was right about that too. After trying to impress Marissa with a few dinner dates at Laguna's newest and most intimate, I had to confess that I couldn't afford to keep it up, Marissa graciously conceded the food wasn't as good as it sounded on the menu, and we settled on sushi once a month.

Which is where we were Friday night after my long day in court. Marissa was in a flirtatious mood. She ordered an expensive glass of wine, playfully kicked me under the table when I looked too closely at the waitress's tight shirt, and told me about the day's excitement.

-This girl came in totally plastered, the poor thing, drunk off her ass. She was supposed to get married tomorrow but her fiancé, what a jerk, he backed out, I mean like the day before. What a bastard. She said her mother made her come to the spa because it was already paid for. So I started the massage, just real light stuff, but it was too much for her. I put a warm towel on her forehead and went to ask my manager if it was okay for her to just sleep there. They get upset if you're kind of taking up space. And then she started puking, like, all over, which guess who had to clean up. I know, gross, huh? So I think I deserve the good Chardonnay this time. You look tired, were you up late?

Was I ever. The emergency room staff had not been impressed by Pete's complaints. No shortness of breath, no chest pains, no urgency. I had expected doctors hustling in with concerned looks, nurses shouting out vitals, like on tv, good-looking nurses, not fill out this form, sign here, sign there, have a seat we'll be with you shortly. Or in an hour. Forty minutes in the waiting room, twenty in an examination room, Pete getting bored, catapulting cotton balls at me with a tongue depressor, and finally Dr. Jekyll sidled in, untamed hair, lopsided glasses on a pinched nose, bewildered eyes. Definitely not prime time.

-You landed on your side, is that right, Mr. Repetti, you didn't hit your head?

-That's correct.

-Repetti. Is that German?

Pete shot me a look of disbelief, like are you kidding me?

-It's Italian.

-Italiano. What were you doing on the roof?

-Getting a frisbee. My friend here can't throw for shit.

-That's not true, Doctor. He can't catch.

-His throws go straight up in the air. He has limp wrists.

Dr. Jekyll ignored our clever repartee.

-You sure you didn't hit your cranium, Mr. Repetti?

-I'm sure. I landed on my side, this area here.

-The only reason he fell off is his ballet slippers couldn't get any traction on the shingles.

-He's lying, Doc. There's no shingles.

-We always want to be careful with the cranium. That's our computer. Any dizziness?

-No. I'm only feeling my side right here and my shoulder.

-Any headaches?

-No headaches. I told you, my side hurts.

Disbelief turning to impatience. I've seen that shift from Pete before, usually when a principal, with inexplicable enthusiasm, is reiterating the latest irrelevant policy change.

-Nausea?

-Not yet. But any minute now.

Pete was at his limit.

-Ever have trouble sleeping?

-Only at night.

With impatience comes sarcasm.

-We might want an MRI, if your insurance will allow it.

-For God's sake, there's nothing wrong with my computer, Doc, it's a Mac, it doesn't crash.

Doc liked that.

-Okay. Let's take your shirt off and have a look at those shingles. Did you ever have chicken pox?

By the time I got Pete—bruised ribs, separated shoulder, arm in a sling—and his van from the hospital to The Cave and drove my old beater back across Laguna, it was two a.m. Leaving the hospital, Pete had finally declared the mission a success. He held a refillable prescription for Ambien and we had a really cool story—the stakeout, the tree, my brush with Sigrid, the insane doctor.

-Was he for real, dude, or just messing with us?

A really cool story, so long as the police didn't come knocking, but sitting in the sushi restaurant, I couldn't tell Marissa a word of it.

-Yeah, I couldn't get to sleep last night.

-Worrying about the trial?

-No. I don't know. This tuna is pretty good.

I was trying to steer away from any discussion of jury duty, but she wanted to talk about day two and wouldn't take contempt of court for an answer.

-You can describe what happened, I mean, I could go to the courthouse and watch, right? Come on, Fletcher, don't hold out on me.

I fed her a few details—I couldn't help it, Your Honor, she was rubbing my shin with her bare foot and I wasn't going to risk contempt of a flirty, tipsy Marissa, but no opinions, I swear, Your Honor, no judgments, just the facts—and she practically exploded.

-That's all they got?

-So far. But—

-Someone thinks they saw Bud Jack a half mile from the place?

She jabbed a chopstick into her plate, flinging rice across the table.

-Marissa, calm down.

-Walking down the street while black—is that a felony now? Someone ought to arrest the fireman for driving under the influence of racism. I bet your all-white jury ate it up.

Another jab, more rice.

-It's not all white.

-Sorry. All white and one Hispanic. A real jury of his peers.

One Hispanic, indeed.

-*Roya* means queen, doesn't it?

-What?

-In Spanish. *Roy* is king, right, so *roya* must be queen.

-I don't know. Why?

-The Hispanic on the jury—that's her name. Roya.

-Is she nice? I mean like sympathetic.

-I guess.

No need to guess really. After hearing of my dog's demise, Roya had been a perfect picture of sympathy.

-That is so sad. I'm sorry. How old was she?

-She was...I'm not sure.

-Oh.

One lie leads to one hundred.

-I got her from the pound.

I should have introduced myself, said something charming or at least pleasant. I should have asked if she had a dog. Instead, I stood there like a fool. She was even prettier close up. I could have stared at her eyes all day.

-You should make friends with her.

-With Roya? Why?

I mean, okay, sure, friends for life, I'll do my darnedest, bosom buddies.

-Just in case.

-In case what?

-You know.

-Marissa, what are you talking about?

-In case she thinks he's guilty.

-You want me to influence her?

-No, I—

-I shouldn't even be having this conversation.

-I want you to make sure the prosecution doesn't confuse the jury. I want you to make sure Bud Jack gets a fair trial. Please. They're framing him, he's not a murderer, he washes cars.

-They have a confession.

-Don't tell me you believe that.

I hesitated. Sloan wouldn't have told us that Bud Jack confessed unless he actually did, right? So that makes Bud Jack either a killer or a liar, and why lie about a murder you had nothing to do with? It didn't look good—not for Bud Jack, and not for me. Marissa was pissed. She pushed her chair back from the table, took her phone from her purse, and started fiddling with it, checking her messages. I didn't need a phone to check my message, it was staring me in the face: fifty dollars on raw fish, and I wouldn't be getting even a warm kiss goodnight.

-No, I don't believe it. I'm giving him the benefit of the doubt.

Her glare subsided into a skeptical frown. I kept going.

-I won't believe it until they prove it, and so far they've only proven that a fireman thinks he saw Bud Jack.

She smiled. No stopping now.

-Thinks. And white people think blacks all look alike, so that's pretty unreliable.

She set down her phone, reached across the table, and took my hands.

-So I'm giving him the benefit of the doubt. Innocent until proven guilty.

-We should get the rest of this to go.

How does the poem go? The last temptation is the greatest treason, to do the right thing for the wrong reason. Well, whatever.

When I woke up the next morning, she was rattling cupboards in my kitchen, trying to find coffee.

-Fletcher, honey, I forgot to tell you, we're going to the theater tonight.

Marissa liked to spring plans on me.

-We are?

Like planning something a week in advance might give me the wrong idea. That was my analysis anyway.

-It'll be fun. Saturday night on the town.

-You mean theater like a play?

-Sigrid and her husband had two tickets they can't use.

-Sigrid? When did you talk to her?

-She called yesterday. They wanted you and me to have the tickets.

-She said me specifically? What else did she say? I mean like anything funny, complain about the neighbors or anything?

-No. I have to go to work. The play's at eight at South Coast Rep.

-Oh, God.

-What?

-Nothing.

I could hear Sharon's *ha!*

-Should I ask somebody else?

-No. No!

Definitely do not ask somebody else, he might say yes, he will say yes, and later he will say he really enjoyed himself let's do this again sometime. I mean if a guy paints Laguna seascapes, he'll love South Coast Repertory. The first play I ever saw there, I forget the name, something Irish, nothing happened, just talking and a brief dance, and I assumed it was my fault I couldn't stay awake, I just didn't appreciate theater. Again, Sharon straightened me out. She took me back a few times, and we always left early with Sharon flailing her arms. Her rant after we gave up on Hamlet was particularly memorable.

-It boggles my mind, I don't know how they do it, take a great script, talented actors, make it dead on arrival. They're geniuses at it really, making Shakespeare bloodless, making Albee cute. Geniuses!

The last time was when a guy came on stage before the show and bragged that this was the most South Coast Rep had ever spent on a production and asked Mr. and Mrs. Somebody to stand, they made this possible, ladies and gentlemen, their extremely generous gift. A nice round of applause, the curtain opened, and twenty minutes later Sharon and I were in the parking lot making a pact.

-No more attending theater in south county, on pain of death, darling, did you see all the bluehairs, they fill the seats, they make donations, they get upset very easily, that's the mission statement, don't dare upset the bluehairs, it's as bad as Laguna Playhouse, it's skim milk, homogenized, pasteurized, and thin.

She chuckled to herself. I suggested the death penalty would be redundant punishment for sitting through their show, she agreed and amended it to full confession and fifty Hail Harry's—for Pinter, darling—and we sealed it with a kiss.

Marissa was on her way out the door.

-I'll be here at seven. You won't change your mind, will you?

Why would I change my mind? When have I ever changed my mind?

-Fletch?

-You promise we won't discuss the trial?

-Not a word.

I slept three more hours, had cold cereal for lunch, and went to the beach. Ahh, the life of a teacher. Of course, while Marissa was rubbing naked flesh all day, I could only ogle it from a distance. It's hard to concentrate on your reading, hard to keep your place on the page, when your eyes won't stay put. Maybe that's why Grishams are so popular—you can read them during jury selection in a crowded courtroom, you can read them seated by the front door of a busy takeout restaurant, you can read them on a boat, you can read them with a goat, and also on a sun-drenched beach, you can read them, can't you, Teach? Near the lifeguard tower on a sun-drenched beach on a warm Saturday in July with half-naked girls lying on the sand, half-naked girls playing volleyball, half-naked girls wading in the surf, screaming and laughing when the cold water reaches their bare stomachs. Read a sentence, look up, read two more, look up, maybe skip a sentence, it doesn't matter. At this rate, I won't finish Grisham number four until September.

A few yards behind me, a woman with disproportionates set up camp—blanket, folding chair, supersize soft drink, cell phone—close to the busy boardwalk for best exposure. I stood, stretched my arms, pretended I was looking for someone, my blatant leer hidden behind dark sunglasses. It wasn't Sigrid, thank goodness. I didn't want to run into her again. I sat back down, opened my cell phone. It took at least six rings before he answered.

-Dude.

-Pete, how you feeling?

-Ambien, dude.

-Guess what I'm doing?

-Hanging at the Boom Boom.

-Funny. Anyhow, it closed.

The Boom Boom Room, Laguna's gay clubhouse, went out of business as the town's renowned homosexual population was getting old and real estate prices kept out the next generation.

-No more Boom Boom?

He sounded groggy.

-It's a family restaurant now.

I could still hear Sharon's lament: The hippies are long gone, darling, and the queers, bless their hearts, are next to go, will the last gay man in Laguna please switch off the lights.

-What time is it, anyhow?

How many sleeping pills had he taken?

-Pete, listen, the other night, was Sigrid by herself in the window?

-Dude, I'm kind of in a nap.

-Okay, but when you climbed the tree, when you said they were getting it on, you were just bullshitting me, right?

-No.

-No?

-I think I'm wasted.

-There was really a guy in the bedroom? Pete?

He was gone. I glanced over my shoulder at the woman by the boardwalk. What if I walked up to her and asked for her phone number, what would she do? Probably say no, probably in a give-me-a-break-I-am-so-sure tone of voice.

What if I asked Roya? Hi, my name is Fletcher, do you like the beach, I could maybe call you sometime, after the trial of course.

What if Sigrid *was* having an affair with Lawson? That would make sense of things. Sigrid knows all about Bud Jack not because of her in-television husband but because of her in-law boyfriend, and that's why he was there late at night, not for a strategy meeting with Mr. Wilhite, who was probably still in LA. No, Lawson was there to see the lovely Mrs. Wilhite.

My phone beeped. A text from Marissa: You up yet? Don't forget tonight. How could I? Sigrid gave us the tickets, mentioned me specifically, because she wants me on her side, wants me sympathetic to her cause. That much is obvious. That's why she pressured Marissa about Bud Jack while I was in jury selection. She wants her pie-faced, limping lover to win the case. Still an astounding coincidence—Marissa's client cheating with the defense attorney from my jury assignment—but plausible. Lawson could live in Laguna. They could have met on the tennis courts or at one of her fundraisers. Maybe Lawson loves sea lions too. Still, that doesn't explain why the Wilhites, if it's true, are funding Bud Jack's defense. So follow the money, look for the greed, like in a Grisham—wherever there's a mystery someone is breaking laws, trying to get super rich. Sigrid and Lawson are extorting money from her husband, or Bud Jack has the dirt on Sigrid's husband and is blackmailing him, or Sigrid's husband hires a hotshot lawyer, gets Bud Jack acquitted, then they sue the Huntington Beach police department and the county for wrongful arrest, violation of Bud Jack's civil rights, and win millions. That's what Sigrid's husband does, not television, he chases ambulances. Would that be legal? He finds poor victims, takes up their cause, speculates in litigation, pockets his cut, and gets rich doing it. Not a bad idea, actually. The last temptation is the greatest treason.

The woman behind me was now in front of me, walking toward the water. If I hurried, I could catch a wave, bodysurf her way, accidentally get tumbled into her. Sorry about that my name is Fletcher what's yours oh that's a beautiful name I teach math Jessica economics actually at the university what about you oh you're in real estate that's fantastic I'm actually looking for a new place in Laguna something bigger oh I see no that's cool I bet you're a terrific office manager how about dinner sometime? Ha! She was standing at the water's edge, still talking on the phone. I could bodysurf into her and knowing me, let's be honest, it would be uh sorry excuse me wrong address.

Why was she standing there alone—Sigrid—the other night, all by herself, as I closed her gate? She had heard a noise, the patio lights came on.

If Lawson was there on a tryst, wouldn't he have chivalrously volunteered to check for intruders? A jaded husband was more likely to let her go it alone, so maybe...no, Lawson was there, he wanted to go, but she said stay inside, don't let the neighbors see you. But his car was there, anyone could see that. The car! Whoever it was—Mr. Lawson or Mr. Wilhite—he drove a new Lexus.

We were driving my old Honda. We parked at South Coast Plaza, a nearby shopping mall, because mall parking is free. The walk to the theater took ten minutes. We held hands. My face was still flush from the sun, my shoulders a little red, and Marissa seemed happy—it was going to be a pleasant evening after a pleasant afternoon on the sand—if the show was bearable.

-The play is about Bach.

So much for that.

-The composer?

-That's what Sigrid said.

-You talked to her again?

-She called to make sure we were going tonight.

Of course she did. Got to help out her favorite lawyer. Got to keep his favorite juror in her debt.

-Are her and her husband having any, you know, trouble?

-I don't think so. Why?

-I don't know. I just thought maybe—I don't know.

-Why don't you ask her yourself? We'll be sitting next to them.

Oh.

Oh, shit.

Nice to meet you, Sigrid, sorry about the other night wasn't that crazy we were looking for this guy's pool party a backyard barbecue but we were confused it wasn't Hummingbird Lane it was Herringbone Lane or Honeybee I forget my friend got it wrong it was his fault I hope we didn't startle you.

The tickets were waiting for us at the box office. I headed for the restroom, told Marissa I would meet her at our seats.

-I can wait for you.

-No, go ahead.

-Are you okay? Fletcher?

-Yeah, my stomach is just a little off.

I waited until the show began, until the theater was dark. An usher with a tiny flashlight guided me to my seat. Marissa patted my hand, asked again if I was alright. The two seats on her other side were empty. No Wilhites? No such luck. They arrived five minutes later, apologizing politely as they stepped past us. While Marissa whispered hellos, I pretended to be deep in the performance, as if cartoonish church intrigue in eighteenth-century Germany really spoke to me. The organmaster had died, the organists-in-waiting were positioning themselves in hope of claiming the prestigious post, they wore enormous wigs, they spouted puns.

-What brings you here?

-Stagecoach, primarily. And, for this last portion, my feet.

I guess it was supposed to be witty, but Hail Harry full of grace, it was torture.

-A crazed bandit tried to steal my luggage.

-It must have been dreadful.

-No, it was very attractive, which is no doubt why he tried to steal it.

It wore me down—the dialogue, the movements of the actors, all painfully stilted. I tried taking comfort in the knowledge that so long as act one dragged on and on, I was safe, Sigrid couldn't see my face. I tried laughing at my bad luck. But a man can only stand so much.

-He has seen you stealing into the choir balcony.

-I go there when I wish to feel closer to God.

-With a young lady.

-She wished to feel closer to God as well.

-I am sure. But which one?

-Which God?

-No, which lady?

Okay, I finally cried, the torment unbearable, I'll talk, I'll tell you everything, I was in the backyard, I was peeping in the window, I'll sign a confession, I'll rat out my accomplice, just please make them stop.

Intermission. House lights up. I whispered urgently to Marissa.

-I need to go. My stomach.

She ignored me.

-Sigrid, this is Fletcher.

-Nice to meet you, Fletcher.

Big smile. Big everything. I avoided eye contact, hoping she wouldn't recognize me. She extended her hand. I grabbed my stomach.

-I'm sorry, forgive me, I have to—

-His tummy is upset.

-Oh. I'm sorry.

I hurried to the restroom, took refuge in a stall. Now what? I couldn't go back in. Ten more minutes with the conniving, mugging organists would finish me off, and when they dragged out my battered, harrowed corpse, Sigrid would get a good long look and gasp, that's him, that's the man who violated my privacy, Marissa, your sort of boyfriend is a total pervert.

In my pocket, my phone buzzed. Are you okay? I waited a little before texting back. No. Bad sushi.

Her next text—the one that offered to drive me straight home forget the play I'll apologize to Sigrid later—never came. Intermission was over, and Marissa wasn't coming out. Nothing to do but sit here on the toilet, play with my phone, maybe write on the door. *Fletcher + Roya*. She would have come out, taken me home, Roya was like that, I could tell. I called Pete, no answer, probably still stoned. Who else could I call?

-Darling, what a splendid surprise, how are you, how's life behind the Orange Curtain, same as ever if you're calling me on a Saturday night, shouldn't you be out with what's her name, your little masseuse?

-Marissa. She's…she's at South Coast Rep.

-Poor dear. Couldn't you stop her? Let me guess, one of those dreadful Greenberg plays.

-Worse. Something called *Bach at Leipzig*.

-Oh, I read about that. Supposed to be like a fugue, keeps repeating itself. Clever, I'm sure, and pointless. Well, at least you stayed home. Good for you.

-Yeah.

-They're Philistines, that theater. What was our word for it?

-Socorepery.

-Yes. I mean, a serious playwright doesn't need formalized gimmickry. Give us human drama. Give us the messiness of life.

Might as well let her ramble. Cell phone calls are free on weekends and I've got time to kill.

-Look at Wallace Shawn's *Designated Mourner*. Look at Pinter's *Caretaker*. That's how you use repetition.

Wait till Pete hears about this. Dude, you were in the shitter for the entire second act? It could have been worse, man, I could have been in the theater.

-That place is a morgue, darling. Theater for zombies. Socorepery—from the Latin for sock—was that my idea or yours?

-Sharon, I want to ask you something.

-Yes?

-If you have a crush on someone—

-A crush? How marvelous.

-Someone you don't even know, does that mean you're unhappy in your current relationship?

-It could mean anything, maybe you're just horny, but, darling, you've been unhappy with her since the beginning and don't tell me otherwise. You've been heroic, putting up with her, above and beyond, and—

-She's—

-I know, I know, she's a good person, she's been through a lot.

-She has.

-We all have. Maybe it's time you look after yourself. What's her name—the crush?

-Roya.

-Oh, she's Persian. Let me guess, dark eyes and pale skin. But listen, I have to go.

-I thought *roya* was Spanish for queen.

-No, that's *reyna*, darling. Roya is Persian. Lots of Persians in southern Cal. I'll call you next week sometime, okay?

Persian?

The US government can't function without a foreign enemy or two, even a high school math teacher can figure that out, and Iran is a perennial favorite. I remember, back in elementary school, pissing with pride on little rubber images of the Ayatollah Khomeini that probably the school janitor had placed in the urinals. Now with the Soviet Union long gone and Iraq in pieces, it's Iran that's once again out to get us, Iran who someday might have a nuclear bomb, Iran the evil in the world that makes military spending and gated communities necessary. At least that's what the experts say on the evening news. The experts and Pete's ex-wife. I tried to reason with her, back before the divorce.

-Think about it, Iran has no nuclear weapons and they're going to attack a country that has ten thousand? That's crazy.

-They are crazy. They're radicals.

-Just think about it logically. It's a big country, like seventy million people. Are they all crazy? I mean, if they try something, we'll blow them off the map.

-Fletcher, you can't use logic with those people, that's their culture, ask anyone.

By anyone, I think she meant anyone in her neighborhood, her church, anyone as afraid of the world as she was. Which is why Iranians in south Orange County can be a bit touchy. Like a student named Ramtin, who angrily corrected me.

-We're not Arabs, we don't speak Arabic, we speak Farsi.

-Oh, Farsi, that must make you Farcical.

-No, Mr. Fletcher, we're Persians.

Persians, as if from the great Persian empire—that's how Iranians in California identify themselves. And according to our principal's convoluted explanation regarding Dana Hills demographics, Iran is the Persian word for land of the Aryans, which means that Persians, though Asians, are counted as Caucasians, which makes Sigrid right, and Marissa, and also The Sophist, they're all right: Bud Jack's jury is all white. One hundred percent.

-Fletcher, is that you in there?

A male voice.

-Uh, yeah.

-Richard Wilhite here. Sigrid's husband. Marissa asked me to check on you.

-Oh.

-Food poisoning?

-Leftover sushi.

I leaned back on the toilet, twisted my neck, and looked with one eye through the gap where the stall attached to the wall. He was standing at a mirror, checking his hair. An expensive haircut, even from my narrow vantage.

-That'll do it. I've been there. Raw fish is always a risk. Can I get you something to drink?

Talking to me, but looking at himself.

-No, that's okay, but thank you.

-They probably have soda water.

How do I get rid of this guy?

-How's the play?

-It's good. If you like that kind of thing.

-You should go back in. Tell her I'm okay.

-Between you and me, I don't really appreciate theater. Sigrid gets the tickets and drags me along. How about a cup of ice to chew on?

What am I thinking? I don't need to hide from this guy. He didn't see me in his driveway. I pocketed my phone, tightened my face into a grimace, and emerged from the stall, one hand on my stomach.

-Pretty bad, huh?

-It comes and goes.

Mr. Wilhite, the mysterious in-television husband, was wearing a light blue pullover and khaki slacks. I splashed water on my face.

-You sure I can't get you something?

-Do you drive a Lexus?

I shouldn't have asked. I already knew the answer. I had imagined a harder, meaner man, like one of Grisham's corporate villains, but he had a soft, blown-dry look, like an evening news anchor, like he might fall over if you bumped into him. Of course he drove a Lexus.

-Yes. Why?

I hesitated. No lie ready.

-I...excuse me.

Quickly back into the stall. I asked about your car because Marissa and I had a bet, no, because I think I saw you driving in Laguna recently I remember the hair.

-Are you okay in there?

Should I make a retching sound? Do I even know how?

-Yeah. False alarm. I think I need fresh air. Will you tell Marissa I'll meet her after the show? Thanks.

I was past him and out the door before he could say anything.

The air outside was cool. Even in July, the evenings cool off. South Orange County does have that going for it, I admit, the world's greatest climate, or so say local license plate frames, in typical south county modesty. Mild winters, no rain all summer. The bored-to-tears weather celebrities report the approach of a potential thunderstorm like the threat of foreign invasion: Bad news, Stu and Linda, we could see heavy precipitation on Friday evening possibly lingering into Saturday morning, stay with us for round the clock updates, coming up next news you can use, how to protect your family in a downpour this could be the big one folks. Usually it fizzles. Just one pleasant sunny day after the next. A guy like Richard Wilhite sports a suntan all year round. A guy like Richard Wilhite was exiting the theater and walking toward me. A friendly wave. Too late to escape.

-Hey, Fletcher, I'm giving you a ride home. Marissa's idea. The girls will come later in your car. If that's okay. Marissa said just leave your keys at the box office.

Are you kidding me? Forty-eight hours ago we were searching for some guy on the internet, and now I'm sitting in his car feigning illness. What next? Will I run into Lawson at the grocery store? Will I track down Judge Silverson? Uh, sorry, Your Honor, excuse me wrong address, since I'm here though can I pound your gavel?

We pulled out of the parking garage and headed for the freeway, two strangers in a new Lexus, searching for conversation topics. Richard scored first.

-I don't understand why that theater doesn't have valet parking.

-Yeah. You'd think.

-In LA, it's standard. Suburbs, what can you do?

-Yeah.

I was nodding my head, trying to be polite, but you can park your own damn car, that's what you can do.

-Where are we headed, by the way? You're in Laguna, right?

-North Laguna.

-Nice. Fantastic area. Some real nice homes.

We didn't speak for a few uncomfortable minutes. Does he feel put out taking me home? Am I pathetic, a charity case, using his theater tickets, getting a ride? Does he think I'm rude not saying anything?

-You're not going to throw up in here, are you?

-No.

-You let me know and I'll pull over pronto. That smell never goes away. No offense.

-I'm feeling better.

-How did you know I drive a Lexus?

-You probably won't believe it.

Long story short, I saw it in your driveway the other night when my buddy and I snuck into your backyard, spied on your wife's fake titties, and broke your tree. I'm serving on a jury right now, and I thought it was the defense attorney's car and that he was having an affair with your wife, but when I met you tonight in the john I immediately sensed there was something effeminate about you so I figured you for the Lexus because the defense attorney is, let's say, more of a BMW man. No offense.

-Believe what?

He looked at me with an odd expression, probably because I was grinning. With fake food poisoning comes giddiness.

-I can look at people and guess their car.

-No, I've heard of that. What's it called? It's called something. Auto-savant?

-I don't know.

-What else can you guess? What line am I in?

-Line?

-Line of work. Can you guess what I do?

-No, just cars. But it's something in television, right?

-Yes. A production company. That's unbelievable. How do you do it? I've got that industry look, right?

I bit my cheek to stifle a laugh. So he really was in television, and it was his Lexus, he was at home with his wife, and when the lights went on in the backyard he stayed inside while she investigated. No affair, no drama. Sometimes my imagination gets the best of me.

-A production company?

-We create shows and sell them to the networks.

-Oh. Like sitcoms?

-Mostly reality shows now. They're easier to do.

-Yeah?

-Cheaper. You don't need to pay professional actors. Sitcoms, you need a big name, right? A star attraction. And a roomful of writers. Everything costs—it's all union. Reality, you just need a concept and a camera.

-Who comes up with the concept?

-Anybody. Me. You. Like here's a concept: a guy can look at you and guess your car, your job. So he walks down the street, meets people, makes funny banter, makes guesses about them. And then, I don't know, you got three contestants, back in the studio, in front of an audience, they guess if he's right or wrong. Like old school What's My Line? meets Who Wants to Marry a Millionaire?

-What are you working on now?

-If I told you, I'd have to kill you. And I would, too, I know people, I'm a serious man.

-Oh.

-When you get a concept, I mean a sure thing, solid money, you protect it like gold, like the Ark of the Covenant, until you're up and running. Then you want to get a buzz going. What line are you in, Fletcher?

-I'm a teacher.

-Nice. I really admire teachers. The basis for civilization. I get sick of these ignorant politicians beating up on the teachers, saying they're overpaid, calling for charter schools, vouchers. That's the end, when you privatize the schools. Then we're Mexico. My daughter went to Laguna High, public schools all the way. Now she's at Stanford, so I guess she did alright. You'll have to direct me to your house.

-We'll turn right on PCH. It's an apartment, actually.

-I used to own an apartment in north Laguna, until I moved up. Got to start somewhere, right? Build that equity.

-Yeah.

-Used to hang out at Crystal Cove. You surf?

-I've got a paddleboard.

-Nice.

Nice. That's what Sharon said—people in south county are nice to you, just not interested, because they've got nothing to learn from you, darling, that's how they see it, either you amuse them or you don't. Richard was nice enough to check on me in the restroom, nice enough to give me a ride home, it's nice that he supports public education, rhetorically anyway, and so very nice that his daughter can attend a fifty thousand per year private university, but he could have at least asked what grade level I teach, what subject, and if I enjoy it, so that settles it, he's not getting a kiss goodnight. A brisk goodbye instead.

-Thanks for the lift, Richard.

I was eager to be out of that Lexus.

-You take care, Fletcher.

None of that we should stay in touch business, nothing about let's get together sometime, not even a nice to meet you. Just see ya.

A big mistake, immediately regretted. Why didn't I ask Richard about his interest in Bud Jack, get it straight from the horse's mouth? I was thinking about it the whole way home, but I didn't want him to know I knew. I was hoping he would bring it up instead, clue me in on his intentions. And why didn't he? Why didn't he ask me about being on the jury, drop hints about Bud Jack's innocence? Probably he doesn't want me to know I'm being used, wants to keep it subtle, just quietly give the juror a ride home, express great admiration for his chosen profession, meanwhile his wife massages the masseuse hoping the masseuse will influence the juror.

I figured I had an hour until Marissa arrived with my car. I cleaned up the kitchen, put fresh sheets on the bed, opened a bottle of wine. Good news, honey, the food poisoning is gone, thank God.

Bad news, honey, Marissa didn't arrive with my car until midnight, she and Sigrid had stopped for a drink, she just wanted to get her keys and drive home.

-I can't stay over.

-You're already here.

She'd rather go out with Sigrid than come home to me.

-I have to work real early.

-I don't mind waking up early.

Maybe I should join the marine mammal rescue society like Sigrid. Or get disproportionates.

-Fletcher, please, I'm tired. I just want to go, okay?

-How was the play?

-It was alright. A little hard to follow. Great costumes.

Great costumes? Maybe I should move to the Bay Area like Sharon, get out of south county. I mean, what am I doing here?

-I'm sorry I got sick.

-It's okay. I'll call you tomorrow. Oh, Sigrid says you look familiar.

There's a spot rich in sea life two miles off the Laguna coast, or maybe it's farther, I just point my surfboard away from shore, stand up, and start paddling. That's what it's called—stand-up paddle surfing—like canoeing, only on your feet, and it's catching on. If the wind is calm, someone is probably out there, paddling the postcard stretch of north Laguna: Bird Rock, Fisherman's Cove, Crescent Bay, Seal Rock, Emerald Bay, El Morro, Crystal Cove. Out in open water, away from the cliff and cove shoreline, you don't see other paddlers, you don't see much at all, until you hit the spot. Pete says it's probably an upwelling zone, cold water rising rich with nutrients from the ocean floor, drawing fish and everything that eats them. First you see birds— gulls, pelicans, skimmers—that's how you find the place, birds mark the spot. Then maybe a few sea lions, out from the Seal Rock rookery in search of a meal. They dive deep, then surface breathing hard. They swim up close and inspect you with strange brown eyes—what are you doing out this far, stupid human? Sometimes you surprise one floating motionless, a flipper extended skyward, napping in the sun. Gray whales pass through, south to Mexico in the winter, northbound with their newborn calves come spring. And there are dolphins.

On Sunday morning, after a disappointing Saturday night, after my date with Marissa had become a date with Richard Wilhite, I was out early. No wind, no choppy waves, the board traveling easily as I dipped the long paddle into glassy water and pulled forward. Maybe it was the smooth repetition, four strokes on one side, then four on the other, or maybe it was because there was nothing to do except paddle—no books or tv, no cell phones, no people—but standing on a twelve-foot plank surrounded by miles of water, I stopped obsessing about Marissa—how does she feel about me today? is she having lunch with that Vincent van Goatee?—I forgot I was a capable though not inspiring high school math teacher and might never be anything else, I got out of my head, as Marissa would say, and just existed.

A squadron of pelicans went gliding by, two feet above the water, and then I saw it, what I was looking for, little dark waves and glints of light barely perceptible on the horizon. I reached out farther with the paddle and pulled harder, it took maybe ten more minutes to get there, and suddenly the ocean came alive with gray and white bodies arching, diving, shooting up again—I was surrounded by dolphins! Dozens of them. Hundreds. One cut across my bow, a curious eye, long mouth, then cut back, the opposite eye taking me in. Pale ghosts flashed underneath me. I heard their whistles and clicks. Five feet to my right, an adult and juvenile burst clear of the water together, parallel torpedoes of glistening skin. Whooo! I whooped and laughed. I looked left and right and over my shoulders, trying not to miss a one. They were after fish. They pulled away, circled back, pulled away again. They didn't swim so much as flow, a river of dolphins, a current of energy streaming across the ocean face. A few stragglers passed me, then the water flattened and calmed. I stopped paddling and watched a long line of dorsal fins shrink into the distance. Okay, so maybe south county isn't so bad.

5

On Monday morning, defense attorney Lawson looked different. Before I entered the fifth-floor courtroom, I ran into him, literally, as he emerged from a restroom, his attention on a folded newspaper. Close up, he appeared even bigger. When we bumped shoulders, I had to step backward to maintain my balance. He apologized and glanced down at me, barely breaking stride. But as I watched him limp down the hallway, he seemed somehow smaller, frail even. It wasn't just that I had noticed sweat stains along his collar and dandruff in his sideburns. In my mind, he was no longer a man of action who held late-night strategy sessions with Mr. Wilhite or late-night straddling sessions with Mrs. Wilhite, no longer the lynchpin in a complex Grisham plot of intrigue and suspense. The late-night ride in Richard Wilhite's Lexus had tamed my wild speculations. Lawson was just another overworked courthouse lawyer. And if Lawson wasn't the superstar I had conjured up, probably I wasn't the focus of his defense strategy, the one juror he was hoping to persuade. That was my imagination too. His face registered no recognition during our brief encounter. He was just another lawyer, I was just another juror, this was just another trial.

When Sloan started the day with a second witness placing Bud Jack at the bus stop, Lawson raised the same issues of viewpoint and lighting that had stymied the fireman on Friday. They were just as effective—the witness couldn't even remember if the suspicious man he saw was wearing a hoodie or just a t-shirt—but, like during jury selection, Lawson now looked bored with the proceedings. I was a little bored too. So what if Bud Jack was at the bus stop? It proves nothing. When Judge Silverson called Sloan and Lawson up to the bench for a hushed conference, I looked over at Roya. She caught my eye and smiled. Forget the courtroom potboiler, never mind the legal cliffhanger, this is going to be a romance.

How do I approach her, what do I say?

-Hi, Roya.

No, too forward, since she never actually told me her name.

-Hi, I'm Fletcher, you're Roya, right?

That's good, I can do that. Then what? I can usually say hi to strangers, even attractive women. I can look them in the eye and smile. It's the second line that throws me.

-Hi, I'm Fletcher, you're Roya, right?

-Yes.

-Okay, I...I just wanted to be sure.

Usually they disappear, suddenly needing to refill their drink or check their phone. Usually that's a relief. Because if I get the second line right, if I don't sound like a total dork, then I've got a bigger problem: the third line.

-Hi, I'm Fletcher, you're Roya, right?

-Yes.

-That's Persian, isn't it?

-Yes. How did you know?

-Uh, my ex-girlfriend. I called her from the men's room, and your name came up. I mean, I thought you were Hispanic.

And away she goes—*sayonara*, Roya. That's the problem: if you're honest, you frighten them away, you ruin everything. No, just be yourself— that's what Marissa says. People who reject themselves in advance to avoid getting hurt, hurt themselves. Pre-emptive rejection. It's better to be honest, honest.

-Hi, I'm Fletcher, you're Roya, right?

-Yes.

-I have a major crush on you.

-Oh.

-Your hair. Your eyes. I can't concentrate on the trial. And my sort of girlfriend says I should make friends with you.

-Why?

-To make sure you vote for acquittal. Wait. You want to get coffee?

Judge Silverson announced a recess. She needed to meet privately with the attorneys. In the Grishams I'd read, the narrator knows everything and would tell you, in simple prose, what the judge and attorneys were hashing out. No such luck here. Silverson just said be back in thirty minutes. Sloan appeared agitated. Lawson was still bored. Roya looked splendid in a yellow shirt and tight black jeans. She clutched a leather handbag close to her side, as if a fellow juror might tear the purse strap from her slender shoulder and make a run for it. Was she nervous? I was. This was my chance, catch her as we left the courtroom, a casual greeting in the hallway. I can do this, I told myself, never mind the stomach butterflies, the racing pulse.

I stood up, took a few deep breaths, I was ready to roll, and…I was stuck. Boxed in. Exiting the jury box was like disembarking an airplane. Roya had a first class seat and was out the door, through the terminal, and staking out a spot at the luggage carousel while I was still trapped near the aft lavatories, waiting for Grandma Strawberry Jam to gather up her carry-ons, delayed by The Elephant as she waddled down the aisle. Something like that. My pulse slowed. The butterflies melted away. The pressure was off. Our second encounter would have to wait. Unless Roya sought me out. That could happen. After all, she was the one who initiated encounter number one on Friday. At the very least, she finds me approachable, and maybe something more. She might be waiting for me outside the courtroom door, hoping I look her way. She wasn't. I took the elevator to the third floor and poked my head into the cafeteria. When I finally spotted her, in the first floor lobby, she was deep in a cell phone conversation and examining her nails.

I found a bench where I could keep an eye on her without being obtrusive, and opened Grisham number five. I had snuck it off Marissa's shelf the evening after jury selection, so why not give it a try, maybe improve my batting average, currently at .250—four Grishams attempted, one completed. I had whiffed on number four on Sunday afternoon. Once the corporate tax lawyer started providing legal assistance to the indigent, the story lost momentum. Nothing bad was going to happen to someone doing something that good, not after he'd already lost everything, not in Grisham's universe. I was catching on, there was a pattern to his stories: greed, suffering, then redemption.

The bad stuff started early in number five. While Roya chatted away, Danilo was kidnapped and drugged. Danilo aka Patrick Lanigan had stolen ninety million dollars—talk about greed—and his abductors wanted to know where it was hidden. They tied him down, taped electrodes to certain sensitive spots of flesh, and hit the switch. Talk about suffering. Roya ended her conversation, fiddled with her phone, made another call. Patrick screamed in pain and begged for mercy. I was hooked. How would Patrick Lanigan, big-time embezzler, find redemption? How would Grisham get him out of this fix? When Roya walked past me, still talking on the phone, heading for the elevators, they were handing him over to the FBI. Even under extreme duress, Lanigan hadn't given up the loot. He couldn't, he didn't know where it was. At the first sign of his disappearance, a woman named Eva had cleverly dispersed the money by wire to different banks around the world. I caught up with her at the courtroom door. Roya, not Eva. She was just turning off her phone, depositing it in her purse.

-Hi, Roya.

She smiled her flawless smile…at Sir No-Sir.

-Oh, hi, Kevin.

The juror with the bad transmission and terse replies had beaten me to punch.

-Ready for more law and order?

She never looked back to see who had held the door open for her, and I was stuck again as more people filed in, including Grandma Strawberry Jam.

-Thank you, dear, you're a real gentleman. How are you this morning?

Slightly nauseated, actually, seeing Juror Number Six, she of the long black curls and first class seat, already on a first name basis with Juror Number Five, he of the crew cut hair and cowboy boots. Sitting side by side in the jury box, they'll exchange knowing glances, whisper clever asides, unconsciously mimic each other's body language. Meanwhile, down in chair one, I'll be stranded next to a little mouse of a man who reeks of cigarette smoke and gives me an awkward nod whenever we make eye contact.

-I'm fine.

Gramma Jamma patted my hand and smiled. Well, at least one woman on the jury digs me.

With Silverson back on the bench, Sloan called to the stand Rex Ruffman, Huntington Beach police officer and street gang expert. He repeated his name for the stenographer—Rex Ruffman, two f's. He had an air of confidence, like he knew his way around a courtroom. He had a good name for socorepery.

-We've got one bank robbery and two car wrecks, Rex.

-It's Ruffman.

-It sure is.

The source of his expertise, he said in reply to Sloan's first question, was ten years interviewing gang-bangers, cataloguing their tattoos and graffiti, learning their sociology.

-It's no mystery. Mostly young men from broken homes, looking for a family to belong to, looking for respect.

Ruffman served on task forces, advised neighboring communities, taught college courses. And, yes, Orange County has gangs.

-Mostly this area. Mid-county. Anaheim, Santa Ana, over in Garden Grove. Not along the coast. The exception being Huntington.

He spoke with professorial authority, but wasn't he forgetting the Laguna Beach gangs? I've seen them—disaffected white teens sporting yin-and-yang tattoos, rampaging through downtown wielding credit cards and firing off text messages, defiantly flashing their gang signs: the two-fingered peace symbol, the ironic thumbs-up. I looked down toward Roya. Would she appreciate my droll wit? The Mouse in chair two saw me looking his way and nodded. I took it as a yes.

Professor Ruffman continued his lecture.

-Southside Huntington Beach is our most established gang. Latinos. They claim the area from Beach Boulevard to Nichols. Call themselves

Playeros. Beach boys. Asian bangers roll through town sometimes, from Garden Grove or Westminster. They're less territorial. Mostly concerned about their Asian rivals. We've got some resident skinheads. White supremacists. Informal links to Nazi Lowriders. Also not territorial. We keep a data base—names, photos, gang affiliation, internal relations like who's giving orders, who rolls with who. Our policy is low tolerance. They act up, we shut them down.

Yeah, but who wears cowboy boots in Orange County? Seriously. Out of the corner of my eye, just past The Elephant in chair four, I could see Sir No-Sir's pointy toes. Is there a gang for white thirty-somethings with tough-guy exteriors and no sense of humor? I mean, besides the police department. I couldn't remember if he was asked his occupation during jury selection. Probably tends bar. Or works in a liquor store. Definitely not a cowboy, wrong kind of jeans. Probably rides a motorcycle since his transmission went out. That explains it. All boots and no cattle. No college degree either, I bet. I could still hear his responses to Sloan: Do you have any independent knowledge of this case? No, sir. Any opinion on his guilt or innocence? No, sir. Can you factor equations, ever take a paddleboard two miles offshore, do you know the difference between Iran and Persia, does Roya go for the macho routine or is she just being polite?

-Tell us about Juan Castro, Mr. Ruffman.

Sloan handed the witness a document identified as a print-out from Ruffman's data base.

-We pegged Juan Castro as a Southside Playero seven years ago, when he was fifteen. Pretty young. He served five months in juvy—juvenile detention—for repeated vandalism, mostly graffiti. Never returned to high school. When he was nineteen, got picked up dealing coke. He was running with a gangster named Sleepy Cedeño, a hardcore Playero with connections to La Eme, the Mexican mafia. That's a major prison gang. Not good.

Not good, indeed, Mr. Ruffman, witness for the prosecution. Shouldn't you be making the victim sound innocent, win sympathy from the jury, not detailing what a troublemaker he was?

-I interviewed Juan Castro last year, after he got popped for a parole violation. No charges were ever filed. He told me he was done slinging dope. He had a baby daughter with his girlfriend.

Oh, okay, Juan Castro was getting out, going straight. The man had a bright future before the dastardly deed. Anything else, Mr. Ruffman?

-We didn't have any more trouble with him, so maybe it was true. Nine months later he shows up dead in a parking lot. Nasty bullet hole in his head. Because of his gang tats, I was called in to have a look.

Sounds rough, man.

His expert testimony, under Sloan's questioning, took up the rest of the morning, and when we recessed for lunch, it wasn't looking good for Bud

Jack. My guess: if we had gone into deliberation right then, the vote goes 12-0, he did it, no shadow of a doubt, send Bud Jack to the big house, send us home. Ruffman knew gangs, Ruffman had even figured out why Bud Jack was hurrying to the bus stop, how could Limping Lawson counter that? I didn't give it much thought. I had other moves on my mind. This time I wasn't getting boxed in, Cowboy Kevin wasn't beating me to the punch. This time, the gloves were coming off. Judge Silverson stood, we stood. She exited the court, the jurors started the slow file leftward. I went right, casually hopped the low railing, and walked unimpeded in front of the jury box. The aisle to the rear door was clear except for a few court spectators. I was the first juror out of the courtroom, and I waited for the others. Gramma Jamma came through, chatting with Lady Yoga. The Cowboy followed—tight jaw, dull eyes. Ever read a novel? No, sir. Not even a Grisham? Then came his lovely neighbor, taking her phone from her purse.

-Hi, Roya.

-Oh, hi.

She smiled her flawless smile…at me.

-How are you doing?

-Good. Hungry.

She laughed. She checked her phone.

-Mr. Fletcher, could I speak with you?

The bailiff, stern and bald—the so little hair left I might as well shave it clean kind of bald—and short, five-foot-six tops—what could he want? A message from the judge, I bet, she wants to sound me out, get a sense of the jury's mood.

-Mr. Fletcher, we don't hop the rail in the courtroom.

Lack of humor to compensate for lack of stature.

-Oh. Sorry. I was—

-Thank you, Mr. Fletcher.

He was gone. So was Roya. The elevator had closed. Now what? Stairs! I hurried down two flights. She was hungry—what an opening! The third line was easy. Should we go to lunch? Feel like getting some lunch? Would you mind some company for lunch? She wasn't in the cafeteria. The escalator to the first floor was crowded and moving in slow motion. She wasn't in the lobby, wasn't near the security checkpoint at the front doors. Maybe she had slipped into a restroom and I was ahead of her. I waited a few minutes, then back up to the cafeteria. Still no Roya. She wasn't with the smokers on the outdoor patio, thank God, but my neighbor in the jury box was, The Mouse, standing in the hot sun, puffing away. I gave up the search, half disappointed, half relieved. She must have gone out for lunch, pork and beans with Cowboy Kev. I had a teacher's sack lunch: yogurt cup, roast beef sandwich, chocolate chip cookies. I found an open seat next to a familiar face.

-Hey, how you doing? I'm Chad.

One of the three moderate men I had chatted with on Friday.

-Fletcher.

We shook hands. In a lunchroom full of strangers, we were comrades, but sitting down next to Chad was a tactical error, immediately regretted. I wanted to eat my sandwich and read, he wanted to talk.

-Didn't know they had gangs in Huntington Beach. Did you? I knew Anaheim was bad.

-Yeah?

-We live in Placentia. Pretty quiet there. Where are you from?

-Laguna.

-We love Laguna. Always try to get down there for brunch when the kids are in town. What's the name of that—?

-Las Brisas.

-Is that it—the restaurant on the cliff? Great view.

Las Brisas—the breezes—Mexican seafood for the weekend crowd. I've never eaten there, but it's always the first thing they mention. That and...

-And the Pageant of the Masters. We've missed the last few years. We need to get down there. Maybe once this trial's over. Ever been on a jury before?

-No.

-It takes longer than you think.

-Yeah?

He lowered his voice and gave me a conspiratorial look.

-These lawyers. We can't discuss the case. They can't shut up.

I forced a smile and scanned the room. Still no Persian dental hygienist. The man sitting opposite us took Chad's bait, started complaining about his jury service.

-Three weeks in, and the defense is still calling expert witnesses, paid by the hour I'm sure. It's unbelievable.

Chad shook his head in commiseration.

-What kind of case?

-We're not suppose to say.

-Actually, you can say what you want, we just can't discuss it.

The man hesitated, worked his eyebrows into a quizzical squint as he pondered Chatty Chad's subtle rendering of the law, then unloaded his grievance.

-These clowns were exiting the freeway and slammed into a retaining wall. They claim the off-ramp was flawed. No one takes responsibility anymore. So we have to listen to everything there is to know about freeway design, traffic safety standards, the braking system on the VW Beetle. Literally clowns. Eleven of them. In one small Volkswagen. It's a joke.

Meanwhile, in Grisham land, coastal Mississippi was in an uproar, Patrick Lanigan the embezzler having returned from the dead. The car accident three years earlier—a Blazer, not a Beetle—was staged. Lanigan had faked his death, changed his identity, stolen the ninety million, and fled to Brazil, leaving behind a widow and daughter. What a creep. I'm guessing Eva, the Brazilian lawyer transferring the loot around the globe, is his lover. And beautiful. If it was my novel, I'd make the hero's girlfriend ugly, even if he's filthy rich, just to confuse the reader.

-I'm not buying it.

Chad was looking at me. So was the guy across the table. With my nose in the book, I had missed something.

-Sorry?

-I'm not saying he didn't do it. But that whole drug story—these lawyers will come up with anything.

Chad was referring to how Sloan, over two half-hearted objections from Lawson, had elicited a complicated thesis from Ruffman. They had started with a second document, which Ruffman barely glanced at.

-Yeah, this is a report from the Long Beach Police Department. They have a big gang task force. Lots of gangs in Long Beach. Most notably Eastside Rollin' Twenties. That's a Crip set. African Americans. Their rivals are the Latino sets, especially Longo 13.

Sloan let him run with this a while, then asked where Juan Castro and Southside Huntington fit in.

-Drugs. Castro's buddy, Sleepy Cedeño, through his ties to La Eme, had connections to Longo 13, moving cocaine from Long Beach to Huntington. Sold it to rich white kids, like from Newport. Longo 13 had a minor turf war going with Eastside Rollin' over control of the cocaine pipeline. If Eastside Rollin' wanted to weaken Longo's position in the south Orange County market, going after Sleepy Cedeño would be a place to start. He was shot and killed in Long Beach. Long Beach PD says it was Crips. Then a carload of Latinos, reportedly flashing Longo signs, shot up two Crips in a drive-by. One dead, one on life support. That was two weeks before Juan Castro was killed.

Chad wiped his mouth with a napkin and gave me his analysis.

-They got a body and a suspect. Anyone can come up with a motive. That's all I'm saying. You're a math teacher, right?

-Yeah. What about you?

-I own a tire shop. Nothing like teaching. No summers off.

They always have to remind you of that, always hard to tell if they're happy for you or resentful. I noticed Chatty Chad's hands—smooth skin, clean nails. Not hands that mount tires for a living. I bet the shop owner takes off whenever he wants. I didn't say it, though. I didn't say anything. I didn't have a second line. I took a spoonful of yogurt to buy time.

-You know how I got my start, Fletcher? Car detailing. Isn't that something? Just like our guy.

Bud Jack ran a car detailing service, Ruffman had explained, gesturing to the Long Beach PD report as he spoke

-Him and this guy working with him. Wash your car in your driveway or your place of business. They come to you. But check your odometer. Sometimes he puts thirty miles on your vehicle, or his guy does, maybe driving to Huntington Beach. Long Beach started getting complaints. They looked into it—the task force did—because Bud Jack has known ties to the Eastside Rollin' Twenties.

Again, Chad knew better.

-I never once took a car out of a driveway. There's no reason. You let a guy detail your car, you unlock the door for him, that's it. He doesn't need to touch the keys. He says he has to take it somewhere, you tell him take a hike. So I'm not buying it. I'm not saying guilty or innocent, you understand. What did you say that restaurant was called—Las Brisas? I need to tell the wife.

Ha! I could hear Sharon's laugh. It's a chum bucket, darling, they seat you like sardines, they toss you soggy shrimp.

-The wife loves their shrimp. I go for the cocktails.

Actually, the shrimp are cocktails—chemical cocktails—that's what Pete had told me one night in his favorite Italian restaurant.

-It's all farm-raised, dude, pumped full of antibiotics, pesticides, algaecides. Toxic shrimp. They put it in everything, including that pasta you're eating, and the more antibiotics we ingest, the more our infectious diseases develop resistance to them. We're creating super germs. You wanna know what else is in that shrimp?

-No, Pete, I don't.

When Pete's in biology teacher mode, he can really ruin a meal.

-Rotenone. It causes Parkinson's. I'm just saying.

I excused myself from the cafeteria table, descended to the first floor, to my favorite bench, and got myself situated: cookies, Grisham, and a clear view of the entrance. When Roya comes through security, does her hotness set off the metal detector? Her Roya Hotness. I was hoping to intercept her, walk with her to the courtroom, but my mind was already headed back there, sorting through the testimony. Did Bud Jack really kill Juan Castro? Did it really go down the way Ruffman posited? Bud Jack takes the bus to Huntington Beach for a meeting with Juan Castro, wants to establish an Eastside-Southside cocaine connection now that Sleepy Cedeño is sleeping for good, but Juan isn't having it, for any number of reasons, so Bud Jack caps him, then catches the last bus home. Lawson had objected to this as farfetched speculation. Sloan insisted that Ruffman was offering an expert opinion. Silverson allowed it, saying Lawson could address this in cross-examination. Maybe it was speculation, but Ruffman had expressed no doubt.

-I've seen enough of these cases, I know the score.

It's the same with algebra students. After a few years in the trenches, you know how they operate, you've heard all their excuses, their pathetic little lies. I couldn't do my homework, Mr. Fletcher, my math book got stolen from my car I got food poisoning and barfed three times my mother said I had to clean my room you can call her if you want. Only they're mostly harmless goofballs at Dana Hills High, not the hardcore gangsters you find farther north. Like Ruffman had said in summary, when it comes to drug trafficking, those crews don't mess around.

The people robbed by Lanigan didn't mess around either. His four law partners, two insurance companies, a federal whistleblower—together they were out ninety million, much of it already spent. They hired some nasty folks who determined Lanigan was still alive and took their pound of flesh when they found him, probably would have killed him too, except the resourceful Eva tipped off Agent Cutter at the FBI. And now Lanigan, rescued by US agents and recovering in a military hospital, faced federal and state indictments and hard time in Mississippi's worst pen, yet he was surprisingly calm. Well, not so surprisingly. This being a Grisham, Lanigan must have a plan.

I waited on the first floor as long as I could, then took the elevator to the fifth. Roya wasn't in the hallway outside the courtroom. If she didn't hurry, she was going to be late. Unless she never left the building. Or maybe there are other entrances. That was my first thought when I opened the courtroom door—there must be other entrances—because court was already in session, the jury was seated, Judge Silverson was on her throne. Halfway to the jury box, I stopped in my tracks. Silverson had grown a beard. The bailiff was eyeing me and he...was a she. What the hell? Oh. I'm in the wrong courtroom. I must be on the wrong floor. I retreated to the elevator. No, this *is* the fifth floor. Am I losing my friggin' mind? It took me a few minutes to work it out: same courtroom, same hallway, wrong damn wing. East Wing, not West Wing. Now *I* needed to hurry. Down to the first floor, over to the West Wing elevators, up to the fifth. Let's try this again. Court was already in session, the jury was seated, Judge Silverson was on her throne. The beard was gone. She was whispering to Bailiff Baldy. They both looked up.

-You're late, Mr. Fletcher.

-I'm sorry, Your Honor. I got lost.

-Lost?

-I can't figure out this building. I was in the wrong courtroom.

Laughter from the jury box. My face flushed hot. Her Honor picked up a pen.

-Take your seat, Mr. Fletcher. Kindly don't climb over the rail.

She turned her attention to writing something. My eyes went to the bailiff. He raised his eyebrows, the only hair on his head, two brown caterpillars girdling a pale pink dome. He pulled his mouth into a smirk. The expression was unmistakable: that's right, I told her, you asshole. The Cowboy pulled back his boots as I shuffled by: make way for the asshole. The Mouse nodded: yep, you're an asshole. I didn't dare look at Roya. She would never agree to lunch with an asshole.

-Which courtroom were you in?

Silverson wasn't through with me.

-I'm not sure.

She studied me over her glasses. Does she think I'm lying? Am I in contempt of court? I needed a second line, and quick.

-The fifth floor, East Wing, I think. The judge had a beard.

-Judge Tompkins.

-The bailiff had hair.

More laughter. A lot more. But it wasn't my fault. The third line had its own momentum, it just came out. I could hear my comrades. The Elephant was snorting. The Mouse was squeaking. Was that a yee-haw from Cowboy Kev? I sat and studied my shoelaces, tightened my stomach muscles, bit down on my lower lip. I was trying to appear oblivious, no laughing, no smiles. Just being honest, Your Honor, just stating the facts, no offense intended toward the skinhead who snitched on me.

-In the future, Mr. Fletcher, please give yourself enough time to find your way back here.

After a moment of anarchy, the authority figure must have the last word, reestablish her dominance, any schoolteacher knows that. I nodded obediently, modestly accepting as sage advice her rather obvious admonition. She returned to writing. I risked another peek at the bailiff. He was waiting. If looks could kill. No, if looks could draw and quarter, if looks could attach electrodes to your inner thighs and hit the switch. He was furious. Why the sour face, kind bailiff, was it something I said?

The truth is I was a little unsettled. I'd read about a tardy juror who spent a night in the slammer. Was Judge Silverson documenting my behavior? Has she just scribbled down my sentence? Attention, attention, Your Honor, the guy in seat one isn't a liar, just another bewildered juror, lost in the halls of jurisprudence. You can't lock him up for that, right? Come on, Your Honor, call the next witness, put this behind us. You'll get no more trouble out of me, I promise, won't even know I'm here. I'll sit attentively, listen to testimony without forming an opinion, exit the jury box respectfully, obey the speed limit the whole way home, and when Marissa demands an update on the trial, mum's the word. I'm going straight. A model citizen.

Except, because he's into science and the environment and everything, I might have to tell Pete how Mount Baldy over there almost erupted.

Silverson was done writing. She looked toward the jury box, the suspicion gone from her face, like maybe my mental telepathy had worked. I relaxed my stomach, took a few belly breaths.

-How's your dog doing?

Oh, crap.

-Mr. Fletcher?

Was my dog dead or alive? Was it a he or a she?

-Sir?

-My dog....

Who did I tell what?

-Yes?

-My dog is better, Your Honor.

-I'm happy to hear that.

-Thank you. Me too.

When my pulse finally returned to normal, Ruffman was back in the hot seat and Lawson was doing the grilling. He asked for a quick review of Ruffman's credentials, congratulated him on his expertise, thanked him for the background on Juan Castro. I'm sure Ruffman realized it was a setup. He affected friendly disinterest and waited for Lawson's sucker punch.

-In your ten years of interviewing gang members, how many have you spoken to from the Eastside Rollin' Twenties?

-None.

-None?

-As far as I know.

-How many from Longo 13?

-None.

Lawson paused, cocked his head, pretended to be puzzled.

-Have you ever interviewed any gang members from Long Beach at all?

-Not that I'm aware of.

-So your expertise is only in Huntington Beach.

-I've studied gang behavior in general.

Ruffman's acting chops were no better than Lawson's. The amiability in his voice didn't match his body language—arms tight to his chest, right hand to his mouth. I'm not having this, his posture said. Maybe that's the definition of expert: someone who thinks he shouldn't be challenged.

-Let me restate. Your expertise—your specific knowledge of gangs and gang members—is confined to Huntington Beach, is that correct?

-That's a fair assessment.

Stick a fork in Ruffman, he's cooked, he's done.

-And your specific knowledge does not apply to Long Beach gangs and Long Beach gang members.

-I receive information from the Long Beach task force.

-But that information is not based on your expertise, correct?

-That's correct. It comes from their expertise.

-And when they—the Long Beach task force—when they tell you something about a specific person in Long Beach, do you have the expertise to verify or refute that information?

-I accept their expertise.

-Why?

-Sorry?

-Why do you accept their expertise?

-They've been studying gangs longer than I have.

Round one to Ruffman. Lawson had him on the ropes, but let him escape. Escape. I wonder what it's like at the beach right now.

At Crystal Cove this morning, where Pacific Coast Highway runs right next to the sand, the ocean was glass, the marine fog layer was already burning off, and, as I drove past, dolphins surfaced a few yards offshore. Another perfect morning for paddling. Or, if you're really lucky, for driving inland to spend the day in a windowless courtroom learning street gang demographics.

-How many Crips are there in Long Beach, Mr. Ruffman?

-How many individuals?

-Yes. In Long Beach.

Sloan stood.

-Objection, Your Honor. The witness has already acknowledged the limitations of his expertise.

-Mr. Lawson?

-Your Honor, I'm trying to establish the reliability of the information from the Long Beach task force, which the witness accepts uncritically.

Poor Judge Silverson, sitting here day after day, listening to these lawyers, handing down her decisions, breathing stale air under fluorescent lights. She ought to hold court on the beach, open air. People would line up for a chance at jury duty.

Her Honor instructed Ruffman to answer Lawson's question.

-Crips is a broad category. A loose alliance. In Long Beach alone, there are at least ten Crip sets. Insane Crips, Original Hood Crips, and so on. Those sets have sub-sets. Blocks, they're called. Or lines. They're all constantly evolving. New members come in, old members fade out. A precise count is impossible.

A precise count—how much money would I need to escape like Patrick Lanigan? Would one million be enough? One million dollars invested at three percent. Thirty thousand a year—I could live on that if I went somewhere cheap, nothing fancy, I hear Belize is nice.

Lawson's next question brought me back to reality.

-What, exactly, did the Long Beach task force say were Bud Jack's ties to the Eastside Rollin' Twenties?

Finally, the heart of the matter. Unless Bud Jack was in a gang, Ruffman's testimony was pretty much a waste of time—that's how it seemed to me.

-Like I said, they documented him in gang colors—black and gold for Eastside, blue for Crips. And his tattoos—

Lawson cut him off.

-That was eleven years ago, correct? In a gang sweep.

-Yes.

-What's a gang sweep?

-You go through a neighborhood, stop any gang-bangers you see, have a talk with them, take down their vitals.

-You've done this in Huntington Beach?

-A few times.

-Is everyone you sweep up a gang member?

-We figure out pretty quickly if they are or aren't.

-Some aren't?

-Correct.

-When Bud Jack was swept up, eleven years ago, was he charged with a crime?

-No.

-Eleven years ago, did he give a statement regarding gang affiliation?

-According to the information I received, he denied gang membership. But—

-This is according to the Long Beach task force—whose expertise you accept.

-Yes.

-Okay. Good. Eleven years ago he denied membership. Now, since then, since that random sweep eleven years ago, has the task force documented any gang activity on Bud Jack's part?

-Not that I'm aware of.

-Did you request they send you information regarding Bud Jack?

-I did.

-And the only information was from eleven years ago?

-Yes.

Round two to Lawson. The big man with the bad hip, ladies and gentlemen, is controlling the fight. His jab—eleven years ago, eleven years ago—is landing, Ruffman's legs are getting wobbly. Why am I rooting for Lawson? Is it the limp? Is he more likable than able-bodied Sloan? I'd like to think I'm rooting for justice, and every time Lawson exposes the speculative nature of the prosecution's case, I lean a little more his way.

Forgive the pun. But let's be honest, I might simply be hoping for a strong reason to vote for acquittal and make Marissa happy.

What would it take to make Roya happy? A house with a pool? A cleaning lady? We could do it for five. Steal five million, head for Brazil. Would she go for it? I looked to my left and caught a whiff of stale smoke. What a deal—Cowboy Kevin is enjoying Roya's sweet perfume, and I'm saddled with the Marlboro Mouse.

-Mr. Ruffman, didn't you say the likelihood of gang involvement decreases as a person gets older?

Round three, and Lawson had come out swinging.

-I did.

-Mr. Ruffman, do you have any concrete evidence connecting Bud Jack to Juan Castro?

-No, I—

-Mr. Ruffman, is your account of Juan Castro's murder supported by facts or entirely speculative?

Stop the fight, Your Honor, this is getting ugly. A few hours ago, Ruffman's version of Castro's demise had made perfect sense. A gangland drug war execution, we've all seen it, in the movies, on tv, and, anyway, Ruffman was the expert. But turns out he made it all up. It was a plausible scenario, an expert's best guess, and nothing more. Thank you, Professor Street Gang, thanks for nothing. Lawson returned to his corner, and Sloan came out to repair Ruffman's bleeding cuts.

-Mr. Ruffman, in your expert opinion, does Bud Jack have ties to the Eastside Rollin' Twenties?

-Yes. When they stopped him, he was with other Eastside homeboys and he had an E.S. tattoo.

-Mr. Ruffman, do gang ties disappear over time?

-Not usually, not if you stay in the community. Involvement may decline. The ties are always there.

So let's do the math: eleven years ago Bud Jack was seen in the company of Eastsiders, if that's what they're called, so he must be an Eastsider, and once an Eastsider always an Eastsider, and since the Eastsiders are at war with Longo 13, and Longo 13 is friends with Southside Huntington, and Juan Castro was a Southsider, Bud Jack must have killed him. QED. What a joke. I've got tenth-graders who would fall over laughing, and not just because they're stoned.

Sloan released the witness, who staggered out, his story in tatters. That was rough, man. Judge Silverson called a fifteen-minute recess.

-I want to meet with counsel in my chambers. Jurors may use the restroom, but stay on this floor. Mr. Fletcher, do you hear me? Fifteen minutes.

Loud and clear, Your Honor, not to worry, the asshole will stay right here in his chair, bury his face in his book, shamefully avoid any eye contact with his fellow jurors, and thank you, Your Honor, for the further humiliation.

Speaking of drug dealers, Patrick Lanigan's wife's boyfriend Lance smuggled marijuana from Mexico in a speedboat she had purchased with the big life insurance payout after Patrick died. Turns out, she and Lance had been hot and heavy the entire time she was married to Patrick and, after his death, they lived extravagantly on the two million dollar policy. But now, with Patrick miraculously resurrected, the insurance company wanted its money back, a lawsuit had been filed, there was nothing to be done, Lance told his newly unwidowed girlfriend, except kill Patrick and this time make it stick.

Fifteen minutes turned into thirty. What are they doing in Silverson's office, having tea?

Lanigan brought suit against the FBI for torturing him, a move calculated to pressure the feds into indicting the real torturers and the angry businessmen who had funded their manhunt. Would Lanigan avoid prison time? Why did I even care about the creep? I cared because my first image of him was as a kidnapping victim, which won my sympathy, had me rooting for him to survive, not give in to those evil sadists. Grisham is clever like that.

The pages were flying by when Her Honor and company returned, teatime over at last. Sloan called the final witness of the day, an accountant from Long Beach who testified that she had hired Bud Jack to clean her car in the parking lot of her office building.

-I know he took it for a long drive because the tank was half empty when I got it back. I have the receipt to prove I fueled up that morning on my way to work. It was a Shell station.

So? Lawson must have been thinking the same thing, or was in a hurry to get home, because he declined to cross examine. Class dismissed.

Again, the slow shuffle out of the jury box. Peering over The Mouse and around The Elephant, I watched Roya's black curls vanish into the hallway.

-I don't think she likes you.

It was Comrade Chad, my pal from the cafeteria, whispering from right behind me in chair seven.

-What's that?

He nodded toward Silverson's empty chair.

-She really gave you the business. I got lost too, the first day. An honest mistake, right?

-Yeah.

-Jeez, give a guy a break.

An honest mistake indeed, Comrade. And when I got outside, happy to have escaped the courthouse with only minor ego damage, one more honest mistake: I couldn't find my car. I walked back and forth. Either I really am losing my friggin' mind or wrong damn parking lot. I should move to a small town, some place where everything doesn't look exactly the same. Some place real. Then, suddenly, there she was, right in front of me, real as rain. Not my vehicle. Roya! She was opening her car door.

-Oh. Hi.

-Hi. I, uh, can't find my car. I thought it was....

-You're having a rough day, aren't you?

-No kidding. I'm not usually like this.

-What kind of car?

-A Honda. I'm Fletcher. You're Roya, right?

Three for three. Three lines, no disasters. Batting 1.000.

-Yes.

A restrained smile, no handshake. She got into her car.

-A green Honda. It's here somewhere. I guess I'll see you tomorrow.

-Okay, see you tomorrow.

I gave her an awkward wave and let her go. Great. She thinks I'm stalking her, thinks I figured out her name and followed her into the parking lot. Either a stalker or just a total loser who can't find his way back to the courtroom, can't find his own car. Four rows over, she pulled up next to me, her window down.

-There's a green Honda back that way. An old hatchback.

-That's it. Thank you. Wait, can I ask you something? Is Roya a Persian name?

-Yes. How did you know?

-I don't know. I have Persian students in my classes, so maybe....

Okay, my ex-girlfriend told me, but I'm not a stalker, I swear.

-It means sweet dream.

Of course it does. Of course it does.

-That's really nice.

She smiled. A real smile.

-Where do you teach?

-Dana Hills High.

-Oh, that's right. You said that during....

-During jury selection.

-Yeah. I thought you said your dog died.

-What?

Great. Crash and burn.

-The other day you told me your dog died, and today you told the judge—

-I just...I didn't want the whole world to know.

I don't want to overstate the case or jump to conclusions, I don't want to speculate, I'm no expert witness, but when Roya looked at me and held my gaze, and I didn't quickly look away or make a joke about how my dog had faked his death for the insurance money, I think she saw me, the real me, not the nervous dork, not the asshole in court. She saw the math teacher who wants his students to succeed. She saw the guy on the paddleboard with tears in his eyes because dolphins are so beautiful. She saw Guillam Fletcher.

-Why don't you hop in. I'll take you to your car.

Guillam Fletcher is sitting in Roya's car! I can smell her perfume. I'm inches away from her and I can't think of a single clever thing to say and it doesn't matter. She likes me. She trusts me. She noticed the book I was holding.

-What are you reading?

-Oh, it's just a Grisham. Something to pass the time. I don't normally—

-Look who's there.

She was pointing to several cars leaving the parking lot.

-What?

-The defense attorney.

-Where?

-In that Lexus.

6

The stratagem always works—that's the other thing I'd come to expect in a Grisham. There will be an elaborate and clever plan, meticulously crafted, which the reader only gradually comes to understand as Grisham reveals it with little twists and turns, and it will go off without a hitch, with no unexpected consequences, no big surprises for the plotter, who has it all laid out from the get-go, he knows what he's doing. Like Patrick Lanigan. Anticipating his eventual capture, before he fled the country Lanigan recorded conversations and acquired documents implicating his law partners, the federal whistleblower, and a US senator in the embezzlement scheme that had produced the ninety million in the first place, and once he was under arrest in federal custody, it went like clockwork. With the incriminating evidence as leverage against his pursuers, Lanigan offered to return the money plus a little interest to its rightful owner, the federal government, if the charges against him were dropped. He would still walk away with over twenty million—craftily hidden by Eva—thanks to careful investing and frugal living while on the lam. The deal was struck, and Lanigan flew to France, a free man, just as he had scripted it. In fact, Lanigan had been so confident of his ultimate absolution that he had allowed himself to be captured just to get it over with.

Is Roya part of Richard Wilhite's plan? Richard gets Sigrid to get Marissa to get me to vote not guilty, and I convince Gramma Jamma and maybe a few other followers, but Cowboy Kevin is a tougher nut to crack. Which is where Roya comes in. With Marissa's encouragement, I befriend the pretty dental hygienist, help her find her way to not guilty, and the male jurors, Cowboy Kev included, come trailing along in her perfumed wake. That's it: I persuade the women, Roya wins over the men, Bud Jack goes free, and Richard laughs all the way to the bank, though how he profits from Bud Jack's release still eluded me.

My thesis had gaping holes, it's true, but just because I'd been reading too much Grisham doesn't mean there wasn't something going on. Too many odd coincidences were popping up. Like on my drive home. As an experiment, I stayed far to the right, in the slow lane, and when traffic opened up, I kept it at sixty—just like I had telepathically promised Judge Silverson. It was relaxing, actually, not feeling hurried, not worrying about switching lanes or getting past slower vehicles or making a phone call without going off the road. I tuned the radio to the classical music station and basked in the glow of Roya. I could still hear her bubbly laugh after I had thanked her for finding my car.

-Maybe you should get a GPA.

-A what?

-One of those things that tell you where you are.

-Oh, you mean a GPS. Good idea.

A shiny black SUV rode up my tail, then cut in front of me and took the next exit, a gas-guzzling maneuver that must have saved the driver all of six seconds. The one-fingered salute as he passed didn't bother me. The poor guy was stressed, he was the one with the problem, not me, and anyhow my mind was still in Roya's passenger seat, admiring the handsome contrast between her dark eyes and creamy skin. Maybe I *will* get a GPS, show her that I take her seriously. When I checked my rear-view mirror, another impatient driver was on my bumper. All these harried people, rushing to work, rushing home, and slowly dying inside. The driver flicked her headlights on and off and raised both hands to signal exasperation and personal affront. Apparently sixty in the slow lane is a public nuisance. Somehow I made it as far as Irvine without inciting a road-rage shooting, stopped at a gas station, and was filling my tank when my phone rang. Marissa. We hadn't talked since our double date with the Wilhites. Maybe she would let me stop by her house on my way home, I was only a few minutes away.

-No, I'm kind of busy. I just wanted to hear how it went today. Any new evidence?

-Not really. Then how about dinner later?

-I have plans.

-Oh.

Plans. Could she be any more vague? Why not just tell me what she's doing?

-Were there any new witnesses?

-I'll call you later.

-Are you upset?

-No, I—

-Fletcher.

-I have to go. Someone's approaching me.

-What? Who?

-This black guy.

I had first noticed him coming out of the convenience store next door. No big deal, just another guy in dark shades, until he started heading my way, looking at me kind of sideways. He was carrying something—a rolled up magazine, I think—I didn't look too closely, didn't want to invite an unwanted encounter. Trying to stay cool, I put the phone in my pocket, removed the gas nozzle from my car, and now he was standing five feet away.

-How's that trial coming?

I knew the voice. The Sophist!

-Hey, how you doing?

The soulful handshake: two hip dudes meeting on the street.

-You taking care of my man?

My phone rang. I dug it out of my pocket. Marissa, again.

-Are you okay? Fletcher?

-Yeah.

-Who was it? Who was—?

-I'll tell you later.

Back to The Sophist, now checking out the gas pump.

-Sorry about that. My girlfriend.

-No worries. Price of gas is insane. Three fifty-nine for the regular.

-No kidding.

-For the regular! What kind of mileage you get? You get thirty?

-I don't know.

-That new Prius gets fifty.

-I heard they're pretty expensive.

-Pay for themselves. Fifty miles per gallon. Still got that all-white jury?

-Yeah. You were right about that.

-Course I was. You gonna convict the brother?

-I...I don't know.

-My man ain't got a chance, right?

-I'm really not supposed to discuss it.

He tightened his mouth and narrowed his eyebrows.

-Alright, you take care.

-You too.

Halfway back to the convenience store, he stopped.

-Hey. I'm still counting on you.

We sit next to each other during jury selection, he gets dismissed, I get selected, when I get to the courthouse parking lot he's still there, says justice is up to you, baby, and four days later—what are the chances?—we run into each other at some random gas station off a freeway exit. Hmm? In a small town, no big deal. In endless sprawling Orange County, one in a million. That's what Pete said when I called him.

-Yeah, one in a million. Same as the chance of coming around a blind curve when two skater punks decide to play chicken.

-What?

-The little shits.

-Pete, what are you talking about?

-Two tons of assault vehicle, dude, doing forty-five.

What he was talking about was that while I was playing court jester, two kids on skateboards tried a mad dash across Pacific Coast Highway, and Pete, too late to brake, swerved left and barely missed them, but with his shoulder still feeling the fall from Sigrid's tree, he couldn't swerve back in time to avoid the oncoming pickup truck which clipped his back end, spun him around, and set him up square for the Hummer, which obliterated the back half of his minivan.

-My backseat totally t-boned, and I'm like, I'm yelling, what's the point, really, do you really need a car like that, what's the point?

-At who?

-The woman in the Hummer. She's all are you okay, I'm so sorry. I wanted to choke her. There was a real estate sign on her car door. Like she needs a Hummer to sell fucking real estate in fucking Laguna.

-But it wasn't her fault, right?

-I know, I was just, I mean, total adrenaline rush. And pissed. Those little shits almost got me killed. And then I'm like, I caught myself and go, ma'am, I think you spilled my groceries. She musta thought I was insane.

-You caught yourself?

-Yeah, I know. But she was hot. This tight t-shirt and short shorts.

-And driving a Hummer?

-I'm telling you, dude, south county. She was nice too. Gave me her number.

-No.

-Swear to God. For the insurance stuff. Does insurance cover food? Because I had beer in the back seat and it went everywhere. First time I ever smashed a six-pack. Usually it's the other way around. Then the cops show up and think I'm drunk.

-Were you?

-Give me a little credit, bro.

-Just asking.

-I was shopping. I tried to tell them, officer, I'm sober, it's the van that's been drinking. Out comes the breathalyzer, count to ten backwards, the whole obstacle course.

-What about the skateboarders?

-Gone. Fortunately, these two guys walking up from the beach, they saw the whole thing. Said the kids came out of nowhere, there was nothing I could do. They said it was a miracle I didn't hit the little shits. So then the cops are like, oh, I guess you're not drunk.

-You saved their lives. The little shits.

-I think I just stayed relaxed because all the drugs.

-You told the cops that?

-No. But fortunately there's no Ambienalyzer.

One shoulder throbbing in pain, doped up on sleeping pills and painkillers, bounced between a truck and a Hummer, beer and broken glass everywhere, and Pete walks away without a scratch.

-Not even whiplash?

-The ambulance guys wanted to take me in. There's no way. I told them not unless you're taking her in too. The Hummer chick. I'll definitely hop in back with her.

-Pete, you know what I think?

-Let me guess—it was all a setup, the skaters, the pickup truck. Someone's trying to kill me. Probably my ex-wife. Or that Wilhite guy. The guy wants me dead. As a warning to you.

-Are you through?

-By the way, I had to cut a deal. The cops overlook the fact I was stoned on Ambien, and I give up the name of the creepy guy who the lady caught trespassing in her backyard. You might want to leave the state.

-I think you got really lucky.

-Lucky? Bruised ribs, busted shoulder, and *then* my van gets totaled. Yeah, I'm having a good week. Not to mention the wasted beer. Lucky would have been if the Hummer chick wasn't wearing a fat diamond on her finger.

-It could have turned out worse. A lot worse.

A pause on the phone.

-Pete?

-Yeah, you're right. When that Hummer was coming at me, dude, I swear, it was lights out, game over. But it's a Yamaguchi, isn't it?

The Yamaguchi Paradox—we made it up when Pete got divorced. A guy named Yamaguchi was visiting Hiroshima when the atomic bomb was dropped. He survived despite serious burns, and the next day went home. To Nagasaki. True story. When the second atomic bomb leveled Nagasaki, he survived that too. Lived sixty more years. The only person known to have survived both atomic bombs. Must be the luckiest guy in the world. Or unluckiest. He couldn't have the incredibly good luck of surviving without the incredibly bad luck of being in both doomed cities. That's the paradox: can you have really good luck without really bad luck?

But that's different than one in a million, which is about likelihood, not fortune. That was still on my mind. One in a million means I could do it all over again—drive home from the courthouse, stay in the slow lane, stop at the gas station—do it over one million times and not run into The Sophist. Pete disagreed.

-No, dude, think about it, three hundred million people in the US, so a one-in-a-million chance occurs here, occurs in America, three hundred times. No big deal. Probably fifty in California alone. I thought you knew math.

-What are the chances that you are one of the three hundred?

-Huh?

-One in a million. So there has to be a better explanation than we just happened to run into each other. Something's going on.

-Dude, you've got Grishamitis.

-I never run into anybody. Not even in Laguna.

-I don't recommend it.

And that's not all. The Sophist went back into the convenience store. I mean, he's in the store, buys a magazine, spies me at the gas station, recognizes me across the parking lot, comes over to say hi—that's the one-in-a-million version—and then goes back into the store. Why would he go back in? Why not just hop in his car and drive away? Unless, I don't know, he didn't want me to see the car he's driving. Because is it possible he'd been following me from the courthouse?

-Grishamitis, I swear. You need to switch to Harry Potter.

We hung up, and I continued home to Laguna, passing the turnoff to the little canyon neighborhood where Marissa was too busy for me to stop by and already had plans. No, Grishams have plans—what she has is called a date. To hell with her. After the verdict is in, I'm asking Roya out. We'll talk about the trial, laugh about how we noticed each other during jury selection. I probably saw her first, sitting in chair six next to the black MBA with the neatly trimmed beard and...the black MBA! Home entertainment systems. USC. That's who I saw on Sunday morning! The prospective juror who sold the stock at the wrong time. When I paddled back to shore, he was watching me—a black man in Laguna, a jacket and tie on the beach, hard not to notice. He looked familiar, but I was walking up the stairs with a twelve-foot surfboard balanced on my head, and couldn't really try for a second look. That's two one-in-a-millions in two days. I called Pete again—he had to hear this.

-You're hallucinating.

-Pete, I'm telling you.

-So all black men look alike to you.

-No.

-Then, dude, you're about to win the lottery.

Yeah, or something strange is going on.

At home, I boiled macaroni, nuked a jar of pasta sauce in the microwave, cracked open a beer, and tried not to think of what Marissa might be having. Can Eddie the Easel afford Laguna's fine dining opportunities? Probably. Probably comes from money. How else do these artsy types manage to live in Laguna? I could call her—would that be intrusive? I told her I would call her back, so it wouldn't be intruding, I'm simply keeping a promise. No, just leave her alone, let her have her fun. I can't force myself onto her. I opened another beer. I dialed her number.

-Hello?

-It was someone from the jury. When you called before. The guy—

-You said he was black.

-He is.

-On the jury?

-He got dismissed the first day. We sat next to each other.

-I thought you were getting mugged or something.

-Because he was black?

I had her. This time I had her.

-No.

-Come on, admit it.

-Because you were so dramatic—Marissa, someone's approaching me.

-I didn't say it like that. Just admit it, you were worried because he was black.

-You're the one who made it about race. Would you have told me, Marissa, it's a white guy?

I can't win.

-What's weird is I saw this other guy, too. On Sunday. At the beach.

-Fletcher, I need to go.

-Wait.

-We can talk tomorrow.

-You asked how it went today. They said Bud Jack is a gang-banger. They said he killed him over drugs.

I knew that would get her attention.

-Do you believe it?

-No. I don't know. I did at first. Then the defense lawyer got the guy to admit there really wasn't evidence. It's like they can say anything.

-That's what I told you. But, really, I have to go.

-Why do you care about this case anyway?

-He's an innocent man.

Maybe it's true. Maybe Marissa, apolitical and safely ensconced in Laguna, is truly concerned, maybe Sigrid really inspired her, the way those movie stars get people passionate about a guy on death row. Ha! Sharon had little use for Hollywood activists, and watching those awards shows usually set her off.

-Darling, don't kid yourself, it's not like they're going to subvert a system that's made them fabulously wealthy, like save the Dalai Lama or whomever, good for them, then back to making titillating movies that glorify violence. Which reminds me, you know how you titillate an ocelot? You oscillate its tit a lot.

Sharon was a hoot, I'll give her that. And she had a philosophy.

-You want to change the world, darling, just love your students. Every one of them is an opportunity to broaden a mind, pry open a heart. Can you do that with math? Can you turn them on?

-Not without getting arrested.

That's probably why she got bored with me—no philosophy. I mean, why teach algebra anyhow? Five to ten thousand students over a career, assuming you don't quit early to broker home loans or become a chiropractor, and how many will ever have need to solve complex equations? Especially now with computers.

-That's the problem with Dana Hills, darling, not enough love.

I should have known then she was moving on.

I washed the dishes in the sink, took a shower, opened another beer, slumped into the couch, and didn't turn on the television. I wanted to finish the Grisham. What is it that makes his books so compelling? I bet I could write one just as good. That's what I'll do: take up writing, pump out a couple of bestsellers, and we'll retire to our beach house in the tropics, *Roya + Fletcher*, no embezzlement necessary. But how does he do it? What's the secret formula? Little violence, no sex, so where's the titillation? Uncovering the master plan keeps you turning pages, I get that, except you can't really figure it out on your own, there aren't enough clues, you have to wait for the author to show it to you. Maybe people prefer it that way.

Out of habit, I kept glancing at the silent television. The ghostly, blank screen's latent energy unsettled the room. The remote control called to me softly, seductively: Fletcher, put down the book and press my buttons, see what's on, just for a minute.

Almost eight o'clock. I could finish this chapter, then catch the sports highlights. There's nothing else on basic cable worth watching. It's all sitcom reruns and celebrity gossip and police procedurals on every other channel. If I can't figure out how to write a Grisham knockoff, I should try a cop show. Or a courtroom drama. And pitch it to my good friend in television, Richard Wilhite. What was it he said?—I know people, I'm a serious man. That was weird. Like halfway between a joke and a threat, trying to impress me, like he doesn't think people take him seriously. Which makes no sense. It's someone like me that people don't take seriously—no wife and kids, no house, an old car, jeans and tennis shoes, hanging out all day with teenagers, no evidence of adulthood on display, an oddball, a goof, and kind of pathetic. Pete takes me seriously, but look at him—the exception that proves the rule.

Look at Juror Number Five aka Sir No-Sir aka Cowboy Kevin, with his earnest demeanor. I bet Roya doesn't think Cowboy Kev needs a Global Positioning Satellite to keep from getting lost in the courthouse. Maybe I should wear a tie tomorrow, like the black MBA—I mean the MBA, the MBA with the beard at jury selection. Everybody liked him, you could tell he was an adult. I have a tie in my closet somewhere. Maybe I should learn how to tie it.

Fletcher, don't neglect me. The remote control was whispering again. Fletcher, you might be missing something good.

Okay, tomorrow, full-on adulthood, arrive early, settle my mind, focus on the testimony, draw no attention to myself. Juror Number One aka Mr. Maturity aka Guillam Fletcher. An adult wouldn't mind being called Guillam, if that's his given name, even if the name sounds archaic and reminds him how little thought his parents gave to his feelings, even if he got tired of being called Kill 'em Guillam as a teenager. Students can call me Fletcher—that's normal, reducing a teacher to his last name—but adult to adult, it should be Guillam. I should start going by Guillam. Anyhow, it's just a name. Better than, say, Richard. Better than Dick.

Psst, Fletch, hit power, turn me on, titillation is just a click away.

I got up from the couch and took Grisham to bed where we could have some privacy for the final chapter, away from the seductive remote control and the looming tv screen. My bedroom, too, didn't exactly scream adult. A queen-size mattress atop an old box-spring on the floor. A florescent floor lamp left over from my college days, six feet tall, clouded with dead bugs. All my clothes crammed in the closet, either on hangers or in boxes on the floor, no need for a chest of drawers. No bedside table, either. No bookshelves, no framed prints on the wall. Bachelor minimal. I could tell Marissa didn't like it, though she never said so. Once again, ex-girlfriend-turned-social-advisor Sharon to the rescue.

-It's all about the message, and your room says I'm not sticking around, I'm not settling down.

-But couldn't it say I don't want to buy expensive furniture I don't really need?

-Same thing, darling, same thing.

-Most people sleep on the floor. I mean around the world.

-You don't live around the world, you live in Laguna. If you want to date women in Laguna, get a real bed. At least get some new sheets and matching pillow cases.

She was right. No, she was wrong. I want to be appreciated for who I am, not what I have. If Marissa doesn't approve of how I live, if Sharon thinks I'm stubborn and clueless, that's their problem. We'll see what Roya thinks. Maybe Persians don't like fancy beds. Maybe that's why they're so into carpets.

I turned the last page. "His journey was over. His past was finally closed." Another Grisham finished, completion rate up to .400— Cooperstown material—and I had to admit I was wrong, there was a surprise awaiting Lanigan. Two, actually. The first was the torture. He knew they'd press him to reveal the location of his bank accounts, he didn't know how bad it would get. Still, he had survived, and the plan did work. Until the final step. Beautiful Eva was supposed to meet him in France, they still had tons of money left over, they would live happily ever after. She didn't show. Surprise number two. She took it all and disappeared, betrayed his trust, gave Lanigan a taste of his own medicine.

My phone rang from the living room. Marissa? I hurried to answer it.

-Dude.

-Dude.

-I'm sitting here watching tv.

-That's great, Pete. Thanks for the update.

-No, listen, I almost got killed today, and now I'm just watching tv, back to normal, like nothing happened. I could be dead. I could be right now nonexistent. And I wouldn't even know it. What a trip.

I hadn't thought about it like that. Pete could be dead and gone. What would I be doing? Not drinking beer and finishing a Grisham. I suppose I'd be calling people from work. Bill, are you sitting down? Carol, I have some bad news. Or I'd be down at the spot, the fatal curve, to see what? Traffic would be moving, no hint of recent tragedy, only little ash piles from burnt-out traffic flares. It would be surreal, I know—my best friend gone—it wouldn't sink in right away. I would stand there trying to make sense of the moment, then go home when students started showing up with candles and flowers and all that teenage sentimentality. It probably wouldn't hit me until the first day of school with Mr. Repetti aka Mr. Spaghetti not in his science room, no balding biology instructor wearing a white lab coat over a floral print shirt, no familiar Repetti smirk when a cute girl, all push-up bra and nascent cleavage, wiggled by.

-Pete, you're right, we should mark the occasion. You could have been a goner.

-Ought to be a national holiday.

A celebration was in order, only Pete was out one vehicle, I was into my third beer, and driving to his place under the influence probably wasn't the best way for me to observe National Pete Didn't Die Day. The risk of tragic irony was too great.

-We can do something tomorrow, after I get home from jury duty.

-Yeah, I'm sleepy anyhow. I hate those stupid pills. I'm done with them.

-Hey, did your life flash in front of you? During the accident.

-No, I only remember thinking I don't want to die like this.

-On Ambien?

-No, in a minivan. The final humiliation. A minivan crushed by a hot babe in a Hummer. When the insurance check arrives, I'm getting a Porsche. Seriously.

-You can't afford to get a Porsche.

-Dude, I can't afford not to.

Pete Repetti wasn't dead. His head hadn't punched through the windshield, his ribs hadn't splintered into his lungs, there was no internal hemorrhaging, no paralysis, no coma on life support, Spaghetti wasn't a vegetable. My dinner was stale macaroni with bland sauce, my sort of girlfriend was out with her sort of guy-friend, Patrick Lanigan's girlfriend had absconded with his millions proving me wrong about Grisham, I was home alone drinking beer in my bare bedroom, and Pete wasn't dead. It was a good night. This was no Yamaguchi, either. There was no bad luck to speak of. Forget the ruined vehicle—an insured minivan is not a sleeping city. Everything turned out fine. A very good night.

That might be the Grisham secret. Everything turns out fine for the hero. Always a good person at heart, he was just greedy, greed got the best of him, and greed can be atoned for—greed, suffering, redemption—so long as he never intended to harm anyone innocent, so long as his antagonists were equally greedy and unrepentantly mean. Good versus evil: that's the magic formula. It's kind of obvious once you see it. Lanigan, the conniving embezzler, had only good intentions, only robbed the bad guys. The wife he left behind was cheating on him, the daughter wasn't even his, still he made sure they got a big insurance payout. The ninety million was dirty money, the federal government had been defrauded, and since the feds would have just wasted the money anyhow, when Lanigan returned it, with interest, the taxpayers came out ahead—that's how Grisham spun it. But what about the charred body in the crushed Blazer? Hadn't Lanigan killed a teenaged loner and used the corpse to fake his own death? Nope. One of Lanigan's clients, an old man nobody cared about, had died naturally, Lanigan alone attended the funeral, the corpse he planted in the Blazer was cold and unwanted, the missing teen was alive and well. In fact, with Lanigan's help, the kid had assumed a new identity and started a new life in a different state, leaving his troubled childhood behind. Lanigan was a good guy, no moral ambiguity, no harm, no foul. He'd paid for his greed, he'd become a better man, an honest man. Jilted at the end, no bank account to his name, he was content to return to simple village life in Brazil.

An honest man—there's an idea: no fake identity, no secret plan.

Would Roya go for blunt honesty? It would be nice to be completely open for a change, not have to be careful and apologetic. Roya, I'm thirty-three years old, I rent a small apartment, I sleep on the floor, that's who I am. I've got a surfboard, but I'm not really a surfer, I don't catch waves, I just stand up and paddle away from shore. And I'm writing a television screenplay, I mean, I'm thinking about it, I've got a pretty good idea going.

BAILIFF BALDY: What are you going to do about Juror Number One?

JUDGE SILVERSON: You mean Mr. Fletcher?

BALDY: I've got a bad feeling about the guy.

SILVERSON: Because of his comment about hair? Don't worry, he's harmless.

BALDY: I overheard him talking to Juror Number Six. The sick dog story was phony.

SILVERSON: You think I don't know that? You think all these years on the bench and I can't detect a lie?

BALDY: Then toss him out. Better yet, let me lock him up for a couple of nights.

SILVERSON: No, the guy wants to serve, let him serve.

BALDY: He's up to no good, I can sense it. I've been at this a long time too.

SILVERSON: Just keep your eye on him for now. And, Bailiff—

BALDY: Yes, Your Honor?

SILVERSON: I like a man with no hair.

The phone rang again—no doubt Pete with more details on life after not death. I spoke first.

-Let me guess, you're still watching tv.

-What?

-Marissa?

-Fletcher, I wanted to say I'm sorry about before. I was in a bad mood. I just…I needed time alone. To think.

-Oh. Okay.

She wasn't out with What's-his-face. She wasn't choosing him over me. Yet.

-I forgot to ask you. Did they get to the confession?

Here we go. Always about the trial. But at least she wants to talk.

-No, but get this, the defense attorney—his name is Lawson—he and Richard Wilhite, they drive the same vehicle.

She waited for more.

-Same year, same color, everything.

Still waiting.

-The defense attorney and the guy paying him—both in a gold Lexus.

-Is that supposed to mean something? Everyone around here has a Lexus.

It means maybe it was Lawson after all who I saw entering your friend Sigrid's front door the night Pete and I snuck into her backyard and broke her tree. But I couldn't tell her that.

-It means…there's just been a lot of strange coincidences. Like the guy at the gas station.

The guy, not the black guy. The guy at the gas station, and the guy with the MBA at the beach on Sunday morning, and Richard and Sigrid Wilhite, why does the trial keep following me home to Laguna? Marissa, too, always asking about details from court. But Marissa wasn't interested in coincidences.

-If the confession was for real, wouldn't they start with that?

I'd had the same thought. In his opening statement, Sloan had told us that Bud Jack confessed. But instead of building his case around that, he gives us two irrelevant eyewitnesses and an expert on gangs who specializes in speculation. Makes you wonder. Unless Sloan was like the Honda salesman who, faced with my hemming and hawing—a young teacher buying his first new car—and sensing I was searching for a reason to say yes, suddenly offered to throw in floor mats and soon had me signing on the dotted line. Because of stupid floor mats. Nothing wrong with the car—140,000 miles and going strong—I just hated the thought of having fallen for such an obvious trick.

-Maybe he's saving it to seal the deal. The prosecutor. We'll probably hear about it tomorrow.

-We should have dinner tomorrow.

Dinner with Guillam or with Juror Number One? Intimacy or information? Courtship or court? Romance or suspense? Hank-panky or Whodunit? Flirtation or—

-Fletcher?

-Yes. Definitely. I'll call you on my way home.

All's well that ends well. Pete didn't die, Marissa stayed home alone, nothing to worry about after all. That's it, that's the formula: Grishams sell because they offer an orderly universe—the plan will work, the good guys will get better, the bad guys will get their comeuppance, just be patient, go along for the ride. What did Marissa need time to think about this evening? Why was I afraid to ask? Don't worry about it, be patient, go along for the ride. I'm one of the good guys. I'm a public employee who helps young people, I don't live extravagantly, I'm not greedy, I've got nothing to apologize for.

So why did I lie to The Sophist about my gas mileage? Of course I know my gas mileage, it's a simple calculation—twenty-six around town, twenty-nine with freeway driving. Better than a Hummer. Not by much, though. Maybe I *should* get a Prius, fifty miles per gallon or whatever. Except I don't want to start making car payments, I just got out from under my student loans. But wouldn't a good person make the sacrifice for the planet—global warming and all that? A Prius—that's an adult car, that says responsibility. And taking on new debt—think of the message that sends: I'm not going anywhere, I'm not planning to quit my job and join the Peace

Corps, I'm in it for the long haul. Hey, ladies, Fletcher Guillam bought a new car, one he can't really afford, a house mortgage must be next, he might be a family man after all. A family man—I fell asleep thinking about that.

The phone rang sometime between two and three a.m.

-Hi, this is Roya, from the jury, sorry to bother you, I heard you were getting the Prius, and I was just wondering what kind of bed you have, a small one I hope.

Yeah, in my dreams.

I'd left my phone next to my bed. I could answer it without opening my eyes, without even waking up.

-Hello?

-Fletcher.

-Marissa?

-I need you at my place right now.

-Really?

I mean, light the candles, pop the champagne, I'm on my way.

-Yes, really. The cops are here.

-What?

-They've got a search warrant with your name on it.

The only shirt I could find was bright pink with the picture of an orange dolphin on the chest. Where did that come from? It was too tight, it pinched my armpits. I cut off the sleeves with a kitchen knife and shoved them into my pants pocket, then grabbed my keys and hurried out. What were the cops looking for? Something connected with Sigrid's backyard? Evidence of a compromised juror? Were they even real cops? How did they wind up with Marissa's address?

I got there fast, told Marissa to fire up her movie camera, and demanded badge numbers. My name was the only one on the warrant, so once the cops were informed that I didn't live there any continued search was illegal.

-And, officer, I'm a lawyer, I'll sue the city, I'll sue you personally, drive you into bankruptcy, my sort of girlfriend is getting this all on video so smile.

Legally, it was a stretch, but it worked. They left, the bald one mumbling something like we'll see you again real soon, dolphin-man.

Then I woke up and couldn't get back to sleep. It was an unsettling dream. Eventually, they will come knocking, I guess I was expecting that. Someone caught Pete's license plate number when we fled Sigrid's neighborhood or Pete opened his big mouth and told somebody hey, dude, check this out, this woman caught Fletch peeping in her backyard. One day soon I was going to need a really good lie. And the bright pink t-shirt was weird. But there was something even more troubling. Legal technicalities. Threats of litigation. I was dreaming in Grisham.

7

I had a college professor who ruined all the historical holidays for me. Labor Day, he insisted, should be May first, international workers day, not some meaningless Monday in September. Columbus Day celebrated genocide. The happy Thanksgiving feast at Plymouth Rock was the beginning of the end for the Indians. I had already developed a serious case of sophomore skepticism, so Professor Hanson's unapologetic iconoclasm was music to my ears, despite the odd articulation, high-pitched and raspy, with a slight lisp that intensified in his more impassioned moments.

-The Fourth of July. Freedom and fireworkth and the Declarathon of Independenth, written by a man who owned thlaveth. Freedom, my ath!

-Professor Hanson, what about Valentine's Day?

-Yeah, what about St. Patrick's?

We knew the answer, we just wanted to hear him say it.

-Candy and beer, people, I told you, candy and beer. And thamrockth.

Professor Penguin we called him. He was pear-shaped, narrow shoulders and rounded hips, and constantly enduring the removal of cancerous spots from a long, splotchy face. But the way he cawed at us— Wear thunthcreen, people, you're not immortal!—he sounded more like the chain-smoking offspring of a crow and a duck. Wear thunthcreen! Don't drink and drive! Practith thafe thex! He concluded his lectures with urgent admonitions that sent us out laughing.

-Now thcram, and don't thpend the entire weekend thtudying!

Since it was widely known that question three on Hanson's final, unchanged in years, would require you to compose an essay making the case for a new holiday, you only had to ask around the dorms to find a time-tested response. John Brown Day, Harriet Tubman Day, New Deal Day—all proven winners. Bob Marley Day—don't bother. Hiroshima worked, it was said, if you proposed a day of mourning and reconciliation and didn't get cute and call it Enola Gay Pride Day. Someone supposedly got an A for a William Henry Harrison holiday, arguing that a president who only lasted one month did the least damage and should be honored. What would Harrison Day look like? Would everyone work one hour and go home? Would there be parties with no one invited? I mean, how do you celebrate the fact that something didn't happen, that nothing was done?

Harrison Day was on my mind when I arrived in the courtroom on Tuesday morning because I had promised Pete we would commemorate his brush with death, and if I left it up to him to plan the evening festivities there would inevitably be some minor lawbreaking, which might be fun for Fletcher, but Guillam, who was sitting in the jury box fifteen minutes early, no tie but gray slacks and loafers instead of the usual jeans and sneakers, had already declared this National Adulthood Day, no occasion for juvenile delinquency, and an adult sticks by his word. I had expected to be the first one in the jury box, not the sixth—what time do these grown-up people arrive? No Roya yet, but Gramma Jamma was working a crossword puzzle and greeted me with a good morning smile.

-You look nice today, dear.

The Elephant was working her cell phone. Chatty Chad was rehashing last night's Angels game with the other two fifty-somethings from north county—three moderate men in chairs seven, nine, and twelve.

-That kid can swing a bat, though.

-I still say he's not worth ten million a year.

-You gotta spend to win anymore.

Sloan and Lawson were talking and chuckling, more like teachers in the faculty lounge before first period than two rivals girding for battle with an accused man's future on the line. Mr. Clean was at his desk, sorting through paperwork, and greeted me with a good morning scowl. I know, I know, an adult would walk over and apologize to him. I'm sorry, sir, I was out of line yesterday. No, he looks busy, an adult wouldn't disturb him, right? Maybe later. He saw me watching him and scowled again.

BAILIFF BALDY: He was early today, and dressed a little better.

JUDGE SILVERSON: Good. See.

BALDY: No, whatever he's selling, I ain't buying.

What about a reverse funeral? I could write a eulogy for Pete and read it to him to acknowledge his not dying. That makes more sense than real funerals, where friends and family say nice things about the deceased, who isn't there to hear it. Pete Repetti, terrific teacher and even better friend, loved life, adored his students, a natural in the classroom, taught tenth graders to appreciate science, taught me how to press pennies between a door and the door frame thereby jamming the latch and trapping the head football coach in his office ten minutes before practice the day after he complained to the vice principal that Mr. Repetti was unfairly refusing to reconsider his starting linebacker's test score. Just for the record, Pete, like any great teacher and colleague, wasn't afraid to admit when he was wrong. He sent the coach an email, a copy of which I kept and will always cherish: Coach Julian, I looked at Kirk's test and you were right, I made some mistakes. I apologize. He should have received a 59 not 61, an F not D-. I've made the appropriate changes in my gradebook. Sincerely, P. Repetti. That was Pete. I miss you, man. I mean, I would if you were dead.

More jurors arrived, like Noah's animals, two by two. First came Lady Yoga with Juror Number Three, a skinny guy with an uneven haircut and bent-frame glasses listing off a long bony nose. Then my neighbor in chair two and a very tall, very blonde woman with large hoop earrings that framed her very long neck—an odd couple if ever there was one: mouse and giraffe. The Mouse greeted me with a good morning nod and waft of cigarette smoke, Giraffe took her place directly behind him in chair eight, Chad and the other moderates—the Mod Squad—making a chivalrous show of standing to help her ease by. And finally, Roya and Cowboy Kev, the last to board the ark. Great. Roya I can understand, but why did God have to spare him from the flood? I leaned forward and watched them settle in, hoping for one more good morning smile, the one that really mattered. She never looked my way.

The side door opened and Bud Jack entered, escorted as usual by two Orange County sheriff's deputies in green uniforms who removed his handcuffs and remained hovering nearby. Bud Jack wore the same dark blue suit every day with a different tie, today a white one. Funny, the gang expert Ruffman had said the Eastside Rollin' Twenties wore black and gold.

Still scowling, Mr. Clean called all rise, Queen Silverson ascended her throne, we were back in business. Her Majesty instructed Sloan to begin, Sloan signaled Mr. Clean, and the side door opened again—two more green-shirted officers, one more brown-skinned prisoner in handcuffs, coat, and tie. Once the cuffs came off, the prisoner took the stand, swore the oath, and told the court his name was Victor Ruiz. I wasn't trying to be snarky, it didn't bother me that the guys they were dragging up from the holding cell were better dressed than the juror driving in from Laguna Beach on this his finest sartorial outing, and anyhow I was trying to be mature about everything, but I wanted to turn to The Mouse and remark that Señor Ruiz must have shrunk. Or his clothes expanded. The sleeves on his sport coat were too long, the shirt was too big, the baggy pants were a joke. *Ropa muy grande.* What was Sloan thinking, bringing him in like that? *Ropa*-dope. Couldn't Orange County taxpayers spring for a visit to the mall to make the witness for the prosecution look halfway convincing? Bud Jack's coat was a perfect fit, measured, no doubt, by Richard Wilhite's favorite tailor, giving the defendant at least a hint of respectability. Mean eyes, cold stare, sharp suit and tie—

could be a murderer, could just be a corporate executive. And Ruiz? Wide-eyed and bewildered, hair to his shoulders, drowning in an ocean of wrinkled fabric—could be an addict, could just be one of Sharon's beloved theater students. Ha!

In what proved to be her final semester at Dana Hills High, Sharon had attempted to stage a play about the Sleepy Lagoon trial—young Chicanos in outlandish clothing harassed by enlisted men and LA cops during World War II. A group of parents calling themselves PWP—Parents With Purpose—convinced our principal to cancel the show on opening night, claiming it encouraged gang behavior. Parents for White Privilege, Sharon called them. It's not racism, they have a legitimate concern, Mr. Worster told her, even though these were the same outraged citizens who disrupted school board meetings with shouts about the dangers—They're a different culture, they have different values those people, they're *rancheros!*—of allowing too many Hispanic students from San Juan Capistrano to enroll at Dana Hills. Livid and verging on spontaneous combustion—Principals Without Principles!—Sharon threatened to give automatic A's to all her students in all her classes or, better yet, not submit grades at all, Worster offered to suspend her, and when she exploded—Worst, Worster, Worstest!—into my classroom where I was quietly grading papers during my lunch hour, I made the colossal mistake, being a man and a math teacher, of suggesting she calm down and think rationally.

-Come on, Sharon, it's only a play.

She screeched and wildly swung her arms. Oops.

-Only a play? What if Worstest banned the quadratic equation? You know, because it encourages geek behavior.

I wasn't disagreeing with her about PWP. I knew that south county was a bastion of white privilege, I knew about white flight. Ever since World War I, when southern blacks began moving to northern cities, moving on up, whites have been moving on out. Professor Penguin taught me that.

-Rathithm, people, the thuburbth were created by rathithm. That will be on the tetht.

Sharon was right, I told her, she was just being impractical.

-Impractical?

I ducked as the chalkboard eraser flew by my head.

-Impractical? Let's see, teach them square roots, help them find imaginary numbers, that's practical. Ha! Or give them words, put them on a stage, help them find their voice.

She grabbed another eraser. I shielded my face with my gradebook.

-No, you're right, Mr. Fletcher, you're right, it's only a play. But algebra... algebra....

She struck a theatrical pose, holding the eraser in a raised hand, studying it as if she'd never seen one, and spoke in a grand, tremulous voice.

-2b or negative 2b, that is the question, whether 'tis nobler in the mind to solve for the sums and averages of outrageous fractions or to take odds against a sea of variables and by opposing add them. Indeed, Mr. Fletcher, algebra is the very stuff of life.

I didn't know whether to applaud or crawl under the desk and call Captain Safety—yes, she's armed, an eraser, hurry before she wipes me out.

But eventually she did calm down and turn practical. She cancelled the annual December production of *A Christmas Carol*, and, with approval from Worster, who thought he was orchestrating a wise and reasonable compromise, replaced it with *West Side Story*. A classic American musical, always a crowd-pleaser, she assured him, not bothering to add that it's about New York gang-bangers killing each other over race issues—Everyone knows that, darling, why should I have to tell him?—or that she intended to set it in 1940s Los Angeles. She would have her Sleepy Lagoon show after all. She also failed to mention the less than subtle lyric changes she had in mind.

> Everything's right in América
> No need to fight in América
> Well, parents' groups might in América
> Keep schools white in América.

East LA Story in South OC, the *LA Times* headline read after Sharon called a reporter to fan the controversy. There was even a photo: Jets in sailor uniforms, Sharks in zoot suits. That's what those oversized outfits are called, that's what our witness Victor Ruiz looked like—a zoot suiter, lacking only the floppy hat.

He sat down and fidgeted nervously while Sloan explained for the record that Mr. Ruiz wasn't currently under arrest for any crime, they just wanted to guarantee he would show up to testify. Was that a smart thing to tell us? Don't worry, jury members, the witness isn't a convict, just totally unreliable. Ruiz looked wired. If Sloan had spent the previous hour pouring coffee into his witness to prepare him for his debut, it wasn't enough. Or it was too much. Sloan's questions were sharp, Ruiz's answers fit as well as his pants.

-How do you know Mr. Jack?

-He told me what happened. That dude over there.

-How did you meet him?

-That's him for sure.

Ruiz pointed toward the defense table. Sloan smiled and took a few steps closer to his witness.

-Let's start over. You were arrested in Huntington Beach, and Mr. Jack, that man seated over there, was in the same cell with you, correct?

-Yeah.

-Good. Okay.

-He said he capped the dude.

Sloan appeared unsure how to proceed. His previous witnesses had known their lines, recognized their cues. Ruiz must have missed the dress rehearsal.

-He told you he shot someone?

-That's right.

-Did he just volunteer this information?

-We was in the cell.

Sloan's smile was getting thinner.

-Did you ask him why he was there, is that how the conversation started?

-Yeah, that's right.

-You were in the cell, they brought him in.

-That's right.

-And you asked what he was arrested for?

-That's right.

Isn't this called leading the witness? Why doesn't Lawson object?

-What did he say?

-That's right.

Maybe because the witness is witless. Let him sink himself.

-Victor, I want you to concentrate, okay? I want you to slow down and concentrate and listen to my questions, it's very important, okay?

The witless witness nodded and tried to hold his hands still.

-When you were in jail, in the cell, and they brought in Mr. Jack, and you asked him what he was arrested for, what did he say?

He clasped and unclasped his hands.

-Victor, what did he say?

-I need a smoke.

Judge Silverson granted Sloan a thirty-minute recess. I had nothing to read because I had finished the Grisham, and I couldn't stalk Roya through the courthouse—it was National Adulthood Day not Halloween—so I went to the restroom, then checked my cell phone. One text message from Marissa: Dinner at six. I'll pick you up. Oh, crap. I had agreed to dinner with my sort of girlfriend on the same evening I had promised my best friend we would celebrate National Pete Didn't Die Day. Someone's going to end up angry. Or maybe Pete forgot. Maybe he took more pills and the new holiday slipped his mind. I hit speed dial.

-Dude.

-Pete, you up?

-I keep thinking about the accident. What time you coming over?

What's a responsible adult to do? My best friend sounded like he needed someone to talk to. My sort of girlfriend seemed more interested in a trial update than anything else. I should hang out with my friend. But if I backed out of dinner with my sort of girlfriend, she might take it the wrong way, and maybe she also needed someone to talk to, she did sound a little depressed yesterday. A responsible adult would just tell his friend the truth, right? A responsible adult would lay out the situation, explain his conflicting loyalties, apologize for any hurt feelings, ask if the celebration could be postponed one more day. And his friend, also an adult, would understand, would say what he always says: She's got you pinched, dude. Maybe an adult should buy time.

-Pete, sorry, I've got to go. They're about to start. How 'bout I call you when I get home?

Zoot Suit, act two: Victor Ruiz back on stage, looking more at ease. Nothing like a nicotine hit to calm the nerves. The Marlboro Mouse in chair two, reeking like a smokestack, nodded. I nodded back. Do smokers know how bad they smell? The Mouse nodded again. Does The Mouse have mental telepathy? He didn't respond. Was he playing coy? I watched him from the corner of my eye. Nothing. I would need a better mousetrap. Sloan apologized for the delay and turned to his witness.

-Okay, Victor, here's where we were. You were in the cell, Mr. Jack came in, you asked him why he was there. What did he say?

-He told me to fuck off.

-Did you?

-I ain't backing down. I said, you got a problem, bro? And he goes, get out of my face, I already popped one Mexican.

-What does that mean—I already popped one Mexican?

-Means he offed him.

-Offed him?

-Killed him, shot the dude, whatever.

-Did you believe him?

-He wasn't clowning, I know that. Said the guy's name was Juan.

There it was, the prosecution's pièce de résistance, a jailhouse confession reported by a nervous prisoner in someone else's clothes who thirty minutes ago couldn't remember what he was supposed to say. Marissa was going to love this.

-And then, Victor, you told a police officer what happened?

-Yeah.

-When did you tell him?

-That same night.

When Sloan sat down, Lawson popped up and took center stage. No limp—he was on the attack, the pie-faced pummeler descending on the witless witness. This should be fun. First a barrage of questions, barely allowing time for a response.

-Mr. Ruiz, did Bud Jack tell you anything more about this guy named Juan that he supposedly killed?

-No.

-Did he say where it happened? When it happened?

-No.

-Did he say how he did it? Why he did it? Mr. Ruiz, did he give any details at all?

No on all accounts. His point made, Lawson took a breath and softened his tone.

-Victor, on the night you talked to Bud Jack, why were you arrested?

-They said I was drunk.

-Were you?

-Maybe a little.

-A couple of beers?

Lawson was slowing down, sounding less accusatory, sounding almost sympathetic.

-Something like that.

-Are you drunk now?

-No.

Maybe it was the way the witless witness glanced over at Sloan or the way he looked down at his nervous hands, but suddenly I knew— physiological certainty—Señor Ruiz had enjoyed more than a smoke during the recess. That fat leather satchel by Sloan's feet held more than just notepads and files.

-Where were you when they arrested you?

No! Lawson! Don't change the subject!

-In the park.

-Were you causing trouble in the park?

-No.

Lawson, ask him when was the last time he had a drink. Ask him if Sloan has a flask or is it those tiny bottles you get on airplanes. Am I the only one who sees this?

-Were you bothering anyone?

-No.

-But they still arrested you.

-That's right.

Lawson was not receiving my telepathy.

-Just for being a little drunk in public?

-It's messed up.

A veteran trial lawyer with superb powers of observation, knows when to nail a witness to the wall, knows what jurors are thinking just by their eyes—that's going in my tv drama. His name will not be Lawson.

-Did you tell them it was messed up?

-I don't know.

-Maybe tell them you're tired of being hassled?

-Yeah. Probably.

-Did you tell them to fuck off?

-The cops? You think I'm crazy? I ain't crazy.

Ha! Good thing it was National Adulthood Day, or I would have laughed out loud.

-Victor, what does fuck off mean?

-Means we're gonna throw down.

-Fight?

-That's right.

-Always?

-If someone disrespects you.

Lawson rested his chin on his right hand and thought for a moment.

-Victor, do you like cops?

-Not those ones.

-So why did you tell them about Bud Jack?

Ruiz hesitated.

-Mr. Ruiz, if you didn't like those cops, why did you help them out?

Suddenly Lawson was impatient again.

-Mr. Ruiz?

One minute a pal, the next he's a jerk.

-I don't know.

-You just told them?

I get it—Lawson is playing good lawyer/bad lawyer all by himself. Ruiz looked flustered. Lawson kept firing.

-Where did this conversation with the cops take place?

-In the cell.

-The same cell with Bud Jack?

-A different one.

-The cops took you to a different cell?

-That's right.

-Why?

-How should I know?

-What did they tell you?

-They said he was dangerous.

-The cops told you Bud Jack was dangerous?

-That's right.

-Are you sure?

-Yeah, I'm sure. They said they didn't want to have to put me back in with that black guy.

Lawson turned toward the jury box, a quick, knowing glance—raised eyebrows, wrinkled forehead—encouraging us to connect the dots.

-They threatened to put you back in with that black guy?

-They said they didn't want to.

-Is that when you told them what Bud Jack said?

-That's right.

Okay, dots connected. I'm with you, Lawson, maybe you don't get my telepathy, but I get yours.

-When Bud Jack told you to fuck off, did he disrespect you?

-That's right.

I get yours loud and clear: the cops pressured Ruiz to cooperate, Ruiz had a grudge to settle with the black guy, take Ruiz's testimony with a grain of salt.

-Victor, do you know anyone named Juan?

-I know a couple guys named Juan. But they ain't dead.

Lawson was finished, Sloan was on his feet.

-Victor, did Mr. Jack tell you he killed someone?

-Yes.

-Did you feel it was important to tell the police about this?

-That's right.

The next witness *was* the police: a Huntington Beach detective who laid out the murder investigation for us. When Juan Castro's body was discovered and the time of death estimated, they went through the logs and discovered that an officer had questioned Bud Jack that same night—stopped him on the sidewalk, asked him what he was doing in Huntington if he lived in Long Beach, didn't get much of an answer but had no cause to detain him. When an off-duty fireman reported having seen a man acting suspiciously and the description matched Bud Jack, they brought him in, put him in a lineup, and the fireman picked him out. While he was being held, Bud Jack bragged to a cellmate about killing a Mexican named Juan, and they knew they had their man. Sloan pressed him on that point.

-Couldn't Mr. Jack just be talking tough?

-The thing is, we arrested him on suspicion of drug trafficking, we didn't say anything about murder, didn't put him in a lineup right away, we were hoping he might let something slip.

The detective seemed convinced, even when Lawson got him to admit there was no physical evidence tying the accused to the crime scene and that the physical description—black guy in hooded sweatshirt—offered by the fireman was rather vague.

-So let me get this straight. A police officer stops him on the street for no real reason except something didn't look right and later you detain him because an off-duty fireman said something didn't look right. Tell me, detective, what does the law in Huntington Beach say about looking right?

-The law allows us to investigate suspicious behavior, and when a murder is committed, we follow up all possible leads.

-How does the law define suspicious behavior?

The detective didn't have a good answer for that. Lawson let it go.

-When Bud Jack was stopped on the street, when you picked him up at his house, when you questioned him, when you put him in the lineup, did he at any time threaten anyone?

-Not that I know of.

-Did he exhibit any dangerous behavior?

-Not that I'm aware of.

-Does he have a record of any dangerous behavior?

-Not that I know of.

-Did you ever tell Victor Ruiz, the drunk prisoner, that Bud Jack was a dangerous man?

-No. But just for the record, he wasn't drunk when I talked to him.

-Do you know which officer, if any, told him that Bud Jack was dangerous?

-No, sir.

I was surprised Lawson didn't dig more into the reliability of the jailhouse confession—it was pretty clear to me that the case hung on that. Sloan brought it up when Lawson was finished.

-Detective, did you ever interview Victor Ruiz?

-Yes. I wanted to hear his story for myself, make sure it was believable.

-What did he tell you?

-He said that the black guy in the cell with him claimed to have killed a Mexican named Juan.

-Was Victor Ruiz drunk when you talked to him?

-I don't believe so. I spoke with him in the morning on the fifteenth, after he'd slept it off.

-Did you find his account believable?

-Very much so.

-The witness is excused.

The witness is excused and the prosecution rests. Silverson checked her watch and sent us off to lunch. Out of the box, down the hall, into the crowded elevator.

-Oh, hi. Fletcher, right?

Roya! Standing right next to me!

-Yes. You remembered.

Did she like my dressier look today? Or did she think I was trying too hard to impress her?

-This is Kevin.

He was there too.

-Nice to meet you, Kevin.

I mean howdy, pardner. Nice boots.

-Hey, how ya doing?

We didn't shake hands. There wasn't really room, the elevator was packed tight. One floor down, even more people got on. Roya moved toward the back, and I slipped in between her and Cowboy Kev, allowing the crush of bodies to push me up against her.

-Tight squeeze. You alright?

-I'm fine.

The familiar perfume or was it the shampoo scent from all that hair? I pretended not to realize my elbow was digging into the cowboy's ribs. I gradually increased the pressure until he leaned away. Sorry, pardner, this county ain't big enough for the both of us. Roya was looking down, avoiding eye contact. I needed a third line, but the only thought in my brain was please, let the elevator get stuck, a five-minute power outage, that's all I'm asking for, five minutes in darkness with her hip pressing against mine. The elevator started down again. Come on, Fletcher, think of something clever to say. No, think of something mature, in the spirit of National Adulthood Day. No, don't think at all, just let it happen, like when she drove up next to me. The lines had come easier then, in the parking lot, and before I knew it I was sitting in her car. That's it!

-Roya, thanks for the ride yesterday. I should—can I buy you lunch?

She laughed.

-Actually, I brought a sandwich. But thank you.

-You know what, I did too. We could sit in the cafeteria.

-Okay.

Simple as that. Straightforward. Mature. Sliced turkey on sourdough meets roast beef on wheat. Or maybe she had felt trapped in the elevator, couldn't find a graceful way to say no. I mean, if she really wanted to have lunch with me, wouldn't she have said yes, love to, and not mentioned the sandwich? Doesn't matter. Bottom line: she said yes to me, and after we exited the elevator, Cowboy Kev disappeared from the scene, out whispering to his horse or something.

-Can I get you something to drink? It's only fair, after you saved me from spending last night in the courthouse.

-Okay. A bottle of water. Thanks.

Dude, those plastic water bottles—shut up, Pete. I blocked his carping voice out of my mind, bought two bottles, and Roya and I were soon sitting across from each other at the end of a cafeteria table. The conversation came easily. She lived in Costa Mesa, worked in a dental office in Fountain Valley, the clientele were mostly senior citizens, and no, jury duty wasn't a problem.

-They brought in a hygienist to cover for me, and I still get paid, so….

-Do people ever bite your fingers? I mean at work.

She laughed. This was going well.

-No. One woman hit me. Not on purpose. I didn't know she had like really sensitive gums, and when I touched them she like jumped and totally smacked me in the stomach.

-Ouch.

-Hi, Roya.

-Oh, hi, Cheryl.

-Mind if I join you guys?

Great. The Elephant squeezed in beside me and unwrapped an egg salad sandwich. A nightmare from back in junior high: trying to ask the cheerleader to the Valentine's dance, and the fat girl with stinky food shows up and grosses you out, but you have to be nice because the fat girl and the cheerleader are friends.

-Hi, Cheryl.

-Hi. How's your dog?

Roya and I looked at each other. We had a secret: there was no dog.

-About the same, I guess.

-Gosh, I really miss Sugar. I wish I wasn't allergic.

I didn't make a joke, it was National Adulthood Day. Roya made it for me.

-I don't eat sugar either.

She was trying to be sympathetic, which made it even funnier. I was trying not to laugh and cough up roast beef.

-No, Sugar was my dog, a cockapoo. I had to give her up.

-Oh.

Roya looked at me and we suppressed grins. This was fun. The Elephant turned to me.

-Yours is a mutt, right?

-Uh, yeah.

Does this woman ever quit?

-You never told me his name.

-Oh, his name—

There's an old African proverb: Don't mention a fake dog to a real elephant. Or there should be, because I swear this woman was determined to catch me in a lie.

-Is there room here for one more?

Blonde hair, big earrings, big lunch. Saved by a giraffe carrying a loaded cafeteria tray.

-Sure, have a seat.

I mean, if I can't be alone with Roya, bring on the whole damn zoo, let her see what an animal lover I am. Giraffe sat down beside Roya, somehow folding all her legs under the table.

-I'm Fletcher.

-Hi, I'm Deborah.

-That's Roya, this is Cheryl.

See, the court jester is actually a gentleman. I still couldn't bring myself to say Guillam, but one step at a time, right? An adult doesn't have to rush into things. An adult can work on just being an easygoing conversationalist, confident and attentive, fun, not obnoxious. Giraffe's tray held yogurt, a baked potato, green salad, a cup of soup, and a banana.

-You must be hungry.

She gave me a funny look. Oops. Was that a faux pas? Did I just call her a glutton?

-I'm eating for two.

Bam!—like a cloudburst, like a traffic light turned green—a flood of instant sisterhood.

-Congratulations. That's so wonderful.

-You look great.

-Thanks.

-Are you comfortable sitting there?

-I'm good.

-Is it your first?

-Yes, and I'm craving everything.

-How far along?

-Five months.

-Wow.

-You can hardly tell.

-You look fantastic.

-Thank you.

-This is so exciting for you.

Instant sisterhood for the ladies, sudden invisibility for the gentleman. I had the urge to go find the Mod Squad and talk baseball. Male sports bond versus female baby bond. I think we know who would win.

-Have you seen the ultrasound?

-A girl.

-Ohhh.

-It's best to have a girl first, isn't it?

-Have you picked a name?

-We're negotiating.

-Oh, wow.

-I know. He wants Jessica, for his mom.

-Jessica is nice.

-I want Mariam.

Mariam? I barely know 'im! I just thought it, I didn't say it. I didn't say anything. They were speaking a foreign language. I mean, how do you see ultrasound? I thought ultrasound was for sore muscles. I chewed my sandwich and smiled, pretending to be elated that a complete stranger got knocked up. Knock, knock. Who's there? Mariam in the white gown. Mariam in the white gown who? Mariam in the white gown, leave him in the red.

-My mother gave us the cutest singlet.

-Ohhh, I love outfits for infants.

-And those little socks, they're sooo adorable.

-And the shoes.

-Ohhh.

-My mother still has my old baby shoes.

Baby names, baby clothes, blah blah blah. What's a singlet? Just give it a blanket, give it some diapers. Givit would be a good name for a mutt. Come here, Givit. Come here, Givit. Give it, Givit. Give it, Givit, damn it! Good dog.

Why did it bother me so much being left out of the conversation? Because I was trying to impress Roya, and the baby talk rendered me mute. Mute and dumb. I hate feeling dumb. I felt eminently dumb back when Sharon first announced her resignation from Dana Hills. At the last sold-out performance of *West Side Story*, Mr. Worster had come up to us and congratulated Sharon on a successful show. I was relieved that he didn't seem miffed about the pointed lyrics. Sharon was in no mood for pleasantries.

-Speaking of sell-outs, isn't it weird that those parents didn't protest the gang violence in this show, it must have been racism after all.

Worster tried to change the subject, asked which plays she had in mind for the spring semester.

-I won't be here in the spring, because the way you did their bidding suggests you're racist yourself or maybe just a coward. Either way, I can't stay at your school.

Sharon felt vindicated, who knows how Worster felt—he turned and walked away—but I was the dumb one. Thanks for the warning, Sharon, thanks for including me in the discussion, I thought we were working toward something. That still hurt whenever I thought about it. Three years gone by, and I was still trying to understand what had happened with Sharon, what I'd done wrong. And then one day on the phone she had the nerve to say my lack of furniture sends a message about not sticking around. Who's the one who didn't stick around? Maybe that's why now I was so frustrated with Marissa. I could never tell where I stood with her, and for all I knew maybe she too was pondering a move to northern California or wherever, maybe her vision of the future didn't include me either. Was it my fault? Did I avoid asking questions for fear of the answer? I'm going to be different with Roya, I'm going to ask the dangerous questions. Are we just friends or is this something more? Do you even want something more? Do you see us together in the future? Assuming, of course, she says yes when I ask her out after the trial is over. Assuming I don't chicken out.

I finally thought of something I could say to the expectant mother.

-Deborah, did you tell the judge you were pregnant?

-I didn't.

-I bet you would have been dismissed right away.

Why didn't I think of that a week ago? Your Honor, my sort of girlfriend is sort of pregnant, expecting any day now, any minute, I don't want to miss it. What's the judge going to do, ask to see the ultrasound? I could be smelling ocean breezes and thuntan lotion, not egg salad. But then I never would have met Roya. Or Giraffe and a Half, a tall pregnant woman who actually wanted to be a on a jury.

-I always thought it would be fun. I guess 'cause of those tv shows. And maybe being in court will inspire my baby.

-Like one day she'll end up on trial for murder?

It just came out. You can't keep a good clown down. The Elephant snorted and said that was mean. Roya didn't say anything. I apologized, said I was kidding. Fortunately, Giraffe and a Half took my gaffe with a laugh.

-I guess you never can know how your child will end up. We're just hoping for the best.

She chewed some greens and smiled at me. Giraffes are forgiving. The Elephant, though, felt obligated to reassure her that being in the courtroom would not push little Mariam toward a life of crime. Again, the expectant mother took it in stride.

-I was thinking more like law school, not prison.

And, again, the clown stuck his big shoe in his mouth.

-Why not both?

After lunch, I looked in the restroom mirror and thought, why do I bother? The long sleeves were too warm, the stiff collar made my neck itch, and nobody was fooled. No matter how nicely I might be dressed, as soon as I opened my mouth the charade was over. I try to have a little fun, try to be an engaging adult, and I end up sounding obnoxious. Or mean, apparently. I'm not mean. Does Roya think I'm mean? When we were walking out of the cafeteria, she thanked me for a pleasant lunch, said we should do it again. No, that's not what happened. What happened was we were all getting up from the table, and I said something like hey, Little Mariam, don't worry, now that you've had lunch with me, I think you'll grow up to be a math teacher. I was hoping Roya would find that endearing, but when I turned to catch her reaction, she was walking briskly away. Sometimes I think I've spent my entire life watching women walk briskly away. Well, forget her. A pretty face, but so what? Cleaning teeth all day—how interesting can she be?

Okay, they don't all walk briskly away. Marissa was walking slowly away. What should I do about her tonight? I got off the elevator on the fifth floor and sent a text message—How about dinner with Pete? He's feeling down—and immediately regretted it. It seemed like an adult solution, except Marissa and Pete didn't really like each other, and I didn't want to play the mediator. I was sick of the adulthood business, sick of feigning politeness. I wanted to relax and be myself. I wanted to go to The Cave, Pete's bare-walled apartment, drink a few beers, be immature and irresponsible. I started typing in a new message, telling Marissa to ignore the previous one. Before I could finish, though, she had already replied: Sounds good. I started typing again, pecking away with my clumsy thumb. Another message arrived: Thai food? She was too quick. I felt tongue-tied, trying to keep up in a texting dialogue with someone who zips off messages like machine gun bullets. It would be a lot easier if we just spoke on the phone, old-school communication, but she was at work, and if I called she wouldn't answer.

-Thanks again for the water.

Roya! Standing next to me in the hallway! I turned off my phone.

-You're welcome. My pleasure.

So she hadn't been fleeing from me. Maybe she had urgently needed to visit the bathroom or escape the smell of egg salad. Like Sharon would say, maybe, darling, it isn't always about you. We entered the courtroom together—two adults in cordial conversation.

-She looks great for five months pregnant, doesn't she?

Roya said it in a whisper, nodding toward Giraffe and a Half, a few long strides ahead of us. I nodded in reply.

-I think all pregnant women look great.

Where that line came from I have no idea, I'm not even sure it was the truth, but judging by Roya's smile, it was a winner. Forget cleverness, forget honesty, from now on, when I'm with Roya, I'm only going to say very nice things, I'll be positive and supporting, kindness to a fault. Cheryl waddled up behind us.

-You still haven't told me your dog's name.

Giraffes are forgiving, an elephant never forgets.

-Givit. My dog's name is Givit.

-Really? That's cute.

-Givitarest.

Lawson began the afternoon session by making a motion for dismissal, citing lack of evidence. Silverson called both lawyers to the bench for a conference. Is this the end? A dismissal would be perfect. I'd get out of these uncomfortable clothes, spend the afternoon at the beach with Pete, pondering life and near-death and bikinis, then still have time for dinner with Marissa, who would be in a good mood after hearing the charges against Bud Jack were dismissed. First, though, I'd have to catch Roya—hey, could I call you sometime, I still owe you lunch—or I'd never see her again, a third one-in-a-million chance encounter being too much to hope for. Would she give her phone number to a guy who means well but can't control what comes out of his mouth? Motion denied. Silverson instructed Lawson to call his first witness.

BALDY: Why didn't you dismiss the case? All they got is that supposed confession.

SILVERSON: I want to watch him sweat.

BALDY: The accused?

SILVERSON: No, Juror Number One. Didn't you notice how uncomfortable he looks in his long-sleeve button-down?

On Professor Hanson's final exam, I proposed a Dorothy Day Day. There was nothing about her in the textbook, but I had found a biography in the library and actually read most of it. Dorothy Day worked tirelessly for the poor, chose poverty for herself, opposed war—I knew The Penguin would approve. Also, there was a girl in the class who I was trying to impress with my broad-mindedness and sensitivity, my appreciation of women. We usually sat next to each other, and when she missed class she would ask to copy my lecture notes. She was cute and funny and I could tell she was interested in me. After the test, I made my move.

-Lori, how'd you do?

-Pretty good, I think.

-What did you put for a holiday?

-My boyfriend had it last semester, and he did Gettysburg Day, so I went with that.

Then she walked briskly away.

8

Traffic in Laguna is an affliction, particularly on summer evenings when the tired, sunburnt masses pack folding chairs, boogie boards, and sandy towels into minivans and SUVs and head home. Because the surrounding hills have been preserved as open space, there are only three ways out of town: inland through the canyon and either north or south on Pacific Coast Highway. The canyon road aka Broadway meets the coast highway aka PCH at Main Beach aka ground zero, a three-way thrombosis where crowds of beachgoers in the crosswalks stymie right turns on green lights, and the HummerSuburbanNavigatorQuestTahoeSequoiaYukonSiennaExpedition backup clogs the narrow arteries of downtown. The short drive to a grocery store drags on for thirty minutes, locals take side roads to avoid the stoplights and can do it in twenty, smart locals don't bother trying until after seven p.m. Marissa picked me up at six. From her place in the canyon to mine in north Laguna was no problem, driving beachward while the outgoers played arrhythmic stop-and-go in the opposite direction. The trip over to Pete's in Dana Point, fighting through high-cholesterol downtown, then joining the plug-along parade on PCH, was misery. I called him and said we'd be there when we got there, that was the best I could do.

-We?

-Yeah. Marissa's driving. You up for Thai food?

-Dude?

Dude can mean a lot of things, it's all in the tone. In this case, the tone said why are you bringing her? I was wondering the same thing. Marissa's driving was grating on my nerves—is she doing this on purpose?—or maybe it was the sense of powerlessness—you call this a free country?—knowing it would take an hour to go eight miles—free country, my ath!—and there was nothing we could do—this is so stupid—except creep along PCH—why don't we have decent public transportation?—past art galleries, hotels, restaurants—you can't even see the ocean, all these buildings—past photography studios, t-shirt shops, day spas—what's a day spa anyway?—and more art galleries—who buys all that stuff?—and still she refused to maneuver her little Saturn—Marissa, maybe you should get over—between the two southbound lanes—Fletcher, relax—even when ours came to a dead stop. Great. She did, however, encourage any and all lane-switchers to cut in front of us—sure, why not?—inviting them over with a friendly wave—we're in no hurry—driving like she had no place to be—is she intent on keeping Pete waiting?—driving me crazy. Experience told me nothing good would come from suggesting a more aggressive approach—you could go a little faster—yes, and you could get out and walk—so I directed my frustration toward other drivers.

-Why didn't he go? He could have made the yellow light. What a jerk.

-Fletcher.

-He's on his cell phone. You see that? Hang up and drive, buddy. This is ridiculous. Bud Jack's grandmother moves faster than this.

She had entered the courtroom in slow motion, a thin, gray-haired woman leaning on a four-legged walker. I wasn't convinced. I was a little sleepy, I needed a nap after lunching with the ladies, still I noticed the old woman looked spry enough, like she could get around fine without the prop. Lawson had put Bud Jack in a tailored suit, and now grandma gets a crutch. If I was Sloan, I would have yelled Fire, everybody out!, just to see how quickly she jumped. Sloan didn't yell anything. The prosecution had rested before lunch, this was Lawson's first witness, and Lawson's limp returned as he helped her into the stand, the lame leading the lame, or so we were supposed to believe.

-Mrs. Wilkes, how long has your grandson lived with you?

-I raised the boy.

-Was he ever in a gang?

-No, sir.

-Did he have friends in a gang?

-There was one or two.

Lawson waited for more. It wasn't coming.

-Why didn't he join? What did you tell him?

-I told him you come straight home, Rudy, don't be messing around.

-Why do you call him Rudy?

-His mother named him Bud, but he reminded me of Durand.

-Durand Jack, his father.

-Yes.

-Your son.

-So I started calling him Rudy.

-Short for Durand.

-Bud isn't a proper name for a child. Not for a man, neither. I tried telling her that.

-Why did you raise him?

-His mother had to work.

-What about his father? Mrs. Wilkes?

-Durand was killed when Rudy was two.

Lawson paused for a moment, as if the unhappy news had caught him by surprise, as if he hadn't intended to bring it up at the first opportunity.

-I'm very sorry.

Good lawyer/bad lawyer was now empathic attorney, deeply saddened by the witness's tragic loss.

-Your grandson—he still lives with you?

The witness stared straight ahead.

-Mrs. Wilkes?

-He does.

-Does he help out around the house?

-He cleans up after supper.

-He cleans the kitchen?

-He cleans everything.

She spoke without animation.

-His bedroom?

-Yes.

-The garage?

-There is no garage.

Lawson waited. She was giving nothing away.

-Does Rudy go to church?

-No.

-Never?

-He'll go if I need a ride.

Again, Lawson gave her time to elaborate. Again, he had to prompt her.

-Usually you drive yourself?

-Joyce picks me up, but sometimes she's not feeling well.

-You don't have a car?

-No.

-Do you know how to drive?

-My husband always took care of that.

Cleaning his room, going to church—what does that have to do with a murder investigation? And here's a bigger mystery: how do you get by in southern California without a car? I'd thought about giving it a try when the price of gasoline started soaring, or at least I'd considered driving less. I could take the bus to work, except that would entail a twenty-mile detour, three transfers, and two wasted hours each way. I could bike to school in under half that time—the only question would be whether I'd be killed on

PCH in the first week of the semester or in the second, sidewalks being rare and bicycle lanes nonexistent. So forget that. This is car country, buddy, like it or lump it.

Marissa allowed a white Excursion to nose in ahead of us. The Ford Excursion—three and a half tons of metal, eighteen feet long, ten miles per gallon but who's counting?—your own private bus for a family of four.

-Would you ever want an SUV? You could…I mean, a person could put two kids in the back of this car just fine, don't you think?

Marissa shrugged. She didn't like discussing the future with me, she especially didn't like discussing *a* future with me, and any mention of children, even incidental, brought a change of subject.

-What happened in the trial today?

Of course.

-The defense started this afternoon. That's all I'm going to say.

I know, Your Honor, I shouldn't have said even that. Because once you start….

-Is that why his grandmother was there? The poor woman. Sigrid said she could lose her house.

-I'm not going to talk about it.

It's bad enough I've got Sloan and Lawson trying to make up my mind for me. I don't need a third voice in my ear.

-Okay, just tell me, did the prosecutor ever bring up the supposed confession?

See what I mean?

-Marissa, I can't discuss it.

I don't need someone telling me if a confession is real or not.

-Are you upset about something?

-No.

Another red light. We're going to be sitting here all night. I should have brought a Grisham. Nothing to look at but the back end of the Excursion. Is it just Orange County, or do they have this elsewhere?—cartoon stickers on the rear window indicating daddy, mommy, and two kids. Sometimes it's on the license plate frame: Final score Boys 2 Girls 2. What if one of the little brats dies?

My phone rang.

-Dude, where are you?

-Almost to Thousand Steps. It's brutal out here.

-You could walk faster than that.

Thousand Steps is a picturesque cove accessible only by a steep, narrow stairway—closer to two hundred steps but who's counting?—because the bluffs overlooking the sea are otherwise monopolized and despoiled by private mansions with private stairs, even private funiculars. But at least there is public access. Other Laguna coves are fully enclosed by exclusive gated communities. By law, California beaches are public land, but what good is public land if the public can't land? If the coastline was open and preserved, if you didn't have to walk across a busy highway to reach the strand, maybe the two skateboarders, the little shits, wouldn't have made their mad dash and Pete wouldn't have swerved and then Marissa and I could have stayed home this evening, we could have walked to the Chinese restaurant near my place for takeout, we wouldn't be stuck in this four-lane parking lot. Or maybe if Pete hadn't survived the accident. Boy, was I in a mood.

Mrs. Wilkes had been in a mood too. I wouldn't say uncooperative, but perfunctory, especially after Lawson had asked about her deceased son, like I'll answer your questions, Mr. Attorney, just don't expect nothing more. If she was a tenth grader in first period algebra on Monday morning, I would have understood.

-Good morning, Jennifer.

-If you say so.

-Finish your homework, Jennifer?

-Leave me alone.

Tenth graders don't care, and why should they? But the grandmother of the accused—didn't she realize the stakes here, didn't she know Lawson was on her side?

He had kept her on the stand for a long time—it was like pulling teeth, every biographical tidbit had to be carefully and patiently extracted from the reluctant witness. We learned that Rudy never cared much for sports after he broke his arm playing Pop Warner football, Rudy liked to read, mostly car magazines, Rudy went back and took the GED to get his high school diploma.

-Why did he do that?

-He never graduated.

-Why did he decide it was important?

-Rudy doesn't like to leave things unfinished.

Good for him, but so what? How about telling us something about the night in question.

-Does your grandson drink alcohol?

-Not in the house.

-Does he get into fights?

-Not any more.

-Does he make much money washing cars?

-Enough to get by.

Where is Lawson going with this?

-Does he pay rent?

-Rent?

-Yes, I mean, how do you—

-Let me explain something.

-Please.

Finally, he'd struck a responsive chord.

-That's not my house, that's *our* house—me and Rudy. One day going to be just his house. My husband, Jeffers Wilkes, when he died, I told Rudy I don't know if I can keep the house, so that's when he started with washing the cars. Between that and the Social Security from Jeffers driving for the city all them years, we make the payments.

That's depressing—her husband spending long hours behind the wheel, probably coming home with a bad back, and now her grandson scrubbing hubcaps and polishing bumpers, just to pay the bank on time. Is that all life comes down to?

-Does your grandson have a girlfriend?

-He has lots of girlfriends. The girls like him. He's a gentleman. His daddy was the same way, girls coming and going.

A green light. Marissa hesitated, like she wasn't sure if it was worth the trouble.

-Did you go to yoga today?

-Yes. It was fantastic. Total release. Why?

-Just wondering.

Just wondering why you're driving in a trance.

-I feel like really centered.

-What does that mean?

-See. I can tell something's bugging you.

-No, people always say that—feel centered. I don't get it.

-It means you're calm.

-So why not say that?

-And you're present. You're in the now. You're focused on what really matters, what you're supposed to be doing.

-What are you supposed to be doing?

-Right now it's driving.

So why not give it a try?

Another fat Ford pushed into our lane. You could tell they weren't locals, probably a nice family from Aliso Viejo or Mission Viejo or some other viejo in the south county sprawl. The good people of Laguna prefer European sedans and European SUVs, and they don't normally sport bumper stickers, particularly not ones that say **WWJD?** What Would Jesus Do—ha!—in a fifty thousand dollar automobile? That had been one of Sharon's favorite rants.

-Darling, didn't Jesus say sell all your possessions and give the money to the poor, or am I thinking of some other first-century Jew?

-Maybe they need an SUV to carry all their possessions to the swap meet.

Sharon and I had these routines—this one triggered by the frequent high-speed collision of conspicuous consumption and conspicuous Christianity: My Boss is a Jewish Carpenter on the back of a Cadillac Escalade, Real Men Love Jesus on a two-ton, monster-tire, lifted pickup truck. She would press her hands against her head like she was trying to compress her brain— another of her strange, dramatic gestures.

-Help me out here, darling, help me understand these bizarre people, does all-wheel traction get you through the eye of a needle?

-You can't fit a cross in a compact car, not a real cross anyway, the nails snag the upholstery.

And away we'd go, amusing each other with obvious jokes.

-The bumper sticker on his SUV says I'd rather be walking on water.

-No, no, Jesus's bumper sticker says My other car is the foal of an ass.

Except one time she had an epiphany.

-I've got it, darling, it's all in the emphasis. They're not asking what would *Jesus* do, that would be ironic, slapping that on your gas-guzzler, and there is no irony in south Orange County, not intentional anyway, I know because I've looked. What they're really saying is what would Jesus *do*? It's not irony, it's certainly not piety, it's contempt, you see?

She chuckled contentedly. I didn't see.

-Think about it, darling. I've got it all, big car, big house behind a big gate, big view of the ocean, I can see Catalina Island, I can see the nuclear power plant down in San Onofre, on a clear day I can see the Marines practicing beach maneuvers down at Camp Pendleton, I'm on top of the world. What would Jesus do? What would Mister Peace and Poverty do about that? Nothing. There's nothing he *could* do. Too bad, Jesus—that's what they're saying—too bad for you.

I still didn't see, but now I caught myself doing it again—thinking about Sharon while I'm sitting next to Marissa. I pointed to the big Ford.

-What do you think of that bumper sticker?

-I always pretend it means Wasn't William Just Deadweight?

-William?

-Bill. My ex.

She had wanted to have children with *him*, she had assumed that's where they were headed, that's what she'd told me. He, apparently, had wanted to have children with her friend, or they went through the motions anyway. I tried to remind myself of that when she was distant and vague, that she'd only had her entire vision of the future obliterated by the person she loved most, that it wasn't always about me.

-But I should change it to something more positive. Wake With Joyful Demeanor. My yoga teacher was saying don't be too happy when something goes well and too unhappy when something goes poorly, because you never know what will come of it.

-Sounds boring.

-Only if you crave drama.

-Sounds like Orange County. Nothing good happens, nothing bad.

-You don't know how good you've got it here.

-No, Pete's got it good. He, at least, gets to almost die once in a while.

In south Laguna, with the gauntlet of traffic lights behind us, traffic finally opened up. Marissa stayed well below the speed limit while encouraging me to exceed the speech limit.

-Did they call Bud Jack as a witness?

-Marissa.

-It's public record.

-I can't have this conversation. How about Waltz While Juggling Daggers?

-It's not a conversation, it's a simple question—yes or no?

-No. That's all I'm saying.

-Do you think he will?

-Weight Watchers Juice Diet.

-You can answer that—it's just a guess.

-Weak Wrists Just Dangle.

-If you tell me, I'll tell you our plans for later.

She had asked me to go somewhere with her after dinner, after we took Pete home, only she wouldn't say where, it was a surprise.

-No.

-No, you don't think he'll testify, or no, you won't say?

-Yes.

For the record, I didn't think Lawson would call Bud Jack. I wanted him to. I wanted Bud Jack to explain what he'd been doing on the street that night. It would be a lot easier to dismiss the prosecution's thin case if Bud Jack said he went to Huntington to buy shammies for car washing there's a wholesale distributor there then my damn car broke down, or my friend was in the hospital in Huntington I caught a ride over with his mother I had to take the bus home—something, anything, a plausible alibi, that's all I needed to hear. But I had a feeling he'd been up to no good. I mean, late night in Huntington Beach, come on. So even if it wasn't murder, he wasn't going to want to answer questions about it, especially not from Sloan. Defense attorneys don't like to put their clients on the stand—I'd read that somewhere, probably in a Grisham—because the prosecution gets a chance to cross examine and will do anything possible to make the accused look like a liar. Probably that's why Lawson called in the grandmother instead.

-Mrs. Wilkes, your grandson was stopped by the police in Huntington Beach. Did he tell you what he was doing there so late at night?

-No.

-Did you ask him?

-That's not my business.

-Does he have a girlfriend there?

-He has girlfriends everywhere.

Bud Jack washes cars for a living, lives with his grandmother—what message does that send, Sharon?—and he has girlfriends everywhere. What am I doing wrong? All I have is a sort of girlfriend who, at this particular moment, is steering with her left hand and texting with her right. I was tempted to ask what was so important it couldn't wait. I was tempted to ask if she was still feeling centered and present, but instead I called Pete to let him know we were getting close. A few minutes later, he met us outside. I greeted him with a hug.

-Glad you're alive, man.

-Watch the shoulder.

I squeezed into the tiny back seat, leaving Pete and Marissa together in the front pretending they were delighted to see each other. How long would it take him to annoy her? I checked my watch.

-Hi, Marissa, haven't seen you in a while.

-Mr. Repetti, how are you?

-Did Fletcher tell you about my accident?

-Scary. Are you nervous about riding in a car?

-I don't know yet.

-I can drive slow.

Yes, you sure can.

She steered out of his apartment complex and back onto PCH, heading south toward downtown Dana Point. So far, so good. At least Pete hadn't opened with one of his greatest hits: Hey, Marissa, still slapping flesh? or What's new at the massage parlor, how's tricks?

-Dude, how was court?

-I can't talk about it. Hey, what exactly is ultrasound?

-High-frequency sound waves.

It's good to have a friend who knows science.

-How come they use it on pregnant women?

-Because they just don't listen.

Look out! Marissa let him have it.

-You're a jerk.

Bingo! Annoyance! Four minutes, twenty-seven seconds. Pete tried to repair the damage.

-That was bad. Sorry. They use ultrasound to check for birth defects.

-Like if it has a penis.

Ouch. There was venom in her voice. And malice on her mind. She abruptly changed lanes, accelerated, and whipped through a yellow light. Like it or not, I was going to have to be the adult this evening.

At the restaurant, a cute Thai waitress greeted us with a cute Thai smile.

-Welcome, come in, okay?

Marissa pressed her hands together as if praying and bobbed her head.

-Namaste.

It's some sort of yoga greeting: nah-mah-stay. The cute Thai waitress namaste-ed back. She had a cute Thai accent.

-Sit down here, okay?

When Pete and I ordered drunken noodles, she advised caution.

-Drunken noodles very much spicy.

But Pete doesn't believe in caution.

-Good, I want very much spicy. You know what, make it extra spicy, like you.

She giggled and turned to me.

-What about you? You want spicy too, okay?

Pete beat me to it.

-No, bring him spicy one. He's not man enough for spicy two.

She looked confused. I tried to help.

-Don't listen to him. He's still traumatized. He almost died. I want like a medium spicy.

-Dude, you can't handle medium spicy.

-Are you kidding? I brush my teeth with medium spicy.

-Fletcher, seriously, last time you got medium spicy you wet your pants.

Okay, Marissa was going to have to be the adult.

-I'm sorry. They don't get out much. Fortunately.

She, of course, wanted zero spicy.

-Come on, Marissa, we're celebrating National Pete Didn't Die Day.

-I'll have a glass of white wine.

The cute Thai waitress tried to sort it out.

-Okay, no spicy, medium spicy, and extra spicy for you, okay? How you almost die?

I couldn't resist.

-He's a very poor driver. He's legally blind in one eye.

Pete protested.

-It wasn't my fault.

-And his other eye is worse.

-Someone crashed into my Ferrari.

That got her attention.

-You drive Ferrari?

-You like Ferrari?

-I like Ferrari driver.

-That's me.

-Good for big tip, okay?

White wine for the woman, beer for the boys, a toast to NPDDD, and all adulthood out the window. Pete insisted that the spice girl had the hots for him.

-Come here, big American, we make happy time, okay?

When I laughed at his bad accent, Marissa said it wasn't funny. Pete didn't quit.

-Happy time with spicy nooder.

When I laughed again, she kicked me under the table and told Pete he was being racist.

-Racist?

Another kick—this one from Pete, demanding intervention. Okay, okay.

-He's not being racist.

-No?

-He's just objectifying women.

Your Honor, my client is willing to plead guilty to a lesser charge.

-Yeah, I'm just objectifying women. What?

Marissa stayed on the scent.

-Would you talk like that if she was white?

Pete's eyes widened, his lips tightened, like thanks for inviting her, Fletcher, great idea.

-Come on, Marissa, cut him some slack, it's NP-triple-D.

Ow. Her second kick was harder than the first.

-Yeah, Marissa, where's your holiday spirit? I could have died yesterday.

-Are we celebrating or mourning?

I laughed and took a second kick from Pete. With friends like these, who needs osteoporosis?

-Okay, how about if we change the subject. And be nice to each other. Marissa?

-Fine.

-Pete?

-Okay. Just make happy time, okay?

I couldn't stifle my laugh, so I swung me legs up under my chair. Her kick caught my knee.

-You're both jerks.

-I'm sorry, Marissa, I can't help it. My prefrontal cortex—tell her, Fletcher—underdeveloped.

-Oh, does that explain the hair loss?

Marissa can be brutal.

-So, in court today, we heard from Bud Jack's grandmother.

-Who?

-The defendant's grandmother. He lives with her. She raised him.

I'm sorry, Your Honor, it was all I could think of, and if I didn't change the subject fast, they were going to cripple me. Pete followed my lead.

-Let me guess—she said he was home watching tv the night of the murder.

-She was more like a character witness.

-My sweet little grandson, he'd never kill no one.

Actually, that's exactly what Lawson had wanted her to say, that's what he was trying to establish—Bud Jack was hard working and responsible, not the kind to shoot a gang member in an unlit parking lot—only Mrs. Wilkes didn't play that way.

-That's the weird thing, she didn't try to win our sympathy.

Marissa gave me a look. *The* look. Great. Either I just said something racist or I'm about to. Fortunately, our meals arrived, and I didn't have to explain myself.

-Okay, extra spicy for Mr. Ferrari, okay?

Mr. Ferrari appeared lost in thought, thank goodness. He didn't speak until the Spice Girl was gone.

-She's black, right? The guy's grandmother.

-Yeah. So?

I inched my chair away from the table. Marissa was on full alert, ready to attack, I could see it in her eyes.

-The judge, jury, the lawyers—all white people, right?

-Pretty much.

I felt like a golf ball, about to get smacked. Pete was teeing me up and pulling out the driver.

-So why should she expect any sympathy? She looks at that sea of white faces and she knows the system is stacked against her.

-I don't know. You could be right.

I was hedging, I didn't want to set Marissa off. She jumped in anyway.

-Of course, he's right.

At first I was just relieved—Pete and Marissa in agreement. Later, I saw it as a revelatory moment. What Pete said about Mrs. Wilkes not only appeased Marissa, it helped me make sense of what I'd seen in the courtroom.

-Mrs. Wilkes, has Rudy ever owned a gun?

-No.

-Maybe just to protect the house?

-I'll tell you what I told him. You bring a gun in the house, somebody in the house likely to get killed, and we seen enough of that.

-Like Rudy's father. Your son.

-Like lots of folk. Everywhere. Kids finding them guns and bringing them to school.

She wasn't hoping for sympathy, she was insisting on respect. And neither attorney understood that. After Lawson had finished trying to paint a reputable portrait of Bud Jack and thanked Mrs. Wilkes for her patience and courage, Sloan began by making a show of being a sympathetic character himself.

-Mrs. Wilkes, I'm going to ask you some questions that might seem obvious or even condescending. I apologize in advance, but we have to make sure everyone is clear about your grandson.

They must teach this in law school—don't appear hostile to the grandmother.

-Where does your grandson wash the cars?

-He goes to them.

-When does he do that?

-Whenever they call.

-When he gets a call, he drives somewhere and washes a car?

-Yes.

Geez, Sloan, glad we clarified that. Next ask her if he uses soap.

-How long does it take? One hour? Three hours?

-It depends.

-Depends on what?

-Sometimes he's gone a little while, sometimes longer.

-Sometimes he's gone all day?

-He's usually home for supper.

-And after supper he leaves again?

-Sometimes.

-Sounds like he's gone a lot.

Sloan waited patiently, hoping she would fill the silence. Hadn't he been paying attention? Silence didn't bother Mrs. Wilkes.

-What I'm wondering about, Mrs. Wilkes, is do you actually see him wash the cars?

Lawson objected, questioning the relevance of Sloan's inquiry. Silverson directed Sloan to get to the point.

-Mrs. Wilkes, when Rudy, your grandson, is gone all day, how do you know he's washing cars and not doing something else?

-He tells me.

-Is that the only reason?

-Isn't that enough?

Halfway through Sloan's interrogation of Mrs. Wilkes, I had figured out what was different when she was on the stand: less fidgeting in the jury box, less movement in the courtroom, you could tell people were concentrating, taking it in. And halfway through dinner, Pete and Marissa chatting harmoniously about Thai food versus Chinese—The difference is the coconut, yeah, that's true, and the snow peas—I finally got it, it all made sense. Sloan's witnesses—the fireman, the detectives, the gang expert, even Victor Ruiz, once he was properly lubricated—were just there to recite lines, to give the prosecutor what he wanted to hear. Did Bud Jack kill Juan Castro? They all swore to tell the truth, but none of them knew the truth. It was all circumstantial, like Lawson had said, all hearsay and speculation—the guy looked suspicious, he has gang ties, he said he killed a Mexican. Mrs. Wilkes, though, didn't have to speculate, she knew her grandson, knew what he was like. She didn't speculate and she didn't equivocate, even when it might have helped, even when Sloan gave her a second chance.

-Mrs. Wilkes, has your grandson told you he has a girlfriend in Huntington Beach?

-No.

-Has he ever told you Grandmother, I'm going to Huntington Beach to see a girl?

She could have just said yes, he's got a girl in Huntington, he goes there all the time. It would have been an easy lie, it would have been a plausible explanation for his presence on that street corner, and who could refute her story? But Mrs. Wilkes wasn't interested in telling stories, that's what I finally understood. She was telling the truth. Hell, she was the truth. I wanted to go to Long Beach, knock on the door of her little house without a garage, and assure her, don't worry, Mrs. Wilkes, you won't lose your home, we're not going to convict your grandson on the testimony of a drunken snitch.

Halfway through his drunken noodles, Pete almost died again. His eyes were watering, his nose was running, his face was bright red. He tried to shrug it off, tried to drown it in beer, but he couldn't go on, he pushed the plate away.

-Dude, my mouth is on fire.

On cue, the Spice Girl showed up with a pitcher of ice water.

-Maybe noodles too hot for Mr. Ferrari.

-This is extra extra spicy.

He gulped the water.

-I told the cook you want it like me, okay?

Marissa clapped her hands with glee and ordered another glass of wine. Tricky Spice twirled away.

-Pete, man, she worked you.

-Holy thit, itth hot. I need ithe cream.

He was sucking on an ice cube and sounded like Professor Penguin.

-Maybe you need to apologize.

Marissa said this with a smile, and Pete, now wiping his tongue with a napkin, didn't hesitate.

-I'm thorry. Believe me, I'm thorry. For everything.

-Not to me. To the waitress.

He gave up on the napkin.

-Yes, to the waitress. And to all Thai people. Asians in general. Even the Chinese. Sorry for raughing at accent.

Look out! But Marissa didn't erupt. She had relaxed and allowed herself to be amused—in fact, she raughed—which is really all Pete needed from his best friend's sort of girlfriend. And if she's happy and he's happy, then I'm happy. Three happy adults, enjoying a pleasant dinner.

Halfway through her third glass of wine, Marissa slid her car keys across the table.

-You're going to have to drive to Sigrid's house.

-What?

So here's a good one: Richard Wilhite told his wife he immensely enjoyed our conversation when he drove me home from the theater, and, not to be left out of the fun, Sigrid Wilhite now wants a second chance to meet Marissa's charming friend, maybe over dessert some night after Richard gets home from LA.

Here's another good one: two hours after she'd agreed to dinner with Pete and me—I just blanked, Fletcher, I'm sorry—Marissa said how about tonight, and Sigrid said tonight would be perfect I just had coffee at the Scandinavian bakery I brought home this absolutely luscious tart.

-Marissa, I can't go to their house. I'm on the jury and they're funding the defense.

-We'll tell them you can't discuss the trial.

-And it's NP3D. We can't just abandon Pete and go have dessert with someone else.

-Who's Sigrid?

Funny, Pete.

-She's one of my clients at the spa.

You know, the one who caught me coming out of her backyard after you broke her tree and your shoulder trying to have a gander at her surgical enhancements.

-Fletcher, you promised you'd go with me.

-Yeah, because I thought you meant a lot later.

And I thought you meant your place, just the two of us. In which case, forget the stupid holiday, I'd dump Pete in a heartbeat.

-Dude, it's okay, you can drop me off.

-No.

-I'm kind of tired anyway.

Pete was loving this—pretending to be doing me a favor while setting me up for disaster.

-No!

I didn't mean to raise my voice—a few other diners looked our way—but it worked. Pete and Marissa got quiet, they could see I was serious. Another crisis averted. Or so I thought.

-Pete can come with us. Sigrid won't mind. I'll call her.

When my friends don't like each other, I get kicked. Now that they're drinking buddies, I'm going to end up in jail. While Marissa made the phone call, Pete put his good arm around my shoulders.

-Relax. I got your back.

He was in adventure mode and couldn't see the perils ahead.

-Sigrid's gonna recognize me and call the cops.

-You can escape in my Ferrari.

As we exited the restaurant, Marissa bowed to Tricky Spice.

-Namaste.

Pete bowed too, then crawled into the back seat of Marissa's car and pretended to be a sensitive and decent human being.

-Marissa, yesterday in the accident I didn't know if I'd ever get to hang out with my friends again, this means a lot to me.

In the front passenger seat, Marissa was a little drunk.

-I'm glad it worked out, Pete, Sigrid's like totally great, she said the more the merrier.

Now I was the one driving slowly on PCH, looking for ways to delay our arrival. If I took long enough, maybe Marissa would fall asleep—three glasses of wine usually puts her out. I found the classical station again and switched on a little heat. It was just getting dark.

-Should we stop and watch the end of the sunset?

-No, Fletcher, we can't be late for Sigrid.

We drove past The Cave.

-Pete, if you're tired, I can just drop you off.

-No way. I want to meet this luscious tart.

A few miles into south Laguna, Pete pointed out the window.

-Right here. This is where my life almost ended.

I pulled over.

-Fletcher, what are you doing?

-We have to pay our respects to the not dead. It'll only take a minute. Everybody out.

There was no sidewalk, so we stood in the short driveway of a three-story house—no front yard, but tremendous ocean view—and Pete pointed out where the little shits ran across the highway, where he swerved into the wrong lane and got Hummer-smacked.

-Right there, dude, the place where I should have died. Unfuckingbelievable.

He shook his head. Marissa put a gentle hand on his shoulder. I told them I wanted to deliver a reverse eulogy and say all the nice things I would have said at a funeral. Marissa checked the time on her phone and told me to hurry.

-We are gathered here tonight to honor Pete Repetti, who we almost lost yesterday at this very spot. If he had died, if Pete's brains had been splattered across the concrete like soup—

-Gross. Fletcher.

Marissa gave me a shove.

-Sorry. Like spicy noodles. I would have stood up in the church and said he was a great friend and a gifted teacher.

-Say I was a scratch golfer.

-I'm not going to lie.

-Say I could have played on the pro tour but I chose to teach high school. At great personal sacrifice.

-Pete Repetti was a great friend and a gifted teacher. He taught me how to engage students. He showed me—

-That is so boring. Say how I turned down the Nobel Prize for my work on embryonic stem cells in mice.

-Pete, shut up. This is my speech.

-And I should have won the peace prize too.

-Pretend you're dead.

-Because my ex-wife is a bitch.

-You guys have it wrong. A reverse eulogy should say all the bad things.

Marissa had a point, and anyway Pete was too amped up to recognize my sincerity, so I started over.

-Pete Repetti didn't die, which is too bad. He cheats at golf. He hits on all the Dana Hills cheerleaders.

-Not true. Not the ugly ones.

-Never cooked a meal his whole life.

-So?

-And I always have to buy dinner.

-That's bullshit.

-Who paid tonight?

-It's my holiday. I almost died.

-Pete Repetti didn't die, which is hard to believe because he is such a wuss.

-You don't always buy dinner. Do you really think that?

-When was the last time you bought?

-Okay, I'll pay for tonight. What did it cost?

-Fifty bucks.

-No, I mean my share.

A man was approaching us from the house.

-Hey, this is private property.

Judging by his tone, he wasn't happy with our little huddle on his driveway. Pete wasn't impressed.

-Who invited him? He didn't even know me.

-Is that your car? You're in a no parking.

Marissa tried to be polite.

-Sorry. We're leaving. We just wanted to see where the accident was.

She took Pete by the arm. The homeowner kept coming.

-Right there. Some asshole driving drunk. What's there to see?

Pete turned to face him.

-He wasn't drunk.

-Sure. Now get off my property before I call the cops.

-Call 'em. He wasn't drunk.

Look out, sports fans, Pete and his adolescent prefrontal cortex can hash up a petty confrontation like this in no time, he has no tolerance for self-righteous bullies, he's seen too many at parent-teacher conferences—You are not going to block my son's ambition, Mr. Repetti, my son will not receive a C—they are endemic to south county.

-Listen, pal, I saw the van before they towed it. Beer bottles everywhere.

-He was coming home from the grocery store.

-You know the guy or something?

-I am the guy or something.

-Pete, come on.

In most cases I can talk him down from the ledge, keep him off the yacht and out of the hot tub, but this time I was ambivalent. The homeowner was kind of asking for it.

-You're lucky you didn't kill someone, pal.

-It's not too late, pal.

And if there was trouble, if cops showed up, maybe I'd get out of dessert with Sigrid. Better Pete arrested than me. Unfortunately, Marissa intervened.

-Listen, he almost died yesterday, and he avoided killing those two kids, thank God, and we just stopped so he could like process his emotions, and you're so like caught up in your property, your stuff, your ego, and that's cool, that's where you are right now, fine, only you can't see how maybe this moment could be critical for you too because believe me you totally don't want a guy with repressed trauma occupying your egoic consciousness.

Yeah. And namaste.

We were two miles down the road when Pete finally stopped laughing.

-Thanks, guys. Great fucking funeral.

9

Why does a criminal return to the scene of the crime? To view the damage he's done? To see if anything has changed? Maybe, if the crime occurred at night, to see what the place looks like in daylight. Or to see if the place actually exists. I mean, if Bud Jack shot Juan Castro in a dark parking lot in a nondescript warehouse district in an unfamiliar city, after a couple of days wouldn't it begin to seem surreal to him, like did that really happen or was it just a bad dream, and wouldn't he want to drive by just to verify yes, there's the dumpster, there's the retaining wall, and wouldn't he be tempted to get out of the car and walk to the fatal spot, trying to make sense of what happened, reshaping his memory, convincing himself that the other guy had threatened him, had gone for a knife, a gun, something tucked in his waistband, it wasn't cold-blooded murder, man, I'm sorry it went down like that, I'm sorry you're dead, but I couldn't wait and see what you were pulling, you shouldn't have moved like that, that's what got you killed, homeboy, should have kept your hands still, and I'm screwed too because no one's going to believe me, I can't prove it, only you and I will ever know it was self-defense. On tv, that's not normally how it happens. On tv, the killer doesn't look back, it's just bang, you're dead, and he goes and gets a burger or something, no remorse, no deep-seated guilt about having broken the ultimate social bond and taken a life. But tv lies. If my conscience kept nagging me about having snuck into Sigrid's backyard and peeked into her windows, then I had to believe Juan Castro's killer, unless a complete psychopath, was carrying a much heavier burden.

She greeted us—Sigrid, not the killer—at the front door in a tight t-shirt.

-Marissa, honey, come in, come in. Fletcher, nice to see you again, no more food poisoning I hope. And you must be Fletcher's friend.

-Sigrid, this is Pete.

I smelled incense and coffee, candles glowed in a window, a crystal vase on an antique table held fresh cut flowers, and, holy Moses, those have to be the two biggest tits I've ever seen! I pretended to be drawn to an oil painting of sea lions and cormorants on Seal Rock. I couldn't look at Sigrid, not without leering. Pete elbowed me. I couldn't look at him either, not without convulsions of laughter. Mission Disproportionates accomplished and then some.

-Fletcher, that painting's by Terrell Hirst, he's local. Marissa, do you know Terrell? I love his work. There's another piece by him back here, this way, let's go into the sitting room, would you like coffee or I could open a Reisling.

The sitting room was only slightly smaller than my apartment, an entire algebra class could sit there, sit there and not learn math, too much distraction, the only figure they'd remember would be Sigrid's. Was that little shirt a power play for our benefit? Did she think to herself Marissa's bringing two men over, better trot out the heavy hitters? While Marissa explained our tardiness...

-All we were doing was standing in the guy's driveway and he goes ballistic. I mean what's that all about? This is Laguna not LA.

...I peered out a back window into the darkness. On the drive over, I had formulated my plan: keep moving, don't let Sigrid get a good look close up, and if she did recognize me from our first encounter, well, I was at Pete's house that night, ask him, Sigrid, he'll tell you.

-Oh, here, this will help. Let there be light.

Sigrid reached for a switch and through the window the patio came aglow—the red lanterns, the luminescent pool. You couldn't see much beyond the deck, which was a relief, two trespassers wouldn't have been visible against the trees.

-Richard had to stay in LA. Emergency production meeting. He sends regrets. Come on, you must see the garden.

She slid open a glass door, and Pete elbowed me again as we stepped out onto the patio. Marissa affected a gasp.

-Sigrid, this is amazing.

-Isn't it? This is my decompression chamber. My oasis.

-I see what you mean about the three boulders.

-I know. You can't design without feng shui, you just can't.

Pete and I didn't speak, there was nothing to say, the beauty of the moment spoke for itself: back in the backyard, just five days after being chased out, and this time as invited guests. Another one-in-a-million? No, it wasn't random like that, just totally unexpected. No one would have predicted this outcome, not when we first began hunting down the Wilhites on the internet, not when Pete was lying in the grass with a bashed shoulder and the lights came on, not when we fled the neighborhood in the minivan with Pete moaning in pain and me trying not to panic at the thought of my fingerprints on the forgotten beer bottle. Since then I had imagined dozens of scenarios, some (unemployment, incarceration) worse than others (probation, community service), none ending with pastry for the prowlers, the deviants getting dessert.

A dog barked next door—woof, woof, it's them, they're back, I smell perverts.

-Okay, Chelsea, good puppy. We had a break-in last week and the neighbors' dogs are still disquieted.

Woof, woof, they're right next to you, Sigrid, get out now!

-Good puppy, Chelsea, it's just us. Usually she doesn't bark at me.

I walked toward the hot tub and scanned the dark yard for evidence of a broken tree limb. Maybe a lawbreaker returns for the thrill, the adrenaline rush of getting away with it all over again.

-A break-in?

Marissa wanted details.

-I caught some creep back here.

-What was he doing?

-I don't know. He ran off. The cops say there's a guy going around peeping into windows and masturbating.

-Gross.

-Sounds like Fletcher.

Thank you, Pete. Maybe Pete is a psychopath. I've read they make up at least one percent of the population—people without conscience—so they must be everywhere, one in a hundred.

We went back inside, and Sigrid proudly unveiled the raspberry chocolate tart.

-Doesn't this look heavenly? It's all organic, even the sugar. In Europe they call it *biologique*.

She poured a cup of coffee for Pete and asked why he kept cradling his elbow. I cradled my breath. A psychopath might just tell her the ruinous truth: fell out of your tree, nearly landed on Fletcher. Thank God he was on good terms with Marissa and didn't feel the need to sabotage our sort of relationship. Thank God he recounted his car wreck instead.

-I can still see that Hummer coming for me.

Marissa had opted for the Reisling and was getting silly.

-Those Hummers are too big. Tooooooo big.

Sigrid took the first opportunity to redirect the conversation to her favorite topic.

-I've never been in a smashup—knock on wood—except when we drove to Mammoth for skiing and Richard slid off the road into a snowdrift. That's why we fly to Colorado now, it's just safer and the snow is better too.

You know what, Pete, you should get a massage for your shoulder. Massage is the best, totally therapeutic, I'd go to Marissa every day if I could afford it.

If only, poor woman.

-The doctor said what I really need is to sit in a jacuzzi.

Pete gingerly raised his arm and grimaced. Nice try, Repetti. I helped myself to a second piece of pie, carefully avoiding eye contact with Sigrid, who had been glancing my way, but now was occupied with Pete.

-Hop in ours, Pete.

Are you kidding me? The other night I had to talk him out of taking your hot tub for a joy ride and now you're handing him the keys. Are you friggin' kidding me? Not to mention he's got three beers and a cup of caffeine in him. Pete feigned reluctance.

-I couldn't. It wouldn't be—

-Nonsense. You need the hydrotherapy. We keep it at a hundred and four degrees, equivalent to a Hopi sweat lodge. Optimal for healing.

-If you really don't mind. Just for a couple minutes. Doctor's orders.

A masterful, if shameless performance, I had to admit.

-Towels are in the steamer trunk next to the wet bar.

-Thank you. I won't be long. Fletcher, you coming?

-I'm not taking a bath with you.

-Oh, come on. Maybe we'll see the peeper.

He flashed what I can only describe as a shit-eating grin—ain't stopping me this time, suckah—and headed out. The dog started barking again, and I was feeling a bit disquieted myself. I couldn't tell if it was too much tart too fast or the way Sigrid seemed to be sizing me up, but something had set my stomach churning. I was searching for a joke about Pete getting into hot water when I caught Sigrid eyeing me again. Officer, it wasn't me, I swear, it's mistaken identity she met me briefly at the theater that's why she thinks I look familiar. For the first time ever, I was glad I'd been to South Coast Rep.

-Fletcher, I told Sigrid you can't discuss the trial.

Thank you, Marissa. Thanks for bringing it up.

-Are you enjoying the courtroom experience, Fletcher?

-It's interesting. But like Marissa said, I can't—

-Of course. Absolutely.

Sigrid refilled Marissa's glass—her fifth, counting dinner. This could get ugly.

-The guy's grandmother testified today.

-Marissa.

I gave her *the* look.

-What? You told us all about it at dinner.

Sigrid sighed and shook her head.

-That must have been heartbreaking. Can you imagine having your grandchild accused of murder?

-Sigrid, he can't talk about it.

I got up and examined another painting: some mermaid-like creature rising from a murky underworld, that's what I saw anyway. Nice tits on her too. Was Lawson ever in here, sitting in Sigrid's sitting room, trying not to stare? It really did look like him, not Richard, entering the front door five nights ago, and since he also drove a Lexus I couldn't rule Lawson out, even if it almost certainly was Richard, who after all lived here. Isn't that Occam's Razor? We had it in my college philosophy class: the simplest explanation is the most likely. But how would Occam explain The Sophist at the gas station and the MBA watching me at the beach and Sigrid, wife of the man funding Bud Jack's defense, inviting Juror Number One and his sort of girlfriend to the theater and now inviting us to her home? The simplest explanation is that the rich guy is running a conspiracy—call it Grisham's Razor. There was a new hardcover Grisham, one I hadn't seen before, on the antique table next to the flower vase when we came in. Was Richard reading Grisham to figure out how to manipulate a trial? Let me guess: a jailhouse snitch, the prosecution's pride and joy, shows up drunk and loses all credibility with the jury. How did Richard pull that off? Or how about a long-lost childhood friend rematerializes and risks self-incrimination to testify for the defense. That had been in the afternoon. His name was Scooter Hopkins. Lawson brought him in after dismissing Mrs. Wilkes.

-Mr. Hopkins, how do you know Bud Jack?

-We was tight back in school.

-High school?

-Elementary, junior high, all the way up.

Scooter Hopkins had on blue jeans, white t-shirt, gold hoop earring, and with his goatee he looked like a pirate, the first witness not wearing his Sunday best. Why didn't Lawson at least get him into a decent shirt?

-Are you a member of the Eastside Rollin' gang?

-Not no more.

-When did you join?

-Probably I was sixteen.

-Did Bud Jack join too?

-This crew tried to jump him in. He ran away.

-Was Bud Jack ever in a gang?

-No. Mostly he stuck to hisself.

I got it! Lawson didn't get Scooter Hopkins a new shirt because he wanted him to appear fresh off the street. Rex Ruffman calls himself a gang expert but, hey, this guy Scooter looks like he's been there. Still, I had a feeling Scooter the pirate might be on Richard Wilhite's payroll. Why else would a gang-banger agree to testify in court, especially knowing one side would want to discredit him? Sloan was ruthless on cross examination, forcing Freebooter Scooter to admit to three years in prison for stealing a car and possession of an unlicensed handgun.

-I got out early. Only got parole now.

And then Sloan nailed Scooter to the wall.

-On parole, but still doing drugs, right?

Lawson jumped to his feet and objected. Sloan claimed to be trying to establish the reliability of the witness. Silverson told him to proceed, but keep your tone civil in my courtroom.

-Ever smoke pot, Mr. Hopkins?

-Once or twice.

-Once or twice?

-Back then, yeah.

-Ever smoke crack cocaine?

Scooter Hopkins hesitated, and the hesitation shouted yes.

-Let me warn you, Mr. Hopkins, that lying under oath is a criminal offense. Have you ever smoked crack?

-Once.

If Mrs. Wilkes was the truth, Scooter was a walking lie.

-Only once?

-That stuff will mess you up.

-Ever sell it?

-No.

His eyes darted nervously. For his sake, I hope Scooter never tries poker.

-Mr. Hopkins, how often have you spoken with Mr. Jack since high school?

-Not too much.

-When was the last time you spoke to Mr. Jack?

-Been a long time.

-So how can you be sure he was never in a gang?

-I would know.

-How would you know?

-On the street that's how it is.

That was it from Scooter the pirate. If Richard Wilhite had paid him five gold doubloons to testify for the defense, it was five too many. Oath or not, no one trusts a criminal.

I took comfort in that thought—no one trusts a criminal—because if Sigrid had recognized me as her backyard intruder, she wouldn't trust me, and if she didn't trust me, she wouldn't have offered her hot tub to my friend, right? My stomach calmed a little. Sigrid seemed in no hurry to get us out of her house, and she hadn't slipped off to a back room to dial 911. She looked rather content, actually, happily complaining to Marissa about the gardeners.

-The Vietnamese guy sits out front in the truck, he just sits there, smoking and listening to the radio, while the two Mexican guys do all the work. It's just wrong.

-No kidding.

Finally, my chance for a careful look. Dark roots exposed her blonde hair as a dye job, the skin around her eyes was unnaturally taut, her teeth blindingly white. *Biologique* she was not. Was she forty? Fifty? Sixty? Had she retained any original parts? Once you got past the gift rack, she was just another skinny Laguna matron trying to cheat time. She looked up and I went back to the murky painting.

-Fletcher, that one's called Venus. A beautiful work, isn't it? Janice James. You've probably seen her work downtown. Janice is always revisiting the female figure.

Lucky her. The way things are going, my sort of girlfriend will be sort of passed out before I get her home, and I'll be revisiting baseball highlights on the sports channel. Marissa wobbled over for a closer look.

-Do you like it, Fletcher?

-Sure.

A big-busted mermaid in mysterious water, what's not to like?

-It does look familiar. The palette, right? Blues and greens. I love how it like flows.

Marissa was trying to sound artsy. Sigrid stood and joined us.

-Richard gave me that painting for my birthday last year.

Marissa cooed approvingly.

-Could you tell Richard my birthday is coming up?

Okay, time for an exit strategy.

-I'm gonna check on Pete, then we should probably get going.

The waterfall was gushing, the hot tub motor was humming, and Pete, splashing around like a kid in a sudsy bath, didn't notice me right away. When he finally looked up, he too started gushing.

-This is unbelievable. Jets for your back, jets for your calves, tiny bubbles from holes beneath your feet, and, dude, if you sit like this they tickle your crack.

-You're naked?

His clothes were in a pile on the deck.

-Yeah. What are you waiting for?

-We need to go. I've got to wake up early.

-Okay, but get in first.

-And Marissa's drunk.

-Two minutes. Just on principle. You'll regret it later if you don't.

He was right, I would regret it, because, knowing Pete, whenever he relived this triumphant moment, he would say something like yeah, and then we ended up buck naked in her hot tub or at least I did, you sissied out. It would get old fast. Better by far just to take the plunge. I shed my shirt and looked back inside through the glass door—the women were still chatting away. I dropped my shorts and tested the water.

-Damn.

-Hot, huh? You get used to it.

I lowered myself inch by burning inch. Once I was up to my shoulders, though, it was marvelous. Pete was right about the bubbles.

-Dude, we need to sneak in here whenever they're on vacation.

-I swear she was looking at me funny.

-She has the hots for you.

-No, seriously, you think she recognized me?

-She was giving you the eye, I saw it. She wants a piece of you. You know she's bored with her husband.

-She's old.

-Not all of her.

After five minutes, I told myself I should dry off, get dressed, collect Marissa, thank Sigrid, and call it a night, but the whirling, bubbling water was immobilizing, and like the metaphorical frog in the cooking pot, there was no hopping out.

-I bet this feels great on your shoulder.

-One word, baby: optimal healing. I need one of these at my place.

-Maybe you should marry a rich guy.

-I'd be out here every night.

-So would he.

-It'd be worth it.

At the ten-minute mark, I told myself five more minutes. For Pete's sake.

-I could be rotting in a box right now, a slab of cold meat. That Hummer had my name on it.

-Must have been surreal.

-Instead, I'm soaking in luxury. Wonder what the footprint is.

-What?

-The carbon footprint. Someone's burning coal to generate the power to heat this water. Probably up on the Navajo reservation. Polluting their air.

-You wanna get out?

-No, the damage is done, the water's been heated, *someone* ought to enjoy it. Out of respect for the Navajos.

At fifteen minutes, sweat was pouring down my face.

-This is friggin' hot.

-Hey, what's up with the Mexican chick? On the jury.

-She's Persian.

-Does she like you?

Does she like me? She offered me a ride (across the parking lot), she ate lunch with me (and two other women), she let me buy her a drink (of bottled water).

-I guess so.

And today after court was adjourned, after Scooter the pirate had walked the plank, I caught up with her in the hallway and she stood real close and spoke quietly.

-I know we're not supposed to discuss it, but that gang guy, didn't it seem like he was lying?

I put my hand on her shoulder, taking care to be appear casual, friendly, not flirtatious, and nodded.

-Yeah, I got that too.

I could smell her wonderful perfume.

-You gonna ask her out?

-I think she has a boyfriend.

Because right then, right after she'd practically whispered in my ear, her phone rang, and something about her voice and smile when she answered made me think it was a guy.

-Yeah, they always have a boyfriend.

And then she gave me a little wave and turned away. I'd been hoping to walk her to her car, but I couldn't stand there waiting for her to hang up, not without looking pathetic.

-You know what, life isn't fair.

-Dude, you're telling me. You're the first person I've been naked with in over a year.

-I mean that woman in court, the guy's grandmother. She lives in Long Beach surrounded by gangs and drug dealers, and Sigrid marries a rich guy and lives like this.

-We should steal something while we're here. Like Robin Hood.

That reminded me of something.

-You remember that old movie, Treasure Island?

-Is it porn?

-No, I saw it in must have been third grade. My whole elementary school watched it, sitting in the gym, and I was walking around in the dark trying to find a teacher to give me permission to go outside because I got scared when the one-legged guy, Long John Silver—

-You said it wasn't porn.

-So this was how many years ago—over twenty?—and today in court it all came back to me, like it happened yesterday. Probably 'cause this witness looked like a pirate.

-You got scared again?

-No, but I felt sorry for that little kid in the gym. No one comforted him.

-Come here.

He stood up on the hot tub steps and spread his arms, offering me a steamy, glistening, naked hug.

-*Now* I'm scared.

At twenty minutes, without warning, and without a stitch of clothing, Pete crawled out of the hot tub and jumped into the swimming pool.

-Whoo!

-Is it cold?

-Oh, dude. You feel tingly all over. You feel alive.

He ducked under, swam to the far end, and disappeared behind the waterfall. I stood up on the deck. It was approximately six steps from tub to pool, which means I was halfway there when I heard a man's voice.

-What the fuck? Don't move, asshole, or you're a dead man.

I recognized the voice. And the fluffy hair.

-Richard, it's me.

I grabbed my shorts off the deck.

-I'm calling the cops, you fucking pervert.

He had his phone out.

-Richard, it's me—Fletcher—remember? I was just…I'm not the…we were in the hot tub. Sigrid said it was okay.

-Never heard of a swimsuit? I walk in, I see a guy naked in my backyard.

-I'm sorry. We didn't think—she said you had a meeting.

-She did? Where is she? Are you fucking around with my wife?

-What? No. She's inside. With Marissa.

-I'll fucking kill you myself.

-Look in the window. See? They're in there.

Richard walked over to the glass door, but didn't go in. He appeared to be studying the scene. He was short, maybe five-seven, I hadn't noticed that at the theater, the hair added a couple inches. When he turned back to me, his tone had changed, the outrage was gone.

-Last week we had this weirdo back here.

-Sigrid told us.

He watched me pull on my shirt.

-We meet in funny places, Fletcher. First the bathroom—

-Now the bath.

He allowed himself a smile.

-Nice. I understand you're on a jury.

-Yeah.

-Who's he? What the fuck? I didn't need to see that.

Pete was back in the shallow end, waist deep in the well-lit water, which would have been alright if he hadn't been in a handstand, and if he hadn't held it so long.

-I have no idea.

I kept a straight face. Richard went for his phone.

-Wait. Richard, I'm kidding. He came with me.

Pete's head finally surfaced.

-Pete, this is Richard. Sigrid's husband.

-Hey. Great pool. You guys coming in?

King Richard looked confused. A man's home is his castle—why were two jesters splashing around in his moat?

-Pete, nice form on the handstand.

-Was I straight?

-No, flaccid.

Richard fled indoors. I watched through the glass. Sigrid didn't stand up to greet him, and he didn't go to her. Stepping out of the pool, Pete was watching too.

-Told you. She's bored with him. She wants you.

He lowered himself by increments back into the hot tub and sighed with exaggerated pleasure.

-I'd like to say this is better than sex, but I can't remember.

When Pete and I, fully clothed, rejoined the party in the sitting room, I had a new explanation: criminals return to the scene of the crime to appear innocent. Reverse psychology. When Richard discovered me and then Pete in his backyard, bare-assed in the oasis, he thought he'd caught the Peeping Tom, but since we turned out to be invited guests, we were now beyond suspicion—it would be too great a coincidence. And now that we were all friends, what difference did it make if we'd been back there uninvited last week? We were legitimate. Nothing left to feel guilty about, I confidently met Sigrid's gaze when she greeted our return with a smile.

-Caught with your pants down, I hear. Serves Richard right not calling to say he was on his way.

Did she just accuse Richard of trying to sneak up on her? Richard had a quick reply.

-I was on the phone talking shop the whole drive home.

-A new reality show?

He ignored my question.

-Besides, Sigrid, you had company.

-You're lucky they didn't think *you* were the prowler.

There was definitely some tension.

-Hey, Richard, here's a concept: plant a nude guy on someone's patio.

He gave me another puzzled look.

-Why?

He wasn't much fun.

-See what happens. Hijinks ensue. Candid Camera meets—

-No, thanks. People call the cops on that. We did, when Sigrid caught that creep.

Richard wandered off. Marissa turned to Sigrid.

-What did they look like?

-There was only one. He—

-I mean the cops. Any hotties?

Richard returned with a bottle of wine and a corkscrew.

-Fletcher, can I offer you a glass?

-Thanks, but we should get going.

-You sure I can't tempt you? This is the good stuff. A major Merlot.

He turned to Pete, who started to accept. I cut them off.

-Really, guys, I've got an early morning.

Marissa waved her hand.

-I'd like one.

I tried to signal Richard—she's way past her limit. He put the corkscrew down.

-Maybe we'll wait on this.

-I mean a hottie. I'd like a hottie. I don't drink red.

Marissa was cracking herself up. And embarrassing the rest of us.

-Marissa, you've got one.

Did Sigrid just call me a hottie? She smiled at me. Marissa smiled at Richard.

-What do you think, Richard? Were you here?

-Sorry?

-She means the other night, dear. The cops.

-Oh. Yes, I was here.

Richard was here, it was him in the doorway. Of course, it was. Occam's Razor. I got Marissa to her feet and her feet pointed toward the front door. Richard followed right behind.

-Court starts early, does it?

-Yeah.

-How's that trial coming?

Does he know I know?

-I can't really discuss it.

Does he know Sigrid told Marissa they were paying for Bud Jack's lawyer, and Marissa let it slip to me? Probably not.

-How are the other jurors? A pretty friendly bunch?

Well, Gramma Jamma is, so is Giraffe and a Half, and Chatty Chad, The Elephant is annoyingly friendly, The Mouse always nods, and then there's Roya.

-I haven't really met them.

-They say you should be affable—if you want to be elected foreman. Wouldn't that be a kick? That's what I would try for.

-Yeah?

-Hey, buddy, next time let's grill some steaks.

He looked at me funny when I laughed out loud, but I couldn't help it. What a night: Marissa unleashes her inner alcoholic and solves the mystery, Sigrid calls me a hottie, and Richard wants to be buds. And Pete is miraculously healed. Earlier in the evening, when we picked him up at The Cave, Pete had flinched at my hug and guarded his shoulder, but now he eagerly threw his arms around Sigrid and thanked her for the soak.

-I feel rejuvenated. I feel alive.

He held on until it almost became awkward. Sigrid didn't seem to mind, seemed pleased actually. I was next—warm hug from Sigrid, firm handshake from my new best friend.

-Good to see you again, Fletcher.

-Likewise, Richard. Thanks for everything, Sigrid.

-Our pleasure. Drive carefully.

-Always.

-Keep your pants on, Fletch.

Good one, Dick. Pete and I folded Marissa into the backseat, where she promptly fell asleep. The Wilhites went back indoors with one final wave from Sigrid.

-Dude, I felt her nipples.

Back onto PCH, where the evening had begun. Traffic was moving freely. In the passenger seat, Pete was mythologizing the epic hug.

-At first I just felt pressure against my chest, like squeezing a balloon, but then I really focused all my attention, like Marissa was saying earlier, look within and place your...your whatever...awareness, and then, dude, man, then there they were.

-She probably felt you too.

-How could she not?

I was trying to focus my own awareness. Richard had come in through the patio, that's why he'd caught me undressed and unawares, he hadn't used the front door. And when we left, no Lexus in the driveway. He must have parked in the garage. If that was his normal routine coming home, then it wasn't him I saw entering through the front door the other night. The mystery had not been solved. And there was more.

-Dude, you didn't feel them when you got a hug?

-No.

-That's because you didn't look within. You weren't in the present moment. That's how I'm going to live, from now on. I'm going to feel life's nipples.

-Pete, did she whisper in your ear?

-No. Not yet.

-She whispered in mine. Seriously.

-Right. What did she say?

-She said, I saw you out back.

-Dude, stop.

-Swear to God.

-No, stop here. I need to do something.

I pulled over. We were back at the site of Pete's accident. He reached under the seat.

-Where did you…did you take those?

He was holding the fresh cut flowers from Sigrid's vase. They had been by the front door.

-Robin Hood, baby. What did you get?

-Nothing.

-No, you got this.

He handed me a book: the hardcover Grisham.

-You're insane, man.

-I'll be right back.

He stood in the same driveway, watching traffic go by. Criminals return to the scene of the crime because they're just plain stupid. I waited in the car with the engine running, watching for the angry homeowner to emerge, and replaying Sigrid's five breathy words: I saw you out back. Did she mean the first time, when I was breaking and entering, or just now, when I was naked? What was she getting at? And what is Pete doing running out into the middle of a four-lane highway? He stopped, waited for a car to zoom past, then placed the flowers on the double yellow line. The next car slowed down, the driver carefully avoiding the crazy man in the street. I rolled down my window.

-Pete, come on.

He ignored me and started shouting at the passing cars.

-I didn't die here! I'm still alive! I'm still alive!

10

According to the newspaper, southern California is in a drought, has been for some time, meaning we've been getting less precipitation than normal. Much of our public water comes from the Colorado River, which drains the mountains of Colorado and Utah, and they too are short on rainfall. So our reservoirs are in danger of drying up. In response, some California cities have enacted half-hearted limits on water use, like no watering your lawn between eight a.m. and six p.m.

-How about no lawns period?

That's what Pete said.

-Seriously, why grow northern European flora in an American desert? What a waste. And all the fertilizers, the weed-killers, straight into the ocean. There used to be more fish, more birds, everything, it's becoming a dead zone.

-So no golf courses, right?

That set him off.

-Dude, don't get cute, lawns are a luxury, golf is a basic human need. But you're right, that day is coming, because all these private lawns nobody sits on, nobody plays on, just a bad habit is what they are, and when things get worse the public golf courses are gonna be the first to go, the tragedy of the commons all over again. I mean like what's the new rule in Laguna Beach—a hundred dollar fine for washing your car without a spray nozzle? Like that's going to make a difference. How about a ten thousand dollar fine if you water your lawn or wash your car or spray down your driveway, and the second violation they chop off your hose?

That was the image that popped into my head—a city employee, like maybe one of Laguna's humorless meter maids, patrolling the neighborhood, binoculars and two-way radio in hand, butcher knife at the ready—when Lawson asked the first witness of the morning about his chosen profession.

-You go to somebody's house and wash the car?

-Wash, wipe, and wax.

-While they wait?

-Ain't no waiting involved. The client just goes on about their business, eating lunch or watching tv, making love to their wife, and we let them know when we're done.

His name, he had informed the court, was Reed Benson—that's Reed with two e's now—and I pictured him and Bud Jack with their buckets and soapy sponges, scrubbing away on a late-model sedan under the vigilant eyes of a uniformed woman with an axe to grind.

-How do these clients find you?

-Word of mouth. Like we're at a house on Ocean, some place prime like that. If the neighbors come out, we ask if they want a car wash. Don't want the wackest-looking ride on the block, see what I'm saying? Or we knock on a few doors, leave our card. They got five dollars off with the card.

Marissa would say this is racist, but Reed With Two E's Now looked almost like a white guy: narrow face, pointy nose and chin, and his curls were loose and round, not tight and kinky. Light skin, too.

-Do you go all over Long Beach?

But you could tell he was black—the way he talked.

-Mostly we're by the water. Belmont Shore. Leisure World.

-Leisure World the retirement community?

-You gotta go where the money's at.

Yawn. I felt suddenly drowsy.

-How much does Bud Jack pay you?

-We go seventy-thirty.

Yawn. My morning caffeine was wearing off.

-You get thirty percent?

-That's right. 'Cause he's got the overhead. Tips is fifty-fifty.

There's an old joke: what's harder than getting a pregnant elephant in the back of a Volkswagen? Getting an elephant pregnant in the back of a Volkswagen.

-Do you do anything besides wash cars?

-We vacuum the inside. Five-star spotless.

Here's a new one: what's harder than getting a passed-out drunk Marissa out of the back of her two-door Saturn? Very little.

-I mean besides cleaning cars.

-Trucks, vans, whatever you got. We done a motor home one time.

After leaving Sigrid's house, I had dropped Pete at The Cave, driven back across Laguna, got lucky enough to find a parking spot right near my apartment, and tried to rouse Marissa. She had a pulse—I checked twice—

but she was dead to the world, deadweight, and even with the driver's seat slid forward I couldn't get enough leverage to pick her up or enough space to drag her out.

-Hey, Marissa.

I was tired, I was getting pissed, I banged my head on the door frame.

-Goddammit! Marissa, wake up.

Nothing.

-Marissa!

Nothing to do but hurry inside, grab some blankets and a pillow off my bed, and hunker down in the front seat.

-Reed, what I mean is does Bud Jack pay you to do anything else, aside from washing and cleaning vehicles?

-You mean like make coffee, open the mail?

-Anything.

-No, man, we don't even got a office.

Did someone say coffee? My attention was fading in and out.

-Would you say you know Bud Jack pretty well?

-I know he gotta have the radio on hip hop. I know he wants fish tacos for lunch.

-What about girlfriends?

Well, a girl in every port, if his grandmother has it right. Meanwhile, I spend the night tossing and turning in my sort of girlfriend's compact car—good on MPG, hopeless for REM. With my head resting against the driver-side window, I caught the headlights of passing vehicles. Flipped around, head on the passenger side, a street lamp blazed in my face. When I tried slumping low, the handbrake between the front seats dug into my thigh or someplace worse, like they should call it a Uranus not a Saturn.

-He got a girlfriend here and there, just like anybody else. He don't say too much about it.

Test drive Uranus today. Uranus seats four comfortably.

-Do you ever go to Bud Jack's house?

-Sometimes.

No mountain's too big for Uranus. Sorry, Uronor, but it's either pathetic jokes or I'm taking a snooze, or maybe you could direct Lawson to get to the point. Heronor didn't respond. No telepathy, that one.

-Sometimes?

-If we got time to kill, we go check on his grandmother, just chill out.

Yawn. Nine in the morning and I can't stay awake. Midnight last night I couldn't sleep, couldn't keep my head out of the light, and couldn't keep Sigrid out of my head. It was the way she had said it—I saw you out back—whispered so no one else could hear and at the last minute, on our way out the front door, so I couldn't respond. I shoved my feet up onto the dashboard and tried outlining the possibilities, the way I do on the chalkboard in class. Was she 1) being flirtatious, implying she had seen me in my birthday suit when I got out of the hot tub, and was it 1a) a friendly, joking flirt, or 1b) did she have something more serious in mind, maybe lighting the candle on my birthday cake? Or 2) was she letting me know she knew it was me she'd caught sneaking out her gate, and, if so, was she 2a) saying all is forgiven, we'll just keep it between the two of us, or 2b) making a threat? I couldn't work out which option Occam would go for, they all seemed straightforward enough, but I was pretty sure Grisham's Razor would have Sigrid 2b) threatening to expose me as the local pervert unless I voted not guilty, it was all part of Richard's secret plan, and meanwhile Richard was inviting me back for a barbecue. Were the Wilhites playing good cop/bad cop?

-Did Bud Jack ever mention a guy named Juan Castro?

Lawson was stuck in boring cop.

-That don't sound familiar.

-Did he ever say anything about having a problem with anyone? Maybe a guy in Huntington Beach.

-No.

My eyelids drooped to half-mast. This was getting painful.

-Maybe a Mexican.

-No. But he don't talk about hisself too much. Mostly he's all business—how many cars we got lined up, if we behind schedule or not.

-How many cars do you wash a day?

Maybe I can listen with my eyes closed.

-Five or six. We could do more but we're real careful. Spit and polish, baby. Five-star clean.

My mind flashed back to Sigrid sitting on her couch, serving up tart.

-They're not really gardeners, not even the Vietnamese guy. They don't know the first thing about flowers.

She threw up her hands in disbelief. Pete elbowed me. Her disproportionates were trying to bust through her t-shirt. *Whoosh-whoosh.*

-I would tend the yard myself—manual labor is good therapy—but who has the time?

A new image: Sigrid in her tight shirt, raking up leaves and sweeping the patio. *Whoosh-whoosh, whoosh-whoosh.* Another elbow from Pete.

Wait, that wasn't Pete. I opened my eyes. It was The Marlboro Mouse in chair two, reeking of cigarette smoke as usual. Had I fallen asleep? The Mouse nodded.

-Reed, does Bud Jack carry a gun?

-I never seen one.

-Is Bud Jack involved in drugs? Buying? Selling?

-Like I said, we wash cars, that's it.

My eyes slipped shut again.

-Is Bud Jack in a gang?

Lawson, please, haven't we been through this?

-Yes.

How long till lunch? I'll never make it. Did he just say yes? Hello!

-He is?

Lawson appeared taken aback.

-SSC, baby. Southside Squeegee Crew. Me and him's a gang of two.

Oh. Two E's Reed was two n's grinning. One E Silverson was one n not.

-Please, Mr. Benson, answer the questions directly.

-Sorry. Just seeing if folks is awake.

Was he referring to me? The Mouse nodded. I swear that varmint can read my thoughts. Hey, Mouse, want some cheese? Honk if you love cheeses. Nothing. Not even a smile.

-I'll ask again. Is Bud Jack in a street gang?

-No, sir. He's a businessman, same as me. Gainfully employed.

Speaking of varmints, across the room a short, hairless rodent had his beady eyes on me. Had he noticed me nodding off? Would he rat me out to Judge Silverson?

BAILIFF BALDY: It was Juror One. He's the sleeper. You want, I could give him a wake-up call. Maybe pull out his fingernails.

JUDGE SILVERSON: I'm a bit drowsy myself today.

A certain scenario came to mind, causing me to smile at the stuffy bailiff. He looked away.

SILVERSON: You were snoring again.

BALDY: I was not.

SILVERSON: Even my neighbors couldn't sleep.

A door next to the jury box opened, and somewhere a giant unseen vacuum sucked every ounce of air from the courtroom.

That was a line straight from Grisham. I had sworn never again after Patrick Lanigan, the ninety-million-dollar man, got stood up and ripped off by the beautiful Brazilian, after the complicated, impossible plan had worked and then Grisham, maybe out of boredom, maybe just to tease his loyal readers, had thrown in one last twist: sorry, people, this time our hero doesn't end up with all the loot, he's still happy though, don't worry, and wiser too. I'd sworn never again will I waste my time with a bestselling legal thriller. But it was two a.m. when I discovered the stolen Grisham beneath the passenger seat where Pete had left it, and I couldn't sleep, and if Pete was right, somewhere on a dark, impoverished Indian reservation black coal was burning to keep Laguna street lamps glowing, so the least I could do would be not let those kilowatts go to waste, right? There was just enough light for reading, and I figured after ten or twenty pages I would drift off.

Lawson sat down. Sloan stood up.

-Mr. Benson, do you and Mr. Jack wash cars in Huntington Beach?

-No. Seal Beach sometimes.

I was hoping the prosecutor would tear into the witness, create some fireworkth, but Sloan had little use for Double E Reed.

-Thank you. No further questions.

Double E departed. Silverson summoned Sloan and Lawson to the bench for a conference. I decided to bait the trap. Forget 2b or not 2b, if Sigrid is 1b) offering me quality time with her triple D's, I'll vote any way she says—not guilty, innocent, pure as Sunday snow—and if she wants two jurors in her pocket I'll bring The Mouse along in mine. Hell, I'll even let The Mouse go first, I'll get down on my hands and knees so the little pipsqueak can stand on my back and reach Sigrid's low-hanging fruit.

The Mouse scrunched his nose. I was watching him out of the corner of my eye. That's right, Cheese Lover, nuzzle up and nibble on that Double Gloucester, I know you're a titmouse. His upper lip lifted, baring two brown teeth. Go ahead, Mouse, double-click.

The startling sound he produced was more an explosive splutter than a laugh, like he couldn't hold it back anymore, and trying to disguise it as a cough only made it louder: *Puh-FAH-kee-koo-KOO-sis*! Something like that. The Mouse had roared.

Judge Silverson asked if he was okay. The Mouse nodded and coughed again. The nerdy guy in chair three offered him a lozenge. I looked over with a grin. Gotcha! That's what you get, Mickey, for having big ears.

The conference at the bench continued, joined by the pinched-nose bailiff. They appeared to be arguing.

BALDY: I wasn't snoring.

SILVERSON: Why do you think I slept on the couch?

LAWSON: Man, you must have been snoring if she crawled out of her own comfortable bed. I've been there, I know.

SLOAN: I'm glad I don't snore.

SILVERSON: No, you're more of a wheeze.

At one point, Lawson gestured toward the jury box, and Bailiff Buzzsaw looked right at me. Now what did I do? Is a slumbering juror grounds for mistrial? Uronor, I just closed my eyes, I swear, I didn't miss anything. Please, Uronor, call a recess, give me ten minutes, a quick nap, and I'll be good to go. Nothing. I heard Chad whispering behind me.

-These guys must get paid by the hour.

A door next to the jury box opened, and somewhere a giant unseen vacuum sucked every ounce of air from the courtroom.

That line bugged me. Isn't unseen vacuum redundant? Unless Grisham meant a giant unseen machine, like a vacuum cleaner. The book's setup had promised a typical Grisham morality tale: a church-going, Mississippi town struggling against a giant, New York-based chemical company that had poisoned their water and made them all sick. One woman sued and, though the lengthy trial bankrupted her small-town lawyers, she won a verdict to the tune of forty-one million dollars. The chemical company CEO was the classic Grisham villain—filthy rich, greedy for more, heartless and conniving. Screw the dying town, with many more plaintiffs lining up against him, the CEO would appeal the decision to the Mississippi supreme court.

Angling the book to catch the yellow glow from the street lamp, I had skimmed through the pages, I wasn't going to get involved in the story, this would only be a one-night fling. After twenty pages and no closer to sleep, I told myself I would read until I uncovered the secret plan. It didn't take long. Court-watchers expected the verdict to be upheld by a 5-4 vote, so, with the help of other heartless connivers aka political operatives, the CEO would throw millions behind a candidate who would run against an incumbent judge in the upcoming elections—supreme court judges being elected in Mississippi. The CEO's stooge would win the seat, change the balance of the court, and see the decision overturned, the case thrown out and buried, future class actions stifled.

I closed the book and closed my eyes. Would the evil CEO get his way? I know, I know, it wouldn't be a Grisham if the plan fails, but if it succeeds, if the CEO's candidate takes the election and swings the court into tossing out the forty-one million dollar decision, then the CEO comes out on top, greed pays, and if the avaricious, unrepentant bastard doesn't get his comeuppance, if there's no greed-suffering-redemption sequence, it couldn't be a Grisham. Did I have it right? If a) the plan works, then b) greed pays, and not c) a Grisham. If a, then b, and not c. And if the plan doesn't work, then it definitely can't be a Grisham—if not a, then not c. Either way, not c, not Grisham. Maybe it *wasn't* a Grisham. Maybe it was a cheap knockoff trading on his bestselling name. It sure looked authentic, with the bright, white JOHN GRISHAM in its usual place of prominence, bigger than the title and superimposed over a shadowy, conspiracy-suggesting cover design. The usual breathless newspaper blurbs too. "The best American storyteller writing today." "Could become its own era-defining classic." "Detrimental to sleep. You may read all night." Perfect: I was looking for a sleeping pill and get a dose of "packs a wallop" instead.

I put the book aside—threw it down, actually—and checked on Marissa. It really was the perfect metaphor for our sort of relationship: me squirming anxiously in the front seat, unable to go anywhere, unable to leave while she needs protecting, waiting for her to wake up. Wake up and what?

-Ladies and gentlemen of the jury, you've listened to the witnesses, you've heard the evidence, the rest is up to you.

The conference was over, and Sloan was standing in front of us, where he had begun six days earlier, back to playing the efficient public servant.

-I'll make this brief. It's pretty simple, really. The defendant confessed.

He ran through his case, and I found myself refuting every step. Mr. Jack seen near the crime scene acting suspiciously. (Not all that near, Mr. Sloan.) Mr. Jack with a history of gang involvement. (Yeah, eleven years ago he got a tattoo.) Mr. Jack confessed to the killing. (Or so says a drunk police informant.) My silent objections didn't slow Sloan's sloganeering.

-I'll say it again, Mr. Jack confessed. Opportunity. Mr. Jack was there that night. Motive. A turf war was heating up—Crips and Latinos—and he shot a rival gang member. Opportunity, motive, and when the police arrested him, Mr. Jack confessed. Your job now is to weigh the evidence and, if you believe Mr. Jack is responsible for the death of Juan Castro, find him guilty and put him away for a long time, get him off the street so he can't hurt anyone else.

As Sloan concluded, I looked over at Bud Jack—steely-faced as always. I still couldn't get a read on him. I knew Bailiff Bonaparte hid his shortcomings in stern self-righteousness. I could tell Judge Silverson had a wild streak behind the schoolmarm façade. Sloan took comfort in the certainty of law. Lawson had a warm heart and little ambition. But the one person I couldn't decipher was the one person I had to judge. Yo, brother, move your right hand if you're innocent, raise your left if you killed him, nod if it was self defense. Nothing.

The Mouse—how far did his telepathy reach? If all this time he's been eavesdropping on Bud Jack's silent thoughts, then I'm voting however he votes, simple as that. Hey, Mighty Mouse, can you intercept brainwaves from across the room? He blinked his eyes. Tell the truth, Mouseketeer, or I'll get you laughing again, I know you're listening, you want to hear more about Sigrid's hooters? He scrunched his nose and turned away. They're bigger than your head.

Lawson approached the jury box, limping slightly.

-Did Bud Jack really confess to murdering Juan Castro? No. Did he confess to killing anyone? Only according to a drunk prisoner who, by his own admission, had exchanged hostile words with Bud Jack and then was pressured by the police.

With his palms splayed open, the same sympathetic pose he had welcomed us with on day one, Lawson now reminded us that we must find his client not guilty unless the prosecution had convinced us beyond a reasonable doubt.

-That means no doubt. No maybe's, no probably's, not most likely, not he might have, not chances are, not he could have, not I bet he did it. Beyond a reasonable doubt. And in this case there is much reason for doubt.

He recited a long list: the absence of evidence tying Bud Jack to the scene of the crime, the so-called gang expert's lack of experience in Long Beach, the inconsistent conditions in the police lineup, the unreliable testimony of Victor Ruiz. Bud Jack, Lawson insisted, was an innocent man on the wrong street at the wrong time.

-Other people have jumped to crazy, unsupported conclusions. Gang member. Drug dealer. Murderer. You know better, don't you? You know he is no threat to society. In fact, he does everything society asks of him. Supports his grandmother. Runs an honest business. Provides another man with a paying job. Bud Jack is regularly welcomed through the gates of Leisure World because they know he does good work and means no harm. And he keeps his room spotless.

A few people chuckled. Lawson limped back to the defense table and put a hand on Bud Jack's shoulder.

-It has been difficult for my client to sit here quietly, keeping his emotions in check, while being falsely accused of terrible things, but now you can do the right thing and find him not guilty.

Lawson sat down and Judge Silverson began giving us instructions. Choose a foreperson. Consider all the evidence. Give everyone a chance to speak. Clean your plates if you want dessert. I wasn't really listening. I was anticipating our cue, and when it came I jumped to my feet. A door next to the jury box opened, and somewhere a giant unseen vacuum cleaner sucked us out of the courtroom. I pushed The Mouse aside, squeezed by The Elephant, darted ahead of several sluggish backbenchers, got my hands on the chair Gramma Jamma was gunning for, and when the dust had settled around the big table in the jury room, Juror One was seated next to Juror Six.

-Roya, how are you?

She giggled and smiled that smile.

-I'm good.

-Have you got this thing figured out?

-No, not really. Have you?

Believe it or not, yes, I had made up my mind. Or, rather, it was made up for me. Not by Lawson's closing statement. Not by Sigrid or Richard or Marissa or anything like that. In retrospect, I guess I had done a pretty good job of not discussing the case, except when a few words were necessary to avoid hurt feelings or kicks to the shinbones, and even then I was careful to stick to factual reporting and not raise the question of guilt. In my mind, too, it was like I had half ignored my own thoughts, didn't put two and two together even though four was staring me in the face. Without really trying, I had suspended judgment, kept an open mind—you were right, Uronor, Juror Number One was a keeper after all—and at the moment the defense rested, I was more focused on where I would sit in the jury room than where I would stand on the verdict. But once the sullen little bailiff had closed the door on us, it was like being set free, like somewhere a giant unseen vacuum cleaner had sucked away every ounce of inhibition, a fog was lifted, truth was revealed, suddenly I knew: Bud Jack was innocent. Not innocent like the evidence is ambiguous, the prosecution failed to make a compelling case, we have to turn him loose. Innocent like he should sue the police for wrongful arrest, ask millions in damages, because there's no way he did it, he never should have been tried. Forget the cold, steely stare, the gang tattoo, the odd behavior at the bus stop—Bud Jack did not kill Juan Castro. Physiological certainty. I'd heard the witnesses, observed their body language, and I just knew.

An awkward hesitation permeated the room—twelve self-conscious jurors unsure how to proceed—and I was just about to say look, there's obviously no case here, let's skip all the hand-wringing, tell the judge not guilty, and get home in time for lunch and a power nap, when Chatty Chad took charge.

-Okay, folks, I guess we need to pick a foreman.

The Elephant objected immediately.

-Fore*person*. The judge said—

-Right. Sorry. Anyone interested in the job?

-I vote for this young man. He's a schoolteacher.

Gramma Jamma, seated to my right, had her hand on my forearm. I shook my head.

-No, I wouldn't be good.

I wouldn't be good because the foreperson has to communicate with the one person who always looks like he wants to teach the teacher a lesson—Bailiff Sourpuss. I leaned over to Roya and whispered.

-You want to be foreperson?

-No way.

-It would be easy for you. Just tell everyone to say ahhh.

Another giggle, but not the vacuous, air-headed giggle so carefully cultivated by girls at Dana Hills High. Is it only in America that stupidity is a virtue?

-Alexis, why don't you have your algebra book in front of you?

-I'm sorry, Mr. Fletcher. I couldn't remember what I needed from my locker.

Giggle, giggle.

-How many weeks have you been coming to this class?

-I know, I'm sorry, I was in a hurry and couldn't think. So I just grabbed my tennis socks.

Giggle, giggle, airy laugh, and a shameless smile for the class because if I can get away with obliviousness and distractedness, I must really be something special.

No, Roya's giggle was different—one part bashfulness and three parts genuine bemusement. Roya's giggle was charming. At least to me.

-Why don't you take it, Chad?

It was like by design: Chad calls for volunteers and then one of his Mod Squad buddies nominates him. No one else seemed particularly interested, and Chatty Chad got the job. Isn't that how dictatorships begin?

Chairman Chad read aloud some additional instructions, and again I was choreographing my next move instead of listening. We could be done before lunch, verdict rendered, jury dismissed, and once she was out the courtroom door with her cell phone to her ear it would be too late. I would have to be ready to move quickly, not get penned in, maybe another leap from the jury box—to hell with Ol' Sourpuss—and I would need a good line. Roya, do you ever hang out in Laguna Beach? Too passive. Roya, maybe we can stay in touch. Too vague. I mean, if she says I don't think so, or I've got a boyfriend, or you've got to be joking, the humiliation will only last until I disappear into the anonymity of the freeway, safe from the embarrassment of ever seeing her again, so might as well just come right out and ask. Roya, would you go out with me, I mean like a date? Roya, I'd love to buy you dinner, get to know you better, have I mentioned my real name is Guillam? Roya, want to clean my teeth? I looked at her. No reaction. No telepathy, thank God. I looked across the table at The Mouse. He looked away.

-I think he did it. I really do.

Lady Yoga was sitting to Chad's right, and he had asked her to speak first.

-Why do you think that?

-I guess because he was there. They saw him, right? And then he told that guy he killed a Mexican.

The Elephant scoffed loudly at Lady Yoga.

-You mean the drunk? That witness was sketchy at best.

Lady Yoga looked confused—had she said something wrong? One of the chivalrous Mod Squadders jumped in to defend the damsel from the advancing beast.

-The detective said the witness was sober.

The Elephant thundered forward.

-No, that was the next day. He was drunk when he talked to Bud Jack. He said so himself.

-That doesn't matter.

-Doesn't matter?

The Elephant wrapped her trunk around a small tree, tore its roots from the ground, and hurled it toward the brave knight, who deflected it with his shield. Or maybe I'm getting carried away. Chairman Chad raised a hand to restore order.

-Let's let her finish, okay?

Lady Yoga shook her head.

-That's really all I had to say.

The gallant Mod Squadder spoke next. We were going counter-clockwise around the table.

-The witness who can't be trusted is the gang member who said Bud Jack wasn't in a gang. I mean, come on, the police said he was in a gang, the police said he was acting suspiciously, the police said he confessed, and who are you going to trust, a gang member or the police? I'm going with the police.

-Thank you, Mike.

Moderate Mike nodded and ceded the floor to Giraffe and a Half.

-My only concern is there's nothing tying him to the crime scene, like fingerprints or DNA or whatever. And nothing about the gun. But other than that, I'm leaning toward guilty.

Oh, other than that. Other than the absence of any material evidence whatsoever. There's an old African proverb: Don't stand near a leaning giraffe. Or there should be, because you could tell she was begging to be toppled. Moderate Mike obliged.

-Don't you believe the confession?

-I guess I do.

What trial did these people see? I thought I was the one who dozed off during testimony, whose mind wandered and made up stories, who got lost and ended up in the wrong courtroom. I thought yoga instructors were open-minded, giraffes forgiving, and moderates reasonable. I thought we would agree to not guilty and be home by noon. But it was like they had tuned out Lawson's entire defense. Chairman Chad signaled the other Mod Squadder.

-You're up, Mark

Moderate Mark agreed with Moderate Mike.

-Yeah, I think he's got it right. It comes down to do you trust the cops on this one, and they wouldn't go to all this trouble unless they were sure they had their man.

Moderate Mike agreed with Moderate Mark.

-Exactly. Those guys know what they're doing. They're the experts.

-That's right. And we're not.

They must have planned this out: Chad, you run the meeting and we'll argue for conviction. That's why I always saw them huddling in the hallway. It was a moderate conspiracy.

-I'm not convinced. Police sometimes...police...they make mistakes.

The Mouse had a nasal voice, high-pitched but cigarette raspy, like Professor Penguin without the lisp, and he squirmed in his chair as he spoke, eyes darting left and right, nose sniffing the air for trouble. Moderate Mark pounced.

-What mistake do you see here?

-I don't know. Just something seems...something's missing...like that proves it...proves he really did it.

Way to go, Mighty Mouse, don't let those cats slap you around. The Mouse nodded nervously. Chad pawed at him.

-So you don't believe the confession?

-Well, what he said was...what the guy said...the witness...he said the...he said Bud Jack said he popped a Mexican. That's kinda vague.

Attaboy, Mouse, you the man!

Moderate Mike wasn't having it.

-But think about it, they arrest a guy they think killed a Mexican, but tell him he's arrested for drugs or something, and then without being asked he says he killed a Mexican. If that's just a coincidence, we're talking like one in a million.

The Mouse shrugged and scurried back into his hole. Wait, Cheese Whiz, don't back down, one-in-a-million happens all the time. To me anyway. The Mouse nodded but said nothing. The Elephant raised her trunk.

-I know it's not my turn, but you said we'd go around the room and have everyone give their first impression, and I'm sorry, but whenever someone expresses a little doubt you guys start arguing with him.

The brave knight drew his sword.

-You did the same thing.

Chairman Chad interceded.

-No, she's right, let's let everybody get their two cents in, and then we'll open it up.

Juror Number Three, the nerdy guy, adjusted his glasses and cleared his throat.

-I agree the case has some holes, by why didn't the defense put Bud Jack on the stand and let him give his side of the story? Pretty damning, if you ask me. Pretty damning.

The Elephant waited a polite, exaggerated moment, making sure El Nerdo was finished, then took her turn.

-First of all, I weighed all the evidence like the judge said to, and right now I'm not convinced beyond a reasonable doubt, and the main thing, I guess you can tell, is I don't believe the confession, not only because the witness was drunk that night, but he and Bud Jack had words in the cell, they didn't like each other, so the witness could easily have made up a story to get back at Bud Jack.

-But still that's some coincidence, saying he killed—

-Let me finish. See, that's what I was talking about.

-Sorry. You're right.

-I think it's very possible that the cops asked him if Bud Jack said anything about trouble with a Mexican guy, and he told them what they wanted to hear. The witness was biased against Bud Jack, and that's a reasonable doubt if you ask me. Now, you're next.

She motioned quickly to Cowboy Kev before the Mod Squad could issue a rebuttal. Turned out, Cowboy Kev was one of them.

-I'm with you guys. I don't got a problem with the confession. The guy was walking around the streets that night acting weird. He was up to something.

Roya followed Cowboy Kev.

-I don't know, I really don't. It's like when the one lawyer talked, I believed in him, and then the other one talked, and I would go back and forth, you know what I mean?

-So it sounds like you're undecided.

Chairman Chad made a note with a pen. Was he keeping score? A quick unofficial tally: with seventy-five percent of precincts reporting, I count six votes for guilty, two for not guilty, and one lovely undecided. But let's be realistic, The Mouse will cave under moderate pressure. The Elephant was a different story. She wasn't going to budge, her body language said it all. While speaking, she kept a thick elbow planted on the tabletop like she was ready to arm wrestle all comers, and when she was quiet, she leaned back in her chair and folded her big-rig forearms in front of her, confident in her inertia: not guilty all the way.

-Okay, Fletcher, whata you think?

Whata I think? One part of my brain was ready with a joke: I can't decide if I'm undecided or not. Maybe that would lighten the mood in the room.

-I can't—

Some other part of my brain, probably my prefrontal cortex, stopped me: don't say it, Roya will think you're mocking her.

Okay then, my prefunny cortex advised, tell them you think the defendant is not guilty and Juror Six is hot.

No, replied the prefrontal cortex, if you say not guilty, I guarantee The Elephant will plop down next to us at lunch with her stinky food and want to commiserate.

Good point, a third sector of my brain chimed in, and I'm getting hungry.

-Fletcher?

Everyone was looking at me, waiting, but my brain was still squabbling with itself.

-*Say not guilty.*

-*Don't do it. Seriously.*

-*What about the physiological certainty?*

-*What about the smell of egg salad?*

-Honey, are you okay?

Gramma Jamma was touching my forearm again. I needed to say something.

-I'm undecided.

It just came out.

-*Way to stand up for what you believe in, Guillam.*

-*I'm concealing my hand.*

-*That's just rationalizing.*

-*No, it's a strategy. Let The Elephant take the heat. Let them think I see both sides.*

-*Be honest. This is really about a need for control.*

-*Be honest. This is really about Roya.*

I leaned in and whispered to her.

-I guess we're in the same boat.

She leaned toward me, we brushed shoulders, and I caught a strong whiff of her fragrance. Wow. No telepathy, but she knows how to send a message. When I started listening again, Gramma Jamma was depositing her two cents.

-He seems like a nice young man, cleaning up after supper, taking his grandmother to church, washing people's cars for them. I don't see how he could kill someone. Isn't it possible they confused him with somebody else?

Okay, the updated tally: assuming Chad follows his moderate pals, that's seven for guilty, Elephant, Mouse, and Gramma J. for not guilty, one undecided dental hygienist with shiny black hair and dark glittery eyes, and one awkward math teacher physiologically certain of the defendant's innocence but pretending to be undecided in order to a) avoid eating lunch with The Elephant, b) appear open-minded and unbiased, and/or, depending on which part of his schizoid mind you choose to believe, c) establish common ground with the uncommon Miss Undecided.

-Can I say something about that, Chad?

It was Moderate Mike. Or was it Mark? They looked alike—unfashionable glasses, slouching shoulders, graying hair—and now I couldn't remember who was whom.

-Go ahead.

-I just figured something out. This guy's a neat freak. His house. His car. You see how he dresses. Maybe that explains the clean crime scene.

The other moderate agreed.

-Yeah, the guy's a professional cleaner.

The Elephant unfolded her massive forelimbs with a snort.

-You want to convict a guy for murder because he cleans his room?

-I was just raising the question.

I leaned toward Miss Undecided.

-Can you believe those guys?

-I know.

Another shoulder touch, another whiff of perfume. Maybe a long deliberation won't be so bad.

Chairman Chad interrupted my swoon.

-Folks, sounds like we've got some talking to do. How about we break for lunch, give everyone a chance to think a little, then come back and really hash this thing out, see if we can't finish up in one day?

I leaned in again.

-Did you bring a sandwich today?

-No. Sorry.

-That's okay. You want to go find a restaurant?

-Actually, I told Kevin I'd have lunch with him.

-Oh.

I pretended to be preoccupied as the room cleared out, then opened my lunch bag—just like back in junior high, eating peanut butter and jelly by myself in a lonely corner of the cafeteria where I wouldn't get pushed around by some eighth-grade bully or teased for having a sack lunch with a milk when all the cool kids bought a hot lunch and can of soda. Sometimes I would find a handwritten note in my lunch bag: I love you, Guillam, hope you're having fun. I never told my mother I wasn't having fun. I didn't want her to know I wasn't the superstar she imagined me to be. Anyway, what could she do to change things? The cheerleader I liked was having lunch with the tough kid who had his own dirt bike, and I'll just hang out here until the vice principal, two-way radio in hand, chases the stragglers out to the playground.

-Mr. Fletcher, you can't stay in here. I'm locking up.

I gathered up my lunch and, carefully avoiding eye contact, stepped past the imperious bailiff.

-You'll find the cafeteria on the third floor.

Yeah, the cafeteria and The Elephant and Chatty Chad. I found an empty bench in the hallway instead, and checked my phone: one text message from Marissa: Just woke up. Hangover.

Around five a.m., with daylight coming on and neighborhood traffic picking up, she had emerged from her coma long enough for me to coax her out of the backseat and get her tucked into my bed. Then I took a shower, ate a bowl of cold cereal—breakfast of champions—assembled my lunch, and when I checked on her before leaving, she was back in never-never land.

I texted a reply: Trial done. Almost immediately, my phone rang.

-You're finished?

She sounded draggy.

-We're in deliberations. How's your head?

-Does anyone think he's guilty?

-Marissa.

-My head's not happy.

-Did you throw up?

-Sort of.

-Did you make it to the bathroom?

-Sort of.

My sort of girlfriend.

-Are you okay now?

-Yeah. Just tell me, how many are holding out for guilty? One?

-Marissa, I can't—

-Two? Give me a number.

-Seven.

-For guilty?

-So far.

-Fletcher, you've got to do something. I'm counting on you. Oh God.

-What? Marissa? Hello?

I waited a few minutes, then called back. Nothing. No doubt too busy puking luscious tart all over my bedroom. At least it's *biologique*.

Speaking of puking, why does Roya want to hang out with Mr. I-don't-got-a-problem-with-duh-confession? Who talks like that? Who thinks like that? Bud Jack, a hard-working businessman, struggling to make ends meet, gets accused of murder because a white fireman and his police friends think a black man at night looks suspicious, and that makes sense to people on an all-white jury, people like Moderate Mike and Mark and Cowboy Kev.

I leaned my head against the wall. I wanted to fall asleep, but when I closed my eyes, there was Cow-pie Kev, yellow grease dripping down his tough-guy goatee, chewing and chewing on a bean burrito while he talked to Roya: you see his eyes, he musta did something, and how 'bout letting me finish off that quesadilla for you? Is she sharing her food with him? Is she letting him pay? I bet he asks her to dinner, offers her a ride on his motorcycle, and she'll sit behind him, arms tight around his waist, black curls flowing out from under her helmet.

To chase that cruel image from my mind, I pulled out the purloined Grisham and skimmed the last fifty pages. The plan was working. The evil CEO got the election result he'd paid for, the new judge swung the state supreme court against big liability claims, and the forty-one million dollar decision against the chemical company would soon be overturned. So a) the plan works, and b) greed pays. But wait, there's one final twist. The judge's young son is injured in a baseball game, hit in the head by a wicked line drive off a high-powered aluminum bat, and there's a liability issue. The baseball bat had been banned as too dangerous. The umpire and the coach should have prevented its use. The sporting goods company, which understood the danger, should have recalled the model. You could see what was coming: personal tragedy causes the judge to discover the wisdom of huge fines levied against negligent corporations. Carefully avoiding subtlety, Grisham tacked on medical malpractice—a screw-up in the ER left the young baseball player with brain damage. So the plan works, it's fundamentally sound, only a last-second, one-in-a-million accident disrupts its flawless execution. Call it an act of God, but at least greed didn't pay: a, but not b, and therefore c—it's a Grisham after all!

But wait again, you're not going to believe this, the final twist was a feint. Despite the illegal bat, the medical malfeasance, the brain-damaged son, and the looming medical bills, the judge's change of heart is tentative, he can't reconcile his new-found sense of justice with his old political instincts—he was elected, after all, on the promise to tame these big lawsuits—so he splits the difference, votes against a negligent nursing home but casts the deciding vote to toss out the case against the chemical company. The evil CEO wins big. Greed pays. Call it an act of Grisham.

I closed the book, closed my eyes, leaned my head back. I guess this ending was more realistic—rich people get what they want. The CEO was narcissistic and mean, yet he had a young, sexy wife. I try to be considerate and kind—I spent the whole damn night in the front seat of a car, for God's sake—and what do I have to show for it? The CEO's trophy wife had fake breasts and patronized the arts with her husband's money, just like Sigrid, only the trophy wasn't interested in art, it was just her way of staying in the spotlight. Sigrid isn't like that, she'd been a college art instructor after all. Maybe that's what captured her attention—the way I appeared to be admiring the paintings in her house—and then she caught a glimpse of me naked, and, bored with little Richard, she called me a hottie and whispered in my ear: I saw you out back. She 1b) knew what she wanted, and what Sigrid wanted she usually got, at least ever since she'd acquired her in-television husband and escaped from the public-employee middle class. She's living large in her big house and resort backyard—heated pool, gurgling waterfall, jacuzzi running day and night—the desirable Laguna lifestyle it's called in the glossy real estate ads. I could see Bud Jack and Double E Reed scrubbing the Lexus in her driveway. *Whoosh-whoosh, whoosh-whoosh.* I could see Sigrid sunbathing on her patio, face down but propped up, bikini top untied, summoning me over to rub lotion on her back.

-Hey, buddy, I think it's time.

I opened my eyes: narrow-toed boots, clunky belt buckle, goatee. Cowboy Kev. And the cowpoke was all by his lonesome. Maybe lunch didn't work out.

-Oh. Thanks.

How long had I been asleep?

-You reading Grisham?

-Not really. Just killing time. Someone left it in my car.

I stood up.

-You were smart staying indoors. It's insane hot out there. Like walking into a furnace.

Yeah, smart, because the last thing I'd want to do is go have a hot lunch with a hot juror on a hot day.

-Oh, did you go somewhere to eat?

-That sushi place across the street. Great sashimi. Have you been there yet?

What kind of cattleman eats raw fish?

-Hi, Fletcher.

Roya had appeared. She smiled at me, and I pretended to be pleased to see her standing next to him. He checked his watch.

-We better get back.

They left together, walking side by side down the hall. At least they weren't holding hands. Yet.

I collected my things—phone, remains of lunch, stolen book. It all made sense to me now. The story of the sickened town, the vile CEO, the judge for hire—a fictional tale, yes, but the situation was all too real, or so said the author in a personal note on the last page. When I read that, I finally understood: that's why he'd compromised his moral formula, that's why he let the greedy guy, without comeuppance or redemption, win in the end. The book was one long discourse, Grisham was making a point: private money in judicial elections corrupts the courts. Which is what I needed to do—not corrupt the courts, but come up with a sustained argument that would carry the day, with clear and cogent logic even smug moderates couldn't refute. Enough with the phony indecision which has gotten me precisely nowhere, it's time for an impassioned plea that will sway the jury, rescue Bud Jack from cowboy justice, and fill Miss Undecided with admiration and longing for this sturdy champion, this bold mathematician aka Juror One aka Guillam Fletcher, because if John Grisham can make a stand for fairness and truth, so can I.

11

I was juiced, inspired, ready to rumble, as I trailed Roya and Cowboy Kev down the hall. I had a bounce in my step, fire in my eyes, my mind was focused, my quarrelsome cortices worked as one. I was fixing to face down the forces of evil—until I took my seat in the airless jury room and, within minutes, like I'd been drugged, my head fogged up and my eyes glazed over, the fire went out. Sorry, Grish.

-Alright, folks, let's figure this deal out.

When Chairman Chad launched the afternoon session, I was half asleep—not closed eyes and snoring like a spent and abandoned Bailiff Baldy in Judge Silverson's bed, more like a somnolent dolphin. Yes, dolphins do sleep, or so I'd been told.

-They're mammals, dude, they have to sleep. But they're also conscious breathers, so like, yo, I can't sleep because I'll forget to breathe and I'll drown, and the only thing more embarrassing for a dolphin than death by drowning is life in Sea World, so half their brain sleeps at a time and the other half stays awake enough to breathe and hold one eye open for sharks and jerks on paddleboards.

That was me—not a jerk on a paddleboard, a half-conscious mammal—surfacing for air then drifting under. Not even Roya's perfume could stir me from my post-lunch haze—fifth-period paralysis we call it at school. The best I could manage was two eyes halfway open and the occasional head shake to keep my chin off my chest and my mind from floating away. *Whoosh-whoosh, whoosh-whoosh.* There were sharks in the water—great white moderates prowling for blood—a dolphin has to stay alert. At the moment, though, the sharks were closing in on the three for not guilty, and mostly left us undecideds (real and pretend) alone, probably figuring Roya and I would drop like dominoes once they'd toppled The Elephant.

The Mouse was the first casualty. He held out for a while, stayed out of sight. I could smell him, of course. How many cigarettes can one little rodent puff down in a lunch break? He nodded his head twice. Yeah, right, Smokey, I'm guessing at least four. But if nicotine is calming, maybe he should have lit up a few more, because once the sharks started circling, when the cats crouched to pounce, he panicked and scampered into the open.

-Maybe you're right, but…I just…what if he…the defendant…I don't know.

The Mouse was squeaking. Moderate Mike (or was it Mark?) and Moderate Mark (or was it Mike?) kept squeezing.

-Let's go through this one more time. They arrest the guy for drug trafficking, right? They don't tell him about the murder, don't put him in a lineup, he's just sitting there, that's what they said, they waited, and then he tells the other prisoner he already killed one Mexican.

-Yeah, what's the saying? Murder will out.

The Mouse looked trapped. Bear down, Smokey. He squeaked again.

-Yes, but police…they could have made….

-Made a mistake. That's true. They're not perfect. Believe me, I know. They gave me a traffic ticket for nothing. But they still try to find the right guy, don't they? Because if they get the wrong guy, the killer's still out there. So do you really think they'd testify under oath if they had doubts? Would they really coerce a confession?

-Yeah, what's their motive?

-I mean, unless this is like some movie where all the cops are dirty.

The Mouse teetered.

-Probably no, but…I just…probably you're right.

-If the rest of us agree to guilty, could you go along with that?

The Mouse tottered.

-I probably…I guess so.

Ka-thump. The Mouse falls. That's eight for guilty, and they'll go after Gramma Jamma next. I felt bad for her, a trusting soul, she's got no chance in this shark tank.

-Anyone else still skeptical about the confession?

Chairman Chad scanned the room. Avoiding his eyes, I looked over at The Elephant, strangely quiet. Did she have a strategy, or was it just another case of afternoon lethargy? Do elephants sleep like dolphins, one eye looking out for lions? As I watched, she hunched the thick folds of her shoulders and came to life.

-I think that's a great point—would the police have a motive to frame the wrong guy?

Are you kidding me, Elephant? Are you agreeing with those guys?

-But like I said before, Victor Ruiz did have a motive. Bud Jack threatened him.

That's more like it, Heffalump. But her body language was different now—no defiant arms, no set jaw. Was she softening? The gallant knight saw an opening.

-I accept that, Cheryl. But if he wanted to frame him, how did he know to say he killed a Mexican? That's my point.

-You're right, that would be quite a coincidence.

Are you friggin' kidding me? Did The Elephant just give up the fight? Come on, Dumbo, what about him being drunk, what about reasonable doubt? Nothing. I had noticed her chatting amiably with Chatty Chad as they returned to the jury room after lunch. I bet he'd sat down next to her in the cafeteria, and that was enough to win a sympathetic hearing. Either way—*ka-thump*—it sounded like nine for guilty and, at this rate, two more weren't far behind.

Okay, this is it, I should come up for air and say something, make my impassioned plea—hey, everybody, he's innocent, trust me, physiological certainty, I can feel it in my bones.

-*They'll think you're loony.*

-*Maybe I am loony.*

-*I just want to sleep.*

Chairman Chad offered me a way out.

-Why don't we take a vote, see where we stand now. Let's do secret ballot. Everyone needs a slip of paper.

If I voted guilty, I could go home and sleep, my head could sink deep into the cool pillow, my burning eyes could finally close. Now I know why CIA torturers use sleep deprivation. I took a deep breath, filled my lungs, and I stood up. Whoa! Head rush! I grabbed the back of my chair to steady myself.

-You okay, Fletch?

-Just getting sleepy.

I handed him my ballot and turned on my phone. Marissa had sent another text: You can do it! Yeah, right.

-Well, folks, I think we're making progress.

The unfolded ballots lay face up on the table in front of Chairman Chad—a dozen white butterflies tacked to a board. There was a joke in there, but my bushed brain couldn't find it. Chad swept the slips over to Lady Yoga for a recount. She was quick about it.

-Nine for guilty, one for not guilty, and two put undecided.

I sat back down, leaned in toward Roya, and whispered.

-Stay strong.

She giggled. Cowboy Kev said something I didn't catch. Roya leaned away and giggled louder. I needed a good line and quick, but nothing came.

Chairman Chad asked for suggestions on how to proceed from here, folks, and Moderate Mike or Mark chimed right in.

-Not to put anyone on the spot, but maybe the two undecided people could say what they're confused about.

Moderate Mark or Mike seconded the motion.

-That seems fair.

But Lady Yoga had a dissenting opinion.

-I don't think people should feel pressured to talk.

-No, but we gotta know what people are thinking if we're gonna get anywhere. Whata you say?

He looked over at Roya and me. I looked down at my lap.

-*They're all staring again.*

-*You want to know what I'm thinking?*

-*Just tell them the truth.*

-*I'm thinking the butler did it. No, the butter did it.*

My brain was fried.

-*The butter and Colonel Mustard. In the dining room.*

-I just can't believe he's a killer.

I looked up, and all eyes were on Gramma Jamma, who smiled as she spoke.

-And his friend—the young man he works with—he seemed very nice. And it sounds like they're together a lot, so I think his friend would know if he was doing bad things. That's why I put undecided.

I surveyed the faces across the table. Giraffe and a Half and Lady Yoga were gently returning Gramma Jamma's smile. Moderate Mike or Mark glanced at Moderate Vice Versa and rolled his eyes. El Nerdo sported a frown. Chairman Chad scratched his head, then gestured to Gramma.

-What would it take to convince you?

-Convince me of what?

-To vote guilty.

-Oh, I couldn't do that.

I laughed out loud. It was the way she said it, smiling sweetly as she sentenced a roomful of people to continued confinement. One of the moderates groaned, El Nerdo checked his big watch, I laughed again. With sleep deprivation comes giddiness. Our Fearless Leader didn't give up.

-But what if he really is guilty, like the police say?

-Oh, I don't know. We should ask this young man.

Gramma Jamma was touching my arm and smiling at me.

-You mean you would go along with whatever Fletcher says?

She ignored Chad's question or didn't hear. She just sat there beaming.

-Fletch, can you help us out here?

-Yeah. I mean no. I mean I can't think straight. I was up all night.

The Elephant snorted.

-Your dog sick again?

-Something like that. I can barely keep my eyes open.

-At least tell us where you're at on this.

Moderate Vice Versa was getting impatient, but my brain was blank—no clever comeback, no honest answer, no ideas whatsoever. I turned my palms up and shook my head—there's nothing I can do, guys, sorry, I can't even tell you two apart anymore. Moderate Verce Visa didn't like my silence.

-You're not even going to answer?

Lady Yoga stepped in.

-We agreed not to pressure people.

-Then what are we going to do, play tiddlywinks?

The room went quiet as the bad news sunk in: the undecided old lady won't budge without encouragement from the smartass teacher, and the smartass teacher won't cooperate until he gets some sleep, so the afternoon session will be a wash, further debate is pointless, a children's game would be just as productive, maybe more so. Chairman Chad shifted the bent ballots around the tabletop—twelve-card monte, not tiddlywinks.

-I don't know, folks.

It was an accusation, like I've done everything I can do and I'm really disappointed that you people aren't cooperating—a passive technique employed by tired, desperate teachers when threats no longer work.

Lady Yoga perked up.

-Why don't we quit for now?

Chairman Chad shook his head.

-We can't. It's only two o'clock.

-Can't we do what we want? We're the jury.

-The judge said we go till five.

-Oh.

More silence. El Nerdo suggested we play charades.

-I'm serious, we've got to pass the time somehow.

Moderate Mark or Mike had a better idea.

-Let's play that old game where you close your eyes and stick up your thumb.

-Heads Up, Seven Up?

-Or Show and Tell. And he can have nap time.

He meant me. The tone wasn't friendly. I met his glare—yeah, buddy, why don't you show and tell us how you stick your thumb up your ass. I didn't say it, but at least my brain was blinking back to life. Sensing trouble, Giraffe and a Half raised her long neck and scanned the savannah for carnivores. As she spoke, she bobbed her head like she was agreeing with herself.

-No, she's right. A jury can do what it likes. I read about it somewhere.

Lady Yoga bobbed her head in reply.

-Yeah, we could tell the judge we're done for the day.

-I think it was in a John Grisham novel.

More head bobbing. Chairman Chad leaned back in his chair and chuckled.

-That's not how it works. Not in real life.

-What can she do, arrest us?

-Yes, actually, yes, she can.

He interlaced his fingers behind his head. His fellow Mod Squadders laughed with him, exchanged wry smiles, and shook their heads dismissively—these women just don't get it! It was the head-shakers versus the head-bobbers. The Elephant joined the bobbers.

-It's in the one where the woman outsmarts the cigarette companies.

-That's right. And her boyfriend's on the jury. And they do whatever they want.

-It's called The Runway Jury.

The Elephant and Giraffe know their Grisham.

-No, it's called…isn't it…it's The Runaway Jury.

The Mouse too, apparently.

-I thought that was the one where the jury gets killed.

And El Nerdo. Grisham fans, one and all. And none of them seemed embarrassed.

-No, that's a different book.

Et tu, Kevin? The cowboy can read? El Nerdo conceded the point.

-Well, they all run together.

Head bobbing all around. The Elephant, Giraffe and a Half, The Mouse, El Rhino, Kudu Kev—must be the whole damn Serengeti reads Grisham. Even Kill 'em Guillam, the great white hunter—I admit it, the renegade jurors sounded familiar. Gramma Jamma, though, had missed the safari.

-Why was the jury killed?

El Rhino filled her in.

-They convicted a murderer, and he's taking revenge, one juror at a time.

-Didn't he go to prison?

-A mental hospital, but they released him.

-Oh.

Her smile was gone. She looked a little worried. Dying jurors—I'd given that one a try too, when I was searching for a way out. Why didn't I say yes when Heronor offered to dismiss me back on day one? I was too tired now to remember.

The Elephant, of course, remembered everything.

-You're supposed to *think* it's the convicted murderer taking revenge one by one, but really it's someone else.

El Rhino slapped the table in mock anger.

-Now you've spoiled it for everyone, Cheryl.

The Elephant apologized and recommended instead the one where the Supreme Court judges get assassinated.

-You'll never guess how that one ends.

-I think I already saw the movie. With that one actress, right?

-You mean Tom Cruise?

-No, the actress. That woman.

Gramma Jamma touched my right arm. Her smile had returned, and she wanted to tell me something.

-Killing jurors one by one sounds like Agatha Christie.

-Who?

-Why don't we vote on it?

Lady Yoga was calling for a show of hands.

-On Tom Cruise?

-No, who wants to go home early?

My hand shot up—hell, yeah! The Elephant and Giraffe were almost as quick. The other women followed, then El Rhino and The Mouse. Attaboy, Smokes!

Chairman Chad laughed dismissively.

-People, this won't make a difference. The judge won't care.

But even Kudu Kev had joined the stampede. Moderate Mike and Mark held out, not wanting to betray Comrade Chad, but it didn't matter, the yoga instructor had taken charge and seemed satisfied with a three-fourths majority.

-That's nine. Nine to three. I'll tell the bailiff.

She left, and Comrade Chad mumbled something about an exercise in futility and getting us all into trouble—so much for Our Fearless Leader's fearlessness—but no one was listening, the entire Serengeti was talking at once, the jury-room debate had finally heated up.

-I can't stand Tom Cruise.

-Oh, I think he's great.

-He's a good actor.

-He plays the same character every time.

-So?

-He never gets killed—have you noticed that?

-That's true.

-It's like in his contract or something.

-Just once I'd like to see him killed.

-Or at least mess up his hair.

-What's his wife's name again?

-Which one?

-Isn't he divorced?

-I can't think of her name.

-Didn't she get remarried to that singer?

-Why do they always marry rock stars? You know it won't last.

The vote to quit early so I could go home and sleep had energized the room, and I found myself wide awake, like maybe I didn't need an afternoon nap after all, my whole brain was working again. I smiled at the irony and kept it to myself.

SILVERSON: They have a verdict?

BALDY: No, they're tired.

SILVERSON: Take them some coffee.

BALDY: They want to go home for a nap.

SILVERSON: Not a bad idea, actually. What do you think? Feel like a nap?

BALDY: I think Juror One is behind this. Let me lock him up. What's so funny?

SILVERSON: I just remembered your handcuffs are still on my nightstand.

When Lady Y returned, she was beaming like Gramma J.

-Okay, she wants us back at eight a.m. sharp.

Later days, Chadster. Out of the room, down the elevator, past the security checkpoint, and—yowzer!—Cowboy Kev was right. The furnace blasted your face once you stepped clear of the courthouse doors. Had to be over one hundred. My car would be broiling hot.

-Hey, what's happening?

The Sophist! I was walking out, he was walking in.

-Oh. Hey.

I mean, are you friggin' kidding me?

-Y'all finished up?

He raised his right hand, palm open, initiating the hip handshake. Moderate Mark or Mike hurried past, pretending not to notice me, but he had to see it—a serious black man publicly acknowledging a white guy as a brother. A brothah. I liked how it felt.

-You find my man innocent?

-We're still in deliberations.

-The all-white jury. Alright, you take care now.

-Wait. What're you doing here?

See, my brain really was working. I was going to get to the bottom of this.

-Taking care of some business.

He took a step toward the doors. I tried to keep him talking.

-You in some kind of trouble? I mean, with the law?

Oops. Was that racist? He didn't seem put off.

-Just got some paperwork. Damn, it's hot.

He wasn't carrying anything, no briefcase, no papers. I studied his face. Was he lying? I tried another angle.

-Let me ask you something. We keep running into each other.

-See you tomorrow, Fletcher.

Black curly hair. Not The Sophist, the Persian Princess, heading for the parking lot, and not a single cowboy in sight.

-Roya, wait.

She stopped. She smiled. The Sophist grinned.

-Looks like you got business too, brother.

I barely heard him.

-Roya, can I walk you to your car?

She giggled. I took it as a yes.

-Maybe we could have lunch tomorrow.

-Yeah, maybe.

What's the old joke? If a lady says no, she means maybe. If she says maybe, she means yes. If she says yes, she's no lady.

-They were really putting the pressure on us, weren't they?

-What?

She was looking at her phone.

-Trying to get us to vote guilty.

Roya had to be the other undecided—her and Gramma Jamma.

-I guess. This weather's way too hot.

-No kidding. I can't wait to get home. I live close to the beach.

I checked to see if she was impressed. She was digging in her purse.

-I hope I haven't lost my keys.

-I can always give you a ride. You're in Costa Mesa, right?

-Here they are, thank God. What? Yeah.

-Ever go to the beach?

-Sometimes.

-Do you come to Laguna?

Because, I mean, I live right there, we could hang out, you could come to my place and we could walk down to Heisler Park or have lunch downtown.

-We usually go to Newport.

She unlocked her car with a remote button and flinched when she grabbed the metal door handle.

-Hot?

-I swear it better be cooler tomorrow.

-I think tomorrow you're gonna really feel the heat.

-I'll come early and get like a spot in the shade. This is crazy.

-I mean from those guys, trying to get you to vote guilty.

-Oh.

-I mean, I'll do what I can. I won't let them bully you.

Because, Roya, I'm not afraid of those guys, it was me who voted not guilty, I was the only one. They want to lock up Bud Jack and throw away the key, but I'm standing up for the truth, and I hope you'll join me.

-Actually, I did vote for guilty.

Ka-thump!

If the CIA was serious about torture, they would take their sleep-deprived victims and force them to sit in a traffic jam on a blistering July afternoon. The southbound 5 was stopped dead. My left arm was in the sun, my legs were in the sun, and even with the air conditioner blowing high I was sweating and feeling carsick and my head was fogging up again. Please, just let me sleep, I'll admit to anything, I trained the suicide bombers, I work for bin Laden, I confess it all. The radio reported a two-car fender bender and a three-mile backup. A fender-bender? Just exchange your damn insurance numbers and get moving, how long can that take? My eyes tried to shut themselves. With my left thumb and middle finger, I stretched my eyelids open. They started closing again. Okay, okay, I am bin Laden, you got me, bring on the lethal injection and let me float away. *Whoosh-whoosh, whoosh-whoosh*. Ninety minutes of stop-and-go agony—we quit early for this?—and when I reached the site of the accident, the dented cars were long gone, which was a good thing because, not owning a gun, I would have had to kill the irresponsible driver with my bare hands. When I finally got home, I was too stressed out to lie down. I took a shower, ate two bowls of cereal, with a bowl of ice cream for dessert—dinner of champions—watched mindless television until I mellowed out, then pulled all the shades in my bedroom and fell asleep. It must have been around five o'clock.

When I finally woke up, it was four o'clock in the afternoon, I'd slept twenty-three hours. I wonder what the world record for sleeping is—that was my first thought. My second thought was oh, shit! I checked my clock again and fell back in relief—a.m., not p.m., I'd only slept eleven hours, Bailiff Buzzsaw wouldn't be busting down my door and serving a warrant.

My third thought was what was she thinking? Before lunch she couldn't decide, and after lunch she votes guilty. It had to be Cowboy Kev, the jerk on the motorcycle, he convinced her to convict an innocent man. Does raw fish make a person pliant? I could just imagine what he'd told her: Bud Jack's a hoodlum, Roya, everyone can see that, except maybe the old biddy and that teacher dork, and they'll get it eventually, mind if I eat this last piece of eel? Well, newsflash, cowpoke, maybe you lassoed Roya yesterday, might even round up the old gray mare today, but it takes twelve to convict, and I'm hanging this jury. And if Roya voted guilty, there's still another undecided besides Gramma Jamma running loose. Way to go, Smokes! Had to be the little pipsqueak, he'd said he'd go along if everyone else agreed, and not everyone else agreed. As long as I hold out, he will too, the Dynamic Duo standing together for justice and truth—Smokey and Sleepy, Mighty Mouse and Superman.

Or Mickey and Goofy. Because what if we're wrong? What if Bud Jack hates Mexicans, capped one in a dark parking lot, threatened another in a jail cell, and what if I'm only arguing for acquittal so Marissa will still occasionally sleep with me, or so Roya won't sleep with Cowboy Kev? Maybe it's true we're hardwired to seek justice—I read that somewhere, not in a Grisham—but we're also hardwired for something else, wired hard, if you know what I mean, and I might be desperate enough to ignore the obvious—the man confessed!—in hope of preventing one more woman from walking briskly away.

No chance of falling back to sleep now, not with my mind starting to regale me with tales of rejection and woe: Sharon choosing northern California over me, this cute woman who lived next door for a while choosing a preppy-looking marketing guy over me, Marissa choosing the beach ball artiste or maybe just aloneness—rather be alone than with ol' Fletcher any day—and now Roya, seated next to me in the jury room yesterday but leaning away.

I opened the front door, the sun wasn't quite up and already the air felt warm, no foggy marine layer this morning, today would be hotter yet, a perfect beach day, and I would be commuting inland to fiery hell. Like I said at the beginning: jury duty in July—I'll die. But I had three good hours before heading to my death, might as well make the most of it.

I saw them as soon as I hit the water: a pod of bottlenose dolphins cruising parallel to the beach just beyond the surfline. Four, five, six dorsal fins. I sat on my knees, paddled through a few ankle-slapper waves, then stood up on my board. The water was flat and glassy, I could see the sandy bottom thirty feet down, two orange fish hovered beside a rocky outcrop. Five minutes of hard paddling, and I caught up to the dorsal fins—six turned into eight turned into eleven or twelve pale gray bodies, scratched, scarred, mottled, and surprisingly big up close, their long mouths set in beguiling grins. They creased the surface with the tops of their heads, took in air, arched back down. I pulled ahead of them, they were hardly moving, they were coasting, I could see them gliding just off the seafloor. We passed Rockpile, the sun broke over the hills behind Laguna, the broad curve of Main Beach came into view. A few early risers were strolling the boardwalk, traffic was moving on PCH, no doubt the homeless crew in Heisler Park was gathering up their dirty sleeping bags and bracing for another bright, unforgiving day. When they surfaced again, I could have tapped the closest one with my long paddle, I was right on top of them, they didn't care—the dolphins, not the vagrants. Three feet to my left, a gray body sensed my presence, rolled onto its back, and contemplated me with its left eye. Why not just open your right eye, Flipper? Why do you think, Jerk on a

Paddleboard? Unbelievable! I was actually seeing it: dolphins at sleep. Half asleep. While downtown Laguna was rising with the dawn, one hundred yards offshore this pod was still on snooze. And I was right there with them, floating past Main Beach, moving south. What a trip! The chatter in my brain subsided, the world dropped away, dissolved, nothing existed beyond the gleaming morning sun, the gently undulating water, the effortless dolphins. We drifted with the current. I only paddled enough to change course when they did, and I was careful to give wide berth when they rose for air because I know what it's like being pressured by strange creatures, I know how it feels when you just want to sleep.

The strange creatures reassembled a few hours later—eight a.m. sharp. Moderate Mike patted me on the back like an old friend and asked how I'd slept. Moderate Mark jumped to his feet and pulled out a chair for Giraffe and a Half. I could tell them apart now—Mike combed his thin hair over, Mark his thin hair back. The Elephant was explaining to El Nerdo that she'd read every Grisham, even the non-thrillers.

-People say they aren't as good, but I think it's his best work. He should get more credit. Those New York critics just resent commercial success. I say more power to him.

El Nerdo said he preferred the movie versions.

-The screenwriters usually tighten up the endings.

The Mouse caught my eye and nodded. How about you, Smokes, you read all of them? He nodded again.

The order around the table was exactly the same. After all those years in school, we're just more comfortable with assigned seating, even as adults. No one remembers the quadratic equation or what year the Civil War began, but form a single-file line, don't take someone else's seat—the lessons of social conformity stick. I wasn't complaining, I still had the best seat in the house. Gramma Jamma greeted me with her irrepressible smile.

-You look rested today, dear, you must be feeling better.

Roya smiled too. I sat down and leaned in.

-Did you get a shady spot?

Giggle.

-No, not hardly.

The smile, the perfume, the hair.

-Are we on for lunch?

-Lunch? Oh. Maybe.

If a lady says maybe, she means yes—unless she gives no indication of having said maybe the day before or even of having considered the invitation, in which case—I'm not stupid—maybe means indifference at best and, more likely, a cold-hearted no. Whatever. It's hard to get upset after starting your day on a calm ocean in the company of half-sleeping, half-grinning cetaceans. Despite having returned to the concrete wasteland, despite the giant unseen vacuum cleaner sucking every ounce of air from the dismal, windowless jury room, despite the Mod Squad's calculated friendliness and Roya's sincere disinterest, my mind was still buzzing with pleasure. Have to ask Pete, but seems like, dude, dolphins trigger endorphins.

-Folks, the bailiff informed me we won't be going home early today.

-What? No more bankers' hours, Chad?

-Nope. Unless, of course, we reach a verdict, and I'm sure none of us want to be back here tomorrow, right? So let's see about wrapping this up today, okay? And that means sorry, but we're gonna have to put some of you on the spot. Like you, Fletcher, we're kinda hoping to hear from you. You back on your game today?

-Yeah, I was even out surfing this morning.

Out surfing—that was for Roya's benefit. Out paddling doesn't have the same cachet. Dogs paddle, surfer-dudes surf, and surfer-dudes are cool, the coolest white guys on the planet—tan, athletic, laid-back, soulful, *biologique*—that's the image anyway, which I don't totally understand because they're really just glorified skateboarders, and skateboarders are dweebs, the little shits, they almost got Pete killed. They almost got Pete killed, which led to NPDDD and Marissa drinking herself silly and me spending a sleepless night in her car, the little shits.

-I was out surfing and the water was super clear, like you could see fish, you could see the ocean floor.

Dolphins too, but that's my secret—I won't betray my sleeping friends, not to this school of hammerheads.

-And I started thinking.

Surfing and thinking, Roya. Would you really choose an uptight, brain-dead, wannabe cowboy on a motorbike over a tan, athletic, laid-back, soulful, *biologique* guy who also thinks?

-Yesterday my brain was in a haze, but today it's like...like I can finally see the fish.

I could hear my teacher's voice emerging—confident, authoritative, insistent.

-And there *is* something fishy about this case.

I'm not sure where my corny little homily was coming from, but I had nothing to lose, and I had the room's attention—no smirking, no patronizing smiles, no passive-aggressive body language from the Mod Squad—maybe because they know I'm a teacher, maybe just because it was still early.

-I mean, the witness from the jail, the drunk guy, if he's telling the truth like most of you seem to think, then the cops threatened to put him back in the cell with the dangerous black man. They told him the guy was dangerous. That's what the witness testified. The cops threatened him, so he told them Bud Jack confessed.

Moderate Mark objected.

-Hold on a second. He didn't say that was the *reason* he reported the confession.

His tone was respectful, and I matched it.

-You're right. And it doesn't prove he invented the confession either. But it does sound like they threatened him, and that's at least a little fishy. Will you grant me that?

Giraffe and a Half and Lady Yoga were bobbing in agreement. The Elephant spoke up.

-That's what I was saying yesterday.

Moderate Mike jumped in, trying to regain control of the debate—or maybe just assert his manhood.

-And what I was saying yesterday was it still doesn't explain how the witness knew to invent a confession about killing a Mexican.

-The police...they could have...the witness...I mean, what if they coached him?

Mighty Mouse to save the day! The moderates scoffed, Cowboy Kev snickered, I raised my voice enough to cut them off.

-I was thinking about this very point when I was on my surfboard. I mean, I've got nothing against cops. So why don't I trust the cops on this one?

-You mean you trust the defense witnesses? A gangbanger and a—

-I mean something's been nagging at me, and yesterday, when you wanted my opinion, I couldn't place it.

I had stayed with the dolphins for almost an hour, watching them thread through the webs of kelp, listening for their spluttery exhales whenever I lost them in darker water. When we passed Thalia Street, they cut away from the beach, making for open water. Reluctantly, I came out of my zone and I remembered I was Guillam Fletcher aka Juror One, and I had some place to be. One last time I counted the dorsals—ten, eleven, twelve, the dozing dozen, you guys take care—then turned and paddled for home, against the current and into a soft breeze.

With the dolphins gone, my mind resumed its obsessive thought production. Driving to Santa Ana is going to suck. At least I get to have lunch with Roya. Maybe I can change her mind about Bud Jack. Is she interested in me? Is any woman interested in me? She did say goodbye to me when I was talking to The Sophist. Yeah, but then she was more focused on her cell phone.

To block it out, I counted the strokes—one-two-three-four-switch sides, one-two-three-four-switch. I found a steady rhythm, leaning forward, knees slightly bent, pulling with my back muscles. One-two-three-four-switch. And suddenly it came to me: the timeline was off!

-Remember what the detective said? He interviewed the witness, Victor Ruiz, on the morning of the fifteenth, after the guy had sobered up. They brought him in drunk the night before, so that must have been on the fourteenth. They brought him in, stuck him in the cell, and Bud Jack confessed, supposedly. On the night of the fourteenth. Right? But there was that other witness, the off-duty fireman who saw the suspicious guy at the bus stop. The fireman said the cops called him in three days later to look at a lineup—on the fourteenth. That's what he testified.

-Wait a second, Fletcher.

I ignored him.

-Do you see the problem? If the witnesses are right, the lineup was on the day of the fourteenth, and Victor Ruiz was arrested and heard Bud Jack's confession on the night of the fourteenth. The lineup came before the confession. But the detective said they didn't put Bud Jack in the lineup right away, they wanted to see if he might let something slip.

-That's true. The detective said the lineup came later.

Excelente, El Nerdo, but what about the others? A good teacher reads the students' eyes, and I was seeing puzzlement and confusion. Still, they were attentive, they wanted to figure it out, even the moderates were waiting for more.

-Let me put it this way: the fireman picked Bud Jack out of a lineup, said he was the suspicious guy at the bus stop, so the police think they've got the right guy, but they don't have any other evidence to speak of. What are they gonna do, let the guy they think is a murderer go free?

The Elephant finally caught on.

-That's it. That's the motive we were asking about. The police threatened Victor Ruiz, or even coached him, because after the lineup they thought they had the killer.

-Cheryl, that's speculation.

-Yes, but it's reasonable. Reasonable doubt.

Moderate Mike looked frustrated—he was running out of arguments.

-So the cop mixed up the order of things? So what?

Bingo! That's what a teacher wants—skeptical students asking the right questions. The only thing missing now was a chalkboard.

-Yes, I think that's what we need to ask: 1) did the detective make an error, and does that 1a) mean he simply misspoke, or 1b) imply a degree of incompetence. Or 2) did the detective intentionally mislead us, and should we conclude 2a) he just wanted to convict a guilty murderer, or 2b) an innocent man was being framed?

With that, I leaned back in my chair and let others do the talking. A good teacher helps students frame a question in a useful way, but also encourages debate, allows them to voice their own opinions, draw their own conclusions. The moderate argument was trust the police, and I'd offered a legitimate reason not to. I hadn't told anyone what to believe, I'd only raised the issue. It was a start. Around mid-morning, we voted again: five for guilty, four for not guilty, and three undecided. When we took a bathroom break, I slowly thumbed a text message for Marissa: Good news jury split. She was at work, but I had a feeling I'd be seeing her tonight, seeing her in a good mood, because the more votes for not guilty, the less likely Sloan would want to retry the case, and I figured I had Gramma Jamma, The Elephant, and The Mouse on my side, plus Giraffe and a Half gave me a big smile and a half in the hallway, and I'd swear El Nerdo winked at me when Chairman Chad called us back to order.

-Folks, I let the judge know where we're at, and she said keep trying, so how are we gonna resolve this?

-Well, I think it's too bad folks don't 5a) trust the cops any more.

Thank you, Mopey Mike.

The room was quiet. I looked over at Roya. Had she changed her vote? I'd be satisfied with a hung jury, I'd happily quit right now and throw Bud Jack's fate to a new panel of jurors, if I knew that I'd at least convinced Roya, that I'd rustled her out of Cowboy Kev's corral.

-I have a question.

Speak of the devil—Cowboy Kev, not Roya.

-Could we agree on a lesser charge? Manslaughter or something.

That got people talking again. Giraffe and a Half said she'd seen a jury do that on tv.

-You sure it wasn't in another Grisham?

Thank you, Mopey Mark.

Gramma Jamma asked what it means, and Chad enlightened her.

-It means we find him guilty, but the sentence could be shorter. For example, you're not comfortable convicting him of first-degree murder and sending him to prison for life, right? So could you say he's guilty if you knew he'd only get ten years max or something like that? But I don't know. We'd still have to ask the judge, because I don't think a jury can just change the charges.

-Why don't we just convict him of being a black man on the street at night?

It just came out. It came out when I noticed some heads bobbing at Chad's mention of a shorter sentence. It came out when I heard Roya tell Cowboy Kev she thought his idea was a good one, really, because like a lesser charge would be fair, right? It came out and kept coming.

-Because that's what we're doing here. We've got a roomful of white people, and we're only going by what the white witnesses said. I'm not accusing anybody here of being racist.

Except maybe Cowboy Kev, and the Mod Squad, and the five others who voted guilty yesterday.

-But step back and see what this looks like. White people versus black people. Our word against theirs. And we're totally ignoring theirs. Ignoring the grandmother. Ignoring the guy he works with. And the guy who—

-We can't trust them. They might be protecting him.

-Exactly. You assume they're lying and you assume the white officers are telling the truth. Like one of you said yesterday, there's no hard evidence, no fingerprints, no bloody clothes, just a white guy saw a black guy on the street and picked him out of a lineup and that makes him guilty. Again, I'm not calling anyone racist.

Why state the obvious?

-I'm saying the prosecutor—it's like he's playing on our prejudices. Remember how quickly he rejected the two black jurors, even the businessman in the expensive suit? And the Latinos too. Is it really an all-white jury on accident? And then he brings this case with flimsy evidence knowing a white jury will fall for it, because white people are automatically suspicious of a black man on the street at night.

-Now hold on.

I waved him off and pointed toward Cowboy Kev.

-This guy said it perfectly, he said Bud Jack was up to something. Right? And now he says we should convict him of a lesser charge or something, anything, like that's a good compromise. Well, I say we send the prosecutor a message. We let him know that we're not racist, we're not prejudiced, and he shouldn't insult us by bringing a case without real evidence, because we can see through shoddy police work and we're not falling for a jailhouse snitch. Yeah, we're average citizens, a bunch of working-class folks, right? But we're not stupid.

How about that, Grish?

After my outburst, the deliberations turned ugly, voices were raised, I was accused of reverse racism and being some kind of crazy, leftwing liberal. I didn't defend myself, I'd said my piece, I wanted to appear above the fray. Moderate Mike said he'd really like to know who he'd seen me talking to outside the courthouse yesterday, was that Bud Jack's brother? The Elephant told him he was out of line. Lady Yoga suggested everyone take a few deep breaths. Moderate Mark suggested how 'bout a few deep reality checks instead? The arguing went on for a while, we were hopelessly deadlocked, the jury was hung. Until two things happened that almost instantly turned the mood around. Gramma Jamma asked everyone to please stop shouting, this isn't right calling people names. She had tears in her eyes and stood up like she was walking out. For a moment, the room was awkwardly quiet. Then Cowboy Kev made an announcement.

-Okay, I gotta say something. I'm not gonna sit here and lie to you, I guess I didn't totally presume innocence and that's not right. I'm a standup guy, and Bud Jack deserves a fair shake same as I would want.

Whoa! The cowboy switches horses midstream—who'da thunk it?

That was the turning point. I could feel momentum shifting, the energy in the room transformed. It took a few more minutes, but eventually El Nerdo found the magic formula that allowed for a graceful change of vote.

-We wouldn't be saying he's innocent, right? We'd be saying the prosecution didn't make their case.

Ka-thump!

After that, it was almost too easy, like a Hollywood fairytale. Everyone was eager to get on board. No one wanted to appear prejudiced. Even Moderate Mike admitted to hasty conclusions.

-Yeah, probably I just wanted to be right, the wife says I do that.

The mood in the room was now satisfaction and relief—we'd overcome our differences, we were doing the right thing—and when we voted again a secret ballot was unnecessary. We returned to the courtroom—single file, no cutting in line—and took our seats. Judge Silverson instructed Chairman Chad to read our decision, asked us one by one to affirm the verdict, and then it was over, just like that. Not guilty.

-Mr. Jack, you're free to go. The jury is dismissed. Court is adjourned.

Whoo-hoo! School's out for summer! The Mod Squadders wanted to shake my hand. Gramma Jamma reached out for a teary hug.

-I knew you'd figure this out for us, dear.

I glanced away from The Elephant's friendly smile—an embrace from her would crush my ribs—and glued my eyes to those long black curls as they headed for the door.

-Hey, Roya.

-Oh.

A quick hug. Her hair smelled like flowers. She was already turning on her phone. This was it. Suddenly my heart was racing, my face was flushing hot, but what the hell?

-Roya, I hate to just say goodbye. I don't know—could I call you sometime?

-Okay.

Okay? If a woman says okay, it means…okay. Okay, okay, okay! Like I said, I was on top of the world. This was all too good to be true. The screenwriters had tightened up the ending. A poem kept lilting through my head.

> Bud Jack acquitted
> Dolphins aslumber
> I can't believe Roya
> Gave me her number.

When I got to my parking space, I spotted The Mouse and Cowboy Kev a few rows over, smoking cigarettes and admiring a motorcycle. I ducked into my car and shut the door. I didn't want to go through more goodbyes and nice meeting you and see y'around and all that. I started the engine, got the air conditioner blowing cold, and checked my phone: Can I come over around six? Silly question, Marissa, we've got some celebrating to do.

As I steered toward the exit, a motorcycle zoomed up next to me. The rider looked over and nodded. Cowboy Kev? No, The Mouse! Hey, nice working with you, Smokes. He gave me a thumbs-up and sped off, the little pipsqueak aka Runaway Ralph. I checked my rearview mirror—sure enough, Cowboy Kev at the wheel of an old Volvo station wagon, a long, blue shoebox on wheels. Might as well be driving a chuckwagon, cowpoke.

> Bud Jack acquitted
> Dolphins aslumber
> Beautiful Roya
> Gave me her number
> Could Cowboy Kev
> Look any dumber?

The greatest morning of my life.

12

There is a certain technique to calling a woman—if only I knew what it was. If I call too soon, she might think I'm pushy or needy. Don't want that. Better to wait, be patient, play it cool, she already knows I like her so let her wonder a little, let her imagine I'm in demand, I've got a cluttered social calendar, I've got important stuff on my plate. But how long can I wait? I should strike while the iron is hot, while it's fresh in her mind that Fletcher is the surfer with smarts who detected the flaws in the prosecution's case, Fletcher is the one who courageously resisted peer pressure, stood up for racial tolerance, and saved an innocent man from a life behind bars, Fletcher is the man I want to father my babies. There must be at least a hint of that floating around in her subconscious mind, right? But when this morning's excitement starts to fade, she'll recall that Fletcher is also the guy who got lost in the courthouse, cracked wise with the judge, couldn't find his own car in the parking lot, what kind of children would that goofball raise? Would calling her tonight be too soon, too desperate, like I couldn't get her out of my mind? What about tomorrow? I guess I kind of need to decide on the message I want to convey. Is it Roya, I'm calling because 1) you seem interesting, I'd like to get to know you, I'm not concerned where it leads, or 2) I have this strong romantic attraction to you and I'm hoping it's mutual? If it's 1, maybe I wait a few days. If it's 2, tomorrow is probably right. Tomorrow evening. But even if 2 is the truth—and I'm not saying it is— should I still go with 1 just to be on the safe side? Yeah, I'll go with 1, wait a few days and relax about it. But waiting a few days to call might come across like I'm nervous and trying to get my courage up, like I'm thinking about it too much. Tomorrow evening then. No, calling on a Friday evening would be really pathetic, like I've got zero social life, and anyway she wouldn't be home. I could leave a message—hey, Roya, just calling to say hi, I'm running out the door in a couple minutes but call me back if you get a chance. Why would I call to say hi if was running out the door? Okay, I'll call on Saturday. Afternoon. No, late morning.

-Dude, shut up and just call her.

-You think? Yeah, you're probably right.

We were at Treasure Island, the ocean breeze was warm, the sun high in the sky. Just another typical day in the fascinating life of Guillam Fletcher: surfing with dolphins at the crack of dawn, a few hours at the courthouse in the morning securing justice for the oppressed and getting a phone number from a beautiful woman—ho-hum, happens all the time—then picking up Pete, my partner in crime, and hitting the beach.

-I mean now. Call her now. You got your phone?

-I left it in the car.

And my car, thankfully, wasn't conveniently close. It was at the shopping center on the other side of PCH, a fifteen-minute trek away. A sign warns no beach parking allowed—customers only, violators towed—and a security guard cruises around in a cart watching for evildoers, but as Pete once put it, if you can't outsmart a minimum-wage rent-a-cop, you've got no business breaking the rules. This was one technique I had down pat: I dropped off Pete and our beach chairs by PCH, parked behind the yoga place, and entered a back door, looking to all the world like I was attending a class. Thirty seconds later, with a confident smile for the receptionist—Namaste!—I exited the front door and hurried across the parking lot to where Pete was waiting. Piece of cake. If the security guard spotted us now, so what? He couldn't know which car was ours.

-Dude, dolphins.

Out beyond the whitewater, a pair of dorsal fins disappeared and reappeared in steady rhythm, too quickly to be sleeping.

-I think she's kinda on the fence with me. I'm just looking for the right approach.

-No, you're looking for plausible deniability. In case she's not hot for you. Then you can pretend you were just being friendly.

Crack. He was eating peanuts from a plastic grocery bag and tossing aside the empty shells.

-I just don't want to come off as a dork.

-That's your mistake. You're trying to be smooth, which is all wrong. You've got to let her see you have too much integrity to be smooth.

Crack.

-I'm supposed to be awkward?

-And a little nervous—out of respect for her. Chicks dig that, the real ones, anyway. Trust me, I know.

-So where's all *your* girlfriends?

He shook his head and threw a peanut shell at mine.

-Just wait till I get my Porsche.

Treasure Island is actually a postcard-beautiful spit of coastline, formerly secluded and hard to reach until the city council approved construction of the Montage resort on the cliff top where an abandoned trailer park had been decaying in the sun—the last vestige of funky Laguna plowed under. Now there are staircases with handrails, a ramp for golf carts, a lifeguard tower, kayak rentals, morning yoga on the sand, and resort staff in conspicuously white shirts handing out towels to wealthy, indulgent vacationers who sprawl in cushioned lounge chairs—hotel guests only, violators towed.

-Check her out. Good God.

Tall and thin and busty in a flawless blonde sort of way, a fashion model a few years beyond her prime, but still a neck-wrencher in a yellow bikini. She had gotten up from her lounge chair and was walking toward the water. Her husband's smoothness—designer sunglasses, silk shirt unbuttoned halfway down, highlighted hair moussed into place, fifty-plus going on thirty—was obvious at a glance from thirty yards away, the diamond ring on her left hand was visible from the moon. Pete stood up for a better look.

-Oh, crap.

He sat back down.

-What?

-Students.

Two teenaged boys toting skimboards were walking up the beach. Skimboarders are skateboarders without wheels, the little shits. Pete pulled his hat down low, tucked his chin, covered his face with his hand. I pulled my beach towel over my head and shoulders like a shroud.

-You know them?

-Had the tall one in class last year.

Dana Hills students usually don't hang out at Treasure Island—no waves, no parking—but these two were wandering up from Aliso Creek, a quarter mile down the sand.

-We should've gone to Main Beach.

In the classroom, students watch our every move—they know our speech patterns, physical quirks, dress habits—and when you're constantly on display, when your successes are made the stuff of local legend and your shortcomings cruelly mocked, you become jealous of your privacy, you carefully limit familiarity. Away from school, you want to relax, be yourself, escape the scrutiny. If you run into students—at the grocery store, going to the movies, at the beach with your shirt off and your guard down—you have to shift back into teacher mode, professionally concerned but emotionally detached. It's like getting called into work on a weekend. It sucks. We stayed under wraps until the boys disappeared around the bend in the coastline, then Pete stood up.

-Let's get out of here.

-They're gone. Let's eat lunch.

The grocery bag also held sandwiches, hastily assembled in my kitchen, and I hadn't eaten since a quick breakfast after paddling.

-No, let's go sit in the jacuzzi.

-It's too hot out.

-Dude, my shoulder. Hydrotherapy.

We put on our shirts, left our chairs and towels behind, and after a slight detour to get a better look at Mrs. Smooth's smooth assets, walked past the eager towel dispenser—Enjoy the awesome afternoon, gentlemen!—and up the ramp. The city council had insisted the resort grounds remain a public park so locals, if they solve the parking puzzle, can stroll the bluff and take in the ocean view. And if they know how to break the rules, they can visit the hot tub. We had a technique for that too. We stopped twenty feet short of the target, where a fat man was having a warm soak.

-Dude needs a bra.

He wasn't moving, so we continued strolling the sidewalk. We passed a woman in a tailored green and brown uniform. She stepped aside and stood at attention, arms at her side—the servile Montage salute.

-Good afternoon, gentlemen.

We nodded and kept walking. Something about her professional politeness made me uncomfortable.

-Dude, our students should stand like that. Heil, Repetti.

I guess I'd rather she was permitted to be fully human. Then we could encounter each other honestly and spontaneously instead of playing prescribed roles. Which, when I thought about it, was really what I wanted with Roya. Why does it have to be so difficult?—asking for a phone number, arranging a date, taking care to present myself as myself, but not too much of myself, a reserved, non-threatening, idealized sampling of myself.

-He's up.

Fatso was toweling off. We quickened our pace—steady but nonchalant—and timed it perfectly, arriving back at the gate just as he was exiting. Pete and I both went for our pockets.

-You got your key?

-Yeah, somewhere. I think.

Our usual routine, probably unnecessary, probably overkill. The big guy held the gate for us.

-Oh. Thanks. How's the water?

-Fantastic. Enjoy.

We had it to ourselves.

-I'm going naked.

-Yeah, right.

We pulled off our shirts and dropped into the swirling water. Ahh—not as hot as Sigrid's, no titillating symphony of ascending bubbles, but jets powerful enough to propel you off the wall. Would Roya sneak into a hot tub? Will she pick up when I call?

-So, if I get her voicemail, what do I say?

-Dude, you're like a tenth-grader, you know that? Hi, this is phone number, my Fletcher is....

Voicemail always throws me. At the beep, I become self-conscious, I can't think of what to say because I'm thinking about how I'll come across. I don't like my voice on recordings, I sound depressed, and if I compensate and try for pleasantness I end up sounding ridiculous. But getting her voicemail might be best. That way if the answer is no, she can spare us both the embarrassment, avoid the need for excuses, and simply not call back.

-Dude, security guard. Don't look.

-Should we bail?

Our escape plan is to grab resort towels left behind by legitimate guests and walk straight into the hotel like we belong there.

-He's leaving.

-Good. There's no way we look suspicious.

That's what we counted on. Two clean-shaven white guys in their thirties, one partially balding. We could be corporate lawyers. We could be investment bankers.

-Does this look suspicious?

Pete lifted his swim trunks out of the water and draped them over his head.

-Are you crazy? Pete, man, seriously, I'm leaving. You say *I'm* the tenth-grader?

-Okay. Calm down.

His shorts disappeared back under the roil of bubbles and foam. I disappeared back into voicemail. Roya, this is Fletcher, your fellow jurist. Too dorky. Roya, this is Juror Number One. Too cute. Roya, this is Fletcher, from the jury, just wondering if you might at all be interested in going out to dinner with me on some evening. Too wordy. How 'bout dinner some time? Too brisk. How 'bout we skip dinner and start with dessert?

-Gentlemen.

Shit. The security guard—coming through the gate.

-Gentlemen, these facilities are reserved for guests of the Montage. I need to ask you to exit the whirlpool.

My first impulse was to play dumb—oh, sorry, my mistake—and be on my way. Pete had a different impulse.

-You're kidding me. Is this a joke? Is this how guests get treated?

Pete has a philosophy on security guards: their authority is limited and depends on your cooperation, you've got to call their bluff.

-Sir, could I see your room key?

Pete turned to me.

-You got yours, Bill?

-No, I—Sharon has it.

Why did I pick Sharon?

-Yeah, it's with our wives. One of the other guests let us in.

-I understand, sir. If I could just have your room number.

I shrugged. Pete gave it a try.

-Three…three-thirty…I don't know. That's what I'm trying to tell you. The wife keeps track of that. I just sign the receipts. You know how that goes.

Two investment bankers who can't remember their room numbers.

-I apologize for the trouble, sir.

He stepped away and spoke into his radio. I couldn't make out the words that came crackling back, but I knew he wasn't finished with us.

-Let's just go. I'm hungry anyhow.

I climbed out of the water and toweled off, trying to appeared bored by the confrontation, trying to keep my unmarried ring finger out of sight.

-Sir, what's the name on the room?

If the guard wasn't giving up, neither was Pete.

-This is unbelievable. Bill, can you believe this? Listen, I know you're just doing your job, but we stay here because it's private and quiet. Otherwise we'd be over at the Ritz.

The Ritz is in Dana Point. Nice jacuzzi there, too.

-No one's ever hassled me here before, everyone's very accommodating, maybe you didn't get that memo, but what exactly do you want us to do, paste the room key to our forehead? This is totally unacceptable.

Pete had worked himself into a fit of agitation, he slapped the water angrily as he climbed out. The guard remained calm and polite.

-Sir, I apologize. If you tell me your name, we can clear up any misunderstanding.

Resort towel in hand, Pete took an aggressive step toward him.

-I'm not giving you my name. I'll go up to the front desk and take care of this myself. I tell you what, why don't you go on about your business, and I'll tell your boss you were very respectful, very discreet and understanding, and I have no complaint about you personally.

It was a convincing show—the Type A corporate lawyer, accustomed to bullying people and getting his way, insulted by the wage worker's insolence, but magnanimously cutting him some slack. The guard studied Pete for a moment, weighing alternatives, but only for a moment.

-Why don't you cut the bullshit and remove yourself from the resort premises, and I won't call in Laguna PD and have you arrested for criminal trespassing.

Pete pulled on his t-shirt.

-Fine. I don't have time for this.

When you're beat, you're beat. Time to get out of Dodge. To his credit, the guard didn't rub our noses in it. He spoke again on his radio, then held the gate open for us.

-Leave the towels here, please.

-What, no salute?

We headed for the beach—steady but nonchalant. Okay, maybe a little chalant. Another security guard was hustling up the sidewalk. He extended his arms wide to block our path.

-Gentlemen, excuse me. Gentlemen.

We stepped around him and kept moving—they rely on your cooperation. I didn't look back until we were halfway down the ramp.

-They're still behind us.

-What can they do? Beach is public.

-What if they called the cops? We should have left right away.

-Dude, I had him going until you jumped out. You flinched.

-No, he knew from the beginning. Probably saw us earlier coming in from the parking lot. I bet they called the cops. And you know how the cops handle things here.

One time the Laguna police were summoned and ended up killing two Montage guests. True story.

-Are they still coming?

-No.

-Okay, then. We're golden.

The guards remained at the top of the ramp. The towel dispenser greeted us at the bottom.

-Good afternoon, gentlemen!

-Could we get a couple towels?

Pete doesn't know when to quit.

-Absolutely, sir. Room two-nineteen, right?

-Yeah, that's right.

-Cool. I remember you from yesterday.

I checked the ramp. They were still up there. The beach attendant handed Pete two towels.

-It's Mr. Haroldson, right?

-Excellent memory. What's your name?

-I'm Dave. You guys need lounge chairs, or are you good?

I interrupted.

-We're good. Thanks, Dave.

-Right on. Enjoy the beach.

-No, dude, let's get lounge chairs.

I should have put my foot down, ended the charade right there, but Pete directed my attention to two unoccupied lounge chairs next to Mr. and Mrs.

Smooth, and soon we were sunbathing in cushioned comfort. Mr. Smooth was fiddling with his phone. The missus was lying face down, her bikini top unattached, a hint of soft white breast squeezing out from under her torso. Leering without Mr. Smooth noticing wouldn't be easy. Not leering wasn't an option.

-That guard was about to fold. If you hadn't shown weakness.

-You watch too much poker.

That's Pete's favorite tv entertainment anymore—sallow-skinned, narcissistic game theorists playing high-stakes tournaments and mugging for the camera when they ought to be lecturing on nuclear deterrence or mapping genomes or otherwise serving the common good.

-It's all about psychology. He didn't want to go all-in—I picked that up right away. I think I'm a natural.

-Yeah, a poker genius. Here they come.

The guards were descending the ramp.

-Relax, dude. We're legit.

Maybe Pete's prefrontal cortex was impaired, but mine was on full alert, warning me to get out now.

-I need a swim. Let's go for a swim.

We could casually walk away, dignity intact, dive into the waves and splash around until the Keystone Kops went back up the hill.

-No, sit tight. Don't flinch.

I watched them trudge across the heavy sand. They looked serious. They looked pissed. They didn't even glance at Mrs. Smooth, didn't do a double take at her yellow bikini. These guys were professionals. Pete fired a preemptive shot.

-Don't tell me you guys came all this way to apologize.

-Sir, these are not public chairs.

-Unbelievable. What's it going to take? Are you going to crawl in bed with me tonight too?

-Sir, we do press charges.

-Room two-nineteen. It's under Harrison. Call it in. Or go ask Dave.

-Who?

-The towel guy. He knows me.

I'd swear Guard Number One showed weakness. He looked over at Dave, he looked at his partner, he looked indecisive. Pete showed strength.

-Call it in.

-I'll do that.

Guard Number One stepped away so we couldn't hear his radio conversation. Guard Number Two remained in place, hiding behind a blank-faced stare, arms folded smugly across his chest. Did the towel guy say Harrison or Haroldson? My stomach growled. Thirty yards away, a roast-beef sandwich was calling my name. Should I retrieve it? A white seagull was cautiously pecking at the peanut shells we'd left behind.

-Gentlemen, I'll give you one last chance to leave quietly.

Number One was back. Pete sat up.

-Did you call it in?

-You're not registered.

-Unbelievable. Go ask Dave.

-I don't need to ask Dave. I need you to get out of the chair.

-Or what?

Again, the guards looked indecisive. They weren't the pitiful, waddling beer bellies in windbreakers you see patrolling time shares and golf courses, but neither were they bouncers—not physically imposing, not looking for a fight. And the cops weren't on their way, at least not yet, or Number One would have said so. Pete was right—they weren't going all-in.

My attention was drawn to Mrs. Smooth as she reached both hands behind her back to tie her bikini top. Then she rolled over, glanced at the security guards, and asked her husband what the fuss was about.

-Don't know, but some idiot's losing his lunch.

Mr. Smooth pointed to our empty folding chairs where two seagulls were now playing tug-of-war with my plastic grocery bag. Three more gulls swooped in, squawking with delight. If I dashed madly into the birds, shouting and waving, I'd look like a total dork, the kind of guy who parks behind the shopping center and sneaks into the hotel jacuzzi, not a well-heeled investment banker staying at the Montage, but so what? At this point I'd rather save my sandwiches than salvage my pride. Only I couldn't do that without abandoning Pete.

-Gentlemen, this is your final warning.

Pete stood up. Was he finally walking away? Nope.

-Dave! Hey, Dave!

He'd found another card to play. As we all watched, the white-shirted attendant came slogging across the sand. I liked that he snuck a peak at Mrs. Smooth—he was one of us.

-Is there a problem, Mr. Haroldson? The chairs okay?

I knew it—Pete had screwed up. Guard Number One knew it too.

-Haroldson? You said you were Harrison.

The house had drawn an ace. Read 'em and weep. But Pete didn't hesitate.

-Get your hearing checked, man. Unbelievable. Dave, can we get food brought down here?

-Absolutely, Mr. Haroldson. Beach service. I'll go score you a menu.

Dave headed back to his post. Number One and Number Two looked at each other—what if we're wrong, what if the guy we're harassing really is a paying guest, and what if he complains? They didn't know their next move.

-Well, call it in, guys. Haroldson. Get it right this time.

They didn't call it in. They huddled a few yards away and tried to appear satisfied with the outcome. They were going to withdraw by increments.

Meanwhile, the squawking was getting louder. More seagulls had arrived and were tussling over the loot, trying to get their yellow beaks around scraps of bread and shreds of beef. Our lunch was being slaughtered.

Mr. Smooth caught my eye and nodded toward the guards.

-You guys bring in call girls or something?

-Just a misunderstanding.

-Yeah, I tell my wife the same thing.

His wife laughed. What does a woman who looks that good see in a man who sounds that stupid?

-What line are you guys in?

Well, we're high school teachers but we stay at the Montage because you only live once and anyhow we've got money to burn he inherited a bundle when his parents died and I if you must know just won the lottery would you believe it one in a million.

-We're in education.

-Excellent. I hear that's really an expanding industry. Testing and whatnot.

-We do okay.

Pete aka Mr. Haroldson joined the conversation.

- Hey, we're ordering some food. You folks want anything?

Mrs. Smooth smiled.

-We just had lunch, but sweet of you to offer.

I thought Roya was pretty and charming, but this woman could sink a thousand ships, or however the saying goes. If she had said she'd love a dolphin sandwich, I would have happily swum out and hauled one in. It must be nice being that attractive. For one thing, you wouldn't have to agonize over asking someone out, you wouldn't have to agonize over anything, you could get whatever you wanted with just a smile, the universe would always say yes. So why would she shack up with Mr. Smooth when she could have someone real, someone—how had Pete put it?—with too much integrity to be smooth, someone like, say, yours truly?

-Hey, Repetti! Mr. Repetti!

The skimboarders! The little shits had recognized their favorite biology teacher and were coming over to say hi.

-What's up, Repetti? How'd you get a chair?

I shot a guilty glance at the security detail. Yes, I showed weakness, I admit it. Number One went for his radio. Number Two started moving in. I showed weakness and then I flinched: I stood up and walked away. I could hear Pete feigning enthusiasm at running into students.

-Great to see you guys. Beautiful day, huh?

The seagulls saw me coming and retreated to a safe distance. I quickly folded our chairs and began gathering up shredded sandwich wrappers. Peanuts were everywhere.

-Dude, leave it.

Pete was right behind me. Somehow, he'd already shed the students and ditched the guards.

-What'd they say?

-The Haroldsons checked out this morning.

He grabbed the chairs, I took our towels, we left the rest for the birds.

-Let's go to Aliso.

We didn't look back. It was going to be a long walk—fleeing down the beach, then back along PCH to the shopping center, but at least we wouldn't have to pass Mr. and Mrs. Smooth or look Dave in the eye—sorry, man, no tip—and we wouldn't have to endure being escorted up the ramp and across the resort property by two triumphant rent-a-cops. And this way Pete could still claim victory.

-I had him. He mucked his cards. Did you see his face when I asked about beach service? Those kids were just a bad beat.

-You should buy me lunch.

-I should go to Vegas.

I expected the cops to be waiting for us in the Aliso parking lot or to catch up to us when we crossed PCH, but they never showed. When we got back to my car, I checked my phone: Something's come up. Tomorrow night instead? What could possibly come up? She never works late. When she wants to come over, she comes over—which is almost never these days. Marissa was so gung-ho about me saving Bud Jack, and now this? I mean, seriously, what the fuck?

-Just call her and ask.

-She's still at work.

-No, the jury chick.

Yeah, maybe Roya's free tonight. We could hang out and talk about the trial, laugh about the Moderates and the rest of the menagerie—The Mouse, Elephant, Giraffe and a Half. But what if Roya says yes, and then Marissa calls and wants to come over after all?

-Dude, if you're not gonna call her, give me her number and I will. I'm not afraid of rejection. It's like my middle name.

I got her voicemail, the usual formula—Hi, this is Roya, I'm away from my phone—only in a soft, enchanting voice. I got flustered.

-Yeah, hi, Roya, this is, uh, this is Fletcher, from the jury. Just wondering...I just...I wanted to say hi.

-Dude.

-Yeah, and maybe we could go out sometime, like dinner.

There. I'd done it—called and asked her out, put my money where my mouth is, the ball's in her court. Way to go, Fletcher!

-At least you weren't smooth.

Pete suggested we go straight to the Ritz for more hydrotherapy—fall off a horse, saddle right back up—but I'd had enough criminal trespassing for one day, and I wanted to get back across Laguna before the late afternoon traffic disaster set in. I dropped him at The Cave and drove home. I called Marissa and left a message saying I was sorry she couldn't make it tonight and asking her to call me, we still needed to set a time for tomorrow night, right? I ate, took a shower, tried napping, but couldn't stop thinking about Roya. Had she listened to my message yet? Would she call back this evening or wait until tomorrow? Like me, she probably didn't want to appear too eager. By six p.m., no one had called, not Roya, not Marissa. If I sat around all evening waiting for the phone to ring, the anxiety would kill me, so I turned the ringer to vibrate, put the phone in my pocket, and walked down to Heisler Park.

The tide was low, the sun was setting, it was the magic hour before twilight when the hazy golden glow draws portrait photographers and their clients to the beach. I walked past a family of five dressed identically in unfaded blue jeans and unwrinkled white blouses, neatly casual in bare feet and Sunday hair, grouped on the sand and smiling for the camera, the usual south county portrait of idealized harmony—we dress the same, we think the same, no problems here, all happy families are alike. Except if they're anything like the families my students tell me about, dad has a bad temper and yells a lot, mom starts the day with gin and ends it with sleeping pills, the fourteen-year-old son spends the day locked in his bedroom playing violent video games, and his two younger sisters will experiment with pot before they even hit their teens and quickly graduate to Vicodin and Ecstasy. Or maybe I'm just being cynical.

A little farther down the beach, I passed an angelic young woman in a wedding dress and her husband-to-be, handsome in black tuxedo, posing at the water's edge. What did he have that I didn't? I mean, besides a woman who loved him. Was he smarter than me or more caring? Did he seem more stable, an obvious family man? The photographer directed them to hold hands as they walked, happily ever after, into the sunset. Tomorrow would be Friday, there would probably be a rehearsal dinner, and late Saturday morning they would become man and wife. What's that like?—knowing from now on someone will be there for you, someone you can count on, someone to plan things with, the house won't be empty when you get home from work.

The vibration from the phone in my pocket startled me, like a mild electric shock. Probably it was Marissa, but be Roya, please be Roya. It was Pete. I didn't feel like talking to him, I didn't want to have to tell him she hadn't called yet, didn't want to hide the disappointment in my voice. I put the buzzing phone back in my pocket and continued walking down the beach, away from the sunset.

13

I'm not very good at parties, especially in a roomful of strangers. I walk in intending to be fun, spontaneous, a hail-fellow-well-met, but as soon as I see all the unfamiliar faces, I become self-conscious, like when I'm leaving a message at the beep, only now it's in person, in a group, with nowhere to hide. I'm not sure what to say, or where to stand, how to stand even, and what do I do with these hands? Ultimately, the issue is small talk. I don't do it well. When I chat with someone—oh, I teach math, what about you?—I quickly run out of things to say and don't know how to make a graceful exit. I stare straight ahead, avoid eye contact, pretend I'm content just taking in the scene—great party, huh?—until the person gets bored or embarrassed and wanders off. Alcohol helps. Not for the intoxication, though, not for letting go of inhibitions. Having a drink gives my hands something to do, gives me an action, an excuse, a raison d'être. What am I doing standing here in the corner not talking to anyone?—oh, I'm enjoying my beer, reveling in this wonderful glass of wine, this here's the best margarita I've ever tasted I love the greenish color I could gaze into it all evening. My other survival strategy, besides working a drink, is to latch onto more skilled conversationalists and use their momentum, draft behind them as they mingle. I'll nod and smile and ask a question now and then, trying to appear relaxed and engaged, hoping we run into someone I can relate to, someone I can talk to on my own, before my guide slips away and I'm left staring into space and wishing I was back home watching tv.

Which I suppose is what Marissa did—got tired of me hanging over her shoulder, listening in on her tête-à-têtes, and ducked off on her own. I studied my glass of wine—a rich, dark red with the promise of black cherry and hints of tobacco, that's what I'd read on the label anyway—then went outside where the host was manning a smoking barbecue grill. Maybe I could latch onto him for a while.

-Fletcher. Glad you could make it. Last minute, I know, but we decided we had to celebrate. Her idea, actually. How do you like yours done? Medium, I hope. Don't tell me you're one of those bloody beef guys.

I had woken up thinking about Roya—wonder what time she gets out of bed, would she call in morning? Probably not. I took the phone into the bathroom anyhow, just in case it rang while I was in showering. It didn't. Maybe she'd call on her lunch break at the dentist's office, so I packed my phone with me while grocery shopping. Nothing. Until I was toting groceries into my apartment, and then I heard the familiar trilling. Is it possible? I dropped the bags onto the sidewalk, dove back into the car, and grabbed the phone off the passenger seat. Be Roya, please be Roya. It was Marissa.

-Fletcher, sorry about yesterday, something came up.

His paintbrush, I hope, and nothing else.

-Fletcher, are you there?

-Yeah.

She doesn't feel obligated to tell me why she backed out last night, doesn't even care enough to make up an excuse. Just drop me, Marissa, get it over with.

-Are you free tonight?

-Yes.

When am I not?

-Good. We have plans.

We have plans! Marissa wants to do something with me. And the trial is over, the verdict is in, so this can't be about trying to influence my vote.

-Fletcher?

-Sorry. I couldn't hear you. My phone.

-We've been invited to a party.

But what if Roya calls? What if she's free tonight?

-Fletcher? Is something wrong?

-No. Sounds great.

I can always fake food poisoning again, or use Marissa's technique— sorry, something came up—and race off to Costa Mesa for a discreet dinner with the pretty Persian. Why hasn't she called? It's been almost twenty-four hours since I left her a message. Probably she was back at work today, probably she already has a date, it's Friday night after all, probably she's going out with friends, or her boyfriend if she has one, but why would she give me her number if she has a boyfriend? Maybe I should try calling her again.

-Don't you want to know who's having the party? I'll give you a hint— they've seen all of you.

-What?

-Naked.

Which is how I ended up back in Sigrid's backyard—third time in nine days—watching Richard attempt to incinerate the steaks. The fire was so hot, the grill sizzled like a frying pan.

-How long have you been doing this?

-Why? Am I doing something wrong?

A dark look flashed across his face—narrow eyes, tight mouth. I'd swear he was about to assault me with his barbecue tongs.

-No, I mean your organization. Public Defense, right? Sigrid said—

-Whoa!

He jumped backwards as the grill flared up, to the obvious delight of one of the other guests.

-Jesus, Richard, should we call the fire department?

-Sammy! Whata you say?

Sammy was dressed for the yacht club—leather deck shoes, white pants, white sweater draped over his shoulders, sporty sunglasses pushed back atop his head, and still not a hair out of place. Who wears sunglasses to a dinner party? I could hear Pete: Dude, some people just need a punch in the face.

-Sammy, this is Fletcher.

Sammy had a sun-burnt face, pale blue eyes, and an aggressive handshake.

-A pleasure, Fletcher. Hey, Richard, heard you had a pervert back here. That's Laguna for you. Queer City. When are you and Sigrid gonna move up to Newport?

He winked at me as he slapped Richard on the shoulder. Pete's right—a good, solid jab to the schnozz.

-Sammy, that reminds me. Here, Fletcher, keep an eye on these bad boys, will ya? Don't let 'em burn.

Richard handed me the tongs, then guided Sammy out onto the lawn for a private conversation. Was he showing him the tree with the broken branch, maybe pointing out the spot where they'd found a discarded beer bottle? Or were they discussing Richard's hot new idea for reality tv?—*Desperate Chefs of Orange County*. I lifted the lid and flames shot up around a dozen slabs of sizzling beef. Are they done? How does one know? A few more people, drinks in hand, wandered onto the patio and admired the feng shui waterfall. Not wanting to appear awkward or strange, standing alone while everyone else huddled, I opted for busy. I turned down the gas to reduce the flames, then started flipping the steaks and rearranging them on the grill, randomly, this one here, that one there, move this one over two—twelve-steak monte. I didn't notice Sigrid until she was right next to me.

-Look at you, Fletcher. The grillmaster.

-No, I—

-Can you make room for these breasts?

I wasn't quick enough to catch myself—my eyes went straight to her insistent cleavage. Actually, I think I stared. I think my jaw dropped. I think the neighbor's dog barked—woof, woof, pervert alert!

-No, these.

She was carrying a platter of chicken. When I took it from her, she kissed me on the cheek.

-Sweet of you to help.

-I…I don't really know how to do this.

I could feel my face turning red.

-Just keep your fire hot.

Here we go again: the double entendre, the ambiguous innuendo spoken for my ears only, throwing me off balance and leaving me dizzy. I watched her go back inside. She has to know what she's saying, has to know what those disproportionates can do. But is it 1a) playful dalliance, or does she 1b) want my meat?

-Hey, Cal, Greg, we need you guys. You too, Rob. We need one more.

Richard was setting up some kind of lawn bowling and summoning participants. I like playing games at parties, it gives you something to do, something to talk about, a reason to interact, but Richard wasn't calling me over, and if I abandoned the grill, dinner gets ruined. I watched with a slight sense of jealousy. Richard was dressed head to toe in black, Hollywood standard, and his friends about the same. In their slacks and long sleeves, strutting about on the grass, they looked like an ad for designer menswear. Standing at the grill in jeans and sneakers, what did I look like? A beer commercial. Only I was the one gazing into the distance, and the fashion models were the ones laughing, slapping hands, enjoying the high life. The guys were communing—the male sports bond—and I was stuck holding the baby. Fine. If Richard wants to play with the boys, I'll work on his wife— who, I reminded myself, had greeted me with an enthusiastic hug when Marissa and I first arrived at the party.

-Fletcher, I'm so proud of you. We all are. This was like the first win for Public Defense since we came on board.

An enthusiastic hug and a quick explanation: it's a nonprofit organization for helping poor defendants.

-I mean, innocent people go to prison all the time because they can't afford a lawyer. Or they get twenty years, thirty years, for stealing a bicycle or smoking a little pot. I told Richard, write a check, save some lives.

And when Sigrid wants something—a painting, a party, disproportionates—Richard provides. Though, at the moment, I was the one meeting her needs. I added her chicken to the fiery grill and tried to come up with a good line for when she returned. Sigrid, this meat's ready, where should I put it? Sigrid, anything else I can warm up for you? Sigrid, should I rub more sauce on those breasts?

-Guillam.

At first it didn't quite register. Did I hear right? Is there another Guillam here?

-Guillam Fletcher, isn't it?

A big hand extended. A round, pink face.

-Russell Lawson.

Attorney for the defense.

-Hey, I know you.

-Nice to finally meet you, Guillam. I didn't expect to see a juror here.

-They needed someone to convict these steaks.

A pathetic attempt at a joke. I was thinking gas grill, death sentence, never mind. Lawson was polite enough to pretend he hadn't heard.

-You disappeared so fast the other day. Didn't get a chance to ask what you thought.

-Not guilty, all the way.

He grinned.

-Thank goodness. I was nervous. Honestly, I thought I could lose this one.

-It was contentious in there, believe me.

-I heard. The jurors I spoke to said it was you who convinced them. So I'm curious, what convinced you?

-Pretty simple. My girlfriend threatened to dump me.

He chuckled, then noticed I was keeping a straight face.

-Really?

-No. She's not my girlfriend. Not full on.

-Oh. Okay.

He turned away from me, probably looking for a way to escape. I'm such a dork.

-No, I thought the prosecution didn't make its case, like you said at the end. The gang stuff was weak. You took that guy apart—the expert. That was good.

-Yeah?

-And it seemed like the police pressured that Ruiz guy, telling him Bud Jack was dangerous. I thought you'd emphasize that more.

-Well, see, I couldn't prove the police misled him, and Judge Silverson can be hostile to that degree of speculation. I could only imply it and hope you guys caught on.

Turns out, Lawson was neither brilliantly incompetent or incompetently brilliant, just a decent lawyer who, with a little luck, with the right jurors, found a way to win his case.

-And what about the timeline error? You never even mentioned that.

-Timeline error?

I recounted the confusion over the police lineup and the supposed confession. Turns out, Lawson hadn't noticed the discrepancy over which came first. Turns out, only Guillam Fletcher, paddling with half-sleeping dolphins at sunrise, had seen the light. Lawson thought about it for a second.

-That's fantastic. You're absolutely right, Guillam. Can't believe I missed it.

Like I said, I should have been a lawyer.

More people were showing up on the patio, people I'd never met, people who wouldn't be overly interested in meeting a high school teacher, I could tell just by looking. But engaged in serious, sober conversation with Lawson, I felt confident and important, like how I felt when The Sophist shook my hand outside the courthouse. I felt adult. And besides, the hostess had the hots for me—that's a pretty good raison d'être. I set down the tongs and folded my arms across my chest.

-I wanted to ask you, why did you keep me for the jury? I mean, after I said I thought he was guilty.

-You said that?

-You don't remember? During jury selection.

-Jurors say lots of things. I don't worry about that too much.

-Oh, I thought you would, like, profile the jurors. I read—

-Yeah, that's big money trials, not little stuff like this.

Sigrid emerged from the house and headed toward me, a smile on her face. I smiled back.

-Russ, sweetheart, when did you sneak in here?

Sigrid didn't kiss Lawson on the cheek and make a suggestive comment. No, Lawson got a kiss on the mouth and a straightforward invitation to help the hostess mix the salads in the kitchen. Which he accepted.

-I guess I'm needed elsewhere, Guillam. Sigrid's the salad queen. And her chicken is legendary. We'll talk more later.

That settles it: Lawson was here that night, it was his Lexus in the driveway, his large frame in the front doorway, case closed, jury dismissed. The mystery was pretty much solved. Sigrid tells Richard to support Public Defense, Public Defense hires Lawson to defend Bud Jack, and Juror Number One just happens to be involved, sort of, with Sigrid's masseuse. A huge coincidence, yes, one in a million, but not a conspiracy. Lawson knows Richard and Sigrid, and stops by their house the same night Juror Number One and his irresponsible friend sneak into their backyard. A twist, a surprise perhaps, not exactly bestselling suspense. No death threats, no bribes, no suffering and redemption. This was no Grisham.

-Aren't those steaks ready yet?

Richard was back, and with his usual charm.

-Here, I better take over. See, these look too done. Damn it. This is expensive beef.

I didn't apologize, I didn't say anything, I hadn't volunteered to cook.

-Hey, don't worry about it, Fletcher. Way I hear, we wouldn't be having this little fiesta without you. You turned the jury, right?

-I wanted to ask you about that. About Public Defense. How did you guys choose this particular case?

-Good question. I'm not involved in day-to-day. They stuck me on the board because I give a little money. Cal over there—he's the guy to talk to. It's his deal. Do me a favor, will ya? Go ask Sigrid for another platter. We gotta put these steaks somewhere. And pour yourself more wine. Don't be shy now.

No Grisham, indeed. More like a gossipy television series. And now, in the not quite breathtaking ending, we all end up in the backyard together for a victory party, everyone but the irresponsible friend. I should call him. I had told him where I was going, and he'd insisted on an update if there was any breaking news. Yo, Pete, I'm with Sigrid in the kitchen, and her husband's outside with his meat getting cold.

Actually, Sigrid wasn't in the kitchen. Neither was Lawson. The salads had been a pretext. They weren't in the sitting room, either, where Marissa was talking and laughing with two women I didn't recognize. Marissa smiled at me, but didn't invite me over. No need to introduce ol' Fletch, he won't be around much longer anyway. I checked the entryway, where a new bouquet of cut flowers graced the antique table. Had the Wilhites noticed the hardcover Grisham was missing? How could they not? The doorbell rang. After a moment, after nobody came rushing to answer it, I opened the front door.

-Hi, I'm Jay.

He looked old enough for Richard's crowd, but no designer labels, just jeans and flip-flops and shoulder-length blonde hair going to gray. Could be a guest, could be swimming pool maintenance.

-Hi, Jay. Come on in.

He shook my hand and held out a bottle of wine.

-I brought this. Are you Sigrid's husband?

-No. Her lover.

It just came out.

-Oh.

He wasn't sure if he should laugh or not. I didn't intend to make him uncomfortable, I liked how he wasn't so pretentious, but for some reason I didn't tell him I was joking. Instead, I directed him toward the sitting room.

-Everyone's back that way.

-Thanks. Nice meeting you, uh….

-Yeah, likewise.

Why didn't I tell him my name? Why am I always such a dork? Do I really look old enough to be Sigrid's husband? I walked down a hallway and met a woman emerging from a bathroom.

-Hi. Have you seen Sigrid?

-She's not in the kitchen?

As she eased by me, I noticed the south county look: a little too blonde, a little too thin, and the skin on her jaw a little too tight.

-Wait, forgive me, I'm Fletcher.

That's better. More charm, less dork.

-You're the caterer, right? Those steaks smell great.

She hurried away. Yeah, I'm the caterer, and you must be Sigrid's mother, nice facelift.

I was standing in front of a staircase. Sigrid and Lawson were somewhere upstairs—where else could they be? I guess my prefrontal cortex was still functioning at that point, because I didn't go up. Instead, I returned to the sitting room just in time to watch Marissa squeal with delight and throw her arms wide for a big hug. Physiological certainty: Mr. Flip-Flops paints seascapes. She was kissing him when she caught my eye, kissing him on the mouth.

-Fletcher, come meet my friend Jay. He's the artist I told you about.

Bingo.

-We've already met, actually.

-You're Fletcher? I've heard a lot about you. Dana Hills High, right?

-Yeah.

I turned to check the expression on Marissa's face. She had already slipped back to the safety of the two women, pretending it was no big deal—her sort of boyfriend meets her sort of guy-friend.

-That's got to be challenging. But rewarding too, I bet. What do you have, algebra? Geometry?

-Algebra mostly.

-Gotta love it. How's your summer vacation?

-I just finished up some jury duty.

-That's right. I heard about that.

-Are you involved in Public Defense?

-No. What's that?

-It's not important. So…did you see the sunset last night?

I was hoping he would clue me in—yeah, I was walking on the beach last night, with Marissa actually, or, no, I had an art opening, Marissa was there—but he didn't oblige.

-I bet it was awesome. We have great sunsets here. This is a great place to live.

-Jay, I'm glad you made it.

The hostess had descended.

-Sigrid, you look terrific.

Another kiss on the mouth. Everyone but me. I interrupted their mash-up.

-Sigrid, Richard asked me to ask you for another platter. I looked in the kitchen.

-Below the microwave. Thanks, sweetheart.

Jay noticed the painting of Seal Rock.

-Sigrid, that's the piece you were telling me about. Terrell Hirst.

She took him by the arm.

-Isn't it amazing? Come on, I'll show you around.

She takes Lawson upstairs, she offers Jay a tour of the house, and all I get is a quick peck on the cheek. Maybe she's only 1a with me after all. Hell, what do I care anyway? An older woman with a fake body—she's all yours, Flip-Flops, just leave me Marissa.

I delivered the platter to Richard. At least it gave me something to do.

-Thanks, Fletcher. Thought I'd lost you. Say, how 'bout Sam—what kind of car does he drive?

-Sorry?

-Hey, Sammy, come here a sec.

Sammy had his sunglasses over his eyes now. The sweater was still neatly in place. He held a glass of wine in one hand and a lawn bowling ball in the other.

-Are you ready, Richard? Championship of the free world.

-Fletcher here can look at you and guess your car.

-No, I can't. That was—

-Like a bar bet kinda thing?

-No, we're gonna turn it into a show. Go ahead, Fletcher.

I didn't know what to say. Sammy laughed loudly.

-Scintillating television, Richard. You've been in Laguna too long.

-Just give him a moment. Come on, Fletch, you're the man.

-*Think of something. Hurry.*

-*Tell him he drives an assholemobile, with extra head room.*

-*What about the car in the driveway?*

-A Mercedes convertible. Two-seater.

It just came out—to my immediate regret. I didn't want to be part of this. Sammy pointed an accusatory finger at Richard.

-You told him.

Richard whooped triumphantly and raised his right hand.

-Swear to God.

-Well, he saw me drive up or something.

-The man's got skills, Sammy. He guessed my Lexus first time we met.

Sammy winked at me again.

-That's pretty obvious, Richard. You're a Lexus kind of guy. Which is why you're about to lose the championship. On your home court too.

-Hundred bucks.

-It's a bet. You hear that, guys?

Sammy headed back to the lawn.

-Is he involved in Public Defense?

-Sammy? Are you kidding? I just invite him to take his money.

-Will Bud Jack be here?

-Who?

-The defendant.

-Oh, right. Bud Jack. I doubt it.

That would be something, though, meeting the defendant. What would I ask him? First thing would be what he was doing on the street that night in Huntington. No, that would be nosy. I'd ask how his grandmother is doing, and how's the car-washing, you must have lost some business when they had you locked up. Maybe I would buy him lunch, get to know him, Marissa would like that. I wonder who she's kissing now.

I went back inside, to the sitting room, where Sigrid was holding court.

-We've talked about putting in native vegetation for drought resistance, but you need a lawn for garden parties, you really do.

Marissa was on the couch next to Jay. No kissing, though—they were too busy seconding whatever Sigrid was saying.

-Absolutely.

Jay absolutely agreed about the lawn. Sigrid held up her wine glass.

-Isn't this white fantastic? It's so summery, like sitting on the boat at sunset.

-I totally get that.

Marissa totally gets that—she spends so much time on the boat at sunset.

There was a little room on the couch next to her, opposite Jay, so I squeezed in. She held out her glass, offering me a sip of nautical twilight.

-No, thanks. Someone has to get you into the backseat.

She laughed and stuck an elbow into my ribs.

-Yeah, you'd like to get me in the backseat.

-I'd like to get you anywhere.

Marissa put her arm around me and kissed me on the neck. Are you catching this, Flip-Flops?

Sigrid was becoming more animated.

-I had wildflowers, but the gardeners thought they were weeds. And the maid—don't get me started on the maid. But they need the work, don't they?

-Absolutely.

Sounds like a yes.

-And try making a living in a foreign country, a foreign language, that can't be easy.

-It's not. I lived in Provence.

-I love Provence. Isn't the light amazing?

If Jay had lived in Provence, and Sigrid loved Provence, what about Marissa?

-I've heard it's wonderful. I really need to go soon.

I noticed Lawson standing alone, checking out Sigrid's art collection. When he got to the big-breasted mermaid painting, I uncoupled from Marissa and joined him.

-Nice fins, huh?

-Guillam. I was just remembering I saw a manatee one time. Down in Belize.

Strange, but I didn't mind him calling me Guillam.

-A manatee?

-They're supposedly where the idea for mermaids came from.

-I wanted to ask you—how did Public Defense choose this case?

-Oh. I don't know the process. I guess if they think the guy's truly innocent. And in danger of conviction.

-What's Bud Jack like?

He hesitated.

-What's he like?

-Yeah. He seemed so—what's the word?—stoic.

-He was on trial for murder.

-No, I know. I'm sure I'd be stoic too. But what's he like outside the courtroom?

-I only met with him at the jail. But he's alright. If I remember correctly, *manatí* is an old Caribbean word for breast.

He was trying to change the subject.

-I'd like to meet him.

-Bud Jack?

-Yeah. Is that allowed? I mean for a juror.

-I guess. If the trial's over.

-Could you help me, I don't know, contact him? You could tell him I'm the one who helped acquit him.

-My guess is he'd like to forget the whole thing.

-Can't hurt to ask, right?

-I'd have to think about it.

Sounds like a no.

-What about Judge Silverson? I bet she's a wild woman.

He laughed.

-You want to meet her too?

Richard entered through the sliding door and announced dinner was ready on the patio. Lawson and I joined the general exodus from the sitting room, but when no one was paying attention, I headed back through the house and out the front door. My car was parked on the street a few houses down, my phone was in the cup holder. No messages, no missed calls. But I didn't really expect any. She'll call tomorrow, Saturday, she'll have more time then.

I sat in the driver's seat, leaned my head back, closed my eyes. It was good to be away from those people. I was tempted to leave, just turn the key and drive away, but I still had work to do. And just then Sigrid and Lawson emerged from the side gate where I'd run into her that first night. She turned to face him. Hello! They kissed hungrily, the big lawyer pushing the hostess with the mostest against the garage door. Mixing salads—that must make you salacious. They stopped abruptly and hurried back to the party. The moment they disappeared behind the gate, like on cue, the front door opened, and, sure enough, Jay and Marissa walked out to the driveway. I slumped down so they wouldn't spot me. I wanted to run up and interrupt them before things went too far, but I knew I needed to see it happen, needed to finally face the undeniable truth. They looked around cautiously, then, as I watched in equal parts belief and disbelief, performed their own passionate two-step. Well, there it is. Absolutely. Totally. Should I honk the horn? Drive past and wave goodbye? With one finger? They gazed into each other's eyes, then Jay went back inside while Marissa waited a few minutes on the driveway, fixing her ruffled hair. Should I confront her now? A noise startled her, and she turned to see the gate swing open. Are you kidding me? Sigrid and Marissa looked at each other—who had caught whom?—then suddenly they were grappling like love-struck grizzlies. Even to my distant eyes, their mutual lust made the previous exhibitions look like, well, a peck on the cheek. Hands were everywhere, grabbing at hips, running through hair, clawing at *manatís*. I noticed myself getting aroused. Only when they slammed onto the hood of Sammy's bright red convertible did they unclench. One more gymnastic kiss, then they retreated, Sigrid through the gate, Marissa via the front door.

Okay, enough. I opened my eyes. Time to end this farce before Richard and Sammy show up—I don't want those two lovebirds taking flight in my overwrought imagination. But seriously, what would I do if I caught Marissa and Jay hot and heavy? I guess wish them all the best and bow out gracefully. Let her go, and then get on with my life. After getting Pete to help me slash some tires.

I dialed his number and got his voicemail.

-Pete, I'm outside the party. Operation Hardcover—ground zero. I'm going back in to deliver the package. I'll call you later with a full report.

I reached down and pulled the stolen book out from under my car seat. With the house empty, returning the Grisham was easy. I slipped it into a bookshelf, between Hemingway and Updike. I'd read them both in college and retained nothing, but still I had to laugh: Grisham loitering in the literary district.

Then I stood at the sliding door, watching the festivities on the patio, listening to the muted murmur of conversations punctuated by laughter. The sun was setting over the neighbor's rooftop, illuminating the backyard. Long shadows from trees brindled the golden glow. Everyone looked vividly alive. Richard and Sammy were happily arguing about something, Lawson had a plate piled with food balanced in one hand, a big glass of red wine in the other, as he chatted with Cal or Rob or whoever it was, long-haired Jay posed for a photograph near the bubbling waterfall, his arms around two bubbling women, and moving through the midst of them all, reveling in her congregation, the amazing Sigrid, her blonde hair a sunlit halo, queen of salads and all she surveyed. And trailing in her royal wake, Marissa—the way the dying sun revealed the reddish hue of her hair and softened her face, I'd never seen her so beautiful. Or maybe I was a little bit buzzed from the wine. Either way, I was in no hurry to join them. From the safety of the house I could simply observe and not have to worry about where I fit in. Because I didn't fit in. I realized that as I watched Lawson set down his wine glass and confidently shake hands with Sammy, as I saw Sigrid slip her arm around Richard and smile at something Sammy said. These were not my people. It was fascinating, though, like seeing animals in the wild, like paddling up near a mass of boisterous sea lions shifting about on an island of rock. They tolerate your presence, just don't get too close, don't stay too long. These were not Marissa's people either, not really, too much smugness, too much unexamined extravagance, but she wanted to be part of it, wanted to wear the clothes and drink the wine, wanted to share the same pleasures, suffer the same angst. There must be no greater joy than having a maid to complain about. Maybe that's Jay's attraction. Maybe he's her ticket to the desirable Laguna lifestyle.

Turns out, no. Turns out, it was a surprise party. For me, anyway. Because the rest of the evening was one shocker after another. And it wasn't my overwrought imagination, I promise. For example, after the sun went down, after the patio glow had shifted from California gold to Chinese lantern red, I stood eating—savoring one of Sigrid's famous salads, enjoying her legendary breasts—while listening to her reflect on the glories of a certain Laguna painter.

-It's not just his art. He uses his fame, his wealth, to promote education, to save our oceans.

A few women nodded their approval, but Jay, in a stunning turnaround, didn't absolutely, totally concur.

-Frankly, I wouldn't call what he does art.

Do I detect a hint of jealousy, Flip-Flops? Sigrid was quick to anticipate his critique.

-Yes, he's a muralist. Yes, he's accessible. Yes, he's commercially viable. But he really captures the gorgeous mystery of sea life. There's no one else like him.

-It's taxonomic illustration—that's what he does. I'm so over it.

Jay is so over it. Who talks like that, besides sitcom characters and the teenagers who watch them? Marissa nudged me toward the hot tub, away from Sigrid's audience. She had something she wanted to ask me.

-What's taxionic elevation?

-I don't know. Are you drunk?

-No. Maybe a little.

Uh-oh. Her tipsy giggle was starting.

-We should go soon.

Before I have to spend another night in your car.

-Do you like Jay?

-Jay? Sure. Is he gay?

It just came out. I suppose I wanted to denigrate his masculinity.

-Duh.

-You're kidding.

-What's the big deal? So's your friend over there.

She pointed across the swimming pool.

-No. Lawson? The defense attorney?

-That's what Jay said. And I guess he would know. He also said you told him you were Sigrid's lover. What's that about?

-Oh. That. I was just—

I looked over her shoulder, out across the lawn, to the dark perimeter of the yard.

-I mean, I know you have a crush on her. But anyone can see you're not her type.

Are you kidding me?

-And besides, she already has a boyfriend. But you can't tell Richard, okay?

Is my imagination running away again? Or is there a man hiding in the bushes?

-Fletcher, are you listening?

-Sorry. Hey, let's go inside, okay? Let's find some dessert.

I escorted her in and handed her off to Jay—hang out with the painter all you want, I think his friendship is good for you—then escaped unseen out the front door again. But instead of heading to my car, I crossed the driveway between the garage door and Sammy's front bumper and found the side gate unlatched. I slowly, carefully, pushed it open and stepped into the darkness. I waited a moment until my eyes adjusted, then crept along the unlit walkway between the garage and the fence. When I reached the end, I poked my head around the corner. To my left: the crowded patio, glowing pool, Sigrid and her oasis. Straight ahead: the footlights at the lawn's edge, the trees, and a familiar figure crouched in the shadows.

-Pete?

He heard my whisper and snuck back along the fence line to the cover of the walkway.

-Dude.

-What are you doing here? Are you nuts?

-Backing you up. In case the mission goes bad. Did you see me wave?

-They're gonna think you're the Peeping Tom.

-No, they know me. Sigrid loves me.

-Come on. You've got to get out of here.

He followed me back through the gate and out to the street.

-Shouldn't we go inside?

I was almost to the point of not caring what mayhem might ensue. Almost, but not quite.

-No, *we* shouldn't. *I* should. Before Marissa gets too drunk.

-Okay, but sneak me some chow. That barbecue smells great.

-Just wait here.

-Dude, and something to drink.

Pete leaned against my car while I went back through the house to the patio and filled a plate. There were lots of leftovers sitting around—charred steak, legendary chicken, green salad, fruit salad, three-bean salad, couscous salad—might as well feed the hungry.

-Oh, I'm glad they're finally letting you grab a bite.

The skinny blonde facelift from the hallway—still assuming I'm the caterer.

-No, I was getting this for you. You look malnourished.

Apparently, I no longer cared what these people thought of me. I didn't even try to disguise my inelegant exit. I could have wandered beyond the hot tub, faded into the shadows behind the garage, and used the hidden walkway, nobody would have noticed. Instead, I carried the heaping dinner plate and a glass of wine unapologetically through the sitting room, where half a dozen people were finishing dessert. Marissa giggled.

-Honey, we could ask Sigrid for a doggy bag.

Jay watched me with raised eyebrows.

-Fletcher, didn't they feed you on the jury?

-Nothing but lies, man, nothing but lies.

I could still hear them laughing when, managing plate and glass with one arm, I pulled the front door closed behind me. Pete was waiting for me in the front seat.

-Sweet ride, dude, or what?

The front seat of Sammy's convertible.

-Pete, no.

-Don't say it. Just hop in. Leather seats, baby. You'll regret it if you don't.

He was leaning back, his left arm extended straight to the steering wheel, his right arm around an imaginary girlfriend in the passenger seat. And I was the drive-in waiter. I handed over the food. I pulled a napkin and fork from my pocket.

-Just don't spill anything.

He tucked into his supper, and I climbed in on the passenger side. I mean, why not? I was going to have regrets either way.

-Great food. Thanks, bro. How's the party?

-Not my crowd.

-I hear ya. But they know how to live, don't they? Red wine, red meat, red Mercedes. Living in the red. And look in the glove box. Living large and in charge.

-No.

-Just look.

He reached over and flipped it open.

-Holy shit.

Sammy's got a gun. Some kind of pistol.

-Good thing I backed you up, huh? This could have gotten ugly. Take it out.

-No.

I shut the glove box, but couldn't help laughing.

-What?

-Nothing.

Nothing, except I'd been wrong about everything, about Marissa and her artist friend, about Sigrid and Lawson, about Richard and a secret plot. The only thing I could say for sure was my best friend is insane.

-Did you complete the mission, soldier?

And worse, he was the only one who made any sense to me.

-It's back on the shelf. They'll find it a week from now and blame the maid.

-Told you, dude, nothing to worry about.

-But we've got a new one.

-A new book? I hope it's better than…what's the guy's name? Grisham.

-No, a new mission.

14

Why would she do this? Why give a guy your phone number and then ignore his calls? The least she could do is call back and say sorry, I can't go out with you. I mean, invent a lie if you have to—I'm Iranian and only date Muslims, I'm Persian and only date perverts—but give a guy a little closure, don't leave him wondering how many times to phone before giving up. A quick return call, not even five minutes of your precious time, then he can quit agonizing and you'll get no more pleading messages. But snubbing him altogether—that's inconsiderate, coldhearted, downright rude.

-Dude, just shoot yourself already.

-One simple phone call.

Like Fletcher, this is Roya, you're a really nice guy, I'm sorry, I'm a lesbian.

-You think you're the first person to get the passive brush-off?

Or Fletcher, this is Roya, you're a really nice guy, I'm sorry I'm a lesbian.

-Try having your wife go visit her parents for a week, and her cell phone's turned off, and when you call her parents they say she can't come to the phone right now, and when she finally comes home its like, oh, I needed space, I needed time to think. Yeah, okay, so why didn't you just say so?

I was driving, Pete was riding shotgun—two guys comparing scars, two dogs licking their wounds.

-And she goes, 'cause you wouldn't understand. Like I'm so stupid I wouldn't understand she needs a little time away from me. And then suddenly she's a true believer.

I tried tuning him out. I knew his angry divorcée routine by heart: everything was great until she started taking her church stuff seriously and her pastor told her the world was only a few thousand years old and anyone who said otherwise—biology teachers, for example—was doing the devil's work.

-She says, you would rather stick with your dinosaurs than with me.

He put his feet up on the dashboard and leaned back. This was his favorite part, his triumphant moment.

-And I told her, at least dinosaurs were rational creatures.

His laughter almost covered the bitterness.

-Not to mention they had nicer skin.

He got the best line, she got the house.

-She had this thing about her complexion.

We were northbound on the 405, heading out of south county on a bright, sunny afternoon, the day after Sigrid's party. Traffic was smooth through Irvine, but started bunching up when we reached Costa Mesa.

Costa Mesa! I switched lanes and exited the freeway.

-Dude?

-Roya lives around here. We're gonna find her.

-At the mall?

We were approaching South Coast Plaza, one-stop shopping and dining destination for folks with money and those who just pretend.

-What else would she be doing on a Saturday?

-Going to the beach.

-Not a beach girl.

-Hanging out with friends.

-Exactly. At the mall.

-What about the mission?

-The mission can wait.

As we circled the parking lot, I started noticing license plate frames: **University of Nordstrom's** and **Follow me to South Coast Plaza** and **Warning: This Car Brakes for Mall Exits.** It took ten minutes to find an open spot. **If the Shoe Fits, Buy It.** A summer afternoon and the mall is jam-packed. **My Other Car is a Shopping Cart.** Don't these people have lives? **So Many Malls, So Little Time.**

-You expect to just run into her? Talk about one in a million.

-Happens all the time.

Once inside, though, Pete's skepticism gave way to thirst for adventure, like a hunting dog finally out of the kennel.

-What's she look like?

-Persian. Dark eyes, long black curls.

-Age?

-Don't know. Mid-twenties. Average height.

With both hands he cupped the bill of his baseball cap, for him the equivalent of combing his hair or straightening his tie.

-Okay, I'm on it. If she's here, we'll find her. Hey, look.

An easily distracted hunting dog.

-What?

-Your favorite pajamas are on sale. Excuse me, sir?

Here we go. Pete signaled a man with carefully parted, salt-and-pepper hair and a sharp three-piece suit—at first glance a corporate executive, not the menswear attendant in a department store.

-Gentlemen. How are we this afternoon?

I felt bad for him. How does a man in his fifties end up overdressed and working retail? He reeked of cologne.

-My friend wants to try these on.

Pete held up something dark purple and shiny.

-No, I don't.

This was a mistake. I should have done this alone.

-Perhaps there's something else I can help you with.

Pete put down the pajamas.

-Yeah, actually, we're looking for this Persian chick. We think she's in the mall. Where do you suggest we try first?

-Oh, I would have no idea. Try mall security.

Sensing no sale to be made, he disappeared behind a row of sport coats. Pete mimicked his resigned tone.

-Try mall security. Like they're going to help us stalk someone.

-We're not stalking her.

We left menswear and found a shopping directory. No Persians, but lots of Italians—Salvatore Ferragamo, Emilio Pucci, Ermenegildo Zagna, Bottega Veneta. Is this the mall or the mafia? Lots of French, too—Vuitton, Piaget, Tourbillon, Chopard, Tourneau, Lacoste. Can a dental hygienist afford to shop here?

-Victoria's Secret. Second level. Dude, let's go.

As we continued through the mall and up the escalator, I felt a faint, creeping nausea, from the sterility of air conditioning, I think, and the blasts of artificial scent—fried food, perfume counters, new shoe rubber, plastic everything. Pretentious and high-end, it still smelled like a mall.

-Hello!

The lingerie store's windows displayed larger-than-life photos of supermodels in skimpy underwear. Let's hear it for soft porn in public spaces—we've come a long way, baby! The flawless, airbrushed girls summoned with come-hither eyes, but neither of us crossed the threshold, it was too daunting, even for the guy who dropped his shorts in the Montage hot tub in broad daylight.

-Dude, she's probably not in there.

-Yeah, let's just split. This is stupid.

-Persians at two o'clock. Lock and load, soldier.

I didn't see them, but the hound was off leash and weaving through shoppers. He waited on point outside a clothing store, and I followed his gaze to two heads of long, dark curls. They were deep in the shop, partially hidden by racks of clothing, and facing away from us, but still....

-That's her!

-For real?

-Wait. Don't go back there. Let her run into us.

We started perusing shirts—Italian labels made in El Salvador and the Philippines. The prices were startling. I positioned myself to watch the back of the store. Either it was my imagination or I could detect Roya's perfume. My thumping heart was trying to escape my chest. I spun around at a female voice behind me.

-If I can help you guys find something, let me know.

She was blonde and thin and, though nobody's supermodel, proudly showing some cleavage. Once again, the dog quit the hunt.

-He needs a birthday present for his girlfriend.

-Well, maybe like a blouse would be cute. What size is she?

They both looked at me.

-I don't know. She's....

-No problem. Guys never know. Is she like my size?

-No, she's big. Fletcher likes big girls.

-So like an eight, maybe?

Pete spread his arms wide.

-Real big. She could eat you for lunch.

-We don't really have much in big sizes. You could try Sears, though.

Here they come—the two raven-haired women. I could see their faces: definitely Persians, definitely not Roya, not nearly as pretty. I felt a wave of relief wash through me. My heart eased up. I shook my head no, but Pete stopped them anyway.

-Excuse me, this is kinda random, do you know a woman named Roya?

I expected them to keep walking, but they were friendly and tried to be helpful.

-What's her last name?

Pete looked at me. I shrugged. I'd never thought to ask. How did I end up such a social dunce?

-Tabatabai?

-What?

-I know a Roya Tabatabai. Does she work in a bank?

-She works in a dental office.

The other woman spoke up.

-I know a Roya in a dental office. Roya Shahrokhshahi.

-Gesundheit.

The woman laughed at Pete's tired joke.

-I know, huh? Persian names sound funny.

-No, they sound romantic.

Pete was trying to be charming. I stayed on task.

-A dental office in Costa Mesa?

-No, down in Orange County.

-Costa Mesa is Orange County.

Always the teacher—I can't help it.

-I mean real Orange County, like Aliso. Or it might be Laguna Hills.

You mean real white Orange County. I could hear Mr. Worster: Persians count as Caucasians.

-So what's the deal with this Roya anyhow?

-We're stalking her.

-We're not stalking her. We're just….

-He got stood up.

The women cooed sympathetically.

-Ohhh.

-How sad.

-Don't worry, you'll find someone else, I can tell. You have a good aura—it's open and welcoming.

I watched them walk away. They weren't laughing, weren't ridiculing the pathetic guy wandering the mall searching for a woman who probably wasn't here. I liked how they were approachable, weren't so guarded like Marissa, or shy like Roya. They were like Sharon, outgoing and confident, only gentler. Maybe I'll find a woman like them. It's funny how a few kind words from a stranger can feel so good.

-Did you hear her? My aura is open and welcoming.

-I think aura is Persian for anus. Seriously.

The bookstore next door had a display of the top ten bestsellers. I took number two off the shelf and checked the publication date: brand new this year.

-Grisham's a machine.

Numbers seven and nine were his also. Incredible. Three of the top ten. I turned to the back flap and looked at his picture. Not only rich and famous, but handsome too.

Pete scoffed.

-It's all ghost writers. He just comes up with the idea to get them started and slaps on his name when they're done. I need a gig like that—sitting on the beach, writing down story ideas. I could do it, you know. I got ideas out my ass.

It was almost believable—Grisham subcontracting out concepts. It's his setups that matter, the legal intricacies. And the formula. The writing style is forgettable.

-Anything I can help you with?

All the hair on the store clerk's head was combed forward, like he walked to work with a stiff wind at his back. Which might also explain the need for the silver plugs that stretched gaping holes in his earlobes.

-Yeah. Have you ever heard that Grisham doesn't write his own books?

His tongue, too, was pierced. *Click-click.* He played the silver ball against his teeth as he considered my question.

-No, but it would make sense. He's totally corporate.

-Told you, dude. Totally.

Pete reached out for a fist bump with the clerk, who motioned to a table stacked high with more number two's.

-They would publish his grocery list if that's what he gave them. Capitalist greed—it's so wrong.

Without meaning to, I found myself defending Grisham.

-His books criticize corporate greed.

That was part of the formula, after all, the evil, unrepentant executives getting their comeuppance. *Click-click.* The clerk nodded his head like he'd heard my argument before.

-Yeah, you read them and think there's justice in the world. That's why they've got it out front like this. Opium for the masses, man.

-Well, since you put it that way.

I returned the book to the shelf and wiped my hands on my shirt in mock disgust.

-That's right, bro. Don't buy it. Just say no.

How did this guy ever get hired? Pete picked up the book.

-What if we stole it?

The clerk looked back toward the checkout counter.

-Right on. But wait till I'm on break, okay?

-Dude, I'm kidding.

And then it was an old-fashioned mall prank: Thrill-'em Guillam standing calmly on a descending escalator, Spaghetti Repetti scrambling down its ascending partner. A race to the bottom. Holding a slight lead as we neared the finish, I watched Pete stumble and grab the rubber rails, watched his arms get pulled back and up while his head continued forward like a sprinter leaving the starting blocks. He released his grip, and, just before diving face first into the rising steel stairs, swung his knees out ahead of his chest and vaulted the final ten feet to solid ground, landing knees bent and palms flat on the ground.

-Let's see Grisham do that!

An impressive recovery, and Pete, like a pro golfer acknowledging the gallery, tipped his hat to the security guard who stood waiting, a radio wire curling down from his ear, another middle-aged man in a dead-end job. The guard shook his head in disapproval, but an upturned mouth betrayed a slight bemusement. He put a friendly hand on Pete's shoulder.

-Usually it's the twelve-year-olds.

-I'm big for my age.

The guard allowed himself a full-on grin.

-Usually we page their mother.

-Mine can't hear anymore.

I gave Pete a shove to shut him up and get him moving.

-Sir, we're on our way out.

Leave 'em laughing, right? Quit while you're ahead. The guard pointed at Pete.

-Don't let your young friend there drive.

-Never. Are you kidding?

A little ways down the mall, Pete looked back over his shoulder.

-He's not even watching us. Where's the fun in breaking the law if nobody cares? And now my shoulder hurts again.

His right hand was carefully cradling his left elbow, just like when we fled Sigrid's backyard.

-You still up for the mission?

-You think I did all that research for nothing?

All that research meant running a few internet searches. I had arrived at The Cave with Mexican takeout at noon, let myself in, and found Pete splayed on the couch, the stereo blasting, the muted tv replaying baseball highlights, homerun after identical homerun. I turned down the music and tossed him a foil-wrapped burrito.

-You ready to play private dick?

-That's all I ever play.

-I know the feeling.

Marissa had kissed me when I drove her home from Sigrid's party—kissed me goodnight and didn't invite me in. She was inebriated, Bud Jack was acquitted, and—forget homeruns—I still couldn't get past first base. Never mind. Doesn't matter. At least she had exited the car under her own power, and I enjoyed a decent night's sleep in my bed.

-Okay, let's track this guy down.

Pete fired up his laptop, and by one p.m. we had what we needed. With a computer and credit card, you can find anybody, there's no privacy left on the planet. A newspaper obituary gave us a date of birth and a former employer. A credit report gave us a street address. Operation Hijack was off to a roaring start.

The quixotic side trip to the mall cost us some time—we got back to my car in the parking lot a little before four—but Pete was pleased, he had a new adventure tale.

-Your escalator was too fast. I knew I had to go airborne.

-You were falling over.

-No way. I stuck the landing.

I opened the car door and went straight for my cell phone. Nothing. No messages, no missed calls.

-Would I be stupid to call her again?

-No. Tell her you're in Costa Mesa and you went to the mall looking for her. She'll like that.

-Yeah, okay. You're right.

I put the away the phone and started the car.

-No, seriously. Tell her about your open aura.

Something about the clerk in the bookstore was still gnawing at me. Not the piercings and silly hair—if a guy wants to look like a freakshow, what do I care? I always have a few students like that, it's just their way of rejecting social norms—though rebellion through self-mutilation, besides suggesting some deep self-hatred, has itself become a cliché. What bugged me was the patronizing way he had nodded, like he thought I really believed Grisham was offering a profound critique of society, like he recognized me as just another Orange County suburbanite, Saturday at the mega-mall, Sunday at the mega-church. No, worse, I was one of Sigrid's crowd, arguing for social justice but living like a king. But I don't own a house or drive a big gas-guzzler with a smug license plate frame, I'm not like that. And you should have seen me in the jury room, Mr. Retail-Store Radical, I turned those people around, I actually made a difference, and the only reason I've read a few Grishams...I caught myself. Marissa says if your mind goes back and tries to change what already happened, you're not living in the now. And who cares what some long-eared mall punk thinks about me anyhow?

I returned my attention to the northbound 405—probably a good idea since we'd left the parking lot fifteen minutes ago and I was the one driving. Pete was still back on the escalator, still crafting the legend.

-If you think about it, I broad-jumped at least twenty feet. Off a moving platform. And walked away like no big deal. That's why the security guard didn't do anything. He was awestruck.

-Don't forget how you jumped over that kid.

-I could've. I had the vertical.

-You're right, you are good at fiction.

He tapped his temple with his index finger.

-I'm telling you, chock full of bestsellers.

-Let's hear one.

-Right now? You want to hear one right now?

While he tried to come up with something, I took the exit for 710 South and got stuck behind a semi truck doing twenty on the tightly curved transition ramp. The truck's mud flaps flaunted the familiar chrome silhouette of a reclining woman. The shape of her hair, flowing back from her uptilted head, reminded me of Roya. Everything reminded me of Roya.

-Okay, so a semi gets pulled over by the cops.

I should call her one last time—after a few more days, after maybe a week. Because maybe she went out of town for the weekend and couldn't call me. Or maybe she caught the flu.

225

-No, it stops at the INS checkpoint in San Onofre. And when they open the trailer, there's two hundred illegal immigrants packed inside. And one of them escapes.

And call her from a different phone, so she doesn't recognize the number and has to pick up.

-You listening?

-An illegal immigrant on the loose in California. Catchy.

-I'm not finished. He ran away from the checkpoint, so…so now he's on Camp Pendleton. So they send out the troops.

-Come on. The Marines?

I could see it—all those trucks and tanks rumbling around the dusty hills, tearing up vegetation, trying to find a migrant worker before he gets to San Clemente and starts mowing people's lawns.

-Yeah, they've got to stop him.

-What exit are we looking for?

We had an address, we had driving directions, we didn't have the navigator's full attention.

-No, dude, he's headed for the nuclear reactors. He's got explosives.

-Oh, that's more believable. He's like give me citizenship, or I'm blowing it up. Give me a job picking strawberries, or Orange County is toast.

-How about this one: a biology teacher's smart-ass friend, maybe a fellow teacher, gets brutally murdered.

I could call her from school. Hi, Roya, this is Fletcher, I don't know if you ever got a chance to call me back because I lost my cell phone, how are you doing?

-No, it's his ex-wife. Chopped into little pieces.

-Pete, you should seek help, you know that?

-No, no, one of his students. A cheerleader. And the police think it's suicide. Yeah, so the teacher starts investigating, using the biology lab to examine evidence from the crime scene. And right before he solves the case, the teacher gets suspended, put on leave, locked out of the lab.

-Ooo! The principal is the killer.

Maybe that's why people write novels—so they can kill off an ex-wife, so they can convict the boss.

-No, the school board's a bunch of right-wingers who want to fire the guy for teaching evolution. Including—wait—the dead girl's mom.

-The mom's on the school board?

-Pretty good, huh? I'm copyrighting it, so don't even think about plagiarizing.

I didn't say so, but anyone can come up with ideas. That's the easy part. Like the screenplay I started—the courtroom drama. I wrote half a page and gave up.

-Dude, I got it. The school board lady wants to fire him for teaching evolution, and then his evolutionary argument proves her daughter was murdered. Something to do with the rate of bacteria reproduction, which can show exactly when the girl was killed. And that proves somebody was lying about when they last saw her.

-The principal—I'm telling you. No, her boyfriend—he killed her. Ex-boyfriend. Because she wouldn't return his phone calls.

-Whatever. The ghost writer can figure that out. I just provide the hook.

We took what proved to be the wrong exit and drove in circles for a while, so it must have been around five p.m. when we finally located the property—a little clapboard house with a half-dead lawn, once owned by a city bus driver named Jeffers, and presumably still the home of his churchgoing widow and her devoted, car-washing grandson. The house was dark.

-Dude, this neighborhood looks sketchy.

-Why, because there's black people?

The street was empty, but we'd passed some rough-looking kids a few blocks over. Pete brushed aside my accusation.

-No, because there's bars on all the windows.

And, he might have added, no late-model SUVs in the driveways, no look-a-like stucco houses, no red tile roofs. South Orange County this was not.

-I'm gonna go knock.

I opened the car door.

-Dude, you're gonna get shot.

I couldn't actually knock—there was a heavy metal screen with iron bars, and it was locked tight. Rich people live in gated communities, the middle class settles for fences around their yards, poor folk put fences on their doors. I pressed the doorbell button and listened—the chime worked, but no footsteps, no barking dog. All quiet on the Wilkeses' front. Back in the car, Pete was glancing around nervously.

-We can't sit here waiting for him to get home. We'll look like cops.

I suggested we go eat dinner and then come back. But if staking out a low-income neighborhood made Pete anxious, driving around Long Beach almost did me in. While I dodged buses and swerved around parked cars and swore at jaywalkers—the little shits—and slammed on the brakes to spare the life of a scraggly drunk on a bicycle, nearly losing my own due to cardiac arrest, Pete called out restaurants.

-Mexican. Mexican. Salvadoran. Mexican. I'm sensing a theme here.

-Just pick one.

-We had Mexican for lunch.

I stopped for a yellow light I normally would have ignored, and hoped for a long red, just to catch my breath and get my bearings. It was all street lights, sidewalks, billboards in Spanish advertising bail bonds and liquor, and one dismal strip mall after another. A red lantern in a storefront window caught my eye.

-How about the Hong Kong Palace?

-There's no parking.

-We'll go down a side street and find something.

-You kidding? Hondas are the number one stolen vehicle in California, you know that? Let's just bolt.

-You mean abort the mission?

Usually *I* was the one suggesting an expedient retreat.

-We did what we could. And it's Saturday night—he might not be home for hours.

-I'm not giving up. We came all this way.

-Yeah, that's what Custer said.

I looked over at Pete. He had his hat pulled low over his forehead.

-I can't believe it—Pete Repetti's scared of Long Beach.

-I'm not scared, okay? Custer wasn't scared either. Custer was stupid.

I thought of Professor Hanson. The way his lisp intensified, you could tell The Penguin loved recounting the Little Bighorn: The Thioux Indianth were led by Thitting Bull. Ththitting there waiting. And then came Cuthter, the real ththtavage. People, Cuthter died for our thinth.

-Dude, we're like the only white guys for five miles. It's gang-banger heaven.

-That guy on the bike was white.

-Barely.

We finally found an Indian restaurant—India Indian, not the Custer-killing kind— where we could sit by the window and keep an eye on the car, though it was hard to imagine a thief taking an interest in my old beater. The waiter nodded a welcome, slid menus onto the table, and walked away without a word.

-Wonder what part of the subcontinent he's from.

-The Mexican part. Same as the cook.

-He probably is the cook.

The room was dimly lit. There were no other diners.

-You get the feeling we shouldn't be here?

A health inspection notice in the window gave Bombay Feast a big fat A, but the sticky seats and faded travel posters didn't inspire confidence, and the name on the menus was Bombay Buffet.

-It's still a little early.

-Dude, if we left right now, we could be eating Thai food in Dana Point by seven o'clock. With an extra spicy waitress. And clean silverware.

-The lamb curry sounds good.

When Pete turns cynical, my tendency is to counterbalance with optimism, and anyhow I wasn't seeking a gourmet experience, I just wanted a place to relax for a few minutes while giving Bud Jack a chance to return home.

-Why do you want to find this guy anyhow?

-I don't know. I mean, I sat there looking at him for five days. The guy never spoke a word. Hardly even moved. And then I had to decide if I thought he was guilty.

-I got it. I know what your problem is.

-It's not a problem. I just—

-Your problem is…you don't know jack.

-No, that's it exactly. If I can say hi to him, that will make him more real. If we just acknowledge each other.

-He'll probably tell you get lost, white boy.

-That's fine. But if I'm going to judge the guy, I should at least find out who he is. At least try. I mean, I practically held his life in my hands.

-Invite him out for a beer.

-Maybe I will.

-Invite him to school. Class, this is how I spent my summer vacation. Couldn't make it with the Persian chick, so I tracked down a black man.

Neither of us cleaned our plates. I paid the bill and we hurried out the door of Bombay Feast aka Bombay Buffet aka twelve-dollar death. The evening sky was slipping toward night and, to be honest, I was relieved to be back in my unstolen Honda with the doors locked. Custer should have been so lucky.

-Exquisite choice, dude. Thanks.

-I wanted Chinese.

-A nice taste of Long Beach. And we've seen where he lives. Whata you say we call it a night?

To be honest, my enthusiasm for Operation Hijack was on the wane. I was tired, my stomach was objecting to the curry, and I could hear Rex Ruffman, the expert witness: Lots of gangs in Long Beach—Insane Crips, Original Hood Crips. It would be pathetic, though, to suffer that meal and then not finish the job. You can't go all the way to LA County just for the salmonella.

-We'll drive by the house. If it's still dark, we're outta here.

Except when we got back to the 'hood, when we pulled up to the Wilkes home—what I assumed was the Wilkes home—the front window was giving off light. I circled the block, then parked across the street. My mind was on high alert. Why is the street so quiet? Is this Crip territory? Are Insane Crips literally insane, or just a little nutty? I took a deep breath and opened the car door.

-Dude, you're asking for trouble.
-If I don't make it back, you can have my paddleboard.
-Awesome. I'll keep my fingers crossed.
-And tell Roya I loved her from afar.
-I think she knows.

15

It didn't seem real, it was dream-like, like I was there, in it, and at the same time I was watching from the outside—watching myself walk up the driveway in the twilight, watching myself ring the doorbell and listen for footsteps and look back across the street at Pete crouched low in the car, no doubt with the doors locked tight. It was the strangeness of the situation, my sense of being out of place, so out of place it didn't feel like me, and wondering what I looked like to whoever might be spying from behind drawn curtains and iron window bars on this oddly quiet street. One thing I knew for sure: I looked white. Conspicuously white. A skinny white guy from Laguna, not even a decent tan, thanks to a week of jury duty. I thought of Custer riding into the Indians' camp and what it must be like when suddenly someone is shooting at you. In the movies there's usually a dramatic build, you see it coming, you see a car creeping by, you see a shotgun swung out the window, it happens in slow motion. I caught myself. In the next yard over, a squirrel was scratching its way down a tree. When its bushy tail disappeared behind some hedges, I turned back to the screen door. I touched the rough metal with my fingers and was happy to see the three familiar tendons, if that's what they are, forming an elongated W on the back of my hand. This was still the real world. It was still me. I laughed at my hyperactive imagination and rang the doorbell a second time. A shout came from inside the house.

-He ain't here!

-Mrs. Wilkes? Hello? Mrs. Wilkes?

Did I have the right address? No garage, just like Mrs. Wilkes had told the court, and no car out front—she'd said she didn't drive. I rang again. I didn't come all this way to be so easily rebuffed.

-I told you, he ain't here!

231

The shout was closer this time, from right behind the door.

-Mrs. Wilkes, I was on the jury. For Bud's trial. Rudy's. You called him Rudy—that's what you told us. Short for Durand. Mrs. Wilkes?

A deadbolt turned and the door opened a few inches, as much as the security chain allowed.

-Mrs. Wilkes? My name is Fletcher. Guillam Fletcher. I'm not a cop or anything.

-What are you?

-A math teacher, actually. But I was on the jury when you were a witness. Do you recognize me?

There was a pause. She was looking me over through the screen door, looking at the white guy.

-So?

-So I was hoping to meet Bud.

-He ain't here.

I guess I'd expected that. Double E Reed had testified that he and Bud drove around in a little pickup truck filled with car-washing supplies, and I'd seen no such vehicle in the neighborhood.

-I was also hoping to meet you. I wanted to introduce myself. I really admired what you said in the witness stand, the way you stood up to those lawyers, you didn't let them put words in your mouth.

I was talking fast, trying to make a connection before she slammed the door.

-I'm sure that wasn't easy for you in front of all those…all those people.

I was going to say all those white people.

-The other witnesses—you could tell they were repeating what they'd been told to say. That's why I didn't trust them. I knew I could trust you.

I paused, hoping she would respond, but she didn't feel a need to fill the silence, same as in the courtroom.

-I guess that's what I wanted to say, that I really respect how you carried yourself.

Again, no response. But the door stayed open.

-Do you know when he'll be back?

-No.

A quick, matter-of-fact no, without hint of apology or encouragement. A conversation stopper.

-Could you tell him I came by? Guillam Fletcher. Juror Number One. I'm sure he'll be as pleased as you are.

-I'll tell him.

I thought I detected a slight softening in her voice, but the door went shut before I could say thank you. Well, at least I'd tried. I'd done the right thing. I turned to watch a car go by—no shotgun barrel, no slow motion—

and then saw Pete's head pop back up. He must have ducked out of view when the car approached.

-Hey, you said you was a math teacher?

The door was open wider. She'd undone the chain. Still safe, though, behind the heavy screen door.

-That's right. Dana Hills High School. In Dana Point.

-You must be good at numbers.

-Not like a genius or anything.

She was smaller than I remembered. She was leaning on her walker.

-Some of the Social Security don't make sense to me.

-Yeah, I bet that stuff is confusing.

-Gives me a headache.

I almost told her I get confused by the teachers' pension program—trying to calculate how many years you need to work and what percent of your salary you'll still get paid after you retire—but then, duh, she's not making small talk, she's asking for help.

-Is there something I could look at for you?

-It's just a few papers. I got them laid out in the dining room.

The air inside was stale, smelling of cigarettes and something that had cooked in a frying pan, but the house was neat and tidy. I guess it was true what she'd said in court—Bud cleans everything. The front door opened onto a small living room with worn green carpet and an angular green couch, like nothing had changed since the 1970s, except for the flat-screen television, turned on too loud. Hobbling along on her walker, she led me down a short hallway and through a cramped kitchen to the dining room. Among the family photos hanging in the hallway was a large one that looked like Bud, the same steely eyes giving nothing away, but a sturdy, rawboned face that suggested a bigger man. It was hard to reconcile, I had to think it through carefully—Bud Jack's deceased father, Durand—because the picture was taken when he was younger than Bud was now. I wondered if Bud found it equally confusing, his father frozen in youth.

-Usually they just send the check the first of the month and Rudy takes it to the bank for me, but now they asking for more information. One letter—I think this one here—no, that's not it. Somewhere here they asking if I'm alive or dead. I ain't been dead for a long time.

It wasn't just a few papers, it was several stacks of letters, some in unopened envelopes.

-This looks like a lot of work. I'm not sure I have time to—

-You got to go already?

-It's just that my friend is out in the car waiting.

-He a teacher?

-Yes. Science. But—

-Might go faster with two.

I was back in the dream and floating above it, watching myself walk to the car to ask Pete to come into this uninviting house in this ominous neighborhood and assist an old woman we didn't know with some vague paperwork.

-You're shitting me.

-Thirty minutes, tops. You wanna wait out here?

-Just get in the car and quit playing.

When he finally realized I was serious, he got out of the car with a show of reluctance and exasperation.

-If I get killed, it's on you, man. And this time I want a real funeral. I want the whole damn school. The marching band. I want you bawling your eyes out, wracked with guilt. 'Cause this is royally fucked up.

The screen door had locked behind me, so Mrs. Wilkes had to let us in.

-Mrs. Wilkes, this is Pete Repetti.

He followed me in and shook her hand.

-Mrs. Wilkes, a pleasure to meet you. What a lovely home.

-Been here thirty-two years.

-Wow. Is it a good neighborhood?

What he meant was is it safe? For two white guys?

-People come and go. The Hastings been here longer than me. Three houses down.

Again, she led the way through the kitchen, not much wider than Pete's one-man galley, to the dining room. This time I noticed the postings on the refrigerator door—a yellow flyer announcing a church rummage sale, an obituary clipped from a newspaper, two coupons for pizza delivery. Comfortingly normal. I also observed that while I'd been outside recruiting Pete, another thick stack of mail had made it to the dining room table.

-Mrs. Wilkes, what exactly do you want us to do here?

-Just tell me what they want. My husband, Jeffers Wilkes—he always took care of it.

The doorbell rang. Pete and I shared a look of concern, like maybe it was Insane Crips coming to find out who had parked on their street. Mrs. Wilkes hobbled out of the room. The doorbell sounded again. Impatient Insane Crips.

-He ain't here!

That seemed to be the end of it. People come and go.

Pete and I took seats at the little round table and began unfolding letters. Behind me, an old grandfather clock, shaped like a skinny wooden coffin standing on end, went *tick-tick, tick-tick*. I tried not imagining who might be prowling around outside. Mrs. Wilkes, I knew, wouldn't put up with any nonsense in her house, but she could hardly prevent angry gang-bangers— Incensed Impatient Insane Crips—from torching my car. Incendiary Incensed Impatient Insane Crips. Was my car insured for arson? Stop it—

focus on the work. Tucked among the Social Security notices sent to Wanda Wilkes were several windowed envelopes from the City of Long Beach addressed to Jeffers Wilkes and various junk-mail alluvia—credit card offers, discount carpet cleaning—targeting Current Resident.

Alluvia—that was Sharon's word for our more listless students, devoid of self-awareness, sleepwalking through their teens.

-Suburban alluvia is what they are, the poor dears, swept along by a culture of conformity in a land of comfort, south county is one broad alluvial plain.

Now, I wondered if Mrs. Wilkes felt like alluvium, dropped by the stream of life into this cubbyhole to live out her years connected to the outer world only by form letters she couldn't follow. Is this her reward for perseverance? And what about her grandson, every day out washing cars so they can pay the mortgage on time—will Bud Jack grow old in the same dreary house, the doors locked tight, the television on? Is this how society deposits its dregs? A desire to be helpful, to show her someone cared, kept me scanning Mrs. Wilkes's mail, but none of it appeared to require a response on her part. Maybe she invited us in simply to have company on a Saturday night.

-Dude, this is fucking ridiculous.

-Shh. She can hear. So can he.

I pointed to a cheaply framed picture on the wall behind Pete. Kindly brown eyes, neatly trimmed beard, shiny blonde locks radiating a warm glow. Sunday school Jesus.

-Good. At least we're not the only white people.

He pushed away a stack of letters—Pete, not Jesus—and stood up. He was getting antsy, which usually means trouble. He peered out a back window into the darkness.

-See anything?

-Dirt.

-No hot tub?

What a trip—last night at Sigrid's pleasure palace and tonight with gentle Jesus in this humble abode.

-Let's get outta here. This place stinks.

-Let me just finish this stack. Hey, here's one from the office of Russell Lawson, the defense attorney. It's a bill—are you kidding me?—for twenty-one thousand dollars.

-I shoulda been a lawyer.

-This is weird, because I thought Public Defense was covering the expenses.

-Maybe the lawyer jacked up his fees. Get it? Jacked. You think she's got beer?

He disappeared into the kitchen. I heard him open the refrigerator door, and a light went on. In my head, I mean. The whole story of Richard and company randomly selecting an accused murderer and funding his defense had never made total sense to me, and now this new piece to the puzzle. Okay, assuming Bud Jack had retained Lawson on his own, how was he planning to come up with that kind of cash? Not from washing cars. Did he inherit some money? Was there a life insurance policy? That was another thing: if his paternal grandparents were Wanda and the late Jeffers Wilkes, how did Bud end up with a different last name? How did he get Jack-ed? That one could have an easy explanation. Occam's Razor: Bud's parents never married, Bud uses his mother's last name, and when his father died, leaving an insurance claim to his only son, Bud banked the payout, saved it for a rainy day. Then the police came knocking with an arrest warrant, and for a black man in sunny southern California, it doesn't get much rainier than that. Or was it something more fraudulent? Grisham's Razor: when Lawson or some other compromised attorney gets a paying customer from the low-income community, Public Defense writes a fat check on the defendant's behalf, the conniving attorney takes his cut, then funnels the rest back to the phony charity crew. That was the best money trail I could come up with. For a math teacher, I admit, I don't really understand finance. But if I was right, Bud Jack might have never even heard of Public Defense, they just used his name. To what end? Does Public Defense exist so Richard and his fellow donors can pad their deductibles column, or are they laundering some illicit income?

Pete returned, empty-handed.

-No beer?

-She's sitting there watching a cop show.

-So?

-So maybe when you're done sorting her mail, houseboy, you can go rub her feet.

-Do me a favor. Look through that stack for anything like this one.

I handed him the invoice I'd found: Russell M. Lawson, Attorney at Law, Irvine, California. How did Bud Jack ever connect with a defense attorney from Irvine, unless Public Defense arranged it for him? So Bud Jack had to know about Public Defense. I wanted to think I was getting warmer, but every explanation I wove for the Bud Jack-Russell Lawson-Richard Wilhite connection had a hole in it. Why couldn't this be like a Grisham, where at the end the conspiracy is revealed and it all makes sense, all the pieces fit?

-This isn't a bill, you know. Look down at the bottom.

Sure enough, I'd missed the fine print: Remit no payment at this time.

-Lawson's the gay one you thought was having an affair with Sigrid, right?

I ignored him and attended instead to the latest tear in my logic. Does Lawson's letter mean Bud Jack isn't being billed, someone else is paying, or that the actual bill will follow shortly?

-And then there's the gay painter you thought was getting it on with your girlfriend. All that time you spent worrying, and turns out he—

-Yeah, I get it, alright?

I couldn't hide the irritation in my voice.

-Sorry, dude.

Tick-tick, tick-tick. We worked in uneasy silence for a few minutes, flipping through envelopes and scanning letters, searching for another clue, another piece to the puzzle. No silence in my head, though, now that Pete had brought up last night. At first I'd felt relief—my sort of girlfriend's sort of guy-friend is a totally gay friend. But what does it mean when she spends the entire time talking to him, flirting with him, and when I drive her home doesn't invite me in? Really enjoyed our evening together, Marissa. Glad we had plans. But I think I'm done being your chauffeur.

The doorbell rang yet again—the Four-I'ed Crips were still out there. And Grandma Wilkes was still ready with her warm welcome.

-He ain't here!

Thirty-two years in a rough neighborhood must take a toll, not to mention burying a son, burying a husband, and now a grandson prosecuted for murder. Watching a cop show, does she root for the detectives or the suspects?

-Dude, how does she know the doorbell's not for her?

Surreal—that's what this was. Like one of those moody, inscrutable films that Sharon—Darling, just let it flow over you—claimed to love. Like cut to two guys going through the mail in a dimly-lit back room, no sound except the clock's oppressive ticking. One guy gets bored, stands up and looks out the window, goes into the kitchen, comes back, sits down, sorts more mail. The doorbell rings and no one answers it. Like the director wants to depict the staleness of modern life. Like we need to see more of that. And when something does happen, the director underplays it. One of the guys quietly slumps over dead—the antsy one, I hope—or maybe the Jesus picture blinks.

-Wouldn't it be trippy if Jesus started talking to us? Hey, Fletcher, it's me, up here on the wall. Hey, Pete, don't pretend you don't know me.

-Dude, you're on drugs.

WWJS?—What Would Jesus Say?—after all he's seen in this airless room.

-Guys, you gotta get me down from here. Take me back to Orange County. Take me to the beach. I haven't seen a hot chick in like two thousand years. You think Jesus goes for disproportionates?

I thought it was a good setup line, but Pete didn't run with it.

-Dude.

He was staring past me, eyes widened like he'd seen something.

-What?

I looked over my shoulder. Nothing behind me except the clock.

-It's drugs. The doorbell—think about it. It's a Saturday night. They ain't looking for a carwash. Bud Jack is selling dope.

I *was* thinking about it, as soon as he said it. A picture was already forming in my head. Some kind of diagram. No, an organizational flowchart. With Richard Wilhite at the top. He was the linchpin, he attracted investors, people like that slimy Sammy. They financed the operation upfront. Bud Jack was a distributor, one of many, selling out of his house at night. And during the day making deliveries to upscale Long Beach neighborhoods under the pretense of washing cars. That's perfect: rich white folks in Long Beach are using, rich white folks in Orange County are raking profits off the top, and poor black folks are doing the dirty work, handling the illegal merchandise, fighting turf wars, dodging cops. And Public Defense is the cover organization that allows Richard and company to defend their operatives in court without revealing their own self-interest. Is it possible Sigrid's art collection was bought and paid for by drug trafficking, her designer tits came courtesy of Long Beach street gangs? I didn't like where that thought took me, how that possibility led unavoidably to the next: Bud Jack was guilty. He killed Juan Castro to protect Richard's market share. I didn't like that conclusion at all.

-It could be his friends, stopping by to hang out.

-They would call him.

-Maybe they don't have a phone.

-He's slinging dope, I'm telling you.

The rattle of Mrs. Wilkes's walker warned us she was on her way through the kitchen. The rattle stopped, replaced by the snap of a lighter. I strained to detect her next movement, but heard only the nagging clock. *Tick-tick, tick-tick.*

When she rejoined us a few moments later, a burning cigarette angled from the corner of her mouth. She smoked like a Hollywood tough.

-Mrs. Wilkes, looks like we're about finished.

-How come they think I'm dead?

The cigarette wiggled as she spoke.

-We haven't found anything like that. These things from Social Security—mostly it's just information, disclosures they have to make. But there is something here from Bud's lawyer.

-That's his business, not mine.

I hesitated. It's not polite to pry. But how else can you get answers?

-It mentions the legal fees. I thought an organization was paying for that.

-I said, that's his business, not mine.

I don't know how else to describe the sensation: I got the creeps. There was something sinister in the way she eyed me, I could feel it in my bones, physiological certainty, something wasn't right. This time I didn't have to work through the implications, it all came to me in a flash. If Pete was correct, if Bud Jack peddled dope out of his home, then his grandmother had to know. How could she not? She might even be involved, mortgage payments were looming after all. *Tick-tick, tick-tick.*

Talk about surreal: ten days ago I was trying to figure out how to avoid jury duty and maximize my beach time, five days ago I was worried the judge in Santa Ana was ready to lock me up for contempt, assuming I didn't first get nabbed for unlawful trespassing in Laguna, and now, tonight, any minute, the cops could bust down the door and—Jesus help me—arrest a suburban math teacher for providing consulting services to a Long Beach drug ring. *Tick-tick, tick-tick.*

-We should be going.

Would Judge Silverson appreciate the layers of irony in my sudden descent into crime? Guilty, Uronor, guilty of liberal guilt. Would Richard Wilhite contribute generously to my defense?

-Don't worry about this stuff, Mrs. Wilkes, you can probably throw most of it away.

She took the cigarette from her mouth, but didn't speak, didn't even appear to exhale. Smoke just drifted up from her nose and mouth as if her brain was smoldering.

-But nice meeting you.

Pete had already slipped out of the dining room and was making for the front door. I was close behind. Adiós, Jesús! Namaste!

The night was noticeably darker than when we'd arrived, and Mrs. Wilkes didn't have any outdoor lights on, but I had managed to park the car under a street lamp. Another scene flashed across my brain: the dark, abandoned parking lot, the lone car in a dome of hazy light, and—*BOOM!*—a fiery explosion blows the doors off. I shook my head to clear my brain. Too many damn movies.

I don't remember crossing the street or clicking the car unlocked, only that we got inside in a hurry. I looked back at the phosphorescent glow coming from the barred and curtained window of Mrs. Wilkes's television room. Had I read her correctly? Could an old grandmother with church flyers on the fridge and Jesus on the wall really be involved in the drug trade? When Mrs. Wilkes was testifying in court, I could sense her honesty, I was sure of it, yet now she gives me this eerie vibe. Either she's a sinisterly brilliant actor or I'm letting my imagination get the best of me. I know what Marissa would say: would you have been spooked by a little old *white* woman?

-Dude, start the car.

-I'll be right back.

-Dude? Fletcher!

This time, no movie scene. This time, I strode up the unlit driveway like it was no big deal. Third time's a charm. No out-of-body sensations, no scary thoughts, I wasn't thinking at all, I was moving, I was a frail white moth drawn to the flickering blue light. A bit precious, I know. Forget the moth. I walked up the driveway. I hesitated before pressing the doorbell. How would I get her to open up? Mrs. Wilkes, I need to use your bathroom. Not a chance. Mrs. Wilkes, I left something in your dining room. She'll just go and look for it. Mrs. Wilkes, I made a quick phone call and I figured out your Social Security issue, I know why they think you're deceased. That should get the door open, that should bring us face to face. Then what? I didn't know my second line, but I knew I wasn't leaving without a straight answer. Because—might as well come clean—I wanted acquittal for the acquittal. That's what Operation Hijack was all about. I was seeking proof I hadn't helped free a cold-blooded killer.

-The fuck you want?

It didn't come from inside the house. I looked left, toward the hedge next door, and suddenly he was in my face.

-I—

I couldn't find words. I started backing up, onto the lawn, and then I was falling. I reached out, grabbed at the air, and slammed into the ground. Things were moving at strange angles. My head might have bounced. I closed my eyes.

-I said, whatchoowant, mothafucker?

If you fall down, they kick you. I'd read that in the Holocaust survivor's book, and here I was, sprawled on the dying lawn.

-I'm talking to you, asshole.

I tucked my face behind my elbow and pulled my knees up to protect my ribs. I could feel it before it happened—I was about to get hurt.

-You deaf?

-I was on your jury.

It just came out. Just in time. Like I was gasping for air.

-Say what?

I looked up. He was standing over me, poised to pounce. I gasped again.

-Juror Number One. Closest to the judge. Judge Silverson.

Our eyes met, and I concentrated on holding his gaze. I'd read that too. If someone's about to kill you, don't turn away, even if you're scared. Make them see you're human.

It took a moment—a very long moment—before something registered, before maybe I caught a hint of recognition in those cold eyes.

-The fuck you doing here?

His voice had changed—still mean, but less threatening, more quizzical.
I think. With my left elbow pressed against the grass, I slowly propped
myself up. I kept my right palm open in front of my head, an obvious gesture
of surrender. I'm sure I looked pathetic. My voice cracked when I spoke.

-We didn't...after the trial...I thought I should say hi.

He kept his eyes on mine, waiting for me to give something away. As
kids, we called it a stare fight, trying not to blink first. For a second, that's
what I saw—a kid, with a missing father and an overwhelmed mother and he
just wanted to be loved, same as I sometimes see, if I look carefully, in the
faces of my students.

I sensed movement. His hand was reaching down to help me up. Or
was he going to grab my arm and kick me in the face? The weird thing is
right then I relaxed, like I knew I could trust him. I looked to his hand, then
back to his face. That's when I saw the gun. It wasn't in slow motion. It
wasn't in motion at all. It was just there, announcing its presence, changing
everything. An unapologetic, unblinking handgun. It was pointed at his
head.

-Move and I'll blow your fucking head off.

A handgun in a hand attached to an arm attached to Pete's shoulder.

-I ain't moving.

-Keep your hands up!

-They up, man. Stay cool.

Pete was almost shouting, Bud was almost whispering, they both
sounded scared. I scuttled backwards, away from the gun, and got my feet
under me.

-Pete, don't.

-Go start the car.

-He was just—

-Start the car!

This time I ran. Maybe I should have stayed and tried to defuse the
situation, but it was turning bad, and I just wanted to get away. My hands
were shaking, the keys rattled, but the engine started right up. Thank God!
Thank Honda! Thank the new sparkplugs installed last month! Funny what
flashes through your brain. I saw the mechanic who had insisted it was time
to replace them. I saw his greasy blue coveralls, his gray, thinning hair. And
then it was a dream again, an hallucination, Pete with a straight arm extended
toward Bud's head, Bud with hands raised to ear height. Neither man
moving, they formed a horrifying silhouette against the tv's blue flare—the
frozen moment before disaster, yet they appear to be steaming. Then Pete is
walking backwards toward the car. He's saying something I can't make out. I
reach across to open the passenger door and can't locate the handle. My own
damn car, and I can't...it opens anyway, and I see Pete, I see the gun.

-Go! Go!

I go alright. Down the street, through two stop signs. I don't see any headlights, and I don't brake. I swing onto the main drag, my pulse is racing, I can feel it in my ears, but I'm focused, absolutely, totally, on the route back to the on-ramp.

-Dude, slow down. Act normal.

-Are you crazy? Are you fucking crazy?

I'm shouting as I accelerate onto the freeway.

-Don't speed. Go sixty.

-You coulda got someone killed. What if he grabbed your arm? What if he had friends with him? Fuck, Pete, I swear.

-What'd you expect me to do, just sit there watching him jump you?

-He didn't jump me.

-Knocked you down. Whatever. This isn't Laguna. They don't fool around.

Could I testify under oath that he knocked me down? Maybe there was some contact, a slight shove—hard to say, Uronor—maybe I was just startled and tripped over my own clumsy feet.

-What if he calls the cops on us?

The scenarios in my head had shifted from what could have happened to what still might. Assault with a deadly weapon. Reckless endangerment. This wasn't my overactive imagination, this was for real. We could get prison time.

-That guy's not calling the cops. Are you kidding?

-He knows who I am. I told him—

-Just calm down, okay? Nothing happened.

-Nothing happened? You pulled a gun on him. Where'd you get a gun?

-Where d'ya think?

He was grinning, and for a moment it was funny—Pete swiping the gun from Sammy's red convertible.

-You're insane, Pete. I mean insane. You had it this whole time—at the restaurant, at the mall?

-It was in here.

And then I was seriously pissed off.

-You had it in my car?

-Under the seat.

I could feel anger sweep across my brain. And Pete was laughing!

-It's not funny, man.

-Fletcher, dude, relax.

-I'm driving around with a stolen gun in my car—in LA—and you don't fucking tell me?

I was shouting again.

-Dude, it's—

-Don't talk to me. Just don't talk to me.

-Fine.

My head was throbbing. I took a few deep breaths, tried to regain composure, tried to concentrate on my driving. It wasn't easy. At best, I was accessory to a serious crime. At best. We needed to ditch the gun—wipe Pete's fingerprints and toss it in a dumpster. Better yet, throw it in the ocean. Park at my place, walk to the beach, heave it out beyond the breakers. No, not in Laguna. Too many scuba divers. Too close to home. The harbor, then, in Dana Point—no one dives there. We drove in silence for five minutes, ten minutes. I noticed my hands trembling. How long had that been going on? I looked over at Pete—still laughing. I shook my head, trying to express disapproval. I mean, I love the guy, but you just threatened to kill someone, pal—crank up the prefrontal cortex and get a fucking clue. Or was it nervous laughter? Was he finally grasping the implications and laughing bitterly, ruefully, at the fix he was in?

-Dude, I think Jesus *would* go for disproportionates. He liked miracles.

That settles it: Pete's a psychopath. A finger twitch away from murder, and now he's all giggles. Alternating images flashed across my mind: Bud's open hand reaching down to me, then Pete's long arm extended to Bud's head. Open hand, long arm, and then I pictured cop cars skidding onto the scene. I checked and rechecked the rearview mirror, expecting the red and blue lights of the highway patrol. Nothing. I felt a slight sense of relief when I stopped seeing billboards along the freeway. That's the sign you've left LA County, you're back behind the Orange Curtain. I saw instead the fake windmills of a tiny amusement park. Usually they struck me as silly, now they seemed reassuring—what could be safer than miniature golf?

-Maybe she's at the mall now.

-What?

We were passing the exit for South Coast Plaza.

-Roya. Your girlfriend. Maybe—

-Don't talk to me.

I'd forgotten about Roya. I mean, for the past hour or so, anyway, I'd stopped wondering what she was doing and why she hadn't called. I hadn't even thought to check my phone. It was in the cupholder. No messages, as usual. The hell with her. Life's too short. I turned the phone completely off—first time in three days. I just wanted to get home—get rid of the gun, get rid of Pete, get back where I felt safe. I wanted to wake up tomorrow morning with the sun shining, walk down to the coffee shop, then break out my paddleboard and go find some dolphins. I needed dolphins. Summer vacation had a few weeks left. I would paddle every day. I would sit on the beach and read. Comedies, not thrillers. Does anyone write comedies anymore?

We passed the quiet business parks and half-lit high-rises of downtown Irvine, and space seemed to open up around the freeway—fewer lights, less congestion. I felt lighter too. We were back in south county.

-Can I talk yet?

-No. Just listen. We're gonna dump the gun in the harbor.

More psychotic giggling from the passenger seat.

-You got a problem with that, Pete?

-No, that's great. Great idea. What if it doesn't sink?

-Yeah, right. Like *The Bagel* didn't sink.

Pete had assured me, when we launched his doomed picnic table, that the harbor water was so polluted we could float a car across it. When did we graduate from harmless pranks to inexcusable crime?

-I think I might have been wrong.

-No kidding.

-He wouldn't be selling drugs out of his house. It's too risky. In that business, you can't let anyone find out where you live.

-Like you would know. Like you would know anything about anything.

-No, I saw it on tv. You make your transactions on the street.

-Remind me never to listen to you again. Ever.

When we finally reached Dana Point, the evening fog was hanging thick. That boded well. I drove across the bridge to the harbor island and found a quiet place to park—no one around except a young couple holding hands. I told Pete to bring the gun and follow me. When he started to say something, I shushed him. I was taking charge, keeping him on a short leash, this was no time for his antics. We followed a sidewalk—steady but nonchalant—until we escaped the streetlights, then picked our way across a rocky embankment, slippery with dew, to the water's edge. Dark, foggy, secluded—the perfect spot for our rotten work. I kept my voice low.

-Throw it far.

-Why are we doing this again?

-Because you stole it. And you held it to someone's head. And threatened to kill him. That's like three felonies right there.

Pete lifted his t-shirt and pulled the pistol from his waistband.

-Here, you do it.

He held it out for me to take.

-Why?

-My shoulder.

I hesitated. I'd never held a real gun. But someone had to chuck it.

-Okay, give it to me.

It was surprisingly small. And light. Too light.

-What is this? Is this real?

Pete leaned against a large rock.

-Dude, I...dude.

He tried to say more, but couldn't. He was shaking with laughter. He was holding his stomach. I was holding a toy.

-Are you fuckin' kidding me?

Aren't toy guns supposed to be bright orange? I pulled the trigger and it went *snap*. A cap gun.

-This is what you pulled on Bud Jack? Are you fuckin' kidding me?

My voice was getting louder. I was losing all composure. I didn't care. The third time was a roar.

-ARE YOU FUCKIN' KIDDING ME?

Equal parts fury, amazement, and relief.

-I…I tried….

Snap, snap—I shot him twice. Strange how it felt satisfying—pointing a pistol, squeezing the trigger. He affected a moan and slid off the rock, clutching his chest. I wiped the gun with my shirt, like I'd seen in the movies, and threw it out over the dark harbor—the gun, not my shirt. It didn't go far and landed with barely a splash. It wasn't going to sink. Then I climbed back up the embankment, leaving Pete to die.

-Dude.

My first impulse was to get in the car and drive away, let him find his own way home, but I needed to think, needed to reconsider what had happened in Mrs. Wilkes's front yard, so I just kept walking through the warm, foggy night, past my parking spot, toward the south end of the island.

One thought stopped me in my tracks: Pete had come to my rescue with a cap gun! Spaghetti Repetti had held a plastic toy to what he thought was a drug dealer's head. Unfuckingbelievable! Maybe Pete was right, he should head for Vegas—talk about going all in.

Then I was walking again, almost blindly, through the fog. I found myself counting steps—one-two-three-four, one-two-three-four—and every step seemed to bring another question. Was Bud Jack actually a drug dealer? Did he kill Juan Castro? What was he doing on the streets of Huntington Beach that night? Had Grandma Wilkes perjured on his behalf? And why did the Wilhites care about his trial? Was Public Defense a charity or a conspiracy? What conclusion do I draw? **WWJD?**—What Would John Do? Hand it off to the Grisham writing stable, no doubt, let them work out the details.

One-two-three-four, one-two-three-four. I was still amped up, still had adrenaline to burn. I crossed the street and passed the rows of yachts asleep in their slips. One-two-three-four, one-two-three-four. And suddenly, like the timeline revelation, it came to me: it didn't matter if Bud Jack was guilty or not, I was innocent. There was no felony in the front yard, the gun was fake. And I had acted in good faith, I hadn't been convinced beyond a reasonable doubt, I had to vote not guilty. If a killer went free in Long Beach—not my fault, not my responsibility.

And with that, a calmness came over me. For a moment I pictured the toy gun ending up in some foamy harbor backwater, floating in a tangle of plastic bags, dead fish, and seaweed. Then I stopped thinking about it altogether. My pace slowed until I felt weightless, like I was floating in still water, neither hot nor cold, only soft—maybe a sensation that goes back to the womb. A foghorn moaned and sea lions barked in reply. I heard the splash and hum of an invisible boat crossing the ghostly harbor. When I ran out of sidewalk, I sat on a damp bench facing west, toward the harbor mouth and out to sea. I think. The harbor channel reaches across to a breakwater, where pelicans often line up by the hundreds, but I couldn't see it. Through the gray-black fog, I could only pick out a green light marking what I guessed was the end of the jetty. My mind felt exhausted. Not sleepy, just spent.

I heard a cough and the scuffle of feet. A figure was emerging from the shadowy soup and gradually finding form. Three feet short of the bench, he pulled up. It wasn't Pete, unless Pete had recently acquired baggage—a sleeping roll, a large plastic trash bag—and grown a bushy beard. The man stood there, perplexed. He hadn't expected to see me. Was I sitting on his bed? Then the foghorn sounded again, drawing his attention seaward.

My instinct is to avoid homeless people, don't want to invite an awkward situation, like he might ask for money and not take no for an answer. But I wanted to greet him, acknowledge his presence, the guy was probably pretty lonely, if only I could think of what to say. Again, the small talk problem. He spoke first.

-We beat on against the current.

Something like that. His mumble was hard to make out, and he said it turning away.

-Sorry?

He didn't answer.

-Wait. You want the bench?

More mumbling, and he faded back into the thick night.

I sat for a while longer—just sat. Lacking vision, my other senses sharpened. I felt the moisture on my arm hair and heard water lapping on rocks. I smelled the guano stench left by pelicans. I became aware of the slow rise and fall of my breathing. Was it my imagination, or was the green light brightening?

It wasn't my imagination, because then the breakwater appeared. And then I spied a signal buoy floating farther out in open water. The fogbank was lifting, like a curtain pulling back to reveal a window on the world. My world. On a suddenly clear night. A few miles up the coast, the hillside lights of Laguna winked at me. Beyond that, I could see the vague glow of Newport and Huntington, and way in the distance the faintest luminary hint of Long Beach. Were we really there tonight? It already seemed so long ago. Some experiences are so foreign there's nothing to hold onto. Yet that moment on the bench—I can still recall how I felt. With a little concentration I can, even now, conjure up the sensation, the softness—quiet, serene, nothing to think about, nothing to do, like I could have sat there forever. Then as quickly as it opened, the curtain closed, fog re-enveloped the harbor, the breakwater vanished. Only the green light remained.

THE PLAYS OF TIMOTHY BRAATZ

In **The Devil and the Wedding Dress** (1994), God's "prosecuting attorney" speaks in rhyme, appears in different guises, and places a curse on four scheming businessmen. It's "The Emperor's New Clothes" in reverse—rather than the proverbial birthday suit, the accursed quartet unknowingly sport wedding dresses. And it's Job updated—the lead character loses wife, job, and home, and struggles to reconcile the essential Judeo-Christian contradiction: an all-powerful Creator allowing human misery. Rather than add to the misery, we'll only say that **Gabriella's Garden** (1996) is about a prisoner trying to write himself out of a Latin American dungeon, and move quickly northward to the more delightful mayhem of **Helena Handbasket** (1999), which includes two Spanish *conquistadores* captured in Yucatán, a timeless Mayan priest, a clueless American grad student, and two policemen employing good cop/bad cop, also smart cop/dumb cop and tall cop/short cop, to interrogate an anthropology professor suspected of blowing up a corporate executive who was angling to exploit a Mayan community. But it's really about a televised cooking show and the commodification of everything. This sprawling adventure wants to get in your face, or at least your kitchen—the cooking show host lobs a raw egg at the audience—while the almost stream-of-consciousness **New and Nobler Life** (2000) tries to sneak up on you. The characters are avoiding, denying, and forgetting something unpleasant—they just talk and talk, even when their heads are mounted on a wall like hunting trophies. When the truth finally emerges—a mass grave, a genocide—they swear never again, then take their bloody revenge. Commodification and revenge are also themes in **One Was Assaulted** (2001). While no eggs are thrown, the audience members, addressed as investors in a dot-com corporation, are complicit in the commodification of storytelling. In the story they are told—and are invested in—a poor black woman shows up on the doorstep of a comfortable white couple who unknowingly own stock in the corporation that recently downsized her. She won't be denied, the homeowners are well-meaning but have their limits, and the ghost of Harry Truman's secretary of state, James Byrnes, wanders in to defend the use of atomic bombs on Japanese civilians. His surprise visit is only strange at first, and one sees a writer's worldview emerging: skeptical of the usual stuff—war-making politicians, corporate greed—but with middle-class citizens as both victims of modern structural violence and also enthusiastic participants. In **Guns, Lies, and Lullabies** (2002), a veteran of the US invasion of Grenada hides the shame of that crime behind a fantasy of battlefield heroism, and the deceit tears his family apart. In **Paper Cuts** (2003), it's a talented, young college graduate who escapes into his imagination, who would rather play the victim than face the twin disappointments of a failing romantic relationship and unfulfilling career options. But what an imagination it is: the police surround his apartment, business envelopes are made from human skin, there's a mole in central intelligence, and, none too soon, the actors step out of character and shoot the playwright. It all adds up to five levels of reality—or is it six?—including a film and a radio broadcast. In this milieu, the crude propaganda of Soviet commissars is unnecessary; we now have "commistars"—celebrity newscasters who show us the world as seen from the top. The centerpiece of **The Commistar** (2004) is a superstar ex-quarterback's rise to the news anchor desk, and subsequent fall to the drunk tank. He'll be rehabilitated, of course, but not before having to brush shoulders with the unwashed masses, some of whom happen to resent what he stands for, and he narrowly escapes a serious beating in the jail cell. Indeed, he's saved by a jailed antiwar protestor who courageously intervenes to neutralize the conflict. Such courage always raises the question, How far would *you* go, how much would *you* risk, for what you believe in? The frustrated sculptor in **Paper Dolls** (2005) wants to raise awareness of the criminal injustice system, which is just fine with his girlfriend, until his artwork takes over her living room and he starts talking about sculptures that will explode in public spaces. He is inspired by the historical example of John Brown, an activist who would go as far as necessary and who would risk everything, but in the end the sculptor must choose between radical art and domestic tranquility. John Brown's story gets more attention in **When Saints Go Marching In** (2007), particularly his historic but unknown meeting with Harriet Tubman. She agrees to lead his raid on the South, but illness keeps her from participating in the doomed adventure. Brown is hanged at the end of Act One; Tubman takes over Act Two. She serves as a Union Army nurse, spy, and expedition leader, and the Emancipation Proclamation proves old John Brown was right all along. Soldiers and actors, farmers and hunters, and an ambitious theater director all come together in **Cossacks Under Water** (2009). The director wants to help a flooded Iowa town, so, naturally, she stages Tolstoy's short story, "The Cossacks," on a nearby farm and recruits locals to join her New York ensemble. Tolstoy's story is faithfully told, albeit with comic interruptions—local resentment, a wannabe Shakespearean, more rain—and the now familiar multiple levels of reality: a play about the making of a film about the staging of a play based on a classic short story, because it's not enough just to exist anymore, self-promotion is everything.

www.lunycrab.com